MURDER MOST MEDICAL

MURDER
MOST MEDICAL

Stories from
Alfred Hitchcock Mystery Magazine
and *Ellery Queen's Mystery Magazine*

Edited by
Cynthia Manson and Cathleen Jordan

Carroll & Graf Publishers, Inc.
New York

Foreword copyright © 1995 by Cathleen Jordan

First edition June 1995

Carroll & Graf Publishers, Inc.
260 Fifth Avenue
New York, NY 10001

Library of Congress Cataloging-in-Publication Data

Murder most medical : stories from Alfred Hitchocock's mystery magazine
   and Ellery Queen's mystery magazine / [edited by] Cynthia Manson and
   Cathleen Jordon. —1st ed.
      p. cm.
   ISBN 0-7867-0198-6
   1. Detective and mystery stories, English.   2. Detective and mystery
stories, American.   3. Medical care—Fiction.   I. Manson, Cynthia.   II.
Jordan, Cathleen.   III. Alfred Hitchcock's mystery magazine.   IV. Ellery
Queen's mystery magazine.
IN PROCESS
823'.087208356—dc20   95-10409
                                                                   CIP

Manufactured in the United States of America

10   9   8   7   6   5   4   3   2   1

Acknowledgments

We are grateful to the following for permission to reprint their copyrighted material:

"**Dr. Coffee and the Other Twin**" by Lawrence G. Blochman, © 1973 by Davis Publications, Inc., reprinted by permission of the author; "**The Problem of the Dying Patient**" by Edward D. Hoch, copyright © 1989 by Davis Publications, Inc., reprinted by permission of the author; "**Lesson in Anatomy**" by Michael Innes, copyright © 1946 by The American Mercury, Inc., © renewed 1973, reprinted by permission of A.P. Watt, Ltd. on behalf of J I M Stewart; "**The Footsteps That Ran**" by Dorothy L. Sayers, copyright 1945 by The American Mercury, Inc.; all stories previously appeared in **ELLERY QUEEN'S MYSTERY MAGAZINE**, published by Bantam Doubleday Dell Magazines.

"**Life After Life**" by Lawrence Block, copyright © 1978 by Davis Publications, Inc., reprinted by permission of Knox Burger Associates, Ltd.; "**Poor Dumb Mouths**" by Bill Crenshaw, copyright © 1984 by Davis Publications, Inc., reprinted by permission of the author; "**Anomalies of the Heart**" by Ashley Curtis, copyright © 1992 by Davis Publications, Inc., reprinted by permission of the author; "**Life or Breath**" by Nelson DeMille, copyright © 1976 by Davis Publications, Inc., reprinted by permission of the author; "**Blood**" by Robert Halsted, copyright © 1990 by Davis Publications, Inc., reprinted by permission of the author; "**One Deadly Sin**" by Anthony Marsh, copyright © 1967 by H. S. D. Publications, Inc.; "**Laura Norder**" by John Mortimer, copyright © 1994 by Advanpress, Ltd., reprinted by permission of Sterling Lord Literistic; "**M Is for Mayo**" by William Pomidor, copyright © 1991 by Davis Publications, Inc., reprinted by permission of the author; "**Aunt Rutabaga**" by Arthur Porges, copyright © 1994 by Arthur Porges, reprinted by permission of Scott Meredith Literary Agency; "**The Quality of Mercy**" by Libbet Proudfit and Mary Monica Pulver, copyright © 1983 by Libbet Proudfit and Mary Monica Pulver, reprinted by permission of the authors; all stories previously appeared in **ALFRED HITCHCOCK MYSTERY MAGAZINE,** published by Bantam Doubleday Dell Magazines.

Contents

Foreword

It's a terrifying, fascinating, adrenaline-raising world, that realm of screaming ambulances, surgeons and anesthetists rushing to emergency rooms, charts with arcane markings hung at the foot of beds, nurses and candy stripers, doctors hung round with stethoscopes, and all the sudden breathlessness of life and death hanging in the balance while most of us untutored mortals stand helplessly by.

It lends itself wonderfully well to the mystery story, to the game of the untraceable poison, for instance. It is a world not only of tension and hurry but also of silent corridors in the nighttime hospital, of doors beyond which we cannot go, of passions within the medical heart too easily able to exploit all that highly specialized knowledge. Those who are inside that world know what the rest of us don't know, about death and all its sources; those outside that world, with motive and ingenuity and daring, can penetrate apparently secret realms.

But so can the sleuth, whether medical or amateur. Among the stories that follow, for example, Lord Peter Wimsey uses what the doctor tells him in Dorothy L. Sayers' "The Footsteps That Ran," whereas in Lawrence G. Blochman's "Dr. Coffee and the Other Twin," pathologist Dr. Daniel Webster Coffee is just the person to have on hand in murder involving twins. English professor Adameus Clay, in Bill Crenshaw's "Poor Dumb Mouths," roped into an investigation of an insurance claim by his brother-in-law Fat Chance, keeps asking questions, while when murder stops a hospital staff picnic cold, Dr. Plato Marley, in William Pomidor's "M Is for Mayo," can give the sheriff a hand.

   Alfred Hitchcock Mystery Magazine and *Ellery Queen's Mystery Magazine* are themselves old hands in the medical mystery business and can recommend these fifteen cases to you. The prescription may be murder, but the side effects are suspense, surprise, and, we hope, satisfaction. And if the heart skips a beat here and there, the reader, we assure you, will survive.

Cathleen Jordan
Editor
Alfred Hitchcock Mystery Magazine

MURDER MOST MEDICAL

THE FOOTSTEPS THAT RAN

by DOROTHY L. SAYERS

M r. Bunter withdrew his head from beneath the focusing cloth. "I fancy that will be quite adequate, sir," he said deferentially, "unless there are any further patients, if I may call them so, which you would wish put on record."

"Not today," replied the doctor. He took the last stricken rat gently from the table and replaced it in its cage with an air of satisfaction. "Perhaps on Wednesday, if Lord Peter can kindly spare your services once again—"

"What's that?" murmured his lordship, withdrawing his long nose from the investigation of a number of unattractive-looking glass jars. "Nice old dog," he added vaguely. "Wags his tail when you mention his name, what? Are these monkey glands, Hartman, or a southwest elevation of Cleopatra's duodenum?"

"You don't know anything, do you?" said the young physician, laughing. "No use playing your bally-fool-with-an-eyeglass tricks on me, Wimsey. I'm up to them. I was saying to Bunter that I'd be no end grateful if you'd let him turn up again three days hence to register the progress of the specimens—always supposing they do progress, that is."

"Why ask, dear old thing?" said his lordship. "Always a pleasure to assist a fellow sleuth, don't you know. Trackin' down murderers—all in the same way of business and all that. All finished? Good egg! By the way, if you don't have that cage mended you'll lose one of your patients—Number 5. The last wire but one is workin' loose—assisted by the intelligent occupant. Jolly little beasts, ain't they? No need of dentists—wish I was a rat—wire much better for the nerves than that fizzlin' drill."

Dr. Hartman uttered a little exclamation.

1

"How in the world did you notice that, Wimsey? I didn't think you'd even looked at the cage."

"Built noticin'—improved by practice," said Lord Peter quietly. "Anythin' wrong leaves a kind of impression on the eye; brain trots along afterwards with the warnin'. I saw that when we came in. Only just grasped it. Can't say my mind was glued on the matter. Shows the victim's improvin', anyhow. All serene, Bunter?"

"Everything perfectly satisfactory, I trust, my lord," replied the manservant. He had packed up his camera and plates, and was quietly restoring order in the little laboratory, whose fittings—compact as those of an ocean liner—had been disarranged for the experiment.

"Well," said the doctor, "I am enormously obliged to you, Lord Peter, and to Bunter, too. I am hoping for a great result from these experiments, and you cannot imagine how valuable an assistance it will be to me to have a really good series of photographs. I can't afford this sort of thing—yet," he added, his rather haggard young face wistful as he looked at the great camera, "and I can't do the work at the hospital. There's no time; I've got to be here. A struggling G.P. can't afford to let his practice go, even in Bloomsbury. There are times when even a half-crown visit makes all the difference between making both ends meet and having an ugly hiatus."

"As Mr. Micawber said," replied Wimsey, " 'Income twenty pounds, expenditure nineteen, nineteen, six—result: happiness, expenditure twenty pounds, ought, six—result: misery.' Don't prostrate yourself in gratitude, old bean; nothin' Bunter loves like messin' round with pyro and hyposulphite. Keeps his hand in. All kinds of practice welcome. Fingerprints and process plates spell seventh what-you-may-call-it of bliss, but focal-plane work on scurvy-ridden rodents (good phrase!) acceptable if no crime forthcoming. Crimes have been rather short lately. Been eatin' our heads off, haven't we, Bunter? Don't know what's come over London. I've taken to prying into my neighbors' affairs to keep from goin' stale. Frightened the postman into a fit the other day by askin' him how his young lady at Croydon was. He's a married man, livin' in Great Ormond Street."

"How did you know?"

"Well, I didn't really. But he lives just opposite to a friend of mine—Inspector Parker; and his wife—not Parker's; he's unmarried; the postman's, I mean—asked Parker the other day whether the flyin' shows at Croydon went on all night. Parker, bein' flummoxed, said no, without thinkin'. Bit of a giveaway what? Thought I'd give the poor devil a word in season, don't you know. Uncommonly thought-less of Parker.''

The doctor laughed. "You'll stay to lunch, won't you?" he said. "Only cold meat and salad, I'm afraid. My woman won't come Sundays. Have to answer my own door. Deuced unprofessional, I'm afraid, but it can't be helped."

"Pleasure," said Wimsey as they emerged from the laboratory and entered the dark little flat by the back door. "Did you build this place on?"

"No," said Hartman; "the last tenant did that. He was an artist. That's why I took the place. It comes in very useful, ramshackle as it is, though this glass roof is a bit sweltering on a hot day like this. Still, I had to have something on the ground floor, cheap, and it'll do till times get better."

"Till your vitamin experiments make you famous, eh?" said Peter cheerfully. "You're goin' to be the comin' man, you know. Feel it in my bones. Uncommonly neat little kitchen you've got, anyhow."

"It does," said the doctor. "The lab makes it a bit gloomy, but the woman's only here in the daytime."

He led the way into a narrow little dining room, where the table was laid for a cold lunch. The one window at the end farthest from the kitchen looked out into Great James Street. The room was little more than a passage, and full of doors—the kitchen door, a door in the adjacent wall leading into the entrance hall, and a third on the opposite side, through which his visitor caught a glimpse of a moder-ate-sized consulting room.

Lord Peter Wimsey and his host sat down to table, and the doctor expressed a hope that Mr. Bunter would sit down with them. That correct person, however, deprecated any such suggestion.

"If I might venture to indicate my own preference, sir," he said, "it would be to wait upon you and his lordship in the usual manner."

"It's no use," said Wimsey. "Bunter likes me to know my place. Terrorizin' sort of man, Bunter. Can't call my soul my own. Carry on, Bunter; we wouldn't presume for the world."

Mr. Bunter handed the salad and poured out the water with a grave decency appropriate to a crusted old tawny port.

It was a Sunday afternoon in that halcyon summer of 1921. The sordid little street was almost empty. The ice cream man alone seemed thriving and active. He leaned luxuriously on the green post at the corner, in the intervals of driving a busy trade. Bloomsbury's swarm of able-bodied and able-voiced infants was still; presumably

within-doors, eating steamy Sunday dinners inappropriate to the tropical weather. The only disturbing sounds came from the flat above,
where heavy footsteps passed rapidly to and fro.

"Who's the merry-and-bright bloke above?" inquired Lord Peter
presently. "Not an early riser, I take it. Not that anybody is on a
Sunday mornin'. Why an inscrutable Providence ever inflicted such
a ghastly day on people livin' in town I can't imagine. I ought to
be in the country, but I've got to meet a friend at Victoria this
afternoon. Such a day to choose. . . . Who's the lady? Wife or accomplished friend? Gather she takes a properly submissive view of woman's duties in the home, either way. That's the bedroom overhead, I
take it."

Hartman looked at Lord Peter in some surprise.

" 'Scuse my beastly inquisitiveness, old thing," said Wimsey.
"Bad habit. Not my business."

"How did you—?"

"Guesswork," said Lord Peter, with disarming frankness. "I heard
the squawk of an iron bedstead on the ceiling and a heavy fellow
get out with a bump, but it may quite well be a couch or something.
Anyway, he's been potterin' about in his stocking feet over these
few feet of the floor for the last half-hour, while the woman has
been clatterin' to and fro, in and out of the kitchen and away into
the sittin' room, with her high heels on, ever since we've been here.
Hence deduction as to domestic habits of the first floor tenants."

"I thought," said the doctor, with an aggrieved expression, "you'd
been listening to my valuable exposition of the beneficial effects of
vitamin B, and Lind's treatment of scurvy with fresh lemon in
1755."

"I was listenin'," agreed Lord Peter hastily, "but I heard the
footsteps as well. Fellow's toddled into the kitchen—only wanted the
matches, though; he's gone off into the sittin' room and left her to
carry on the good work. What was I sayin'? Oh yes! You see, as I
was sayin' before, one hears a thing or sees it without knowin' or
thinkin' about it. Then afterwards one starts meditatin', and it all
comes back, and one sorts out one's impressions. Like those plates of
Bunter's. Picture's all there, l—la—what's the word I want, Bunter?"

"Latent, my lord."

"That's it. My right-hand man, Bunter; couldn't do a thing without
him. The picture's latent till you put the developer on. Same with
the brain. No mystery. Little grey matter's all you want to remember

things with. As a matter of curiosity, was I right about those people above?"

"Perfectly. The man's a gas company's inspector. A bit surly, but devoted (after his own fashion) to his wife. I mean, he doesn't mind hulking in bed on a Sunday morning and letting her do the chores, but he spends all the money he can spare on giving her pretty hats and fur coats and what not. They've only been married about six months. I was called in to her when she had a touch of flu in the spring, and he was almost off his head with anxiety. She's a lovely little woman, I must say—Italian. He picked her up in some eating place in Soho, I believe. Glorious dark hair and eyes: Venus sort of figure; proper contours in all the right places; good skin—all that sort of thing. She was a bit of a draw to that restaurant while she was there, I fancy. Lively. She had an old admirer round here one day—awkward little Italian fellow, with a knife—active as a monkey. Might have been unpleasant, but I happened to be on the spot, and her husband came along. People are always laying one another out in these streets. Good for business, of course, but one gets tired of tying up broken heads and slits in the jugular. Still, I suppose the girl can't help being attractive, though I don't say she's what you might call standoffish in her manner. She's sincerely fond of Brotherton, I think, though—that's his name."

Wimsey nodded inattentively. "I suppose life is a bit monotonous here," he said.

"Professionally, yes. Births and drunks and wife-beatings are pretty common. And all the usual ailments, of course. God!" cried the doctor explosively, "if only I could get away and do my experiments!"

"Ah!" said Peter, "where's that eccentric old millionaire with a mysterious disease who always figures in the novels? A lightning diagnosis—a miraculous cure—'God bless you, doctor; here are five thousand pounds'—Harley Street—"

"That sort doesn't live in Bloomsbury," said the doctor.

"It must be fascinatin', diagnosin' things," said Peter thoughtfully. "How d'you do it? I mean, is there a regular set of symptoms for each disease, like callin' a club to show you want your partner to go no trumps? You don't just say: 'This fellow's got a pimple on his nose, therefore he has fatty degeneration of the heart—' "

"I hope not," said the doctor dryly.

"Or is it more like gettin' a clue to a crime?" went on Peter. "You see somethin'—a room, or a body, say, all knocked about anyhow, and there's a damn sight of symptoms of somethin' wrong, and you've got just to pick out the ones which tell the story?''

"That's more like it," said Dr. Hartman. "Some symptoms are significant in themselves—like the condition of the gums in scurvy, let us say—others in conjunction with—"

He broke off, and both sprang to their feet as a shrill scream sounded suddenly from the flat above, followed by a heavy thud. A man's voice cried out lamentably; feet ran violently to and fro; then, as the doctor and his guests stood frozen in consternation, came the man himself—falling down the stairs in his haste, hammering at Hartman's door.

"Help! Help! Let me in! My wife! He's murdered her!"

They ran hastily to the door and let him in. He was a big, fair man, in his shirtsleeves and stockings. His hair stood up, and his face was set in bewildered misery.

"She is dead—dead. He was her lover," he groaned. "Doctor! I have lost my wife! My Maddalena—" He paused, looked wildly for a moment, and then said hoarsely, "Someone's been in—somehow—stabbed her—murdered her. I'll have the law on him, doctor. Come quickly—she was cooking the chicken for my dinner—ah-h-h!"

He gave a long, hysterical shriek, which ended in a hiccupping laugh. The doctor took him roughly by the arm and shook him. "Pull yourself together, Mr. Brotherton," he said sharply. "Perhaps she is only hurt. Stand out of the way!"

"Only hurt?" said the man, sitting heavily down on the nearest chair. "No—no—she is dead—little Maddalena—oh my God!"

Dr. Hartman had snatched a roll of bandages and a few surgical appliances from the consulting room, and he ran upstairs, followed closely by Lord Peter. Bunter remained for a few moments to combat hysterics with cold water. Then he stepped across to the dining room window and shouted.

"Well, wot is it?" cried a voice from the street.

"Would you be so kind as to step in here a minute, officer?" said Mr. Bunter. "There's been murder done."

When Brotherton and Bunter arrived upstairs with the constable, they found Dr. Hartman and Lord Peter in the little kitchen. The doctor was kneeling beside the woman's body. At their entrance he looked up and shook his head.

"Death instantaneous," he said. "Clean through the heart. Poor child. She cannot have suffered at all. Oh, constable, it is very fortunate you are here. Murder appears to have been done—though I'm afraid the man has escaped. Probably Mr. Brotherton can give us some help. He was in the flat at the time."

The man had sunk down on a chair and was gazing at the body with a face from which all meaning seemed to have been struck. The policeman produced a notebook.

"Now, sir," he said, "don't let's waste any time. Sooner we can get to work the more likely we are to catch our man. Now, you was 'ere at the time, was you?"

Brotherton stared a moment, then, making a violent effort, he answered steadily:

"I was in the sitting room, smoking and reading the paper. My—*she*—was getting the dinner ready in here. I heard her give a scream, and I rushed in and found her lying on the floor. She didn't have time to say anything. When I found she was dead, I rushed to the window, and saw the fellow scrambling away over the glass roof there, I yelled at him, but he disappeared. Then I ran down—"

"Arf a mo'," said the policeman. "Now, see 'ere, sir, didn't you think to go after 'im at once?"

"My first thought was for her," said the man. "I thought maybe she wasn't dead. I tried to bring her round—" His speech ended in a groan.

"You say he came in through the window," said the policeman.

"I beg your pardon, officer," interrupted Lord Peter, who had been apparently making a mental inventory of the contents of the kitchen. "Mr. Brotherton suggested that the man went *out* through the window. It's better to be accurate."

"It's the same thing," said the doctor. "It's the only way he could have come in. These flats are all alike. The staircase door leads into the sitting room, and Mr. Brotherton was there, so the man couldn't have come that way."

"And," said Peter, "he didn't get in through the bedroom window, or we should have seen him. We were in the room below. Unless, indeed, he let himself down from the roof. Was the door between the bedroom and the sitting room open?" he asked suddenly, turning to Brotherton.

The man hesitated a moment. "Yes," he said finally. "Yes, I'm sure it was."

"Could you have seen the man if he had come through the bedroom window?"

"I couldn't have helped seeing him."

"Come, come, sir," said the policeman, with some irritation, "better let *me* ask the questions. Stands to reason the fellow wouldn't get in through the bedroom window in full view of the street."

"How clever of you to think of that," said Wimsey. "Of course not. Never occurred to me. Then it must have been this window, as you say."

"And, what's more, here's his marks on the windowsill," said the constable triumphantly, pointing to some blurred traces among the London soot. "That's right. Down he goes by that drainpipe, over the glass roof down there—what's that the roof of?"

"My laboratory," said the doctor. "Heavens! to think that while we were at dinner this murdering villain—"

"Quite so, sir," agreed the constable. "Well, he'd get away over the wall into the court be'ind. "'E'll 'ave been seen there, no fear; you needn't anticipate much trouble in layin' 'ands on 'im, sir. I'll go round there in 'arf a tick. Now then, sir—" turning to Brotherton "—'ave you any idea wot this party might have looked like?"

Brotherton lifted a wild face, and the doctor interposed.

"I think you ought to know, constable," he said, "that there was—well, not a murderous attack, but what might have been one, made on this woman before—about eight weeks ago—by a man named Marincetti—an Italian waiter—with a knife."

"Ah!" The policeman licked his pencil eagerly. "Do you know this party as 'as been mentioned?" he inquired of Brotherton.

"That's the man," said Brotherton with concentrated fury. "Coming here after my wife—God curse him! I wish to God I had him dead here beside her!"

"Quite so," said the policeman. "Now, sir—" to the doctor— " 'ave you got the weapon wot the crime was committed with?"

"No," said Hartman, "there was no weapon in the body when I arrived."

"Did *you* take it out?" pursued the constable, to Brotherton.

"No," said Brotherton, "he took it with him."

"Took it with 'im," the constable entered the fact in his notes. "Phew! Wonderful 'ot it is in 'ere, ain't it, sir?" he added, mopping his brow.

"It's the gas oven, I think," said Peter mildly. "Uncommon hot thing, a gas oven, in the middle of July. D'you mind if I turn it out? There's the chicken inside, but I don't suppose you want—"

Brotherton groaned, and the constable said: "Quite right, sir. A man wouldn't 'ardly fancy 'is dinner after a thing like this. Thank you, sir. Well now, doctor, wot kind of a weapon do you take this to 'ave been?''

"It was a long, narrow weapon—something like an Italian stiletto, I imagine," said the doctor, "about six inches long. It was thrust in with great force under the fifth rib, and I should say it had pierced the heart centrally. As you see, there has been practically no bleeding. Such a wound would cause instant death. Was she lying just as she is now when you first saw her, Mr. Brotherton?''

"On her back, just as she is," replied the husband.

"Well, that seems clear enough," said the policeman. "This 'ere Marinetti, or wotever 'is name is, 'as a grudge against the poor young lady—''

"I believe he was an admirer," put in the doctor.

"Quite so," agreed the constable. "Of course, these foreigners are like that—even the decentest of 'em. Stabbin' and suchlike seems to come nateral to them, as you might say. Well, this 'ere Marinetti climbs in 'ere, sees the poor young lady standin' 'ere by the table all alone, gettin' the dinner ready; 'e comes in be'ind, catches 'er round the waist, stabs 'er—easy job, you see; no corsets nor nothink—she shrieks out, 'e pulls 'is stiletty out of 'er an' makes tracks. Well, now we've got to find 'im, and by your leave, sir, I'll be gettin' along. We'll 'ave 'im by the 'eels before long, sir, don't you worry. I'll 'ave to put a man in charge 'ere, sir, to keep folks out, but that needn't worry you. Good mornin', gentlemen.''

"May we move the poor girl now?" asked the doctor.

"Certainly. Like me to 'elp you, sir?''

"No. Don't lose any time. We can manage." Dr. Hartman turned to Peter as the constable clattered downstairs. "Will you help me, Lord Peter?''

"Bunter's better at that sort of thing," said Wimsey, with a hard mouth.

The doctor looked at him in some surprise, but said nothing, and he and Bunter carried the still form away. Brotherton did not follow them. He sat in a grief-stricken heap, with his head buried in his hands. Lord Peter walked about the little kitchen, turning over the various knives and kitchen utensils, peering into the sink bucket, and apparently taking an inventory of the bread, butter, condiments, vegetables, and so forth which lay about in preparation for the Sunday meal. There were potatoes in the sink, half peeled, a pathetic witness to the quiet domestic life which had been so horribly inter-

rupted. The colander was filled with green peas. Lord Peter turned
these things over with an inquisitive finger, gazed into the smooth
surface of a bowl of drippings as though it were a divining crystal,
ran his hands several times right through a bowl of flour—then drew
his pipe from his pocket and filled it slowly.

The doctor returned, and put his hand on Brotherton's shoulder.

"Come," he said gently, "we have laid her in the other bedroom.
She looks very peaceful. You must remember that, except for that
moment of terror when she saw the knife, she suffered nothing. It is
terrible for you, but you must try not to give way. The police—"

"The police can't bring her back to life," said the man savagely.
"She's dead. Leave me alone, curse you! Leave me alone, I say!"

He stood up, with a violent gesture.

"You must not sit here," said Hartman firmly. "I will give you
something to take, and you must try to keep calm. Then we will
leave you, but if you don't control yourself—"

After some further persuasion, Brotherton allowed himself to be
led away.

"Bunter," said Lord Peter as the kitchen door closed behind them,
"do you know why I am doubtful about the success of those rat
experiments?"

"Meaning Dr. Hartman's, my lord?"

"Yes, Dr. Hartman has a theory. In any investigation, my Bunter,
it is most damnably dangerous to have a theory."

"I have heard you say so, my lord."

"Confound you—you know it as well as I do! What is wrong
with the doctor's theories, Bunter?"

"You wish me to reply, my lord, that he only sees the facts which
fit in with the theory."

"Thought-reader!" exclaimed Lord Peter bitterly.

"And that he supplies them to the police, my lord."

"Hush!" said Peter as the doctor returned.

"I have got him to lie down," said Dr. Hartman, "and I think
the best thing we can do is to leave him to himself."

"D'you know," said Wimsey, "I don't cotton to that idea,
somehow."

"Why? Do you think he's likely to destroy himself?"

"That's as good a reason to give as any other, I suppose," said
Wimsey, "when you haven't got any reason which can be put into
words. But my advice is, don't leave him for a moment."

"But why? Frequently, with a deep grief like this, the presence of other people is merely an irritant. He begged me to leave him."

"Then for God's sake go back to him," said Peter.

"Really, Lord Peter," said the doctor, "I think I ought to know what is best for my patient."

"Doctor," said Wimsey, "this is not a question of your patient. A crime has been committed."

"But there is no mystery."

"There are twenty mysteries. For one thing, when was the window cleaner here last?"

"The window cleaner?"

"Who shall fathom the ebony black enigma of the window cleaner?" pursued Peter lightly, putting a match to his pipe. "You are quietly in your bath, in a state of more or less innocent nature, when an intrusive head appears at the window, like the ghost of Hamilton Tighe, and a gruff voice, suspended between earth and heaven, says, 'Good morning, sir.' Where do window cleaners go between visits? Do they hibernate, like busy bees? Do they—"

"Really, Lord Peter," said the doctor, "don't you think you're going a bit beyond the limit?"

"Sorry you feel like that," said Peter, "but I really want to know, about the window cleaner. Look how clear these panes are."

"He came yesterday, if you want to know," said Dr. Hartman, rather stiffly.

"You are sure?"

"He did mine at the same time."

"I thought as much," said Lord Peter. "In that case, it is absolutely imperative that Brotherton should not be left alone for a moment. Bunter! Confound it all, where's that fellow got to?"

The door into the bedroom opened.

"My lord?" Mr. Bunter unobtrusively appeared, as he had unobtrusively stolen out to keep an unobtrusive eye upon the patient.

"Good," said Wimsey. "Stay where you are." His lackadaisical manner had gone, and he looked at the doctor as four years previously he might have looked at a refractory subaltern.

"Dr. Hartman," he said, "something is wrong. Cast your mind back. We were talking about symptoms. Then came the scream. Then came the sound of feet running. *Which direction did they run in?*"

"I'm sure I don't know."

"Don't you? Symptomatic though, doctor. They have been troubling me all the time, subconsciously. Now I know why. They ran *from the kitchen.''*

''Well?''

''Well! And now the window cleaner—''

''What about him?''

''Could you swear that it wasn't the window cleaner who made those marks on the sill?''

''And the man Brotherton saw—''

''Have we examined your laboratory roof for his footsteps?''

''But the weapon? Wimsey, this is madness! Someone took the weapon.''

''I know. But did you think the edge of the wound was clean enough to have been made by a smooth stiletto? It looked ragged to me.''

''Wimsey, what are you driving at?''

''There's a clue here in the flat—and I'm damned if I can remember it. I've seen it—I know I've seen it. It'll come to me presently. Meanwhile, don't let Brotherton—''

''What?''

''Do whatever it is he's going to do.''

''But what is it?''

''If I could tell you that I could show you the clue. Why couldn't he make up his mind whether the bedroom door was open or shut? Very good story, but not quite thought out. Anyhow—I say, doctor, make some excuse, and strip him, and bring me his clothes. And send Bunter to me.''

The doctor stared at him, puzzled. Then he made a gesture of acquiescence and passed into the bedroom. Lord Peter followed him, casting a ruminating glance at Brotherton as he went. Once in the sitting room, Lord Peter sat down on a red velvet armchair, fixed his eyes on a gilt-framed oleograph, and became wrapped in contemplation.

Presently Bunter came in with his arms full of clothing. Wimsey took it and began to search it, methodically enough but listlessly. Suddenly he dropped the garments, and turned to the manservant.

''No,'' he said, ''this is a precaution, Bunter mine, but I'm on the wrong tack. It wasn't here I saw—whatever I did see. It was in the kitchen. Now, what was it?''

''I could not say, my lord, but I entertain a conviction that I was also, in a manner of speaking, conscious—not consciously conscious, my lord, if you understand me, but still conscious of an incongruity.''

"Hurray!" said Wimsey suddenly. "Cheer-oh! for the subconscious what's-his-name! Now let's remember the kitchen. I cleared out of it because I was gettin' obfuscated. Now then. Begin at the door. Fryin' pans and sauce pans on the wall. Gas stove—oven goin'—chicken inside. Rack of wooden spoons on the wall, gas lighter, pan lifter. Stop me when I'm gettin' hot. Mantelpiece. Spice-boxes and stuff. Anything wrong with them? No. Dresser. Plates. Knives and forks—all clean; flour dredger—milk jug—sieve on the wall—nutmeg grater. Three-tier steamer. Looked inside—no grisly secrets in the steamer."

"Did you look in all the dresser drawers, my lord?"

"No. That could be done. But the point is, I *did* notice somethin'. What did I notice? That's the point. Never mind. On with the dance—let joy be unconfined! Knife board. Knife powder. Kitchen table. Did you speak?"

"No," said Bunter, who had moved from his attitude of wooden deference.

"Table stirs a chord. Very good. On table. Choppin' board. Remains of ham and herb stuffin'. Packet of suet. Another sieve. Several plates. Butter in a glass dish. Bowl of drippins—"

"Ah!"

"Drippins —! Yes, there was—"

"Something unsatisfactory, my lord—"

"About the drippins! Oh, my head! What's that they say in *Dear Brutus,* Bunter? 'Hold on to the workbox.' That's right. Hold on to the drippins. Beastly slimy stuff to hold on to— Wait!"

There was a pause.

"When I was a kid," said Wimsey, "I used to love to go down into the kitchen and talk to old cookie. Good old soul she was, too. I can see her now, gettin' chicken ready, with me danglin' my legs on the table. *She* used to pluck an' draw 'em herself. I reveled in it. Little beasts boys are, ain't they, Bunter? Pluck it, draw it, wash it, stuff it, tuck his little tail through its little what-you-may-call-it, truss it, grease the dish— Bunter?"

"My lord!"

"Hold on to the drippings!"

"The bowl, my lord—"

"The bowl—visualize it—what was wrong?"

"It was full, my lord!"

"Got it—got it—*got* it! The bowl was full—smooth surface.

Golly! I knew there was something queer about it. Now why shouldn't it be full? Hold on to the—"

"The bird was in the oven."

"Without drippings!"

"Very careless cookery, my lord."

"The bird—in the oven—no drippings. Bunter! Suppose it was never put in till after she was dead? Thrust in hurriedly by someone who had something to hide—horrible!"

"But with what object, my lord?"

"Yes, why? That's the point. One more mental association with the bird. It's just coming. Wait a moment. Pluck, draw, wash, stuff, tuck up, truss— By God!"

"My lord?"

"Come on, Bunter. Thank heaven we turned off the gas!"

He dashed through the bedroom, disregarding the doctor and the patient, who sat up with a smothered shriek. He flung open the oven door and snatched out the baking tin. The skin of the bird had just begun to discolor. With a little gasp of triumph, Wimsey caught the iron ring that protruded from the wing, and jerked out—*the six inch spiral skewer.*

The doctor was struggling with the excited Brotherton in the doorway. Wimsey caught the man as he broke away and shook him into the corner with a jiu-jitsu twist.

"Here is the weapon," he said.

"Prove it, blast you!" said Brotherton savagely.

"I will," said Wimsey. "Bunter, call in the policeman at the door. Doctor, we shall need your microscope."

In the laboratory the doctor bent over the microscope. A thin layer of blood from the skewer had been spread upon the slide.

"Well?" said Wimsey impatiently.

"It's all right," said Hartman. "The roasting didn't get anywhere near the middle. My God, Wimsey, yes, you're right—round corpuscles, diameter $\frac{1}{3681}$—mammalian blood—probably human—"

"Her blood," said Wimsey.

"It was very clever, Bunter," said Lord Peter as the taxi trundled along on the way to his flat in Piccadilly. "If that fowl had gone on roasting a bit longer the blood corpuscles might easily have been destroyed beyond all hope of recognition. It all goes to show that the unpremeditated crime is usually the safest."

"And what does your lordship take the man's motive to have been?"

"In my youth," said Wimsey meditatively, "they used to make me read the Bible. Trouble was, the only books I ever took to naturally were the ones they weren't over and above keen on. But I got to know the Song of Songs pretty well by heart. Look it up, Bunter; at your age it won't hurt you; it talks sense about jealousy."

"I have perused the work in question, your lordship," replied Mr. Bunter, with a sallow blush. "It says, if I remember rightly: *'Jealousy is cruel as the grave.'* "

THE QUALITY OF MERCY

by LIBBET PROUDFIT AND MARY MONICA PULVER

Brichter punched the license number of the black Torino into his computer and continued to follow the weaving car while he waited for the glowing amber screen to tell him something. He was a uniformed cop of ordinary appearance, slimmer than average, with pale brown hair. He was working alone in a business area of Charter, near the airport. The drunk had pulled out from a side street without stopping and was now swooping dangerously at oncoming cars.

The screen abruptly advised Brichter that there were no wants on the car, that it was leased to Walter J. Smith of 1134 Oslo Street, who likewise had no warrants. Well, I'll be damned, he thought.

Brichter flicked on his red lights, and to his surprise, the Torino immediately sped away. He hit his siren and told Dispatch he was in pursuit.

Two blocks later he came bending around a corner to find the Torino had climbed the curb halfway down and hit a light pole, one of the old-fashioned cast-iron kind that don't break away. The car was steaming all over its crushed front end.

There was only the driver inside. He had spidered the windshield with his forehead and his face was a bloody mess. "Sorry," he apologized as Brichter helped him out. He was a meek little man, dark and balding. He wiped clumsily at his face, spreading blood into his sideburns. "Terrible thing. Pay for the damage, of course." His breath smelled strongly of alcohol, but he didn't talk or move drunkenly.

"Yes, sir. Do you hurt anywhere besides your head? Your neck? Your back?"

"Huh-uh. Jesus, look at my car!"

"Yes, sir. May I see your driver's license, please?" Not that he

17

needed to. This was Wally Smith, all right. Walter J. Smith, late of Smith's Drugs, was a celebrity in Charter. He'd been for years a nonentity, a Caspar Milquetoast complete with termagant wife. Then the wife died last year after a brief bout with cancer. Smith quit his hardshell Baptist church and became a Methodist. A vacation in the Bahamas, his first vacation in years, resulted in his purchase of an enormous potted palm which he kept in his store window. A chatty columnist saw the palm and wrote a story about a little man who wanted to live in an exotic tropic clime. It took a while, but fired by the cheers and encouragement of the whole town, Smith reached for his dream. His business was sold last week, and by the smell of him, his going-away party had been a dilly.

"Gonna miss my flight," hinted Smith nervously.

Brichter checked his watch. "The Scooter to Chicago left a few minutes ago," he said.

"Oh, Christ; she'll kill me—!" He stopped abruptly, and said, "I didn't mean that."

"No, sir. Mr. Smith, you are under arrest for fleeing the police and for driving while intoxicated. I want you to accompany me to the hospital, to get that head taken care of; and while we're there I want you to have a blood alcohol level test. Do you understand?"

"C'mon, the cut's not that bad!" Smith fished for a handkerchief with a bloody hand and pressed it to his forehead. He pulled it away, looked at the result and hastily folded the handkerchief before covering the wound with it again. "If you let me go, I can still get to Chicago in time to catch my flight to Nassau." He smiled nervously. "Have a little mercy on a future beach bum, okay?"

"No, sir." Brichter led him back to the squad car, from which he produced a four-by-seven orange metal box. He fitted a clear plastic mouthpiece to it and asked, "Will you blow in this for me?"

"Hey, I've had a few, but dammit, I'm not drunk!"

"All right, show me. Blow in here."

Mr. Smith blew and the green pass light switched to red so promptly that Brichter reset the device and had Smith blow again. If anything, the change was faster. Scared apparently sober, thought Brichter, pulling loose his handcuffs—he was not going to drive to the hospital with an unfettered, scared drunk. Smith's eyes widened and, although he made no objection, fastening his hand reduced him to lip-licking silence.

A tow truck came for the Torino, and Brichter set off with Smith for County General Hospital. There, he parked and led his suspect across the parking lot to the emergency room.

It was a busy Saturday night; the long reception area was densely populated with people waiting for treatment or waiting for people being treated. Under an enormous sign that said, "ALL Emergency and Out Patients Must Stop Here" sat a middle-aged, competent-looking nurse with protuberant eyes and wavy brown hair. She was taking into a red phone.

"If your child has swallowed Inderal, I suggest you call Poison Control and bring him in," she was saying briskly. "Yes, I can give you the number. You're welcome." She hung up, turning to smile at Brichter. Her plastic name tag said Jackie Bauman, RN. "Good evening, officer," she said formally. "What have we— Good heavens, is that Wally Smith? In *handcuffs?*" She reached for an eight by three card.

"Yes, he's been in an accident, needs his laceration looked at," said Brichter, unlocking the cuffs. "And I want a blood alcohol."

"If I miss my Nassau flight, officer, I'm going to be very upset," said Smith tightly.

"Blood alcohol? He doesn't look—" The phone rang and the nurse lifted the receiver. "County General Emergency Room. Nurse speaking." Her attention quickened. "How far out?" She wrote something on a pad. "Family coming? Just . . . just Mrs. Iver." She wrote again. "Got it, thanks." She hung up. "Obie, we've got a cardiac arrest due in about three minutes. I may have to help, so let's keep this short."

"Okay."

She looked at Smith. "is your first name Wally or Walter?"

He stared at her.

"Huh?"

"What is your first name, please?"

He appeared distracted by some overwhelming thought or idea. "Walter James Smith," he said, and gave his address.

"Mr. Smith, who is your private doctor?"

"Samuel Lundquist." He looked at Brichter worriedly. "Think I'm gonna be sick."

Nurse Bauman instantly produced a kidney-shaped emesis pan. "Here," she said, pushing it into his hands, then spoke over her shoulder to a candy striper sitting behind her. "Jinny, take this patient back to Main Six." He was gone before he had a chance to splash the contents of his stomach on Nurse Bauman's clean counter.

She said to Brichter, "Maybe we can get him patched up in time to catch the late Scooter. Unless you seriously intend to take him downtown and book him?"

He said quietly, "Jackie, he failed the breath test. He nearly side-swiped a truck, and he wrecked his car in a getaway attempt. I don't care who he is, he's under arrest."

"Well, *excuse me!*" she said loftily. "Don't you want to go watch him so he doesn't try to run away?"

"He's too preoccupied with his upper digestive tract right now to think about escape. I'll be in the nurses' lounge when you need me."

Brichter walked through double doors into the back and turned left into a small room. It was at one end of a corridor splitting the emergency area in half. A tiny, pretty, dark RN whose long black hair was tied back with a plaid ribbon was in the room, drinking a Diet Pepsi and smoking a cigarette.

"Hi, Stephanie," he said.

"Don't talk to me," she snapped.

He smiled a sideways smile. "Why not?"

She displayed a forearm marked by two red semicircles. "A two-year-old bit me, and they won't let me impound him for ninety days to see if he's rabid."

The rest of the smile appeared. "Too bad."

"Yeah, well, find one night this week—two nights this month—that haven't been rough." She pulled on her cigarette. "I'll be stupid and ask: what did you bring in?"

"DWI. Ran into a lightpole." He went to the twenty-cup coffee maker and selected a Styrofoam cup.

"Ha!" she said crossly. "Serves him right. I hate drunks. Their breath is disgusting, and no matter where you stand, they breathe all over you."

"Stephanie to Red Room One," said an intercom voice. "Stephanie to Red Room One, please."

She quickly stubbed out her cigarette. "That'll be the cardiac arrest. I want to hear a nickel drop every time you fill that cup."

Brichter filled his cup and dropped a coin into the coffee can. He wanted very much to get closer to Stephanie, but whenever he tried, she bristled with wisecracks. God, wait till she found out he'd arrested Wally Smith.

He sipped the hot, fragrant brew and began to wonder if there might not be repercussions downtown as a result of this arrest.

From the other end of the corridor there was the hissing sound of electric double doors opening and a cadenced count from a breathless man: "... and one, and two, and three, and four, and five, and one, and two ..."

A woman was begging, "Stop it, stop it; he's dead, can't you see that?" Other voices spoke. "Crissake, outa the way, can't you?" "Here, in here!" "Start ventilating—where's anesthesia to ventilate?" "I'm right behind you, doctor."

He wandered casually out to watch. He probably should go check on Smith, but this was more interesting. He remembered this sort of emergency from his paramedic days. It was nice to be able just to observe.

The patient was whipped into Red Room One, the cardiac room. Even as Brichter approached, the wheeze-click of Thumper, the automatic CPR device, began. The woman's voice rose again, "Please, stop that! You're hurting him!"

A man ordered briskly, preoccupied, "Can someone take this woman away? Now?"

Two fire department rescue squad members and a uniformed policeman were conversing in the corridor. They glanced through the open door into the room but ignored the request. Jackie Bauman led a weeping woman out. The woman was streaky blonde and deeply tanned, exceptionally beautiful, dressed in bright blue silk. The nurse was speaking in a soothing undertone as they went down the corridor; the woman was shading her eyes with a trembling hand. The firemen and the policeman watched them go out a door.

"Ain't that a luxury item," said one of the firemen.

"Too rich for me," agreed the other.

"Oh, I dunno," said the cop, a veteran whose belly hung over his garrison belt. "Take her clothes off and whatcha got?"

"A lovely woman who wouldn't give us the time of day, Billy," said Brichter, stopping beside him. "What's going down?"

"Well, if it ain't the boy genius!" said Billy, with a broad grin. "You're an ex-nurse, ain't you? You tell me!"

Brichter's pale eyes glinted, but he said calmly, nodding, "I guess a man who shot an innocent garter snake because he thought it was a copperhead can't be expected to know the difference between a nurse and a paramedic. Was that a Mrs. Iver that Jackie just took out?"

"Yeah," said one of the firemen. "I think it's her old man in there on the table."

"Did you really shoot a deadly garter snake, Billy?" asked the other fireman gleefully, and Brichter, feeling he'd gotten more than even, walked into Red Room Two.

It was also an emergency treatment room, with a functional-looking wheeled table and glittering electronic machinery. Glass cupboards held the blue-paper-wrapped instruments necessary for doing diagnostic and resuscitative procedures.

To the left was a plate-glass window that took up half the wall. There was a sink under the window and a paramedic was at it, wringing out a towel he had soaked under a high curved faucet. He was looking through the window, watching with professional interest the concentrated efforts going on next door to resuscitate the cardiac arrest victim. Brichter went to stand beside him.

"He had a down time of at least six minutes before we were called," said the paramedic, beginning to swipe at his spattered brown slacks with the towel, "and she didn't know how to do CPR. Rescue was there in three minutes and we were right behind them. Not a chance, Obie, not a wiggle, the guy was asystole, never got a thing." He began to rinse the towel and observed, "Down time was too long, he'll never make it." He wrung out the towel in a series of strong twists. "Why the hell don't more people learn CPR? She could've saved him. She said he had a bad stroke maybe seven months ago, but there was no history of heart trouble." He began to wipe at himself again. "He must've just finished dinner; he puked all over me."

Brichter looked through the window. The victim was a healthy looking man, somewhere in his middle fifties, naked except for electrodes stuck to his chest, his color a nice pink. There were six people in the room with him, crowding it without getting in each other's way. An orderly stood beside the patient, supervising Thumper, a C-shaped machine whose black foot was compressing the patient's breastbone, squeezing his heart. A sturdy nurse with copper curls was injecting drugs into the IV line. Stephanie was writing things on a clipboard, calling out the time and watching the monitor scrawl a crooked, humping line. The anesthetist, a homely lady in bluegreen operating room scrubs, was squeezing the ambu bag, breathing for the patient. A skinny young doctor with a close-cropped brown beard stood by the victim's feet, in tense conversation with the paramedic by the door.

"Did you ever get anything?"

The paramedic rubbed his sweating face—he'd been the one counting when they came in—and replied, "Asystole; just one long, flat line." He wiped his hand on his trousers.

"Nothing at all?"

"Not that I could tell."

Dr. Anderson swore and said, "Well, let's see what we got. Turn off the thumper."

The click-wheeze stopped and all eyes turned to the monitor, where a perfectly straight line was drawn in green across the bottom of the charcoal screen. Stephanie switched on the recorder and it began to emit paper with the straight line written on it.

"Restart," ordered the doctor. The wheeze-click began and again the peculiarly-shaped series of lumps crossed the screen, still interspersed by none of the sharp jags that meant heartbeat.

"Hell," said Dr. Anderson. "When was his last bicarb given?"

The paramedic said, "He's had two, the last one five minutes ago."

"Push another," the doctor ordered. "And an Epi. Maybe this is fine fib, not asystole." He glanced at the monitor on the wall. "Is the monitor at full gain?"

"Yup," said Stephanie.

"Epi and bicarb in," Coppercurls said, pushing the syringe.

"Seven fifty-three. No change, doctor," intoned Stephanie, writing.

Dr. Anderson looked anxiously at the screen. Sometimes the fibrillating heart was in a tremor so fine it could not be detected on the monitor. He turned to the anesthetist. "Linda, how are his breath sounds?"

Linda put her stethoscope in her ears and listened to each lung as she ventilated the patient. "Lungs clear bilateral." He had not inhaled any vomitus.

The patient was looking very pink, but there had been no effort on his part to breathe or pump blood. And it had been at least forty minutes since his heart had stopped. "Stop Thumper." The line again became perfectly flat, a fact the recorder verified. If there were anything left of the man, the injections should have roused it. Dr. Anderson wiped his forehead. "Damn."

"Well, shall we call it?" asked Stephanie.

"Yeah," sighed Dr. Anderson.

"Seven fifty-eight," noted Stephanie, and wrote it down. This would be the victim's official time of death.

The tension instantly went out of the room. The recorder was shut off. Thumper was pulled out and put on the floor. Linda removed the ambu bag and began to pack her gear.

"Any family?" asked Dr. Anderson.

"I think that was his wife Jackie took out," said Stephanie. She turned off the monitor and began to collect the readout tapes while the sturdy redhead knotted and cut the IV lines. Stephanie took a white sheet off a shelf.

Linda, her work done, left, saying, "Don't call me for a while, okay? I've got two mothers in labor upstairs." Dr. Anderson went out behind her, bound for the family lounge and the giving of sad news. Coppercurls made a "too bad" grimace at Stephanie on her way out.

"I told you we'd never save him," said the paramedic to Brichter. The beeper in his pocket went off. "Christ!" he muttered. "Gotta run!" Brichter followed him less hurriedly out into the corridor, to find Billy and the firemen also gone.

He went to lean in the doorway of Red Room One and drink his coffee. "Who was he?"

"He didn't say." Stephanie was picking up used syringes from the counter, breaking off their needles and throwing the parts away.

"Dumb question?"

"I just treat 'em, Obie. I don't care what somebody calls 'em when they're well."

"Cherry Ames you ain't."

"Especially not when I'm childbit." She glanced at him. "Your eyes are gray, aren't they?"

"Yeah, why?"

"They're so pale they look almost silver in this light. Weird." Brichter did not think to retort—he really liked her—and she said, "Are you scared of bodies?"

"Not particularly. Why?"

"If you can find the strength to pry yourself away from that door, you might give me a hand moving him. The family will probably want to come take a look."

Brichter put his cup on a counter and came to stand across the cart from her. The man's shoulders were propped up, but his head had been arranged to hang back over the support to make a straight line for the endotracheal tube. Brichter lifted a flaccid arm and grabbed a shoulder. When she nodded, he heaved. The body slid heavily, then stopped short, and Brichter fell across the chest. "Hey!"

"What?"

"Funny smell, like nuts or something. On his breath."

"Pbie, he hasn't got any breath."

"Well, take a sniff and see for yourself."

She bent over the quiet face and said, "Hmmm. Vomit and—okay, almonds? I think this will do. Better go check on your drunk." She turned away and began to unfold the white sheet.

Brichter sighed and walked back to the nurses' station and stuck his head in the door. "Suzy, how's Mr. Smith?"

"I might've known it was you who brought Wally Smith in. He's okay. They're stitching his head now in Main Six. Did you really have to arrest him?"

"Yes, ma'am."

One of the clerks at a desk up the way turned and said, "He smells strong, but none of us thinks he's even legally drunk."

"We're doing a pool on his B.A.," said Suzy, "so call us the results, okay? Dr. Holland says he's only a point oh six, but he always guesses low. Tommy says he's point oh eight, and I've got a dollar on oh nine. He better be one oh, legal, Obie, or the whole town is going to be asking for your head. Want to put your money where your handcuffs are?"

Brichter grimaced. "No, thanks." He didn't like drunks, but he didn't find this sort of game funny, either. Especially this time, since it included a swipe at him. Dammit, they were wrong. Smith's blood would test pretty high. It was the scare of the accident and the arrest making him seem more sober than he was.

"He'll be ready in about half an hour, Obie," Suzy said. "The tech will come get you to draw the legal B.A."

He glanced at his watch; that would put him well past quitting time. He'd have to call in soon. "Fine; I'll be in the nurses' lounge."

He went back to the lounge and refilled his cup, dropping a nickel ostentatiously into the can. He reached into his back pocket, pulled out his notebook and sat down. Brichter had an eye for detail and a cultivated habit of making frequent, thorough notes about on-the-job incidents. For the next few minutes he was absorbed in writing a careful account of Mr. Smith's apprehension and subsequent behavior.

A shadow appeared in the doorway, but he didn't look up until it made an exasperated noise. It was Stephanie. "Am I in your chair?" he asked.

She waved a clipboard at him as she approached. She was wearing a wreath of monitor strips and looking very grim. "I need the whole table—*if* you don't mind!"

"Sure. It's your lounge." He stood, closing his notebook. "You finally heard, then?"

"Heard what?"

"I arrested Wally Smith. He's my DWI."

"Oh, that. Jackie told me." She slapped her clipboard onto the table and went to open the little refrigerator under a counter. "Was he really drunk?"

"Stinking."

"No one else thinks so." She found a Diet Pepsi and popped it open. This fuss about Smith did not seem to concern her very much.

"If it wasn't my arresting Mr. Smith, what's got you mad?"

She came to sit down, kicking a second chair aside and putting her feet up on it. "That grieving widow—I don't think!" she said.

"No? She was crying and upset when I saw her."

"It was humiliation, Obie. She had in mind a dignified declaration of death at home and a respectable mortician taking the body away in a decent hearse. She found our resuscitation team and its efforts unseemly and common. You should hear her. I did, at length. Dr. Anderson left it to me to tell her the medical examiner might want to do an autopsy. She blew up all over me. Christ. I tried to tell her the M.E. gets a look at anyone who dies in the emergency room, but it was like trying to talk a Roman candle back onto the ground."

"I've heard of that reaction. It's normal."

"Hey, you've got to know this chick isn't sentimental. There have been stories about her ever since her husband had that stroke." She grinned. "I saw her myself giving old Wally Smith the treatment in a dark corner at the hospital's fundraiser in February. 'Oh, Wally, I think it's so wonderful when a man just reaches out to take what he really wants,'" she mimicked in a breathless little voice. "No, it's like he's her personal property, and we're bodysnatchers or something."

"Is she mad—or scared?"

Her thickly-lashed dark eyes glanced at him. "You're all cop now, aren't you? Don't answer; I've got work to do." She pulled off a monitor strip and began to search along it.

He was silent, but watched her covertly, hoping she'd finish before he had to go back to his drunk. An unsentimental widow who didn't want an autopsy was always a matter of interest.

Dr. Anderson came in to get a cup of coffee, taking a ceramic mug out of a cabinet. "That was a stinker of a case," he remarked to no one, filling it and adding sugar and creamer. He put a coin in the can saying, "And he came in so nice and pink too."

"Maybe he's normally high-colored," said Brichter, joining automatically in the verbal postmortem.

"Nah, I saw the guy a month ago; he was upstairs for an evaluation. No progress, poor bastard." He gestured with a thin hand. "You know him, Obie?"

"Never saw him before."

"Used to be in my racquetball club. Late fifties but keeping himself in good shape for that new young wife. Sailing, travel, tennis, the works. Then pop goes a blood vessel and he's an intelligent cucumber." He came to prop a flat buttock on the counter and taste his coffee. "Well, maybe a little more. His speech was understandable, and he could move an arm. But no walking, much less racquetball. And no poon tang, either, to keep the young bride at home. God, he must have hated that. He was fighting hard to come back, but the prognosis was bad. So maybe it was a mercy, huh? All the same, I would have thought we could have resuscitated him."

Stephanie looked up from her work. "After a down time of forty minutes? She'd've found the cucumber a real fireball next to what we'd've stuck her with."

"It wasn't all down time, Steffie. The squad got to him in nine minutes, and it was CPR all the way from then on."

Stephanie snorted and kept writing. This was a sore point among emergency room personnel, but one not often discussed. Why bring back someone whose forebrain is essentially destroyed, who will have no measurable awareness?

"Anyhow, that pink didn't look real," said Stephanie. "Maybe it was sunburn or something. From a sunlamp, maybe."

"No, it wasn't sunburn," said Dr. Anderson. "It was deeper than that." He smiled. "Almost as if he was blushing."

"A modest corpse?" remarked Stephanie dryly.

Brichter put down his cup, his hands suddenly cold. "Did you notice that smell about him, doctor?"

"What do you mean, what smell?" Anderson asked sharply.

"A nutty smell. What the hell do bitter almonds smell like? Because if I'm right, that would explain the pink, too, wouldn't it?"

"Cyanide," breathed Anderson. "Jesus, how would he get a dose of cyanide? No, Obie, that would make it murder! Are you sure about the smell?"

"Yes, it was very distinct."

Stephanie stopped rolling a monitor tape around her hand. "I smelled it, too, doctor. But what has his color got to do with cyanide?"

Brichter said, "The oxygen stays trapped in the blood, it can't get into the tissues. So the venous blood turns as red as the arterial, and the body glows a healthy pink while the victim suffocates at a cellular level."

"Christ, Obie!" she said. "Do you think that's what happened?"

"I'm going to go take a whiff," announced Dr. Anderson, putting down his mug and starting out of the room.

"See if Mrs. Iver is still in the family consultation room," Brichter called after him. "Damn, I wish Billy hadn't left. I'd like to hear what she told him."

"You think she did it," said Stephanie.

"I didn't say that. But there's a lot of money in the Iver family, you and the doctor agree she hasn't exactly been the devoted wife, and you said she strongly objected to an autopsy. It isn't good police procedure to let someone with that background walk off without a chance to explain herself. I think I ought to go talk to her."

Suzy stuck her head in the door and said, "Obie, if you want to get that blood alcohol, you better come now. We got a whole beach party of teenagers on their way in, so go sign the log." She ducked out again.

"Hell." Brichter thought briefly and asked, "Stephanie, is there some way to detain Mrs. Iver?"

She put down her work. "Far be it from me to keep you from putting poor Mr. Smith in jail on his last night in America!"

"Thanks. I'll come to her as soon as I finish up." He stopped at the nurses' station to sign the log and borrow a phone. He called the Safety Building to tell them about Mr. Smith, and listened patiently to a lecture from the watch captain, who had already received an inquiry from a local radio station that paid twenty-five dollars for new tips. Brichter asked for a team of detectives from Homicide to come over, and explained why. Then he went to Main Six.

The ten-by-six curtained-off area contained a wheeled cart, a shelf with examination equipment, and Mr. Smith. He was sitting up on the cart, gray and scared, a little man with a round bald head whose dark fringe was graying above his ears. The emesis basin, unused, was lying on his suitcoat, neatly folded beside him. There was a large bandage across his forehead, and the blood had been washed from his face.

Brichter said briskly, "Mr. Smith, we need a blood alcohol test. You have the right to refuse; however, if you do refuse your driver's license will be revoked for six months. Will you consent to the test?"

Smith asked nervously, "Is it Mr. Iver they brought in?"

"Yes. Will you—"

The curtain opened and a lab tech came in. "I'm here to draw your blood." He put his tray on the cart and began to roll up Smith's left sleeve.

Smith frowned as the tech wrapped a rubber tourniquet around his upper arm. He pulled his arm away.

"What do you think you're doing?"

"Drawing some blood, for the B.A." The tech, working quickly, rescued the arm and wiped off the inside bend of the elbow with a betadine swab, leaving an orange stain. He held up a vacuum tube syringe. "This may sting a little," he said.

"What's the B.A.?" asked Smith.

Brichter sighed. "Hold it a second, Tommy. Mr. Smith, we want to take a blood alcohol test. You have the right to refuse the test; however, if you do, you driver's license will be revoked for six months. Do you understand?"

Smith stared at Brichter for several seconds, then said, "You already told me all that, didn't you?"

"Then we have your permission to draw the blood?"

"Hell, no! First of all, I'm not drunk. Second of all, I don't give a damn about a driver's license. I'm going to be walking the beaches from now on."

But Brichter was determined to have the test. "Tell him, Tommy."

"Tell him what?" asked Tommy, giving Brichter a look.

"About the pool. Betting on the results of the B.A."

Tommy said nervously, "It was just a joke."

"But you don't think he's drunk, either."

"Hell no! None of us does!"

"Here's your chance to prove me wrong in front of everyone," said Brichter to Smith.

Smith grimaced. "Attaboy," said Tommy encouragingly.

Smith held out his arm. "Take the blood."

Tommy said again, "This may sting a little," and inserted the needle under the skin.

"Ow," said Smith automatically. He stared a moment at the bright upsurge in the tube. "Uh," he said, tearing his eyes away to look at Brichter, "y'see, officer, I know Mrs. Iver. I mean, she brought Mr. Iver's prescriptions to me. Poor old guy's had a hard time of it. So when I heard her name out there I sort of wondered. That's why I didn't pay any attention when you first told me about the blood test. I mean, I don't know her as a friend but she's a nice lady, and life's been hard on her. So naturally I'm concerned."

"Sure," said Brichter, no longer in quite so much of a hurry. Smith sure was anxious to explain himself. "But your drugstore isn't in the Iver neighborhood, is it? Sort of inconvenient, I'd think."

"Bend your arm, please." The tech lifted Mr. Smith's bent elbow and put the blood sample into a small Styrofoam box, which he handed to Brichter. "That's all, sir," he said insolently.

"I went all-generic on my drugs a year or so back," said Smith. "So my prices are low. Everyone likes to save money, even rich people." He cleared his throat. "He's dead, isn't he?"

"Yes, a few minutes ago." Brichter reached for his pen to mark the box and said, "I'm sorry you missed your flight to Chicago. Why don't you get someone to call and cancel your ticket to Nassau? You can make new reservations later."

"You're not going to let me go?"

"No, sir."

"I'll call the airline for you," said Tommy. "Or Suzy will. Or anyone, for that matter."

"Thank you," said Smith. He moved the emesis basin with trembling hands and fumbled in his suitcoat for the plane ticket, found it and gave it to Tommy, who put it on the tray. Smith asked Brichter, "How long will the rest of this take?"

"We're done here. I've got to check on one or two things and then I'll take you back to the jail and get you booked. You'll be free as soon as you make bail."

The tech gave Brichter a dirty look, then unbent Smith's elbow and put a Band-Aid over the puncture site. "I'll let you know when the ticket's cancelled," he said.

"Thanks," Smith said.

Suzy came in holding a sheaf of papers. "Obie, Dr. Holland's decided he wants some X-rays of Mr. Smith's head. Can't send him out of the country with a concussion, can we? We'll take care of it. I'll come get you when we're finished."

Good, he wouldn't have to handcuff the little man to a drainpipe. "All right," he said, and hurried out.

The family consultation room was softly lit, deeply carpeted, and arranged with two distinct clusters of very comfortable chairs. There was a phone on top of a stack of phone books, and boxes of Kleenex were everywhere. In the grouping by the window, Stephanie was taking a very detailed history from Mrs. Iver, her voice quiet and gentle. Brichter stood in the open doorway a moment—he'd never heard Stephanie sound like that before—then knocked once on the doorframe.

Mrs. Iver's blue eyes widened at the sight of his uniform and she pressed a handkerchief to her pale mouth.

"Mrs. Iver," said Stephanie, rising, "this is Officer Brichter. He's been talking with Dr. Anderson about your husband's death. I think he'd like to ask you some questions, so I'll leave you two alone."

"No, please!" Mrs. Iver clutched at Stephanie with long brown fingers. "Stay, please!"

"Of course I'll stay if you want me to. I'll sit over there so I won't disturb you." She sat in the chair farthest away.

Brichter sat down beside Mrs. Iver, notebook in one hand. "Mrs. Iver, do you know of anyone who might have a reason to harm your husband? Perhaps someone who had a serious quarrel with him recently?"

She frowned and shook her head. "Everyone liked Rob." Her voice was sweet and breathy.

"I don't know how to tell you this other than plainly: It appears your husband has been poisoned."

"No!" she said. "It was his heart; he had a heart attack! I went to check on him and I saw he wasn't breathing. And I checked and there was no pulse. I called his doctor, and next thing I knew those terrible men came in and began slapping him and beating on his chest . . . and more came, and they made him throw up . . ." She sobbed once. "Couldn't they see he was dead? It was horrible to watch!"

Brichter made a short note. "I'm sorry, Mrs. Iver. If it's poison, then it's possible your husband has been murdered."

She paled under the tan. "I don't believe you," she whispered harshly. "No, that's impossible. No one hated him. He was too weak to quarrel with anyone, and anyway he didn't have many visitors. He looked so dreadful, with his face all crooked, I couldn't stand the way they'd stare at him."

Brichter was writing. "There are some police detectives on their way down here. Will you talk with them?"

"No. No, I don't think so. I've called my attorney, and he's coming. I won't have Rob cut open, I won't! He was an important man.
Please—" She put a strong brown hand on his arm and looked at
him, tears like diamonds clustered under her frightened blue eyes.
"I'm very tired; I think I'll go home now."

"I'm afraid I have to ask you to stay until we've completed our
preliminary investigation."

She blinked at his cool tone without dislodging the tears. He
waited for her to ask indignantly if she were under arrest, but she
said, "Then perhaps you can leave me alone."

Stephanie said gently, "I don't think you should be left alone just
now. I'll get someone to stay with you. Would you like some
coffee?"

Mrs. Iver gave Stephanie an unreadable look. "No, thank you,"
she said.

"Whew," said Stephanie, as she and Brichter went back up the
corridor. "Was that all right, getting someone to watch her?"

"Yes," he said, absentmindedly brushing the sleeve Mrs. Iver had
touched. "And neatly done, too, not giving her a chance to say no."

"Do you think she did it?"

"I can't say."

"Yes, you can."

He didn't like discussing his job with civilians. But she was interested, concerned—and he really liked her. "Well, it wasn't suicide.
Dr. Anderson said he was angry and fighting, which are not symptoms of depression. And she said herself there were no quarrels, no
enemies, not even much by way of visitors." He pulled an ear. "This
is less concrete, but you noticed earlier how all her tears were for
herself. Same thing now. Not one bit of sympathy for the poor bastard on the receiving end of his friends' pity, only for the poor
woman forced to watch it. I'd hate to be at the mercy of someone
as egocentric as that."

"Dr. Anderson told me he thinks it's cyanide all right. He said to
lean on Mr. Iver while inhaling is to take your life in your hands.
I've never been that close to a real murderer before.

He smiled crookedly. "What makes you think that?"

She went into the nurses' lounge ahead of him. "Well, it isn't
likely, is it?"

Brichter thought of the kid he'd shot a few months ago when he
accidentally interrupted a liquor store robbery. "People kill people
all the time. They just don't talk about it to their friends."

"You have a very ugly way of looking at life, you know that?"

"Comes with the uniform, I guess," he said. "Coffee?"

"No, but you can hand me my Diet Pepsi." She sat at the table and looked resentfully at her clipboard.

"Where did she get it, I wondered?" Brichter asked, taking the opened can out of the little refrigerator and handing it to her.

"What, the cyanide? I don't know. We don't have any around; it has no true medicinal purpose, the laetril pushers notwithstanding."

"Yes."

"It's in peach pits, isn't it? Maybe you should search her garbage for peach pits."

"We probably will. And check her passport. Maybe she's been to South America lately, buying lima beans. Lima beans grown in the tropics are full of cyanide."

She smiled, took a drink of her diet soda. "You know the damnedest things."

"I know."

"Obie?" said Suzy, leaning into the room. "We're finished with Mr. Smith."

"Could you hold him a while?"

" 'Fraid not. Don't forget to call me with the results of the B.A." She left without waiting for an answer.

Brichter said thoughtfully, "Smith. Registered pharmacists can buy poisons. And Mrs. Iver got her prescriptions filled at his store. Maybe he's ordered some cyanide lately."

"Now *that's* ridiculous!"

"Is it? You said she put the make on him. Maybe he didn't say no."

"There's that ugly imagination again."

"Yes." He pulled out his notebook and consulted a page. "When I told him he'd missed his plane he said, 'She'll kill me.' I thought he was so drunk he'd forgotten he was a widower, but he's acted perfectly sober ever since. Ask anyone." He closed his eyes. "There was just a little break on the end of that when he said it, like he barely stopped himself from adding 'too.' "

"You're serious!"

"Is there some place I can talk to him in private?"

She hesitated, then said. "The head nurse's office. She's gone home, won't be back until tomorrow."

"I'll come and see you before I leave," he said. "Will you be here for a while?"

"No, the elves are going to come and do this work while I'm asleep in my little bed." She picked up her neglected clipboard.

As he walked down the hallway he made a bet. The scare of the accident and the shock of the arrest had scared Smith sober, right? If so, by now the sympathy of the staff should have greatly alleviated the false sobriety.

He pulled back the curtain. Smith turned his head alertly and said, "Can we go now? Do you know if the jail will take traveler's checks?"

Still sober. You lose. "Yes, I think they do. Mr. Smith, may we delay going for just a few minutes? Something has come up with regard to Mr. Iver, and I'm hoping you can help us clear it up."

Smith rubbed his chin with a finger. "I don't know anything about it."

"Well, it's kind of a pharmaceutical question."

"Oh. Oh, well, all right, if you think I can help."

Brichter began reviewing in his head the techniques of interrogation as he led the little man to the cosy office beyond the nurses' station. He flipped on the lights as they went in, and shut the door.

He put a chair at the side of the desk so he could observe Smith's entire body during the interrogation. "Sit here, please." Smith sat in a single contained motion in the chair and grasped his knees with his hands to stop their trembling.

Brichter went behind the desk, took out his long fat notebook, and sat down. "I'll try to keep this short," he said. "It appears Mr. Iver was poisoned with cyanide."

"The nurse at the desk said cardiac arrest," said Smith instantly.

"Yes, cyanide induces cardiac arrest. I'm hoping you'll agree to help us determine how he might have gotten hold of the poison. You can refuse to talk to me, if you like; that's your right. And you have a right to discuss this with an attorney before we go on, and to have an attorney present while we talk. If you want one, but can't afford one, I'll get one assigned to you before we continue. Do you understand?"

Despite his gentled-down paraphrase of the standard Miranda warning, Smith looked thoroughly terrified. "Yes."

"Will you answer some questions for me?"

"Yes."

"Cyanide is a deadly poison. It would be difficult for anyone to obtain it, even a registered pharmacist."

"Yes, you have to say why and sign a poison log book."

"Have you ever ordered any, for any reason?"

"No! I mean, no, but my grandfather used to. To fumigate houses with, and kill mice. There are substitutes today, less dangerous. But ag agents—agricultural agents—still sometimes offer it. There are some old farmers around here who use it in the barnyard, to kill vermin."

"I see." Writing, "Did Mrs. Iver ever ask you about cyanide or any other poisons?"

"My God, you think *she* did it?"

"She's our chief suspect," admitted Brichter. "I'm trying to determine if she could have purchased or otherwise acquired it."

"That's crazy! She's a kind woman, a decent person! You can't possibly think she did such a thing!"

"You seem very sure of that."

"I am, I am!"

Brichter turned back a few pages in his notebook. "Then you admit you know her better than you said earlier, when you said she wasn't a friend."

Smith stared at the notebook. "No." He swallowed, and gestured feebly. "You don't have to know her well to know she isn't capable of such a thing."

"Did you attend the February fundraiser for County General Hospital?"

Smith opened his mouth, closed it, and tried again. "No," he said.

"Mr. Smith, if you are going to lie to me, we might just as well discontinue this right now." Brichter put down his pen and waited.

The silence grew and grew. Smith said softly, "She is very beautiful."

"I know. If she'd come on to me like that, I might have been so flattered it wouldn't have occurred to me to say no."

"Yes." Smith sighed, a very gentle sigh, laden with admissions.

Brichter tried a rare bluff. "How long has your affair been going on?"

Smith hesitated, but Brichter had gotten just the right matter-of-fact tone. "Just a few months. We were very careful; I don't know how you found out. Her husband can't—well, he can't. He was very ill, sicker than almost anyone knew. And very unhappy. She said he told her once that if he wasn't going to get better he wanted to die. She was brave, but she needed a respite, you know? It just sort of grew."

"You discussed marriage?"

Smith wriggled uncomfortably. "No." Brichter put down his pen and Smith said, "Well—yes."

"Did she consider divorcing him?"

"Yes, but that would seem like she was deserting him. Better or worse, and all that. And anyway—" He paused, glanced at Brichter. "Anyway, she wouldn't have gotten any money, she said. I'd do anything for her, but I'm not a wealthy man, and she's used to nice things."

"I see," Brichter said. "The real reason you said you were going to get sick was so you wouldn't have to see her, right?"

"Yes. I was scared—she thinks I'm in Chicago by now."

"Yes, sir."

"I love her, you know."

"Yes, I believe that you do."

Smith gingerly tried out the idea: "If you think I got it for her, they'll put me in prison for the rest of my life."

Careful, thought Brichter. "No, sir, I doubt that. She's a beautiful young woman and she'll hire the best defense money can buy. I doubt if she'll spend a long time behind bars. And any accessory could hardly be given a longer sentence, could he? It wouldn't be fair."

Smith looked at the baby palm on the head nurse's desk and said sadly, "I really want to go to Nassau. Everyone expects me to go."

"And you probably will. You've got a lot of friends in Charter."

"The whole town will hate me if they think I helped her kill him."

"Well, but what if they think you let her face it alone?"

Smith bowed his head. "Is she under arrest?"

"There are detectives on their way now."

"She's a remarkable woman. And he was really suffering. It was a mercy—" He stopped, boggling, and went abruptly off on a tangent. "Y'know, I must've drunk a gallon of Gary's fishhouse punch at my party, but I didn't feel a thing. Then I got in my car and pow! All of a sudden I'm singing."

"Yes, sir."

"Then I saw your red lights, like to scared me to death. And when you pulled me out of the car, I could see it in your eyes. I thought, Oh, God, she messed it up somehow and I'm screwed. I was right, huh?"

Don't lie. "No, sir, it was an ordinary DWI, driving while intoxicated—and fleeing the police."

"Shouldna run, should I?"

"That's right."

"All those people out there, sayin' how sorry they are for me—dammit, what the hell do they know?" There was a long silence with Brichter refused to break. Smith sighed. "Wouldna liked it anyhow," he said. "Every time I heard an American voice, I'd've jumped ten feet, prob'ly."

"Yes, sir."

"So I'm not mad at you for arrestin' me. Jus' as well, prob'ly."

"Yes, sir." Here it comes; he's ready now.

Smith shrugged unevenly and his tongue thickened. "I signed my name with my lef' hand, and burned all my copies of the tranzaction."

"Where did you order it from?" Brichter was careful not to change the tone of his voice, to make the confession just a natural continuation of the interrogation.

"Drug house in Cincinnati. Tol' them we had a yard boy who used it to kill gophers."

"Was it prussic acid?"

"Huh-uh, p'tassium cyanide pellets." His terror gone, Smith was relapsing into drunkenness. "I groun' a few of 'em up and put the powder into some capsules I'd emptied his antibiotics out of." He frowned heavily. "She made me do four, though I told her one would do it and two were ample." He studied the baby palm in its yellow pot. "She was goin' to fly to Nassau after the funeral and we'd meet as if by accident. We'd take it slow, not marry for a year or so."

"Yes, sir. What did you do with the leftover cyanide?"

"Put it in a cookie tin and buried it under hydro-dydrangeo bush inna back yard. The flowers'll be a nice cyanotic blue this summer. Only isn't cyanide, o' course. The metal does it."

Dig under the hydrangea bush, wrote Brichter. 'Whose idea was it to use cyanide?"

"Mine. She wanted somethin' fast an' sure an' hard to rekanize. I went all through my PDR lookin' an' lookin' and cou'dn't fin' nuthin' as good—"

There was a soft knock and the door opened. Suzy stuck her head around. "Obie, those detectives are looking for you. Hi, Mr. Smith!"

"H'lo, Suzy!" he said, waving cheerily.

"Wow, you are drunk after all! That's all right, celebrate! Life for you is going to be one sweet dream, right?"

"Well, first this p'liceman is taking me to jail."

She groaned, "Obie, do you *have* to?"

"Yes, ma'am."

"You *are* a merciless bastard, aren't you?"

"Yes, ma'am. Send the detectives along."

The door slammed. Smith said humbly, "Thanks for not telling her."

"That's all right." There was, after all, mercy and mercy. "May I offer you a little advice?"

"Sure."

"Don't eat anything Mrs. Iver might send or have sent to you. And if you make bail, don't accept any dinner invitations from her."

Smith gave this ponderous consideration. "Y'know, I tol' her two was plenny, but she wanted four."

"Yes, sir."

"Women, huh?"

"Yes, sir."

"I sure can pick 'em."

"Yes, sir." Brichter turned back the leaves of his notebook in a review and they sat in companionable silence, waiting for the boys from Homicide.

LESSON IN ANATOMY

by MICHAEL INNES

Already, the anatomy theater was crowded with students, tier upon tier of faces pallid beneath the clear shadowless light cast by the one elaborate lamp, large as a giant cartwheel, near the ceiling. The place gleamed with an aggressive cleanliness; the smell of formalin pervaded it; its center was a faintly sinister vacancy—the spot to which would presently be wheeled the focal object of the occasion.

At Nessfield University Professor Finlay's final lecture was one of the events of the year. He was always an excellent teacher. For three terms he discoursed lucidly from his dais or tirelessly prowled his dissecting rooms, encouraging young men and women who had hitherto dismembered only dogfish and frogs to address themselves with resolution to human legs, arms, and torsos. The Department of Anatomy was large; these objects lay about in a dispersed profusion; Finlay moved among them now with gravity and now with a whimsical charm which did a good deal to humanize his macabre environment. It was only once a year that he yielded to his taste for the dramatic.

The result was the final lecture. And the final lecture was among the few academic activities of Nessfield sufficiently abounding in human appeal to be regularly featured in the local press. Perhaps the account had become a little stereotyped with the years, and always there was virtually the same photograph showing the popular professor (as Finlay was dubbed for the occasion) surrounded by wreaths, crosses, and other floral tributes. Innumerable citizens of Nessfield who had never been inside the doors of their local university looked forward to this annual report, and laid it down with the comfortable conviction that all was well with the pursuit of learning in the district. Their professors were still professors—eccentric, erudite, and amiable. Their students were still as students should be, giving much of their thought to the perpetration of elaborate, tasteless, and sometimes dangerous practical jokes.

For the lecture was at once a festival, a rag, and a genuine display of virtuosity. It took place in this large anatomy theater. Instead of disjointed limbs and isolated organs there was a whole new cadaver for the occasion. And upon this privileged corpse Finlay rapidly demonstrated certain historical developments of his science to an audience in part attentive and in part concerned with lowering skeletons from the rafters, releasing various improbable living creatures—lemurs and echidnas and opossums—to roam the benches, or contriving what quainter japes they could think up. On one famous occasion the corpse itself had been got at, and at the first touch of the professor's scalpel had awakened to an inferno of noise presently accounted for by the discovery that its inside consisted chiefly of alarm clocks. Nor were these diversions and surprises all one-sided, since Finlay himself, entering into the spirit of the occasion, had more than once been known to forestall his students with some extravagance of his own. It was true that this had happened more rarely of recent years, and by some it was suspected that this complacent scholar had grown a little out of taste with the role in which he had been cast. But the affair remained entirely good-humored; tradition restrained the excesses into which it might have fallen; it was, in its own queer way, an approved social occasion. High university authorities sometimes took distinguished visitors along—those, that is to say, who felt they had a stomach for postmortem curiosity. There were quite a number of strangers on the present occasion.

The popular professor had entered through the glass-paneled double doors which gave directly upon the dissecting table. Finlay was florid and very fat; his white gown was spotlessly laundered; a high cap of the same material would have given him the appearance of a generously self-dieted chef. He advanced to the low rail that separated him from the first tier of spectators and started to make some preliminary remarks. What these actually were, or how they were designed to conclude, he had probably forgotten years ago, for this was the point at which the first interruption traditionally occurred. And, sure enough, no sooner had Finlay opened his mouth than three young men near the back of the theater stood up and delivered themselves of a fanfare of trumpets. Finlay appeared altogether surprised—he possessed, as has been stated, a dramatic sense—and this was the signal for the greater part of those present to rise in their seats and sing *For he's a jolly good fellow.* Flowers—single blooms, for the present—began to float through the air and fall about the feet of the professor. The strangers, distinguished and otherwise, smiled at each other benevolently, thereby indicating their pleased acquiescence in these time-honored academic junketings. A bell began to toll.

"Never ask for whom the bell tolls," said a deep voice from somewhere near the professor's left hand. And the whole student body responded in a deep chant: *"It tolls for THEE."*

And now there was a more urgent bell—one that clattered up and down some adjacent corridor to the accompaniment of tramping feet and the sound as of a passing tumbrel. *"Bring out your dead,"* cried the deep voice. And the chant was taken up all round the theater. *"Bring out your dead,"* everybody shouted with gusto. *"Bring out your DEAD!"*

This was the signal for the entrance of Albert, Professor Finlay's dissecting-room attendant. Albert was perhaps the only person in Nessfield who uncompromisingly disapproved of the last lecture and all that went with it—this perhaps because, as an ex-policeman, he felt bound to hold all disorder in discountenance. The severely aloof expression on the face of Albert as he wheeled in the cadaver was one of the highlights of the affair—nor on this occasion did it by any means fail of its effect. Indeed Albert appeared to be more than commonly upset. A severe frown lay across his ample and unintelligent countenance. He held his six feet three sternly erect; behind his vast leather apron his bosom discernibly heaved with manly emotion. Albert wheeled in the body—distinguishable as a wisp of ill-nourished humanity beneath the tarpaulin that covered it—and Finlay raised his right hand as if to bespeak attention. The result was a sudden squawk and the flap of heavy wings near the ceiling. Somebody had released a vulture. The ominous bird blundered twice round the theater and then settled composedly on a rafter. It craned its scrawny neck and fixed a beady eye on the body.

Professor Finlay benevolently smiled; at the same time he produced a handkerchief and rapidly mopped his forehead. To several people, old stagers, it came that the eminent anatomist was uneasy this year. The vulture was a little bit steep, after all.

There was a great deal of noise. One group of students was doggedly and pointlessly singing a sea chanty; others were perpetrating or preparing to perpetrate sundry jokes of a varying degree of effectiveness. Albert, standing immobile beside the cadaver, let his eyes roam resentfully over the scene. Then Finlay raised not one hand but two—only for a moment, but there was instant silence. He took a step backwards amid the flowers which lay around him; carefully removed a couple of forget-me-nots from his hair; gave a quick nod to Albert; and began to explain—in earnest this time—what he was proposing to do.

Albert stepped to the body and pulled back the tarpaulin.

"And ever," said a voice from the audience, "at my back I hear the rattle of dry bones and chuckle spread from ear to ear."

It was an apt enough sally. The cadaver seemed to be mostly bones already—the bones of an elderly, withered man—and its most prominent feature was a ghastly *rictus* or fixed grin which exposed two long rows of gleaming white and utterly incongruous-seeming teeth. From somewhere high up in the theater there was a little sigh followed by a slumping sound. A robust and football-playing youth had fainted. Quite a number of people, as if moved by a mysterious or chameleonlike sympathy, were rapidly approximating to the complexion of the grisly object displayed before them. But there was nothing unexpected in all this. Finlay, knowing that custom allowed him perhaps another five minutes of sober attention at this point, continued his remarks. The cadaver before the class was exactly as it would be had it come before a similar class four hundred years ago. The present anatomy lesson was essentially a piece of historical reconstruction. His hearers would recall that in one of Rembrandt's paintings depicting such a subject—

For perhaps a couple of minutes the practiced talk flowed on. The audience was quite silent. Finlay for a moment paused to recall a date. In the resulting complete hush there was a sharp click, rather like the lifting of a latch. A girl screamed. Every eye in the theater was on the cadaver. For its lower jaw had sagged abruptly open and the teeth, which were plainly dentures, had half extruded themselves from the gaping mouth, rather as if pushed outwards by some spasm within.

Such things do happen. There is a celebrated story of just such startling behavior on the part of the body of the philosopher Schopenhauer. And Finlay, perceiving that his audience was markedly upset, perhaps debated endeavoring to rally them with just this learned and curious anecdote.. But even as he paused, the cadaver had acted again. Abruptly the jaws closed like a powerful vise, the lips and cheeks sagged; it was to be concluded that this wretched remnant of humanity had swallowed its last meal.

For a moment something like panic hovered over the anatomy theater. Another footballer fainted; a girl laughed hysterically; two men in the back row, having all the appearance of case-hardened physicians, looked at each other in consternation and bolted from the building. Finlay, with a puzzled look on his face, again glanced backwards at the cadaver. Then he nodded abruptly to Albert, who replaced the tarpaulin. Presumably, after this queer upset, he judged it best to interpose a little more composing historical talk before getting down to business.

He was saying something about the anatomical sketches of Leonardo da Vinci. Again he glanced back at the cadaver. Suddenly the lights went out. The anatomy theater was in darkness.

For some moments nobody thought of an accident. Finlay often had recourse to an epidiascope or lantern, and the trend of his talk led people to suppose that something of the sort was in train now. Presently, however, it became plain that there was a hitch—and at this the audience broke into every kind of vociferation. Above the uproar the vulture could be heard overhead, vastly agitated. Matches were struck, but cast no certain illumination. Various objects were being pitched about the theater. There was a strong scent of lilies.

Albert's voice made itself heard, cursing medical students, cursing the University of Nessfield, cursing Professor Finlay's final lecture. From the progress of this commination it was possible to infer that he was groping his way towards the switches. There was a click, and once more the white shadowless light flooded the theater.

Everything was as it had been—save in two particulars. Most of the wreaths and crosses which had been designed for the end of the lecture had proved missiles too tempting to ignore in that interval of darkness; they had been lobbed into the center of the theater and lay there about the floor, except for two which had actually landed on the shrouded cadaver.

And Finlay had disappeared.

The audience was bewildered and a little apprehensive. Had the failure of the lighting really been an accident? Or was the popular professor obligingly coming forward with one of his increasingly rare and prized pranks? The audience sat tight, awaiting developments. Albert, returning from the switchboard, impatiently kicked a wreath of lilies from his path. The audience, resenting this display of nervous irritation, catcalled and booed. Then a voice from one of the higher benches called out boisterously: "The corpse has caught the dropsy!"

"It's aswelling," cried another voice—that of a devotee of Dickens—"It's aswelling wisibly before my eyes."

And something had certainly happened to the meagre body beneath its covering; it was as if during the darkness it had been inflated by a gigantic pump.

With a final curse Albert sprang forward and pulled back the tarpaulin. What lay beneath was the body of Professor Finlay, quite dead. The original cadaver was gone.

The vulture swooped hopefully from its rafter.

"Publicity?" said Detective-Inspector John Appleby. "I'm afraid you can scarcely expect anything else. Or perhaps it would be better to say notoriety. Nothing remotely like it has happened in England for years."

Sir David Evans, Nessfield's very Welsh vice-chancellor, passed a hand dejectedly through his flowing white hair and softly groaned. "A scandal!" he said. "A scandal—look you, Mr. Appleby—that peggars description. There must be infestigations. There must be arrests. Already there are reporters from the pig papers. This morning I have been photographed." Sir David paused and glanced across the room at the handsome portrait of himself which hung above the fireplace. "This morning," he repeated, momentarily comforted, "I have been photographed, look you, five or six times."

Appleby smiled. "The last case I remember as at all approaching it was the shooting of Viscount Auldearn, the lord chancellor, during a private performance of *Hamlet* at the Duke of Horton's seat, Scamnum Court."

For a second Sir David looked almost cheerful. It was plain that he gained considerable solace from this august comparison. But then he shook his head. "In the anatomy theater!" he said. "And on the one day of the year when there is these unseemly pehaviors. And a pody vanishes. And there is futures—fultures, Mr. Appleby!"

"One vulture." Dr. Holroyd, Nessfield's professor of human physiology, spoke as if this comparative paucity of birds of prey represented one of the bright spots of the affair. "Only one vulture, and apparently abstracted by a group of students from the zoo. The director rang up as soon as he saw the first report. He might be described as an angry man."

Appleby brought out a notebook. "What we are looking for," he said, "is angry men. Perhaps you know of someone whose feelings of anger towards the late Professor Finlay at times approached the murderous?"

Sir David Evans looked at Dr. Holroyd and Dr. Holroyd looked at Sir David Evans. And it appeared to Appleby that the demeanor of each was embarrassed. "Of course," he added, "I don't mean mere passing irritations between colleagues."

"There is frictions," said Sir David carefully. "Always in a university there is frictions. And frictions produce heat. There was pad frictions between Finlay and Dr. Holroyd here. There was personalities, I am sorry to say. For years there has been most fexatious personalities." Sir David, who at all times preserved an appearance of the most massive benevolence, glanced at his colleague with an eye in which there was a nasty glint. "Dr. Holroyd is dean of the faculty of medicine, look you. It is why I have asked him to meet you now. And last week at a meeting there was a most disgraceful scene. It was a meeting about lavatories. It was a meeting of the Committee for Lavatories."

"Dear me!" said Appleby. Universities, he was thinking, must have changed considerably since his day.

"Were there to be more lavatories in the Physiology Building? Finlay said he would rather put in a path."

"A path?" said Appleby, perplexed.

"A path, with hot and cold laid on, and an efficient shower. Finlay said that in his opinion Dr. Holroyd here padly needed a path."

"And did Dr. Holroyd retaliate?"

"I am sorry to say that he did, Mr. Appleby. He said that if he had his way in the matter Finlay's own path would be a formalin one. Which is what they keep the cadavers in, Mr. Appleby."

Dr. Holroyd shifted uneasily on his chair. "It was unfortunate," he admitted. "I must freely admit the unfortunate nature of the dispute."

"It was unacademic," said Sir David severely. "There is no other word for it, Dr. Holroyd."

"I am afraid it was. And most deplorably public. Whereas your own quarrel with Finlay, Sir David, had been a discreetly unobtrusive matter." Dr. Holroyd smiled with sudden frank malice. "And over private, not university, affairs. In fact, over a woman. Or was it several women?"

"These," said Appleby rather hastily, "are matters which it may be unnecessary to take up." Detectives are commonly supposed to expend all their energy in dragging information out of people; actually, much of it goes in preventing irrelevant and embarrassing disclosures. "May I ask, Sir David, your own whereabouts at the time of the fatality?"

"I was in this room, Mr. Appleby, reading Plato. Even vice-chancellors are entitled to read Plato at times, and I had given orders not to be disturbed."

"I see. And I take it that nobody interrupted you, and that you might have left the room for a time without being observed?"

Sir David gloomily nodded.

"And you, Dr. Holroyd?"

"I went to poor Finlay's final lecture and sat near the back. But the whole stupid affair disgusted me and I came away—only a few minutes, it seems, before the lights went out. I composed myself by taking a quiet walk along the canal. It was quite deserted."

"I see. And now about the manner of Finlay's death. I understand that you have inspected the body and realize that he was killed by the thrust of a fine dagger from behind? The deed was accomplished in what must have been almost complete darkness. Would you say that it required—or at least that it suggests—something like the professional knowledge of another anatomist or medical man?"

Holroyd was pale. "It certainly didn't strike me as the blind thrust of an amateur made in a panic. But perhaps there is a species of particularly desperate criminal who is skilled in such things."

"Possibly so." Appleby glanced from Holroyd to Sir David. "But is either of you aware of Finlay's having any connections or interests which might bring upon him the violence of such people? No? Then I think we must be very skeptical about anything of the sort. To kill a man in extremely risky circumstances simply for the pleasure of laying the body on his own dissecting table before his own students is something quite outside my experience of professional crime. It is much more like some eccentric act of private vengeance. And one conceived by a theatrical mind."

Once more Sir David Evans looked at Dr. Holroyd and Dr. Holroyd looked at Sir David Evans. "Finlay himself," said Sir David, "had something theatrical about him. Otherwise, look you, he would not have let himself become the central figure in this pig yearly joke." He paused. "Now, Dr. Holroyd here is not theatrical. He is pad-tempered. He is morose. He is underpred. But theatrical he is not."

"And no more is Sir David." Holroyd seemed positively touched by the character sketch of himself just offered. "He is a bit of a humbug, of course—all philosophers are. And he is not a good man, since it is impossible for a vice-chancellor to be that. Perhaps he is even something of a *poseur*. If compelled to characterize him freely—" and Holroyd got comfortably to his feet "—I should describe him as Goethe described Milton's *Paradise Lost.*" Holroyd moved towards the door, and as he did so paused to view Sir David's portrait. " 'Fair outside but rotten inwardly,' " he quoted thoughtfully. "But of positive theatrical instinct I would be inclined to say that Sir David is tolerably free. Good afternoon."

There was a moment's silence. Sir David Evans' fixed expression of benevolence had never wavered. "Pad passions," he said. "Look you, Mr. Appleby, there is pad passions in that man."

Albert was pottering gloomily among his cadaver racks. His massive frame gave a jump as Appleby entered; it was clear that he was not in full possession of that placid repose which ex-policemen should enjoy.

Appleby looked round with brisk interest. "Nice place you have here," he said. "Everything convenient and nicely thought out."

The first expression on Albert's face had been strongly disapproving. But at this he perceptibly relaxed. "Ball-bearings," he said huskily. "Handles them like lambs." He pushed back a steel shutter and proudly drew out a rack and its contents. "Nicely developed gal," he said appreciatively. "Capital pelvis for childbearing, she was going to have. Now, if you'll just step over here I can show you one or two uncommonly interesting lower limbs."

"Thank you—another time." Appleby, though not unaccustomed to such places, had no aspirations towards connoisseurship. "I want your own story of what happened this morning."

"Yes, sir." From old professional habit Albert straightened up and stood at attention. "As you'll know, there's always been this bad be'avior at the final lecture, so there was nothing out of the way in that. But then the lights went out, and they started throwing things, and something 'it me 'ard on the shins."

"Hard?" said Appleby. "I doubt if that could have been anything thrown from the theater."

"No more do I." Albert was emphatic. "It was someone came in through the doors the moment the lights went out and got me down with a regular rugby tackle. Fair winded I was, and lost my bearings as well."

"So it was some little time before you managed to get to the switch, which is just outside the swing door. And in that time Professor Finlay was killed and substituted for the cadaver, and the cadaver was got clean away. Would you say that was a one-ma job?"

"No sir, I would not. Though—mind you—that body 'ad only to be carried across a corridor and out into the courtyard. Anyone can 'ave a car waiting there, so the rest would be easy enough."

Appleby nodded. "The killing of Finlay, and the laying him out like that, may have been a sheer piece of macabre drama, possibly conceived and executed by a lunatic—or even by an apparently sane man with some specific obsession regarding corpses. But can you see any reason why such a person should actually carry off the original corpse? It meant saddling himself with an uncommonly awkward piece of evidence."

"You can't ever tell what madmen will do. And as for corpses, there are more people than you would reckon what 'as uncommon queer interests in them at times." And Albert shook his head. "I seen things," he added.

"No doubt you have. But have you seen anything just lately? Was there anything that might be considered as leading up to this shocking affair?"

Albert hesitated. "Well, sir, in this line wot I come down to since they retired me it's not always possible to up'old the law. In fact, it's sometimes necessary to circumvent it, like. For, as the late professor was given to remarking, science must be served." Albert paused and tapped his cadaverracks. "Served with these 'ere. And of late we've been uncommon short. And there's no doubt that now and then him and me was stretching a point."

"Good heavens!" Appleby was genuinely alarmed. "This affair is bad enough already. You don't mean to say that it's going to lead to some further scandal about body-snatching?"

"Nothing like that, sir." But as he said this Albert looked doubtful. "Nothing *quite* like that. They comes from institutions, you know. And nowadays they 'as to be got to sign papers. It's a matter of tact. Sometimes relatives comes along afterwards and says there been too much tact by a long way. It's not always easy to know just how much tact you can turn on. There's no denying but we've 'ad one or two awkwardness this year. And it's my belief as 'ow this sad affair is just another awkwardness—but more violent like than the others."

"It was violent, all right." Appleby had turned and led the way into the deserted theater. Flowers still strewed it. There was a mingled smell of lilies and formalin. Overhead, the single great lamp was like a vast all-seeing eye. But that morning the eye had blinked. And what deed of darkness had followed?

"The professor was killed and laid out like that, sir, as an act of revenge by some barmy and outraged relation. And the cadaver was carried off by that same relation as what you might call an act of piety."

"Well, it's an idea." Appleby was strolling about, measuring distances with his eye. "But what about this particular body upon which Finlay was going to demonstrate? *Had* it outraged and pious relations?"

"It only come in yesterday. Quite unprepared it was to be, you see—the same as hanatomists 'ad thcm in the sixteenth century. Very interesting the late professor was on all that. And why all them young varmints of students should take this particular occasion to fool around—"

"Quite so. It was all in extremely bad taste, I agree. And I don't doubt that the coroner will say so. And an assize judge, too, if we have any luck. But you were going to tell me about this particular corpse."

"I was saying it only come in yesterday. And it was after that that somebody tried to break into the cadaver racks. Last night, they did—and not a doubt of it. Quite professional, too. If this whole part of the building, sir, weren't well-nigh like a strongroom they'd have done it, without a doubt. And when the late professor 'eard of it 'e was as worried as I was. Awkwardnesses we've 'ad. But body-snatching in reverse, as you might say, was a new one on us both."

"So you think that the outraged and pious relation had an earlier shot, in the program for which murder was not included? I think it's about time we hunted him up."

Albert looked sorely perplexed. "And so it would be—if we knew where to find him. But it almost seems as if there never was a cadaver with less in the way of relations than this one wot 'as caused all the trouble. A fair ideal cadaver it seemed to be. You don't think, now—" Albert was frankly inconsequent "—that it might 'ave been an accident? You don't think it might 'ave been one of them young varmints' jokes gone a bit wrong?"

"I do not."

"But listen, sir." Albert was suddenly urgent. "Suppose there was a plan like this. The lights was to be put out and a great horrid dagger thrust into the cadaver. That would be quite like one of their jokes, believe me. For on would go the lights again and folk would get a pretty nasty shock. But now suppose—just suppose, sir—that when the lights were put out for that there purpose there came into the professor's head the notion of a joke of his own. He would change places with the cadaver—"

"But the man wasn't mad!" Appleby was staring at the late Professor Finlay's assistant in astonishment. "Anything so grotesque—"

"He done queer things before now." Albert was suddenly stubborn. "It would come on him sometimes to do something crazier than all them young fools could cudgel their silly brains after. And then the joke would come first and decency second. I seen some queer things at final lectures before this. And that would mean that the varmint thinking to stick the dagger in the cadaver would stick it in the late professor instead."

"I see." Appleby was looking at Albert with serious admiration; the fellow didn't look very bright—nevertheless his days in the force should have been spent in the detective branch. "It's a better theory than we've had yet, I'm bound to say. But it leaves out two things: the disappearance of the original body, and the fact that Finlay was stabbed from behind. For if he did substitute himself for the body it would have been in the same position—a supine position, and not a prone one. So I don't think your notion will do. And, anyway, we must have all the information about the cadaver that we can get."

"It isn't much." Albert bore the discountenance of his hypothesis well. "We don't know much more about 'im than this—that 'e was a seafaring man."

The cadaver, it appeared, had at least possessed a name: James Cass. He had also possessed a nationality, for his seaman's papers declared him to be a citizen of the United States, and that his next of kin was a certain Martha Cass, with an indecipherable address in Seattle, Washington. For some years he had been sailing pretty constantly in freighters between England and America. Anybody less likely to bring down upon the Anatomy Department of Nessfield University the vengeance of outraged and pious relations it would have been difficult to conceive. And the story of Cass's death and relegation to the service of science was an equally bare one. He had come off his ship and was making his way to an unknown lodging when he had been knocked down by a tram and taken to the casualty ward of Nessfield Infirmary. There he had been visited by the watchful Albert, who had surreptitiously presented him with a flask of gin, receiving in exchange Cass's signature to a document bequeathing his remains for the purposes of medical science. Cass had then died and his body had been delivered at the Anatomy School.

And after that, somebody had ruthlessly killed Professor Finlay and then carried James Cass's body away again. Stripped of the bewildering nonsense of the final lecture, thought Appleby, the terms of the problem were fairly simple. And yet that nonsense, too, was relevant. For it had surely been counted upon in the plans of the murderer.

For a few minutes Appleby worked with a stopwatch. Then he turned once more to Albert. "At the moment," he said, "Cass himself appears to be something of a dead end. So now let us take the lecture—or the small part of it that Finlay had got through before the lights went out. You were a witness of it—and a trained police witness, which is an uncommonly fortunate thing. I want you to give me every detail you can—down to the least squawk or flutter by that damned vulture."

Albert was gratified and did as he was bid. Appleby listened, absorbed. Only once a flicker passed over his features. But when Albert was finished he had some questions to ask.

"There was the audience," he said, "—if audience is the right name for it. Apparently all sorts of people were accustomed to turn up?"

"All manner of unlikely and unsuitable folk." Albert looked disgusted. "Though most of them would be medical, one way or another. As you can imagine, sir, a demonstration of a sixteenth century dissecting technique isn't every layman's fancy."

"It certainly wouldn't be mine."

"I couldn't put a name to a good many of them. But there was Dr. Holroyd, whom you'll have met, sir; he's our professor of human physiology. Went away early, he did; and looking mighty disgusted, too. Then there was Dr. Wesselmann, the lecturer in prosthetics—an alien, he is, and not been in Nessfield many years. He brought a friend I never had sight of before. And out they went, too."

"Well, that's very interesting. And can you recall anyone else?"

"I don't know that I can, sir. Except of course our vice-chancellor, Sir David Evans."

Appleby jumped. "Evans! But he swore to me that—"

Albert smiled indulgently. "Bless you, that's his regular way. Did you ever know a Welshman who could let a day pass without a bit of 'armless deceitlike?"

"There may be something in that."

" 'E don't think it dignified, as you might say, to attend the final lecture openly. But more than not he's up there at the far doorway, peering in at the fun. Well, this time 'e 'ad more than 'e bargained for."

"No doubt he had. And the same prescription might be good for some of the rest of us." Appleby paused and glanced quickly round the empty theater. "Just step to a telephone, will you, and ask Dr. Holroyd to come over here."

Albert did as he was asked, and presently the physiologist came nervously in. "Is another interview really necessary?" he demanded. "I have a most important—"

"We shall hope not to detain you long." Appleby's voice was dry rather than reassuring. "It is merely that I want you to assist me in a reconstruction of the crime."

Holroyd flushed. "And may I ask by what right you ask me to take part in such a foolery?"

Appleby suddenly smiled. "None, sir—none at all. I merely wanted a trained mind—and one with a pronounced instinct to get at the truth of a problem when it arises. I was sure you would be glad to help."

"Perhaps I am. Anyway, go ahead."

"Then I should be obliged if you would be the murderer. Perhaps I should say the first murderer, for it seems likely enough that there were at least two—accomplices. You have no objection to so disagreeable a part?"

Holroyd shrugged his shoulders. "Naturally, I have none whatever. But I fear I must be coached in it and given my cues. For I assure you it is a role entirely foreign to me. And I have no theatrical flair, as Sir David pointed out."

Once more Appleby brought out his stopwatch. "Albert," he said briskly, "shall be the cadaver, and I shall be Finlay standing in front of it. Your business is to enter by the back, switch off the light, step into the theater and there affect to stab me. I shall fall to the floor. You must then dislodge Albert, hoist me into his place, and cover me with the tarpaulin. Then you must get hold of Albert by the legs or shoulders and haul him from the theater."

"And all this is in the dark? It seems a bit of a program."

Appleby nodded. "I agree with you. But we shall at least discover if it is at all possible of accomplishment by one man in the time available. So are you ready?"

"One moment, sir." Albert, about to assume the passive part of the late James Cass, sat up abruptly. "You seem to have missed me out. Me as I was, that is to say."

"Quite true." Appleby looked at him thoughtfully. "We are short of a stand-in for you as you were this morning. But I shall stop off being Finlay's body and turn on the lights again myself. So go ahead."

Albert lay down and drew the tarpaulin over his head. Holroyd slipped out. Appleby advanced as if to address an audience. "Now," he said.

And Appleby talked. Being thorough, he made such anatomical observations as his ignorance allowed. Once he glanced around at the corpse, and out of the corner of his eye glimpsed Holroyd beyond the glass-paneled door, his hand already going up to flick at the switch. A moment later the theater was in darkness, and seconds after that Appleby felt a sharp tap beneath the shoulder-blade. He pitched to the floor, pressing his stopwatch as he did so. Various heaving sounds followed as Holroyd got the portly Albert off the table; then Appleby felt himself seized in surprisingly strong arms and hoisted up in Albert's place. Next came a shuffle and a scrape as Holroyd, panting heavily now, dragged the inert Albert from the theater. Appleby waited for a couple of seconds, threw back the tarpaulin, and lowered himself to the floor. Then he groped his way through the door, flicked on the light, and looked at his watch. "And the audience," he said, "is now sitting back and waiting—until presently somebody points out that the cadaver is the wrong size. Thank you very much. The reconstruction has been more instructive than I hoped." He turned to Holroyd. "I am still inclined to think that it has the appearance of being the work of two men. And yet you managed it pretty well on schedule when single-handed. Never a fumble and just the right lift. You might almost have been practicing it."

Holroyd frowned. "Yachting," he said briefly, "—and particularly at night. It makes one handy."

And Albert looked with sudden suspicion at Nessfield's professor of human physiology. "Yachting?" he asked. "Now, would that have put you in the way of acquaintance with many seafaring men?"

Of James Cass, that luckless waif who would be a seafarer no longer, Appleby learned little more that afternoon. The cargo vessel from which he had disembarked was already at sea again, and a couple of days must elapse before any line could be tapped there. But one elderly seaman who had recently made several voyages with him a little research did produce, and from this witness two facts emerged. There was nothing out of the way about Cass—except that he was a man distinctly on the simple side. Cass had been suggestible, Appleby gathered; so much so as to have been slightly a butt among his fellows. And Appleby asked a question: had the dead man appeared to have any regular engagement or preoccupation when he came into port? The answer to this was definitive. Within a couple of hours, Appleby felt, the file dealing with this queer mystery of the anatomy theater would be virtually closed for good.

Another fifteen minutes found him mounting the staircase of one of Nessfield's most superior blocks of professional chambers. But the building, if imposing, was gloomy as well, and when Appleby was overtaken and jostled by a hurrying form, it was a second before he recognized that he was again in the presence of Dr. Holroyd.

"Just a moment." Appleby laid a hand on the other's arm. "May I ask if this coincidence extends to our both aiming at the third floor?"

Holroyd was startled, but made no reply. They mounted the final flight side by side and in silence. Appleby rang a bell before a door with a handsome brass plate. After a perceptible delay the door was opened by a decidedly flurried nurse, who showed the two men into a sombre waiting room. "I don't think," she said, "that you have an appointment? And as an emergency has just arisen, I am afraid there is no chance of seeing Dr.—"

She stopped at an exclamation from Appleby. Hunched in a corner of the waiting room was a figure whose face was almost entirely swathed in a voluminous silk muffler. But there was no mistaking that flowing silver hair. "Sir David!" exclaimed Appleby. "This is really a most remarkable rendezvous."

Sir David Evans groaned. "My chaw," he said. "It is one pig ache, look you."

Holroyd laughed nervously.

"Shakespeare was demonstrably right. There was never yet philosopher could bear the toothache patiently—nor vice-chancellor either."

But Appleby paid no attention; he was listening keenly to something else. From beyond a door on the right came the sound of hurried, heavy movement. Appleby strode across the room and turned the handle. He flung back the door and found himself looking into the dentist's surgery. "Dr. Wesselmann?" he said.

The answer was an angry shout from a bullet-headed man in a

white coat. "How dare you intrude in this way!" he cried. "My colleague and myself are confronted with a serious emergency. Be so good as to withdraw at once."

Appleby stood his ground and surveyed the room; Holroyd stepped close behind him. The dentist's chair was empty, but on a surgical couch nearby lay a patient covered with a light rug. Over this figure another white-coated man was bending, and appeared to be holding an oxygen mask over its face.

And Nessfield's lecturer in prosthetics seemed to find further explanations necessary. "A patient," he said rapidly, "with an unsuspected idiosyncrasy to intravenous barbiturates. Oxygen has to be administered, and the position is critical. So be so good—"

Appleby leaped forward and sent the white-coated holder of the oxygen mask spinning; he flung back the rug. There could be no doubt that what was revealed was James Cass's body. And since lying on Professor Finlay's dissecting table it had sustained a great gash in the throat. It had never been very pleasant to look at. It was ghastly enough now.

Wesselmann's hand darted to his pocket; Holroyd leaped on him with his yachtsman's litheness, and the alien dentist went down heavily on the floor. The second man showed no fight as he was handcuffed. Appleby looked curiously at Holroyd. "So you saw," he asked, "how the land lay?"

"In my purely amateur fashion I suppose I did. And I think I finished on schedule once again."

Appleby laughed. "Your intervention saved me from something decidedly nasty at the hands of Nessfield's authority on false teeth. By the way, would you look round for the teeth in question? And then we can have in Sir David—seeing he is so conveniently in attendance—and say an explanatory word."

"I got the hang of it," said Appleby, "when we did a very rough and ready reconstruction of the crime. For when, while playing Finlay's part, I glanced round at the cadaver, I found myself catching a glimpse of Dr. Holroyd here when he was obligingly playing First Murderer and turning off the lights. There was a glass panel in the door, and through this he was perfectly visible. I saw at once why Finlay had been killed. It was merely because he had seen, *and recognized,* somebody who was about to plunge the theater in darkness for some nefarious, but not necessarily murderous, end. What did this person want? There could be only one answer: the body of

James Cass. Already he had tried to get it in the night, but the housebreaking involved had proved too difficult.''

The benevolent features of Sir David Evans were shadowed by perplexity. "But why, Mr. Appleby, should this man want such a pody?''

"I shall come to that in a moment. But first keep simply to this: that the body had to be stolen even at great hazard; that when glimpsed and recognized by Finlay the potential thief was sufficiently ruthless to silence him with a dagger secreted for such an emergency—and was also sufficiently quick-witted to exploit this extemporaneous murder to his own advantage. If he had simply bolted with Cass's body and left that of Finlay the hunt would of course have been up the moment somebody turned the lights on. By rapidly substituting one body for the other—Finlay's for that of Cass—on the dissecting table, he contrived the appearance first of some more or less natural momentary absence of Finlay from the theater, and secondly the suggestion of some possible joke which kept the audience wary and quiet for some seconds longer. All this gave additional time for his getaway. And—yet again—the sheerly grotesque consequence of the substitution had great potential value as a disguise. By suggesting some maniacal act of private vengeance, it masked the purely practical—and the professionally criminal—nature of the crime.

"And now, what did we know of Cass? We knew that he was a seaman; that he traveled more or less regularly between England and America; that he was knocked down and presently died shortly after landing; and that he was a simple-minded fellow, easily open to persuasion. And we also knew this: that he had a set of rather incongruously magnificent false teeth; that in the anatomy theater these first protruded themselves and then by some muscular spasm appeared to lodge themselves in the throat, the jaw closing like a vise. And we also knew that, hard upon this, a certain Dr. Wesselmann, an alien comparatively little known in Nessfield and actually a specialist in false teeth, hurried from the theater accompanied by a companion. When I also learned from a seaman who had sailed with Cass that he was often concerned about his teeth and would hurry off to a dentist as soon as he reached shore, I saw that the case was virtually complete.''

"And would be wholly so when you recovered Cass's body and got hold of these.'' Holroyd came forward as he spoke, carrying two dental plates on an enamel tray. "Sir David, what would you say about Cass's teeth?"

Nessfield's vice-chancellor had removed the muffler from about his jaw; the excitement of the hunt had for the moment banished the pain which had driven him to Wesselmann's rooms. He inspected the dentures carefully—and then spoke the inevitable word. "They are pig," he said decisively.

"Exactly so. And now, look." Holroyd gave a deft twist to a molar; the denture which he was holding fell apart; in the hollow of each gleaming tooth there could be discerned a minute oil-silk package.

"What they contain," said Appleby, "is probably papers covered with a microscopic writing. I had thought perhaps of uncut diamonds. But now I am pretty sure that what we have run to earth is espionage. What one might call the Unwitting Intermediary represents one of the first principles of that perpetually fantastic game at its higher levels. Have a messenger who has no notion that he *is* a messenger and you at once supply yourself with the sort of insulating device between cell and cell that gives spies a comforting feeling of security. Cass has been such a device. And it was one perfectly easy to operate. He had merely to be persuaded that his false teeth were always likely to give him trouble, and that he must regularly consult (at an obligingly low fee) this dentist at one end and that dentist at the other—and the thing was practically foolproof. Only Wesselmann and friends failed to reckon on sudden death, and much less on Cass's signing away his body—dentures and all—to an anatomy school." Appleby paused. "And now, gentlemen, that concludes the affair. So what shall we call it?"

Holroyd smiled. "Call it the Cass Case. You couldn't get anything more compendious than that."

But Sir David Evans shook his beautiful silver locks. "No!" he said authoritatively. "It shall be called *Lesson in Anatomy*. The investigation has been most interesting, Mr. Appleby. And now let us go. For the photographers, look you, are waiting."

M IS FOR MAYO

by WILLIAM POMIDOR

"You haven't taken any of the crab Louis." Cal scolded her husband as they walked from the buffet. Choosing a picnic table beneath a copse of trees, she asked, "Have you tried it? It's delicious, Plato."

It was a stunning summer Sunday, a cool crisp Midwestern rarity. Either divine providence or the fickle hand of fate was blocking Erie humidity from the Appalachian foothills. Plato wouldn't let his wife's appeal for a healthier diet spoil his breezy mood.

"All that mayonnaise!" he chided her with a self-righteous *tsk!* "I wouldn't think of it."

Cal frowned at her plate as she sat down. Dwarfed by a pair of radishes, the tiny smear of crab was barely visible—hardly enough cholesterol to clog the arteries of a mouse. Some carrot slices and a light salad completed her meal. "Maybe you're right. I'll eat the crab last." She brightened. "You're doing so well with your Healthy Heart diet. I feel guilty sometimes . . ."

Plato glanced at his wife's wispy figure and meager serving and felt his own twinges of guilt. Hidden under a flimsy Caesar salad disguise lurked a cut of prime rib thick enough to choke a horse. Under the table, a steak knife sliced through his pants pocket.

"Ahh, the Doctors Marley!" A beefy hand slapped Plato's back.

"Rufus!" Cal bounced from her seat across the table and gave the intruder a warm hug. "The party is wonderful. Fantastic food. I was just telling—"

Her husband tried to rise, but his knife threatened vital organs.

"No, don't get up." Rufus Thorndyke squeezed Plato's shoulder reassuringly. Back at the buffet tent, he had witnessed Plato's cattle-rustling behavior with raised eyebrows. "That diet of yours must have left you pretty weak."

59

"It's a sacrifice at first," Plato acknowledged with a brave smile. "But after a while, you hardly notice the difference."

Rufus grinned back. Tipping the scales at three hundred pounds, he was something of a stranger to dietary sacrifices. But on his mooselike frame, the extra weight looked natural.

Tailoring, Plato told himself.

"Cal, I've got Brownie all saddled up and ready to ride."His light green eyes chuckled at Plato. "Sanchez is ready, too, if you want to accompany your wife. He's a gentle horse. Really."

Plato suppressed a groan. Old Sanchez, the Venezuelan hellhorse. Rufus had rescued the ancient Thoroughbred from some Caracas glue factory. "Sure. Can't wait."

Thorndyke glanced up the hill. Near the buffet canopy a hand waved, accompanied by a voice carried high and thin on the breeze. "There's Jan. She was driving the lobster down from the airport." Turning, Rufus waddled up the hill to greet his lovely young wife.

"What's he talking about?" Plato asked when Thorndyke was out of earshot. In his confusion, he wondered if he had heard correctly. "Jan's on a lobster drive? Is that what the horses are for?"

Cal just rolled her eyes.

He snapped his fingers. "I've got it! We all know there's something fishy about how Rufus got his money. Maybe 'The Lobster' is a mob kingpin. Works out of Maine—Bangor, Rockport. Commands with a claw, trafficks in tail."

"Plato!" She glanced around, made sure no one had heard her husband's lunatic ramblings. "The lobster's for us, silly. Rufus had a hundred of them flown in fresh from Nova Scotia. It's amazing. Each year the hospital staff appreciation dinner gets bigger and better."

"And each year Andrew Cleeford gets closer to retirement."

"This has nothing to do with hospital politics. Rufus is already on the board of directors."

"Think about it, Cal. The chairmanship. You think that's not the apple of his eye? The culmination of his career? He's no spring chicken, you know."

Cal squinted at her husband from beneath lowered eyebrows. They weren't really as bushy as she thought. To Plato, they didn't mar her prettiness at all. Except when she squinted. "Sometimes you can be so . . . *cynical!*"

She was right. Plato knew he was being hard on the guy. After all, before the dinner, Thorndyke had publicly donated ten thousand dollars to the hospital's drug rehabilitation center. Some DEA official had lectured about the drug menace, focusing on a Mexican product called "sleeper" that was hooking a lot of local kids. And Rufus's seed money bore fruit through impromptu donations from his wealthy friends.

So Plato kept his mouth shut as he followed Cal around the Thorndyke grounds, chatting amiably with dozens of doctors, nurses, and other hospital staffers.

"Plato and Cal Marley," he heard repeatedly, "an obstetrician and a pathologist. Plato brings them in, and Cal wheels them out."

Ho, ho, ho.

Worse yet were the inevitable questions. "What made your wife want to become a pathologist?"

"She eats people," Plato finally replied to Mrs. Cleeford.

The wife of the venerable board chairman patted his hand and nodded sagely. "We all need people, son. She just has to find another outlet—church, social organizations. I'm a member of the Buffalo League Women's Auxiliary."

Cal dragged him to the stables before he could comment. A few miles of old Sanchez's bone-jarring canter brought him back down to earth. He'd never be sarcastic or cynical ever again. He'd eat salads and pine nuts and herbs and sunflower seeds and grass. If only someone would help him off the horse.

"Wasn't that a glorious ride?" Cal asked, holding Sanchez's bridle.

Cautiously, Plato lifted one leg from a stirrup. His backbone had been pulverized, ground to a fine powder, then mixed into a heavy concrete. He toppled to the ground.

Shuffling along the path through the woods, Cal stopped suddenly, squeezing his hand. Beads of sweat broke out on her pale forehead. "I don't feel so good."

"You don't look so good, either." Plato pulled her arm across his shoulder. "Come on. Maybe you should lie down inside."

"Yeah, maybe."

She hobbled beside him for a while, then stopped and winced. "God! It's my stomach, Plato. I've never hurt this bad before."

The hairs on the back of his neck came to attention. A tiny voice in his head spoke: "Acute appendicitis. Perhaps accompanied by peritonitis. In situations like these, time is of the essence."

He swung a surprised Cal into his arms, thankful for once that she ate chipmunk food. They bounced down the path until he jolted to a halt.

"Plato dear, you're sweet," she gasped. "But I don't feel *that* bad. Just put me down, okay?"

He nodded dumbly, slipped her back onto her feet. She turned up and gaped at the clearing. Up the hill, the huge form of Rufus Thorndyke blunted the horizon. Several guests were lying down as well—sprawled on the grass or picnic tables or lawn chairs. A few walking wounded rushed from person to person, checking pulses and palpating abdomens. An ambulance keened from the driveway.

The couple's eyes met.

"Food poisoning," they whispered in unison. "The crab Louis."

Plato's aversion to seafood had been vindicated.

The doors marked INTENSIVE CARE UNIT—AUTHORIZED PERSONNEL ONLY sighed open like the gatestones of a crypt. After helping the crab victims into their respective ambulances, Plato had tucked Cal into bed at home. She would page him if she felt worse.

He hobbled into the hospital sanctuary just as the doors closed, nearly dismembering him with their ponderous weight. He paused to catch his breath, still stiff from the afternoon's glorious ride. While his eyes adjusted to the gloom, he heard the soft, thrusting rhythm of ventilators, the muted mechanical bleeps of monitors, and the low sigh of cool, dry air from invisible outlets.

Intensive care, Plato thought. Where lives are saved or lost and doctors are scheduled in cynicism.

"Excuse me, sir, can I please see—" The voice was as harsh and sharp as a splinter beneath a fingernail. A penlight stabbed Plato's eyes while a hand frisked his coat for an I.D. badge.

"Oh, it's you. Marley." Mrs. Leeman, head nurse of the ICU. Tough, experienced, and brutally competent, her only fault was a bit of night blindness. "Come right in."

"I came to see Mr. Thorndyke."

She led him past a row of glass-walled rooms to the nursing station. Deftly, she spun a gleaming carousel of stainless steel and blue vinyl binders. "You were at his party last night?"

"Yeah. But I don't like crab." Plato retrieved Thorndyke's chart and flipped through it. There was nothing unusual about it; he'd half expected a special red binder, stars and stenciled warning labels: "Authorized Personnel Only—Government Clearance GP-10 or Higher!"

Mrs. Leeman showed him to Thorndyke's cubicle, directly across from the nursing station. The huge man was almost invisible beneath a web of machines, tubes, wires, and cables. Overhead, CRT's traced the frantic heart rhythm, lowering blood pressure, and measured sighs of mechanical respiration. But one look at the flabby, waxen face told far more than numbers on a screen.

"I don't believe we've met before. Doctor—?"

In the murky shadows, Plato hadn't noticed the room's other occupant. Gage, the gastroenterologist. White hair manicured to perfection, navy sports jacket, freshly pressed gray pants, and a sharply knotted tie. Looking at him, you'd never guess it was two A.M.

Plato looked down at his rumpled, coffee-stained lab coat and tennis shoes. Tailoring, he told himself again.

"Plato Marley," he replied, awkwardly shaking hands across the bed. Glancing down at Thorndyke's pale form, he wondered: Is someone awake in there, listening, aware?

He hoped not.

"I was at the party last night," he continued. "I wondered how Mr. Thorndyke was doing. After I got home, I did some thinking. Some of his symptoms seemed a bit unusual. I'd like to talk to you about it."

"Yes, yes, of course." Gage nodded his head and led the way to a door marked PHYSICIANS' CONFERENCE ROOM. "You look familiar—"

"I did my residency here several years ago, then did an infertility fellowship in Chicago," he replied, taking a seat at the table. Blazing fluorescent light bounced painfully from white walls, pearl file cabinets, beige carpeting. Some obscure kidney function calculation was scribbled on the whiteboard. In the corner, a skeleton wearing a top hat browsed through a faded copy of the *Wall Street Journal*.

"Marley, Marley," Gage whispered to himself, as though he were turning through a dictionary. "Seems I've heard that name before."

"My wife's a doctor as well," Plato said. "One of the hospital pathologists. She's in forensics. Tecumseh County coroner."

Gage's eyebrows blossomed in surprise. "Do they really need a forensic pathologist in TC? How long since there's been a murder there?"

"A *people* murder?" Plato shrugged. "Not since Cal took office. But she had a hit and run on a Holstein just last week. We've got the body down at the lab. Well, part of it, anyway."

"Seneca General isn't exactly a center of academic medicine, either," the digestive specialist agreed. "But we provide pretty good care here. And this is a good area to raise a family."

His smile dissolved suddenly. "I don't know if you're aware, but Jan Thorndyke is my daughter." Gage grimaced, raised his voice.

"That makes Rufus my son-in-law, though at his age, it's hard to think of him that way. We were in college together, back East . . ."

The door burst open suddenly, and a stocky figure in white blew into the room.

"Thanks for calling me, Dr. Gage! Sorry I'm late." The intern pulled a ragged mop of hair back from her forehead. Panting, she explained, "I got a dump admission from Urology. It took *two hours*. I got here as soon as I could."

Gage chuckled and pulled out a chair. "That's quite all right. Have a seat. Linda Zamiella, I'd like to present Dr. Plato Marley. He's an infertility specialist, but he was at the Thorndyke party last night and thought we might need his help."

They shook hands. Zamiella's white laboratory coat was spotless. The only flaw in her appearance was a menagerie of dogeared journal articles spilling from her pockets.

"I was explaining that some of Mr. Thorndyke's symptoms seemed unusual for food poisoning," Plato told her, ignoring Gage's sarcastic introduction. "It's hard to put a finger on it, but his case seemed different. Excruciating abdominal pain, far worse than the other victims. Pain on swallowing. Later, as you know, he became delirious."

"There've been some cardiogram changes as well," Linda added, tugging a tattered heart monitor tracing from her pocket. She handed it to Gage. "I think Dr. Marley's right. I saw a lot of the other victims last night. Most of them have already gone home. The few who were hospitalized are doing well. Except Mr. Thorndyke."

"And Felicia Martinez, Thorndyke's maid. She's even worse." Gage frowned, then glanced at Plato. "Linda hopes to become a specialist in digestive diseases, like me. What's your impression, Dr. Zamiella?"

Linda paused for a moment, eyes unfocused. She recited as it from a formula, "Mr. Thorndyke is a sixty-year-old male in otherwise good health who presents with sudden onset of abdominal pain and dysphagia, eventually lapsing into delirium. Signs of shock have been accompanied by an abnormal heart rhythm, but peritoneal signs are absent. My impression is that Mr. Thorndyke's symptoms cannot be explained solely by spoiled food."

"What can account for them?" Gage challenged.

Linda shrugged and knuckled her forehead. "What about some kind of non-bacterial poisoning, like mercury?" She dredged her capacious pockets again. Like hamsters pouching food, interns often tuck entire reference libraries into their coats. "I just read an article last month in the *Archives.* Abdominal pain, nausea, vomiting, and shock are common symptoms.''

Gage chewed a fingernail. "But where would Mr. Thorndyke have received such a dose of mercury? Even hatters don't see much of it these days.''

"It's common in some insecticides. And, well . . .''

"Besides, Linda, how are our patient's kidney functions?''

She squirmed. "Umm, well—''

The old physician touched her arm gently. "It's a good thought, but it doesn't seem likely. At his age, those nonspecific changes could mean just about anything. Excessive stress. An underlying medical condition.''

He snapped the chart shut like a judge rapping a gavel, then delivered his verdict. "I think our diagnosis is very simple. Food poisoning, a la the crab Louis. Just like all the other patients.''

"Has he been worked up for an infection?'' Plato asked, feeling like an intern again. Even though Seneca General was a community hospital, Gage had a national reputation.

The old physician laughed. "There's nothing he *hasn't* been worked up for. It's a race with only one loser. Every specialist in the hospital's afraid he'll screw up. Poor Thorndyke's going to die from loss of blood with all these tests we're doing.''

Mrs. Leeman cracked the door open. "Dr. Gage?''

The two conferred for a moment in low whispers. As the nurse closed the door again, Gage sank into a chair, put his head in his hands.

Linda's wide forehead wrinkled with concern. "What is it, Dr. Gage?''

"Apparently, the cardiologist also wondered about the strange heart rhythm.'' Gage's pale eyes were focused somewhere beyond the far wall. "He ordered a toxin study on Mr. Thorndyke and Felicia Martinez.''

On the table, his bony hands clutched the air. "Both of them are suffering from massive arsenic toxicity.''

Over the public address system came a woman's carefully measured voice. "Code Blue, Intensive Care Unit. Code Blue, Intensive Care Unit.''

They scrambled from the room.

"Thorndyke was flatline when we got there, and he never came back,'' Plato told Cal later that morning. "We tried everything. There wasn't even fibrillation. He was long gone.''

Even though she didn't know Thorndyke very well, Cal was visibly shaken. She was camped out in an old pair of sweats on the living room sofa; the color in her face matched the vanilla pillowslip.

A pharmacopoeia of stomach remedies was scattered on the coffee table. Propping herself gingerly on an elbow, she closed her eyes and pointed randomly at the drugs. Opening them again, she chose a bottle of pink fluid, swigged a few gulps, then sank back with a groan.

"Why don't you go to someone about that?" Plato asked. He hated seeing sick people. Just watching her made him queasy.

"I'm doing fine," Cal sighed. Her bright brown eyes had faded to a shade somewhere between dirt and old asphalt. Beneath them, her cheeks were dark hollows. Frizzled brown hair crackled when she moved.

"If that's what you call fine, I'd hate to be one of your patients."

"That's the beauty of pathology," she said, with a grin that was more like a grimace. "None of my patients whines about my 'setting a poor example.' Besides, staph food poisoning is self-limited, as long as dehydration is controlled. I'm maintaining my fluids."

"Yeah. With Pepto-Bismol and Mylanta. Bismuth and aluminum and magnesium. You're going to rust."

"Lucky dog. Just because you don't like seafood." Cal sobered suddenly. "What about the maid—what was her name?"

"Felicia Martinez," he answered. "She did all right, at first. For a while, we almost thought she was going to make it."

He shivered, remembering.

"What's wrong?"

"The last time we shocked her. Right before we lost her for good." Plato frowned, trying to picture it. "I've never seen it happen before. Her eyes—they opened up, and she was awake. Just for a second or two."

He shoved a few bottles aside and sat on the coffee table. "She grabbed the arm of the poor intern doing CPR. Grabbed her coat. Looked right into her eyes and started mumbling something. Over and over again."

"What was it?" Color had suddenly returned to Cal's face. "Did you hear it? What did she say?"

"Well, it was pretty hard to make out. Something like 'Chant' or 'Chan-ger.' "

"She spoke with an accent. Chan ..." Cal gasped. "How about 'Jan'?"

Her husband nodded. "You're not the first to think of that. There were eight people in that room. Half of them are convinced Felicia was saying 'Jan.' I'm not so sure."

She shook her head. "I can't see it. To kill her husband that way. Jan just isn't that kind of person. Is she?"

"Who knows?" he replied. "But it provides a very simple solution. Jan Thorndyke was a pharmacist at the hospital before she met Rufus."

Cal nodded her head, sank back in the sofa. "But maybe the solution's a little *too* simple."

They were quiet for a while, and Cal's eyes drifted closed. Watching her in the stillness, Plato heard the soft ticks of the grandfather clock by the fireplace, the gentle hiss of a summer shower on the courtyard outside the open french doors.

A slamming car door interrupted his thoughts. He walked to the front window. A blue and white police cruiser with gold county sheriff's stars was parked in the drive. Up the walk slumped a red-haired, gray-bearded dwarf in a rumpled mackintosh he wore summer or winter, rain or shine.

Ian Donal Cameron. "Don" when they wanted to irritate him. "Ian" when they didn't.

Plato opened the door before he could knock.

"Marley, my lad!" Cameron's teeth gleamed in a tobacco-stained grin.

"Come on in."

The sheriff doffed his hat inside the doorway, shrugged his coat onto a chair, and scavenged his pockets for a pipe. Lighting it, he glanced at his friend.

"Put on a bit of weight, haven't you?" he snickered, tapping Plato's paunch with the back of his hand. The smoke circled his head like fog over a low hill, almost obscuring the bald spot. A frostline of white roots surrounded the peak.

Plato chuckled appreciatively. Ian was a friend of the family, and Plato owed him a favor. Otherwise, the sheriff's own proportions were easy marks for a witty riposte.

But when Plato was growing up in Seneca, his father and Ian had been partners on the force. Years later, when Plato was a local obstetrician and Cameron was Tecumseh County sheriff, the coroner had died in office. Although Plato wasn't qualified, he'd temporarily filled the post at Ian's request. It wasn't difficult—he signed death certificates and forwarded the tough cases to experts in Seneca.

Cal had been one of those experts. A year later, she and Plato were married. Ian was best man. And that November, she was elected TC's coroner.

Ian frequently recalled his matchmaking role.

"And how are the two lovebirds today? No, no, I forget. This isn't a social call." Long sideburns wagged ferociously as he puffed on his pipe. Walking down the foyer, he peered into the living room. Cal had dragged the blanket over her head. Whispering, Ian observed, "She doesn't look so well."

"I know. She's all right, though."

"Good." The old sheriff squared his shoulders, marched across the room, and took Plato's chair. "Good morning to you, Cal."

No reply. She was probably asleep. Plato sat on the couch at her feet.

"I've come for an official reason today," the sheriff began, a hint of pride in his voice. He sat forward, eyes glowing brightly. "The Tecumseh County sheriff's office is handling the investigation of the Thorndykes' case. I'd like the coroner's report as soon as possible."

From under the blankets came a groan that could have been the furniture settling. Ian frowned.

"Of course, if the county coroner is ill, the assistant county coroner will aid in the investigation," he conceded.

This was going too fast for Plato. "Assistant? I didn't know Cal had an assistant."

"That's the beauty of it, laddie!" The sheriff stabbed his pipestem at his friend. *"You're* the assistant. Don't you remember? You've been part of the office ever since Dr. Eddings passed on."

"Wait a minute. That was years ago."

"Of course, if you refuse, I can work with Cal alone on the case. It wouldn't be like working with a *man,* but she might be able to help out here and there."

Plato was still confused. "But I haven't signed any papers or worked for the coroner's office in years." He gasped as Cal's foot jarred his kidney. Trust a pathologist to locate just the right spot.

"Of course not," Cameron replied. "You didn't have to. Cal and I automatically renewed your employment agreement. You've been the TC coroner's assistant for five years now. Didn't Cal tell you?"

Plato ground his elbow into the soft spot behind her ankle, where the nerve passed through. There was another groan from beneath the pillow.

"Does she always sleep like that?" asked Ian.

"She's in a lot of pain," Plato replied sympathetically.

The sheriff shook his head and clucked.

"It's tough for women these days," he confided with a wink. He grinned down at Cal's blanket. "They put so much pressure on themselves to make it in a man's world. Especially here in the States. I don't understand it, but it's probably good for them to try."

"Teach them a lesson, you mean."

"Exactly!" Ian beamed in agreement. "They don't realize how good they had it."

"In the home."

"Right!"

Beneath the blanket, Cal's toe was probing, moving up the spine, hunting for the kidney again. Plato changed tacks. "So how can I help?"

Ian's forehead wrinkled thoughtfully. "Well, this is hardly a typical case of murder."

"How do you mean?"

He leaned back, crossing his stubby legs. Mud covered the soles of his boots. "I'm sure the spoiled food wasn't just coincidence. I've talked with a few of the doctors at the hospital—because it seemed odd. That they didn't pick up the arsenic until it was too late. The murderer hoped old Thorndyke's death would seem like severe food poisoning."

Plato had been there. It had almost worked.

"So we have to look for someone with that kind of medical expertise." Ian squinted through the flare of another match. "That's why I want you or Cal involved. You've heard the old saying, 'Send a thief to catch a thief.' "

Plato thought he knew what was coming next.

"I want to start with Thorndyke's son, Homer," Ian said, flipping through a pocket notebook.

"What about Thorndyke's wife?" Plato asked, startled.

"Jan?" he mused absently. "Oh, yes, that business with the maid. Mrs. Thorndyke's in the hospital—she's not going anywhere."

"So what's so special about Homer?"

Cameron slapped his notebook shut, waddled to the door. "I checked up on him. He's a microbiologist at the medical school. I'm driving up there now."

He slipped on his coat and turned. "Coming?"

"Gee, Ian, I'd really like to, but—" Plato thought of his office appointments. Sure, the schedule wasn't that full. Sandy, his partner, could cover.

Still . . .

"Could you get along without me today? Maybe Wednesday I can find some time. Or this weekend."

The sheriff stood there for a moment, puffed furiously on his pipe. A smoky thunderhead rose from the bowl. "There's something else I didn't want to bring up, laddie . . ."

He took a deep breath, gestured at the four walls. "Look around this room. Here you have the entire staff of the Tecumseh County sheriff's office. I have no deputies per se. Technically, as coroner, Cal is a deputy and can even act as sheriff in my absence."

Cameron sighed. "Maybe someday our commissioners will hire me a deputy. But until now, you two are all I've got. There were dozens of people at that party . . ."

Plato wasn't buying it. Rufus's home was outside incorporated city limits. So it was in Ian's jurisdiction. But the county sheriff could always turn the case over to the state police.

Unfortunately, Ian would never give up. The case would never be solved. They'd lose the next election and be driven from town in disgrace. All three would end up working in some two-bit Jersey doc-in-a-box. Ian would be night security and part-time maintenance. Cleaning toilets and scraping gum from floors.

Clearly, Plato was needed.

"In a minute," he replied generously. "Just let me get changed."

He dashed up the stairs, grabbed a clean shirt and tie, ran a comb across his receding hairline, and zipped down to the door. On the way, he caught a glimpse of Cal. She was awake, folding her blanket.

"What are you doing?" Plato asked. "You're supposed to be sick."

She flashed a wan smile. "I've got an autopsy to do."

Beardmore Medical College was named after Dr. Elias Beardmore, whose political skills far outpaced his medical abilities. Good land was scarce even during the Depression, so the school was built on the scenic banks of the Tecumseh River. Property there was cheap because every two or three springs the river escaped the banks to claim the valley flatlands.

Administration occupied the third floor, while computers and research facilities claimed the second. The first floor was mostly classrooms and sump pumps. No one had been in the basement for years.

Homer Thorndyke's door was open, but a bank of files blocked most of the office from view. The hiss of a ventilator was accompanied by a sliding noise, then a thump. The sweet smell of ether made Plato slightly nauseated.

Cameron knocked hesitantly. "Dr. Thorndyke?"

"Yes?"

Slip-thump.

"Come on back here, please. I'm rather busy at the moment."

Around the corner, Homer Thorndyke sat in his wheelchair, fiddling with something like a paper cutter. Or a tiny guillotine. A rush of disgusting animal lab memories swept over Plato. The sheriff stepped around the corner before his partner could warn him. On the counter beside the sink, eight rat bodies formed a neat line. Eight tiny heads were stacked in a gruesome pyramid nearby. A ninth subject slumbered beneath the blade.

Slip-thump. This time, the blade failed to make a clean slice. Instead, the animal squirmed sluggishly, like a sleepwalker with nightmares.

"Damn!" Thorndyke slapped the blade up and down again, driving it home. He tossed the severed parts into a waste can like a master chef who'd found a bad mushroom. "Cheap Japanese blades. A clean kill is *essential* to this experiment. I just sharpened them, too . . ."

Still ignoring his visitors, he packed the sixteen specimens into a plastic casserole and stuffed it in the freezer. Gloves and goggles were tossed away, and he slid his wheelchair over to the sink.

While Thorndyke washed his hands, Plato glanced at the sheriff. He was down in a chair, eyes glazed, skin grayer than fish scales.

Surely, Plato thought, Ian has seen worse during his long career. "Are you all right?"

His voice was a thin squeak, and his Scotsman's brogue thickened. "I hate rats. I keena why, but they make me sick as a dog."

Thorndyke finally glanced at them. Dressed in a white coat, with pale skin and chalky hair, he resembled one of his subjects. A thin mustache drooped over his upper lip.

"The county sheriff." He smiled mockingly. "How good of you to come. Has the Animal Protection Fellowship requested another tour of the dog lab?"

"No, Dr. Thorndyke. This is about something completely different." Cameron bobbed to his feet like an underinflated balloon. But his voice was steadier. "It's about your father."

"My father?" Thorndyke shrugged. "Then I wouldn't say it's very different at all. We're all animals, sheriff. Some more than others."

"Then it wouldn't surprise you to learn that your father was murdered." The sheriff watched Thorndyke through narrowed eyes.

The reaction was disappointing. Another shrug. "No. I assure you, surprise would be my last reaction. I was at the party myself, you know. And I heard from the hospital. Are you planning to indict the caterer?"

From the boredom in his voice, his level tone, the researcher might have been discussing the Gram stain with a pair of high school students.

"Hardly." The sheriff retrieved his pipe, gestured at the refrigerator with it. "Your father was poisoned, just like one of your friends there. He didn't die from spoiled mayonnaise. We think the food was intentionally contaminated, in order to cover the real poisoning."

Homer whistled appreciatively. "Brilliant! Author, author!"

"You mentioned that you were at the party—" Cameron said. He struck a match and dipped it to his pipe bowl.

"Yes, I was. Along with about seventy-five others. Have you questioned them?" His smile faded. "Oh. By the way, I wouldn' light that if I were you. Unless you want to blow us all to kingdom come."

The match was quickly extinguished. "I've checked on most of them already. But no one else has a very good motive, I'm afraid."

"Unfortunately for you, I don't have one, either. It's very unlikely that I'm mentioned in my father's will. But we keep up appearances."

Plato opened his mouth at last. "The two of you weren't close?"

Thorndyke's eyebrows raised imperiously. "And who are you?"

"Dr. Plato Marley," Ian answered. "Representing the coroner's office in this case."

Thorndyke harrumphed and turned to his bench. Red spray patterns marred the white linoleum surface. With a damp rag, he scrubbed vigorously while he talked. "Close? Never. But there was no animosity between us. In fact, there was nothing at all between us."

He looked up, met Plato's gaze with pale pink irises. "If you're asking if I killed my father, the answer is no."

With both hands, he lifted a thigh and shifted it in the canvas seat. "I wish I had. Arsenic would be an excellent technique. Painful, too. The trouble is, I don't have enough *feeling* left to have killed him. Gentlemen, good day."

Cameron stopped with one hand on the door. "The wife, of course, is the obvious suspect."

After a long pause, the researcher replied. There was warmth and bitterness in his tone. "Jan? I don't think she's capable. Besides, she and my father were very . . . close."

"These are rumors about your father and the Martinez woman. She died last night as well, you know."

"Yes, I heard." For the first time, there was a tinge of regret in his voice. "Such a shame. So you think that perhaps Jan poisoned them both? Out of jealousy? Ridiculous!"

"How long was Miss Martinez with your father?" the sheriff asked. They stepped back inside the office.

"Five years or so. Since just after Mother died." He considered. "Perhaps there was something between them at first. But when Jan came along, everything changed. More likely, Felicia killed my father out of jealousy."

"Clumsy of her to kill herself as well." Cameron sucked absently on the unlit pipe. "How about work? Your father's company was very successful. Might he have made some enemies along the way?"

"Mardyke Pharmaceuticals? Successful?" The microbiologist snorted. "At selling health foods and vitamins, maybe. But they'll never make it in the big league. With the lousy researchers they have, it's a miracle they've survived this long. But somehow they're already showing quite a profit. Martin Callahan must be one sly businessman."

"Callahan?" The notebook came out again.

"That man could squeeze carrot juice from a stone. He was in health foods when he conned Father into investing." Thorndyke sighed wistfully, picturing grant dollars and pharmaceutical research sponsorships. "Two years ago, they tried coming out with a new drug. Synthetic painkiller/anti-anxiety combination. Called Hypnocose. But it was a little too successful."

"*Too* successful?" Plato asked. This was a new concept for him.

Thorndyke nodded. "People liked it a little too much. Know what I mean? The FDA squashed it. Let me tell you, the market's tight for new products right now. The FDA approval process is amazingly tortuous, especially for drugs like Hypnocose."

He glanced down at his watch. "Two thirty! I'm already half an hour late."

As they backed out the door, Cameron apologized. "Sorry to have taken so much time, doctor."

"Not at all. If you have any more questions . . ."

Plato stopped Ian in the hallway. "Wait. I want to look for something."

After navigating the maze of corridors from several decades of building additions, they stopped. The bulletin board read:

Hot Off the Press!
Our Latest Research

A number of articles were tacked to the board, including a paper by Homer Thorndyke, Ph.D. The work was titled, "Response to Staphylococcal Pneumonia to Gamma Globulin in the Splenectomized Rat."

"What's it mean?" The sheriff frowned.

"Seems our friend is playing with the same bacteria that ruined Thorndyke's party."

Back at the hospital, Jan Thorndyke had a visitor. "I'm sorry, but Dr. Gage is seeing her, and he's asked for privacy," the charge nurse told Plato and Ian. She had a harried look. The shift was nearly over.

They took seats in the visitors' lounge. Near the window, a gray-haired man snoozed in a recliner. His shoes lay beside the chair, and a pink toe poked through one of his white socks. A fat man with a face like melted rubber sifted through the ancient magazines in the rack. Oprah Winfrey barked from a television hanging on the wall.

"What do you think about young Thorndyke?" Ian asked softly. "Rather interesting—his mention of arsenic."

Rubber-face scowled at them, then took his seat.

"Possibly," Plato conceded. "On the other hand, he may have guessed when you pointed to the rats."

"Oh. Rat poison." Ian grinned sheepishly. "Stupid of me, wasn't it?"

"Not really. He might have figured it out anyway. He seems to be very intelligent."

The sheriff sat back, scratched his nose thoughtfully. "Belligerent bastard, though. He sure did get friendly all of a sudden, didn't he?"

"Yeah. When you asked him about Jan. Do you think he suspects her?"

Ian shrugged. "I do know one thing. He doesn't want *us* suspecting her."

They sat watching the screen until a commercial came on.

"You have to wonder what makes a son hate his father so," Ian mused. "It isn't natural."

"Neither is murder."

"I might do a little research into that lad's past." Out came the black notebook again.

An angry shriek came from Jan Thorndyke's room, accompanied by a throaty growl. It sounded like a bobcat arguing with a bear. A nurse rushed to the room, listened, then returned to her desk.

Plato recalled the only time Homer had volunteered information. "What about the business partner? What did you find out about that?"

"Dead end. The man was in San Diego on Sunday." Cameron scratched a bedraggled sideburn. "And the killer had to be at the party, right?"

"How else could he give the arsenic at just the right time—when everyone else was getting sick from spoiled food?" Plato frowned. "Of course, it could be a wild coincidence. How about some random killer lacing storebought medications?"

"We thought of that, checked all his medicines when we checked the dishes. So far, everything's negative."

The charge nurse appeared in the doorway. "Mrs. Thorndyke will see you now."

There was no answer to their knock. "Mrs. Thorndyke?"

"Yes?"

"It's Sheriff Cameron and Dr. Marley. May we ask you a few questions?"

There was a pause, then a quavery answer. "Come in."

It was hard to find a chair. Scarce pinpoints of light trickled through the Venetian blinds to throw a pattern of dots across the sheets. Jan Thorndyke looked even more fragile in the thin hospital gown than she had at the party. Wispy blonde hair hung in disarray about her angular face. She fiddled nervously with the plastic line running between the IV bag and her arm.

Tissues were flung in a pile on the nightstand beside a vase of red roses. Her eyes were puffy and glistening.

"You are aware that your husband's death wasn't accidental."

"My doctor told me about it—about the arsenic," Jan replied quietly. "Who would want to kill Rufus?"

"That's what we're here to ask you, Mrs. Thorndyke." Ian glanced at the nightstand. "Nice flowers."

"Hmm? Oh, those." She looked away quickly, tipped her head back. "My father just brought them to me."

"First of all, I want to say how sorry we all are—about your husband's death." The sheriff took a seat beside Jan's bed, placed his hand over hers. For a moment, Plato forgot she was Ian's primary suspect. "Did your husband mention any problems here at the hospital? Or at his company? Unhappy employees, people who were harassing him?"

"No. There was nothing like that." The sun was setting, and the dots on her bed were disappearing, one by one. "Rufus was very well liked, both here and at Mardyke."

"Money problems?"

"None. He was doing very well." She brushed a stray wisp of hair from her forehead. "The company was close to releasing its newest drug. Rufus was very excited."

"Was he?"

"Oh, yes. In fact, Martin Callahan had us over on Saturday for dinner and a swim. To celebrate." Jan smiled briefly. "Rufus failed at medical school, you know. He tells—*told*—everyone about that. Still, he was trying to make a contribution. To medicine."

"Speaking of medicine," Plato interrupted, "did your husband get along very well with his son?"

"He tried. Believe me, he tried." She sighed. "He's made more contributions to the school than you can imagine. And he was always calling Homer, asking him to social functions, being interested. And always getting the cold shoulder."

"What caused the falling-out in the first place?"

"I don't know. I asked Rufus about it once." The widow shivered. "I got the impression it was something he'd rather not talk about. Other than that, we didn't have any secrets."

"A good marriage, then," Ian concluded.

"Yes," she agreed emphatically. "Two years now, and it still felt like our honeymoon. We used to joke about it. How it would last forever . . ."

"You have our sympathy, ma'am." The sheriff patted her hand. "Your father—he's probably a great source of comfort—"

Jan smiled patronizingly, like a True Believer. "He's never understood. About Rufus and me. My father and Rufus were great friends. Until we fell in love. Daddy was furious. Jealous, I think. I tried to ignore it."

Jan stopped. Fiddling with the tape on her arm, she looked at them. Tears welled up and threatened to spill.

"Three nights ago—the Friday before the party—Daddy came to visit. He implied . . ." She bit her lip, took a deep breath. "He implied that Rufus was having an affair. I was very upset. Rufus came home late, called Daddy, and told him he wasn't welcome in our house any more. So of course he wasn't at the party."

She twisted the IV line back and forth between her thumb and forefinger. "Today I thought he'd come to apologize. But it was just more of the same."

"This must be very difficult for you," Ian said.

Jan nodded and blinked quickly, but failed to catch an escaping tear.

The door swung open, and the charge nurse poked her head inside. "I'm sorry, but visiting hours are over. I'll have to ask you gentlemen to leave."

"If you want a good crab Louis, don't skimp on the mayonnaise," Mrs. Reiss preached. "These days, so many people are concerned with lowering fats that they use too little. And the green pepper can be overpowering."

"It certainly can," Cal agreed.

"What's that?" Mrs. Reiss fiddled with her hearing aid until feedback squealed from her ear.

"I said, it certainly can," Cal shouted.

She was looking much better. Plato was amazed at what a couple of good autopsies could do.

It promised to be a long interview, though. He had been up all night with a rough delivery that led to a Caesarean section. His brain was an expanding glacier inside his fragile head. The shouting match would crack his skull like an egg.

Plato glanced out the window of Mrs. Reiss's kitchen. Tuesday morning had dawned bright and clear. At the back of the yard, a whitewashed fence marked the edge of the cliff high above the Tecumseh River. Just inside it, a perfectly tended garden glittered with dew. Beans, tomatoes, and romaine lettuce stood in tight ranks, as though waiting for dress inspection. Even the violets and daffodils fringing the yard were meticulously arranged.

The caterer's kitchen was equally precise. Two ovens, wide oak counters, and stainless steel sinks glistened under bright fluorescent lights. A menagerie of pots and pans with burnished copper bottoms hung from a rack over the window. Beside the deep freeze gleamed a collection of knives that surely rivaled Galen's.

"Is there any way that the mayonnaise you used Sunday could have been spoiled?" Plato cringed, waiting for her reply.

"I understand, Dr. Marley, that you have to ask that question. Still, I tolerate it only to preserve the good name of Reiss's Nice Foods. It's a scandal for my business." She pressed a plump hand to her chest and sighed. "You can't imagine how embarrassed I was Sunday night when people started getting ill. I hope you catch the scoundrel who's responsible."

From the tone of her voice, she seemed to feel that apprehending a murderer was purely incidental.

"Still, we all make mistakes," Cal said. "Sometimes the unavoidable happens—power failures, for instance. What about last Thursday? Wasn't there a thunderstorm then?"

"Oh, my dear! Of course I couldn't make the mayonnaise on Thursday! You know that."

Cal gazed at her blankly.

"Under those conditions, the mayonnaise simply won't bind." Mrs. Reiss's pencil-thin brows formed a V on her forehead. "But then maybe you've never tried making mayonnaise during a thunderstorm."

"I've been lucky that way, I guess," Cal admitted, casting a warning glance at her husband. She hadn't made mayonnaise during snow, heat, or gloom of night, either.

"Ordinarily, I make fresh mayonnaise on Thursdays because Francella brings the eggs straight from the hens that day." She touched Cal's arm. "I've found that the freshest eggs make the smoothest mayonnaise. In fact, when Francella delivers them, they're often still warm and there's no need to bring them to room temperature."

"So you made the mayonnaise on Friday," Plato concluded.

"No. Friday was the University Club luncheon. I didn't need mayonnaise for that, so I made it Saturday morning." Mrs. Reiss thought for a moment. "Even if my refrigerator was off a few degrees, mayonnaise doesn't spoil that quickly. And it certainly didn't smell bad."

"Staph food poisoning can be very subtle," Cal explained. "Especially with such a flavorful food as crab Louis."

"My, my, my. This is certainly complicated."

"Is there any way someone could have tampered with it Saturday? Did you leave the house at all?"

"No, I didn't," she assured them. "I'm certain of it."

"You had visitors?" Cal asked.

Plato was shocked. Stern, broad shouldered, competent, and practical though she was, Mrs. Reiss actually blushed.

"Well, I . . ." For once, she was at a loss for words. She wrung her hands feverishly across the broad expanse of apron covering her middle. Finally she took a deep breath and explained. "He started calling on me when I took sick."

"Who did?"

"Dr. Gage. It's my stomach, you see. It's so sensitive. Well, he was just wonderful—no other doctor made house calls anymore. So I invited him over one Saturday, and it got to be a regular thing. Every Saturday afternoon for two years now."

The portly cook sighed wistfully.

"You won't tell anyone, will you?" she begged. "It's been our secret for a long, long time. Not even Leonard knows."

"Leonard?" Cal asked.

"My son. You've probably read his articles in the *Herald Press*. He's the medical editor," she boasted.

"Yes, now I remember," Cal said. "He interviewed me once about Seneca General's pathology department. Strange that he hasn't asked us about the case yet."

"The life of a newspaperman," Leonard's mother chuckled. "He was very upset when I called to tell him what had happened. He's been away this weekend, down at the capital. Looking at substances. Wait. Is that what he said? That's awfully strange."

"I imagine there are quite a few substances down there in the capital," Plato agreed.

"I think it's all a fable. He's got a girl down there. I'm sure of it."

"How about Sunday?" Cal asked. "Did anyone help you with the catering?"

"Just the maid—Felicia. She always helps when I cater at the Thorndykes'. Such a tragedy. Of course, she wasn't involved."

"Not likely," Plato admitted.

The caterer turned to Cal again. "Now that we've finished, dear, there's a dish of mine that you must try on Plato. I call it Sauce Simpliste because it's so easy to make. Wonderful with beef dishes. I've got the recipe written down here somewhere."

She led them to her living room and riffled through a drawer in the television stand. "Here it is, here it is. I want to submit it to the *Grande Cuisine Home Cooking Show*. Have you seen it?"

"I'm afraid not," Cal confessed.

"Then I have to lend you one of my tapes." On the shelf above the TV squatted a new VCR. Mrs. Reiss patted it proudly. "My Leonard bought it for me. We have the same kinds of VCR's, stereos, and televisions. Even the same kind of cars. That way, Leonard can fix them when something goes wrong. He's quite handy."

Plato sighed. Years from now he and Cal would be discovered rooted to the floor, cobwebs swaddling their ankles and knees, Mrs. Reiss's filibuster still in full swing.

Miraculously, the telephone rang, and they bolted for the door.

"Thank you for the tape. And the recipe," Cal called.

"Certainly," the caterer replied with a wave. "Come back again if you have any questions. Or just to talk . . ."

As they closed the door, Mrs. Reiss's hearing aid gave a farewell squeal.

"This won't take long," Cal assured her husband. "Turn left here."

Plato complied. "I don't understand why we have to do this at all. What's Ian up to? Why can't he handle this?"

"He's busy getting depositions from the guests," she answered. "Callahan gave his statement at the courthouse this morning. But Ian wanted us to drop by the plant, just to get an impression."

Mardyke Pharmaceuticals was a sprawling one-level brick and granite complex at the end of a mostly vacant industrial park. From its exterior, Mardyke's prosperity was obvious. Perfectly manicured lawns, rolling hills, and shapely hedgerows were surrounded by a ten foot chain link fence topped with barbed wire. All around the grounds was the Mardyke trademark, an interlocking M and D.

The guard waved them in at the gate. As they drove the battered Nova down to the visitors' lot, Plato lusted for a car with air conditioning. Black asphalt gathered the midday heat, focusing it on the underside of the car, where it passed through the seats to scorch their backs and legs.

At the main entrance, they were rescued by a wash of cool, dry air. The foyer had a polished slate floor and rough sandstone walls. Cal's heels echoed in the darkness as the pair navigated the cave to a pink marble reception area.

"Drs. Plato and Calista Marley?" asked a platinum blonde receptionist. When they nodded, she rose. "This way, please."

Plush pile carpeting replaced the slate, and tastefully neutral paintings under track lights lined the corridor. At the end of the hall, their guide opened a door. "Mr. Callahan will see you now."

The chairman of Mardyke Pharmaceuticals stood with his back to the door. He pretended to admire the view through tinted windows that made the outside look cloudy, cool, and inviting.

When people want to make an entrance and can't, they try the next best thing. Martin Callahan spun around gracefully.

"Ah, Dr. Marley. And Dr. Marley." Circumnavigating his desk took him a while, so Plato and Cal met him halfway and shook hands. "A pleasure to meet you both. Have a seat."

They sat in a pair of matching chairs covered in a surprisingly supple black leather. Callahan scrutinized them across the vast teak desk. Though their chairs were comfortable, his visitors had to tip their heads back to look up at him. A standing halogen lamp behind him cast a halo over his head, making it hard to read his eyes.

"Sheriff Cameron explained the purpose of our visit," Cal began.

"Well, yes and no. The sheriff explained that you needed to talk to me concerning Rufus's death. But I don't see that I have much to add. I wasn't even there at the time." Though Callahan had a boyish face, Plato placed him in his mid-forties. Sleek black hair like an otter, and some of the mannerisms, too. His grave concern seemed artificial, like the spray that held his hair in place.

"You've already given your statement to Sheriff Cameron," Cal explained. "But we wanted to talk to you in a less formal setting, perhaps get your impressions on a few things. We hope to learn a little more about Mr. Thorndyke from the people who knew him best."

"Thank you. I'll take that as a compliment. Rufus was a very good man, and I was proud to be associated with him."

"How long had you known him?"

"Just three years. I met him at a health care conference down in San Diego, shortly before my old company folded. He had always been interested in health foods, holistic healing, that sort of thing." Callahan chuckled. "We had some very interesting conversations. A couple of months after disaster struck my company, I gave him a call. He invited me up here to talk things over."

He spread his hands to encompass the office, the building, the grounds. "Our partnership was quite successful. Of course, the market is much more open here. And Mardyke does much more than health foods now."

"Strange," Cal commented. "I never knew Rufus was into health foods."

"Neither did most people. But he was a closet fanatic. It was our little secret." He adjusted a gold cufflink. "People would frown upon a hospital board member who held those kinds of alternative health beliefs."

"Interestingly put. To Plato, it almost sounded like a religion.

"You weren't at the party?" Cal asked.

"No, I wasn't." He sighed regretfully. "I was in California on business. I'd planned to come later in the evening, but the plane was delayed. Perhaps if I had been there . . ."

Plato could picture it. Rufus Thorndyke lying on the field like a corpulent Arthur while this holistic Merlin made passes over his face and stuffed his mouth with roots and berries.

"Was there any trouble with business? Disgruntled employees? Money problems?"

"Money was the least of our worries. For the third year in a row, the company's revenues have continued to grow." He shook his head sadly. "As for disgruntled employees, I'm afraid that's very unlikely. Rufus was something of a silent partner. He almost never visited the plant. We'd meet informally, generally at my house. The day-to-day routine was left to me."

"He and Jan visited you the day before the party—" Plato prompted.

"Yes." Callahan frowned momentarily. "A celebration. Our research department has found a 'loophole modification.' With a subtle alteration, we can legally manufacture a certain very popular drug still under patent. It could be a big breakthrough."

"And that was the last time you saw Rufus?"

He nodded. "We had a poolside dinner. I'm something of a chef myself, though not of Mrs. Reiss's caliber."

"I see." Cal smiled apologetically. "This may seem an offensive question, but what were the terms of the contract? Your answer is purely voluntary."

"Oh, believe me, I have no trouble answering that," Callahan replied. "There was no survivorship clause. Rufus's shares reverted to his widow upon his death."

That night, Plato was energizing Salisbury steak/broccoli/cheddarmac combination dinners when the telephone rang. He didn't even hear it. Their microwave had crossed the Atlantic on the *Mayflower*.

It had no light, the timer was broken, and the fan sounded like a jackhammer. Cal took the call in the other room.

"What's up?" Plato asked when she returned to the table.

"It was Ian," Cal replied. She removed the plastic lid from her dinner. The broccoli had apparently caught fire during reentry. It was smoking, and there was a charred hole in the dish. Frost still adorned most of the steak. She glanced at her husband. "We need a new microwave."

"What did he want?" Plato replied. "Through a freak accident, his dinner had come out perfect. "I can do yours again if you'd like."

"I'd rather not." Cal's lip curled in disgust as she sawed the broccoli and melted plastic from the remainder of her meal. "Leonard Reiss was in an accident."

"You're kidding." From her nonchalant tone, Plato honestly thought she was. But then, it was hard to tell with Cal. When she was really famished, very little could distract her. It was ten o'clock, and they had just finished their regular work at the hospital. "Is he all right?"

"Moderate concussion," she mumbled through a mouthful of macaroni. "Hasn't waked up yet. Wrecked his car coming down Sandy Ridge from his mother's house after dinner. Sheriff was thinking it might be related."

"Maybe he was just in a hurry to leave," Plato said. "Any sign of tampering?"

"Plus-minus," Cal replied. With the butt of her knife, she hammered her fork into the steak and gnawed it like a Popsicle. "The brake fluid was pretty low. Air in the lines. But the lines themselves were intact. Ian thinks someone might have messed with the master cylinder."

"But why would they want to kill Leonard Reiss? His writing's bad, but that's true for most of the *Herald Press*."

"Guess again."

Crunching his broccoli, he considered for a moment, then snapped his fingers. "Of course! Mrs. Reiss drives exactly the same kind of car. She told us."

"Bingo. The sheriff asked for a state cop to guard her. Seems she might be very important to this case." Cal frowned at her steaksicle. "This is really awful."

With a grunt of resignation, she slipped it into the microwave, holding the power button down for a minute or so. The meat emerged steaming, juicy, and appetizing.

The phone rang again, but Cal just placed it inside the refrigerator. It bleated faintly like a lost sheep. Plato rose to answer it.

"No!" Cal ordered. "Whatever it is, it can wait. If the hospital wants you, they'll use your pager."

While she wolfed the rest of her meal, Plato summarized the interviews with Homer and Jan Thorndyke.

"She seems to have sold you," Cal noted.

He shrugged. "Maybe. She certainly has the motive—Rufus was worth a few million at last count. And who knows how much the Mardyke stock could bring? But she seemed too upset. It couldn't be an act."

"You may be an obstetrician, but you don't know women," Cal said. "When we put our minds to it, we can be the best actors in the world."

"You weren't there, Cal," he reminded his wife. "You didn't talk to her."

They were at an impasse until the doorbell rang.

Ian again. Plato showed him into the kitchen, asked if he'd eaten.

"No." He sat at the table, scrutinized Cal's plate. "But I've been trying to trim up a bit."

"What about you, Ian?" Cal asked. "Are you convinced Jan's innocent, too?"

He threw his hands up in exasperation. "There are so many suspects in this case, I'm not buying anything yet. I've been hoping you might have a bone or two for me. Do you have those autopsy results?"

Cal nodded. "Unfortunately, it's nothing you don't already know. Death was due to arsenic in both cases. Analysis of the stomach contents was basically inconclusive—we're pretty sure the arsenic came in food, rather than a beverage. There's very little excoriation of the mouth or esophagus. No signs that force was used, no external entry wounds or needle punctures. We *can* say that the arsenic was taken orally. But that's about it."

"So much for modern science," Ian complained. "I checked up on Callahan—though he doesn't seem to have a motive. His alibi's solid. He was in San Diego from Sunday morning until late Sunday evening. He was scheduled to arrive at five thirty, but his plane was delayed in St. Louis."

"That fits what he told us," Cal agreed.

"How's Reiss doing?" Plato asked.

"About the same. Not awake yet. But they seem confident that he'll pull out of it."

Cal started. "Ian, is there any possibility that someone was after Leonard? What was he investigating in the capital?"

"Pretty sharp of you to think of that. The thought had crossed my mind, too. I called his editor at the *Herald Press*." The sheriff sighed, put his feet up on a chair. "Nothing doing, though. Something about substance abuse problems in Mexico. Pretty far from home. More likely, someone wanted to kill Mrs. Reiss and got the wrong car. They're practically identical."

He brightened. "I did find out something interesting, though. Remember what I said about Homer?"

They nodded.

"Well, I did some research of my own. Down at the library in Seneca." Ian pulled his beard thoughtfully. "Seems young Homer does have a motive after all. He lost the use of his legs back when he was fifteen. In a water skiing accident on Lake Cantauck. And guess who was driving the boat?"

"Rufus Thorndyke," Plato answered.

"Right. Worse, he was drunk as a skunk. There was a scandal, but he never was charged."

"How awful," Cal whispered softly.

"Do you think he did it?" Plato asked.

Ian shrugged. "Maybe. He's a microbiologist. He was at the party all day. Plenty of means and opportunity. And all the motive in the world."

"What about the attempt on Mrs. Reiss, though?" Cal asked. "I mean, in his wheelchair it might be hard to sneak up and drain that brake fluid."

The sheriff shuddered. "I've seen him in action, lass. I wouldn't put anything past him."

The next morning, the telephone jangled Plato from a fitful sleep. Blearily, he rubbed the fog from his eyes and glanced at the clock. Nine thirty. He was late for morning rounds.

"Hello?" His voice was still fuzzy.

"Plato? Sorry to wake you, dear, but it's time for work anyway."

"Yes, Cal."

"I talked Sandy Aaronson into seeing your patients this morning. I have a favor to ask."

"What now?" Plato groaned, lying back and pulling the pillow over his head. This investigation was getting out of hand.

"Well, you remember our talk about Jan Thorndyke? I think you're right. She didn't kill Rufus."

"Thank you," he replied warily.

"But you see, Plato, she's going home this morning."

"That's nice."

There was a pause. "And she doesn't feel safe. I don't blame her. Somewhere out there, the person who killed her husband is walking around free. Someone already tried to kill Mrs. Reiss. Jan's worried that they might come after her."

"Mmph."

"Plato? Could you come, please? She asked me to go to the house with her, to be sure it's okay. I'd like you to come along."

What could an obstetrician do against a murderer? Wave a pair of forceps at him? Threaten to suture his nose to his lips? But there was no use arguing. "Okay. Let me shower first."

Before the Thorndyke house, a pale silver Cadillac waited in the swirling morning mist. Jan sighed, put her head in her hand. "Someone you know?" Plato asked.

"My father."

From the back seat, Cal patted her shoulder. "If you'd like, Plato and I can—"

"No." She turned to face them. "Please come in with me. I may have given you the wrong impression. Daddy isn't such an ogre. It's just that since Mother died, I'm the only family he's got. He's terribly lonely."

Cal glanced at her husband. "Okay. At least we can help you get settled."

Gage emerged from his car as they mounted the steps and rushed to help with Jan's bag. "Good to see you again, Plato. And this is—"

"Calista Marley," Cal answered, shaking his hand. "I'm Plato's wife. I'm also a pathologist at the hospital."

"Such an interesting name. And so appropriate."

Cal blushed.

"In Greek, it means 'beautiful,' " Plato explained, seeing Jan's confusion.

She smiled and showed them to the study. "This was always my favorite room."

Heavy oak shelves lined the walls. Two full-length windows

looked east across the fog. Red leather chairs squatted in the corner, near an antique globe.

After they were seated, Jan asked, "Would you like some coffee or tea?"

"Nonsense," Cal admonished, rising to her feet. "You just show me where things are; I'll get them ready."

"How is the investigation going?" asked Dr. Gage. He sat back and crossed his legs.

"I don't really know much about it," Plato lied. "Of course, you heard that Leonard Reiss was in an accident last night."

Gage's face darkened. "No, I hadn't."

"Mrs. Reiss is a patient of yours?"

"Yes. Yes, she is."

Cal returned shortly with a silver tea set. While she was serving, the doorbell rang. A moment later, Martin Callahan appeared in the doorway beside Jan. Dressed in a suit of glossy black silk, he looked as sleek as ever.

"Good morning, everyone. I hope I'm not intruding."

"Father, this is Martin Callahan," Jan said. "My father, Nicholas Gage."

"A pleasure," Gage muttered, rising and shaking hands. It was clear that he was losing patience with his daughter's visitors. "Jan, you're tired. Perhaps we should all—"

"That's okay, Father. Really." She addressed the group. "Please stay for a while. I don't want to be alone just yet."

"Certainly. I wanted to offer my condolences, er, about Rufus." For once, Callahan's voice lacked its customary smoothness.

"Thank you, Martin." Taking a seat across from her father, Jan grimaced. Sipping her tea, she complained, "Since I got home, my stomach's been bothering me again."

"All this activity." Gage waggled a finger. "You should be in bed. Your system's had a nasty shock."

"I'll be just fine." Jan smiled, and her blonde hair glowed in the lamplight. She reached into her purse, pulled out a pill bottle. "Remember how Rufus always made me carry these stomach pills around? The ones you prescribed for him? Rufus would hunt through my purse for them whenever he felt sick. I don't know why I didn't take one at the party."

It was like a slow-motion sequence. Before anyone could move, she unscrewed the lid and tipped a capsule into her hand. Cal caught her arm before she could raise it to her mouth.

"Wait!"

Jan looked at her, startled.

"Has Sheriff Cameron checked those pills?"

She shook her head dumbly.

Softly, Cal said, "I think he'd better."

Like an obedient child, Jan glanced down at the pill in her hand and gave it to Cal. A dam of tears broke and flooded her cheeks.

Gage sat still as a statue. The blood had drained from his face.

"Daddy," Jan murmured. It sounded like an accusation. Head lowered, her voice caught. "You hated Rufus. You hired a private investigator to follow him. But I didn't believe you. I still don't."

She looked up at him for the first time. "Can't you see? Sometimes you don't *want* to believe. All that, I could forgive you. I could forget. But this—"

Her voice was perfectly calm, level, lifeless. Slowly, she rose from her chair and walked out of the room.

Gage was stunned. Cal sat staring at the pill in her hand. Callahan looked uncomfortable.

Plato walked to the telephone and dialed the sheriff's office. Ian was out, but the dispatcher would radio his car and send him over.

He hung up. For the first time, all the pieces had fallen into place. Gage's embarrassment at his son-in-law. The bitter confrontation, that Friday before the party.

It must have seemed ridiculously easy to the gastroenterologist. The symptoms of food poisoning and arsenic were remarkably similar. Perhaps one day, long ago, he had filed that away in his mind.

When his daughter didn't want to see the truth about her husband, he removed her problem with cold, clinical precision. Like excising a cancer. A simple matter. Wait for the right moment, open her purse, and dust the pills with arsenic. It wouldn't take much. When Rufus got sick at the party, he'd turn to the medicine Gage had prescribed. Unexpectedly, he'd offered his remedy to Felicia as well.

Gage's friendship with Mrs. Reiss was a stroke of luck. Contaminating the mayonnaise was pathetically easy. Too bad he'd mixed up the cars, draining Leonard's brake fluid instead.

But then Plato had a disturbing thought. He turned to his wife, who was examining the pills more closely. "Cal, you won't find any arsenic on those."

"Don't say anything." Her voice was hard with warning.

He ignored her. "Think about it. Gage had every chance to switch the pills Monday when he visited her. Or during the night, when she was asleep.''

Cal glanced at the old physician. He was motionless, a pale white ghost trapped in ice.

"Plato," she said quietly, "Dr. Gage didn't kill Rufus.''

Her husband crossed his arms, lifted his chin belligerently. "No? Then who did?''

Just then, Martin Callahan rose and headed for the door.

"Wait," Cal cried.

Like a black leopard spotting an antelope, Callahan burst into a run. He was nearly to the hall when Plato stretched his leg across the threshold. The chairman of Mardyke Pharmaceuticals crashed into an ornate china cabinet. Astonishingly, he emerged from the wreckage and took off down the hall before Plato could stop him.

But as he opened the door to freedom, a voice met him. "Hold on a minute, laddie! What's your hurry?''

A raincoated dwarf blocked the doorway. Surprised, Callahan paused for a moment, then tried to push past him. But the sheriff packed quite a bit of inertia. Before Plato could blink, a chubby paw flipped into the mackintosh and reappeared with a .38 caliber police special.

"Now, let's all head back inside and have a little chat, shall we?''

Back in the study, Cal held a handful of capsules. On one side they were stamped with the letters "ginrt." On the reverse they bore an interlocking M and D.

"Ginger root," Cal said. She cracked one open. "Heavily laced with arsenic.''

The sheriff nodded his head at Callahan. "Maybe you'd better have a seat.''

Gage finally spoke. It took him a while to get his voicebox lubricated again. "She thought—she thought that I—''

He went after his daughter.

Callahan sat sullenly, scowling at the carpet.

"By the way, Cal," Ian remarked, "Reiss woke up this morning. He's still pretty foggy, but he said he was investigating some new street drug called sleeper. He'd met with Rufus about it last week.''

"Sleeper," Cal whispered.

"Indeed," the sheriff answered, but Plato waved him to silence.

He watched his wife's face. She was sitting back in her chair, frowning, eyes closed. Her nose crinkled subtly like a rabbit sniffing alfalfa. It was her pose of intense concentration. The poisoned capsules still rested in her hand.

To Plato, it didn't make any sense. Why would Callahan want to kill Rufus? What did sleeper have to do with it?

"Hypnocose." Cal opened her eyes, gazed at Callahan. "One and the same. Oh, maybe there were a few of your special modifications so the drug couldn't be traced. Synthetic narcotic plus an anti-anxiety drug. Both highly addictive."

Ian pulled out his Miranda card and read it to the prisoner.

"Reiss was investigating sleeper," Cal noted. "He probably suspected that Mardyke was the source."

She turned to Plato. "Remember the DEA agent at the party? He thought sleeper was coming up from Mexico. Just the reverse. Callahan was probably sending it down there. He had connections in San Diego. Rufus probably wanted to talk to the DEA before Reiss blew the story."

"Thorndyke would have asked his partner about it first," Plato noted.

"Oh, yes," Cal agreed bitterly. "After all, he was such a trusting person. Callahan probably reassured him, then moved to get rid of him. Easy enough for him, since Rufus's addiction to health foods was their 'little secret.' "

"I don't have to listen to this," Callahan exclaimed. When he rose from the chair again, Ian produced a pair of handcuffs.

"I don't have to use these, Martin. But if you make me, I will."

Callahan sat down again.

"There was no breakthrough at the plant, was there?" Cal asked rhetorically. "The celebration at your house was just an excuse. While Rufus and Jan were swimming, you switched the pills in her purse. I'm sure Rufus had told you how he hid the ginger root in Gage's bottle. Another 'little secret' you shared. When he got sick the next day, he took one. And probably offered one to Felicia as well.

"Unfortunately for you, your plane was delayed. You probably planned to switch the pills back again during the confusion at the party. But you couldn't."

"Hold on, lassie." Ian turned to Callahan, began searching his pockets. He pulled out a small plastic bag. Inside were several capsules identical in appearance to those Cal held. "Is this why you came today? And why you were leaving in such a hurry?"

Callahan ignored him. Like a patient martyr, he looked up at the ceiling, then out the window at the mist clearing in the valley.

"There's only one thing I can't figure out," Cal concluded. "Martin Callahan wasn't at the party. How did he contaminate the food?"

"I can answer that." Jan Thorndyke's voice was clear and confident. She stood just inside the room.

Gage was beside her, an arm over her shoulder.

Salad spray?" Plato cried. "Never heard of it. Who'd want hairspray on their salad anyway?"

"Not hairspray," Cal corrected him. "Salad freshener. All the good restaurants use it these days. Keeps the lettuce from wilting."

"I still don't get it." Plato rummaged through the freezer. It had been another long day. But Callahan was safely in the county hotel, so it looked as if Plato was done with the case. "We need a vacation. Maybe a cruise. There's good food on cruise ships, isn't there?"

"Yeah. But you'd be too seasick to eat." Cal sat before the portable electronic typewriter on the kitchen table. One finger at a time, she plinked out the final draft of her coroner's report.

"Mmmph." Her husband made a fist and hammered at the ice inside the freezer. With a satisfied grunt, he wrestled a plastic bag free. Inside, barely discernible through a coating of frost, were breaded chicken fillets. "Explain it to me again."

"Well, the day before the party, when Jan and Rufus went over to Callahan's, he'd made a salad." Plink, plonk. "He's quite a gourmet, you know. Anyway, he was raving about this salad freshener, and how it keeps the lettuce from wilting. Jan was interested, since their party was the next day. He gave her his bottle. Jan agreed that it might offend Mrs. Reiss, so she added it herself. Of course, it was full of live staph."

"So why didn't they get sick on Saturday?" Plato dumped the bag's contents into a bowl and placed it inside the microwave. "For that matter, why didn't I get sick? I had salad Sunday."

"Yes, but staph needs something to grow on. Crab Louis is a sauce over a base of lettuce." Plink-beep. "It grew in the mayonnaise of the crab Louis, but not in the ordinary salad."

He opened the microwave, turned the bowl, then closed it again. "So how did Callahan know what crab Louis contained? And how could he be sure they were serving it?"

"Silly," she chided him. "He's a gourmand. And in case you

haven't noticed, that dish is Mrs. Reiss's specialty. She's made it for the hospital appreciation dinner for years now.''

"No. I hadn't noticed," Plato pouted. "If you'll recall, I didn't have any. I just had salad.''

"Uh-huh.'' Cal stretched her arm, patted her husband's ample waistline. "Salad and prime rib—don't act so shocked. It's my job to notice things.''

"Well, fine, Sherlock. Just fine.'' Plato couldn't think of a better rejoinder until he recalled his own bit of deductive genius. "Going back over the case today, I figured something out. About Felicia.''

"What's that?''

"Well, she must have realized that she and Rufus were the sickest. And she must have wondered about it.'' Plato gave a satisfied smile. "See, she wasn't saying 'Jan' at all when she died. She was saying 'ginger.' ''

"Good work,'' Cal praised.

"Well, aren't you going to put that in your report?''

She hesitated, then pointed at one of the sheets. "It already is in. On page four.''

"Oh.''

"Cheer up, honey. At least you're a better cook than I am.''

She was right. The chicken smelled wonderful. Plato pulled the bowl from the oven again. Inside, the breaded fillets floated in a bath of melted frost.

"Chicken soup,'' he announced.

"Really? I'm famished!'' She tore that last sheet from her typewriter, peered at the concoction. The breading had separated from most of the pieces, leaving a crusty scum on the surface of water.

She squeezed his shoulder gently.

"We haven't saved enough money for a vacation yet.'' Cal smiled at her husband. "But I think we can afford a new microwave.''

BLOOD

by ROBERT HALSTED

ila Wilson had been dead half a year, give or take a bit. Since somewhere between the time the funeral director had handed her Tibby's ashes and the day she and the lawyer had stood there in the hospital room, weeks later, while they unplugged the machines from Tom's mindless, battered corpse and let his poor weary heart stop its pointless beating.

Nobody could have told you with more authority than Lila that it isn't true the dead don't hate. She had hated doctors, lawyers, undertakers, all the petty vultures that descend on the bereaved, the governor who vetoed the right-to-die bill. She hated herself for living and suffering. She wasn't ready to admit that she hated Tibby's body for being damaged beyond a mother's recognition and Tom's for breathing when it should have stopped, hated them for going together and leaving her alone, though she knew in the depths of her mind she would have to confront all this some day.

But even more than herself, she hated the drunk who had destroyed her family. Who had smirked in the courtroom when he got his license revoked for a year and six months' suspended sentence for involuntary manslaughter. At a time when love and hope were dead, it was perhaps this hatred that had kept her alive . . . for which scant thanks.

She listened to the dying scream of the centrifuge, something deep inside her resonating to it. Automatically, robotlike—her way of life since the accident—she lifted out the plastic bags, sterilely decanted the plasma into empty sterile bags. Add normal saline, sterile. Remix packed red cells. Trickle it sterilely back into the donor, the only non-sterile thing in the room. Herself included.

So long as she kept her mind sterile, it didn't play tricks on her.

93

She no longer started to tell Tom something before she realized he wasn't there, she no longer looked in Tibby's room to remember with a start that she wasn't coming back.

She still needed a shrink, but with sheer guts and gritting her teeth she had weathered the most intense of it. At the price of sterility and wrinkles. Wrinkles were beginning to show on her face, reflecting the sterile mind behind it. Her heart was sterile and wrinkled. She imagined her uterus, the womb that had borne Tibby, wrinkled like a shriveled apple. And sterile for sure; she would never let another man, another child, get inside her feelings again. One living death per lifetime was enough.

"Today you have the choice of OJ or OJ," she said to the donor. "And we're out of chocolate cookies, so you get your choice of plain." The donors thought she smiled, any stranger would have. People who had known her before the accident wouldn't have been fooled.

As soon as the fifteen minutes were up she hustled the donor out. His breath, his skin, his clothes smelt of yesterday's stale booze, tomorrow would smell of today's.

My God, what am I doing here? she asked herself. Drunks and druggies and bikers, losers and boozers, down-and-outers. She shucked off the disposable gloves and tossed them into *Contaminated*, absentmindedly washed and dried her hands twice before she started setting up for the next donor.

The girl was an obvious druggie, everything from eye motion to skin texture shouted of it, so Lila marked a red D in a circle on the corner of the card. This one, she thought, could have been checked closer at the front desk. When they were this heavy into it, the probability of hepatitis, AIDS, and God knows what else was 'way up there, and a minute but still frightening number of these slipped past the lab.

After the druggie she took her brief, asocial lunch break and went back to the floor. The other phlebotomists and techs had no objection to her covering for them—which she preferred, without hostility, to socializing with them—so they could have more leisurely breaks.

While she was Lysoling the furniture and straightening paperwork, a donor approached the back room desk holding his card. At the sight of him she came back to life, though she managed to conceal the fact from him.

She was sure he hadn't recognized her, but her hands trembled as she interviewed him, stuck his finger, and scrubbed his elbow. She fumbled the manometer reading twice, and took three deep breaths before she dared insert the big needle. She wanted him to think this was the most pleasant plasma bank he'd ever seen.

"Are you going to be a regular donor, Mr. Dunivan? You get a bonus, you know, if you come in regularly twice a week." Lila's smile was real now, almost seductive.

"Sure, as long as I get a sweet little thing like you to poke me."

"I'm here every day but Thursday. We're open Saturdays till three." With no home life and no social life, she didn't mind the Saturday shift.

As Lila put the patch on his arm, there flitted through her mind what she thought was a fragment of a psalm: "The Lord hath delivered mine enemy unto mine hands." She was as if possessed: some hitherto unknown aspect of her had taken over, blithe with only a trace of brittleness showing, and was charming the hell out of Sam Dunivan, murderer.

She did her best to conceal her exhilaration from the rest of the staff; she wanted no comments, no observations, no connections made.

Her high stayed with her, in a kind of afterburn or halo effect, through the rest of the afternoon. Her last donor, in shabby wrinkled clothes and with a two day beard on his face, was so smiling and cheerful she felt he must be reflecting her elation at the sudden revelation of purpose in her life.

"Your heart must be very warm," he said as she took his pulse. "Your hand's cold as ice."

"It's the air conditioning. They keep it cold in here so the blood won't curdle."

He chuckled dutifully. "What's a nice girl like you doin' in a place like this?" he asked, flashing a wide, toothy grin. It was the kind of question she usually didn't respond to, sometimes allowed a peremptory and sarcastic answer. "Same as everybody else. Trying to survive." Then before she could stop herself she added, "What's *your* excuse, Mr. Bridges?"

He winked a roguish wink at her. "Same as everybody else. Doing research for a novel."

"You're impossible." She realized how insipid and adolescent a response that was and resumed her frosty veil. She finished scrubbing him, jabbed the blood needle in.

"Ouch. Was that to punish me, or is this your first day on the job?"

"I have inserted thousands of needles into human flesh. There are times when I simply don't care whether the donor finds it pleasant or not. This is one of those times."

The curtain of coldness had come down so abruptly he found himself off balance and was silent for a while. When she finished replacing his red cells he said, "Well, at least you didn't refill me with something lethal. Unless you used a slow poison."

Off guard, she let a quick tight smile cross her face. "I may try that the next time. Mr. Bridges, I have no desire to be approached. By a bum or by a millionaire. I have one purpose in life, and it has no connection whatsoever with you."

"You intrigue me."

"If you knew me better, I would dismay you more than I intrigue you. Would you like orange juice, fruit punch, or cyanide?"

"Dealer's choice. Better to die quickly with you holding my hand than linger on all alone and bereft."

"The hand-holding part was over long ago." She poured him a drink. "The fruit punch is full of toxic carcinogenic additives and tastes like vomit. I hope you enjoy it."

He took the disposable cup, carefully not letting his hand touch hers. "Any gift from your sweet cold fingers would be ambrosia, mavourneen."

"You *are* Irish."

"Sure, and me mither was an auld sod. That's where I got me gift o'baloney."

She slammed two cookies on a paper napkin onto the tray beside the donor couch. "You can leave in ten minutes." She walked briskly away to hide in the lab till he was gone. With anger and fear she realized that, until she caught herself and stiffened her spine, he had had a rear view of swinging hips as she left.

Damn the bastard. The last man who had made her laugh was in his little jar beside their daughter's, silently reproachful on the library shelf.

She felt the tears coming, bit her lip till she tasted blood. Then she scuttled to the staff Ladies' and threw up. After a while she came out, white-faced, and went into the administration office. "Gotta go. Bad PMS or a virus or something. I'll call if I can't come in in the morning."

They tried to drive her home and she waved them away. She almost ran a stop sign, she went off the shoulder one time, but she got home.

She took a tranquilizer, wept and cursed and brooded till it took effect, then lay down for a nap. She woke after dark, choked enough food past the anorectic constriction in her throat to keep the organism going, took another tranquilizer and a hot bath, and went to bed. "Too much all at once" was the last thing she heard herself say. She got up once toward morning, went to the bathroom, came back to bed and went right back to sleep.

At first light Lila stepped out of bed, still a little mellow and fuzzy from the medication but feeling good physically, and under the circumstances surprisingly sharp mentally. She fed herself a decent breakfast, took as chilly a shower as she could stand, put on a crisp fresh uniform instead of trying to get another day out of the old one.

She went in the back door, signed in, and was finished setting up for the day before any of the other staff arrived. She carefully fended off questions and comments on her health—"My lunch must have disagreed with me"—and kept her mind and body working at top efficiency all morning. Though they were doing totally different jobs.

By late morning she had, in basic outline, the remaining weeks of her life planned. She looked forward, with more zest than she had known since the accident, to filling in the details.

"At least you didn't refill me with something lethal," he'd said. Thank you, Mr. Bridges.

She worked singlehanded, since Wednesday was a light day, through the early lunch hour, and consequently had the lounge all to herself at second lunch. She wanted to plan, but it was too dis tracting—background noise and jittery Muzak, smells, no freedom to talk aloud to herself or write things down—so she simply unplugged her mind and went blank, conserving herself. Half a year before she would have thought that an Eastern mystic might be able to do that, never would have suspected she would spontaneously learn to.

At a little before two o'clock Michael Bridges glanced at his bare wrist, then looked at the bank clock across the street. He handed the little nosegay of flowers he was holding to a surprised passing child and walked rather wearily away.

Thursday she made lists, turned old and new thoughts upside down and right side up, evaluated and reevaluated with a crystalline objectivity that astounded and pleased her. This was the home stretch.

Friday she spent more time than usual in the lab, just surveying. It wasn't time, yet, but she wanted to inventory available resources.

The drug cabinet was disappointingly sparse, though she did still have the prescription pad she had been meaning for months to take back to Dr. Quincy's office. As many times as she had forged his signature by instruction in the course of a normal day's business, this was a possible resource.

Dr. Quincy was one of her few guilts and regrets. After Tom's funeral, when she realized how deep in debt the medical industry had left her, she'd gone back to work for him. The healthy children brought tears to her eyes, and the first sad terminal case completely devastated her. She had to quit after three days.

She turned that thought off, too, and went on with her planning.

As the framework of her whole plan, she laid out a set of guidelines for Dunivan's death. He must not die in the plasma bank, but must die soon after her treatment. Not because of who he was but because of who she was, his death was not to require extreme or prolonged pain. It must not reflect badly on anyone else: to the extent that she used plasma bank facilities or Dr. Quincy's prescription forms, she would have to make their noninvolvement clear in her confession.

The confession was virtually written in her head, succinctly explaining her thoughts from the time of the accident, the methods used to terminate Dunivan. She knew she could lapse into logorrhea, so she set herself a limit of one typed page.

There had to be, too, funeral instructions and some disposition of property, in memory of Tom's hatred of lawyers and undertakers and the government picking at people's remains like vultures. A bother, but not insurmountable.

She wished she could be as neat and precise in planning Dunivan's death as her own. The final scenario spread out before her:

The evening of the day she did away with Dunivan, she would go home, shower and dress in something comfortable and nice. She would have a light, pleasant, and tasty supper. Two glasses of wine with supper. As a matter of courtesy to those who had to clear up her remains, she would void her bowels and bladder and take one tranquilizer, both for comfort and, with the alcohol, to depress vital functions a bit and help her along on the way out.

Her confession and instructions would be on the night table.

She considered first an overdose of her own prescription drugs, but there was a dark and smothering quality to the rest they brought that she really didn't want as her last earthly experience.

She thought of a neat longitudinal incision in a vein down her wrist, but there was a possibility she might clot too quickly—she had good platelets—and totally embarrass herself by surviving. Besides, she would have to collect the blood in an open container, a dishpan or such, and someone could step in it or kick it over.

Above all, she must die for sure. She couldn't handle a courtroom scene, time in jail, then—she was pretty sure—a couple of years in a state hospital, then back where she started from. She knew she was coldly sane, but didn't think a jury would see her that way.

She finally decided on a blood needle and tube leading to a five-liter jug she could get hold of without trouble. And she could load up on aspirin before supper to thin her blood.

She wanted them to find her not too soon and not too late. She had to be good and dead, but not decomposed and noxious. She could leave a message on her answering machine for the plasma bank to hear when they called to see why she hadn't shown up, but there was too much risk of premature discovery. She could leave an overnight message on someone's office answering machine for the morning, but it might get garbled, erased, overlooked, or prematurely audited.

A letter could get lost or delayed in the mail. But she could use the postman in another way: leave a note in the mailbox with the flag up asking him to call the police and telling him where the key was. It would be inconvenient for him, but not an unforgivable imposition under the circumstances. She would be found by late morning, and all would be neatly wrapped up. She smiled a thin smile of satisfaction, as if she'd solved a puzzle or balanced an equation.

That left the specifics of killing Dunivan, basically what toxin to use. When she first conceived the plan, she thought of an aeroembolism, but that would kill him on the couch and possibly result in her being held for questioning and unable to implement her own death. No, it had to be a slow but not too slow poison. Thanks again, Mr. Bridges.

Something in his juice, possibly—but she really wanted to inject the seeds of his death into his life's blood. As he had done to her.

Pathogens, maybe a little staph for septicemia: no, that could poison recipients before it was detected. Antabuse seemed more hopeful: that or something analogous that would react with the alcohol he would ingest as soon as the front desk paid him for his plasma. It wouldn't be wise to try to get the Antabuse itself on a pediatric prescription blank, but the principle was sound.

She started smuggling various things home from the office: bags and tubing and needles, last year's *Physician's Desk Reference*, which was quite recent enough to contain the drug interactions she needed to know about.

During the time she was planning, both Dunivan and Bridges kept coming in. Bridges was coming in clean-shaven now, and dressed not too badly. She assiduously courted Dunivan and did her best to avoid Bridges, but one morning he sneaked up on her blind side.

"Sure, me dear, and it's weary I'm gettin' o' bein' stuck by strangers twice a week in vain hopes of a glimpse of you," he said as she came up to his couch.

Mellowed and relaxed at having her life in order for the first time since her death, she laughed before she could stop herself. "You idiot," she said. "You're a complete fake. You're not a bum and you're not even Irish—your dialect keeps slipping."

"Have lunch with me and I'll confess all." She scrubbed his inner elbow with more vigor than necessary. "I think you've got that top layer of skin off now."

"*If* I went to lunch with you, it would be for the food, *not* for the company."

"Sold! I'll be outside the front door at twelve thirty."

"I take the early lunch hour."

"Very well, I'll be outside the front door at eleven thirty."

"But I brought a sandwich today."

"You may bring it with you if you don't like fresh local seafood or prime rib. I'm not easily embarrassed."

She missed the vein and plunged the needle deep into the flesh. He gasped but didn't shout. "Oh, Lord, I'm sorry. Michael, I *didn't* do that on purpose."

His face was blanched and beaded with sweat, but he grinned a tight grin. "In heroic epics, one always expects an ordeal or two on the way to the fair maid. Though, regrettably, it's often the fair maid herself who imposes them."

"Hush." She shut him out, focused her full attention on the needle, got it in straight and painlessly. "I'm not a fair maid, I'm a miserable secondhand person. I'm going to lunch with you out of guilt and remorse. Or for food. Or to get away from this miserable place. Whatever. *Not* to get to know you, or for you to get to know me. I don't plan to be particularly pleasant. If you ever did get to know me, you would not like what you saw."

"Eleven thirty?"

"All right." She didn't get off till eleven forty-five. She wasn't quite sure why she had done that to him.

She was more pleasant than she intended to be. In her new frame of mind, she found she was as curious about Bridges as she had been about methods of murder and suicide.

"*Are* you writing a novel?" she asked over salad.

He shook his head. "Not at the moment, though I find my . . . literary *maturity* rapidly approaching. It started as a feature story, it worked into a series of documentaries—on street people, drugs, prostitution, runaways, unpunished crimes—they're all in one string, there's no stopping place between them. My patient editor is helping me negotiate national syndication, we've got an agent trying to pre-sell a rewrite of the series in hardback. There's a novel in it, and more, when I . . . get my literary and philosophical perspectives better established."

"Unpunished crimes I could tell you a lot about." She quickly changed the subject. "I'm quite serious about avoiding any and all personal acquaintance. You're a free lunch. And now that you've blown your cover, you're no longer even an intellectual challenge." She drew back down the frosty curtain. For a moment he was afraid she was ready to leave.

"Ah, but there are unexplored depths you'll never be sure of until you investigate them." He spoke as lightly as he could, but she could tell he was bruised, and had a twinge of remorse. Why do I feel guilty and want to laugh around him? she asked herself. "But enough about me. Tell me all about your own charmin' self."

"Closed book. If you want, for whatever masochistic reason, to watch me finish eating lunch, you'll leave it closed." Another brief wince on his face, another twinge of guilt on her part.

"Very well. I'll just amuse meself watchin' the dust collect on your lovely binding."

She nearly choked on a piece of lettuce suppressing a laugh. "*Damn* you!" The waiter put another glass of Chablis before her.

By the end of the meal he was mellow, solemn inner thoughts crowding his brow, and she was tipsy or the next thing to it. He lightly laid his hand on hers, and she pulled quickly away, shaking her head.

"Uh-uh," she said. "Don't try to get close. I let you get me drunk enough to get me off guard. But you're not drunk enough to handle what you might turn up."

"Burdens weigh less when they're shared."

She lifted her chin and stuck it out, flared her nostrils, lifted the corners of her mouth in what was more rictus than smile. "Knight in shining armor."

"Don't belittle what's real and honest."

She was near tears, but not for the old reasons. "My life expectancy is very short. Like weeks."

This time, when he took her hand, he held it in a deathgrip, his eyes wide. "Did you catch something from one of your . . . clients?"

She shook her head impatiently. "Nothing the least bit like that. And, as I've said before, none of your goddamned business." She had strength to fight off tears, but not for much longer. She was poised on the edge of the chair, ready to walk out on him.

He took the exit line away from her. "Time to sober you up," he said, glancing at his watch, "so they won't think you're one of the donors. Hurry up and finish your coffee." She obediently drained the cup and they left. He walked her the long way round back to the plasma bank.

That night she nearly wore the *PDR* out, and at last settled on what the patent medicine commercials called a combination of ingredients: a slow-acting, long-lasting depressant that she could administer in the juice, a faster-acting one she could transmit through the reconstituted blood by way of treated saline solution. Half an hour or so after Dunivan left, they would begin interacting with each other in his bloodstream. They would both interact with alcohol, and at about the same time, according to her estimates of his probable behavior. Her mix wouldn't quite kill him without his contributing the third element of the lethal dose. Poetic justice. She checked and rechecked her arithmetic and was satisfied.

The next morning she wrote herself a nice prescription on Dr. Quincy's blank for one of the medications, and that afternoon called her own doctor with symptoms that, with subtle leading, brought her a phone prescription for the other. She picked up both on her way home, her prescription for "Mary Ann Wilson"—she couldn't use Tibby's name—unquestioned.

Thursday she experimented, recalculating, measuring and tasting. By early afternoon she had exactly what she wanted: a saline bag— no longer sterile, but she said to herself, "Frankly, my dear, I don't give a damn!"—spiked with a sublethal dose of Drug A; a one-ounce vial with an easy-mixing solution of Drug B, also sublethal;

and her new handbag with spacious inside pocket, which now contained both drugs ready to use. She could have them out between the time she saw Dunivan at the doorway and the time he got to her couch.

Sober and serious as she was, she was also exalted. Full of energy, she outlined, wrote, edited, and final-typed her confession, leaving underlined blanks for filling in final details of time. It gave all the reasons and means, exonerated all others, and left barely enough room for her signature.

The burial instructions were brief and simple: cremation, with her ashes, Tom's and Tibby's to be mixed and spaded into the rose garden, law permitting, otherwise to be entrusted to her executor(s) for future disposition. Tom believed you could never put too much bone meal on roses, and she smiled; for an instant, a smile of warm memory.

This left one final knotty question. Her divorced father hadn't been heard from since she was in her teens, her mother had died a year before Tom and Tibby, and she had no siblings.

Tom's widowed mother had never accepted her. She had done no more than duty gestures for Tibby, had flown in for Tom's memorial service and taken the next flight back, and was hardly worth bothering with. As a matter of social propriety she would expect, Lila supposed, a farewell note. She laughed a dry shallow laugh at the thought.

She shut the door on the whole subject when she realized how near tears she was, seeing herself as a friendless orphan. As the friendless orphan she was. Not egocentric tears, but a kind of third-person compassion for this suffering self. She couldn't handle that right now, with the mother-and-daughter flavor of it.

Lila was digging in the freezer for supper ideas when it hit her, with laughter. She giggled in quiet hysteria, tears starting down her cheeks. She realized the calmness and satisfaction on one side were balanced precariously with being near the ragged edge on the other; she shut the door on the laughter, but held back a sardonic smile.

"He wants inside the book of my life. Okay, he gets the whole thing. In memoriam." She put the lamb chop and box of peas back in the freezer, forgetting all about food, and went to her desk. In minutes she had a holograph of her will roughed out, naming Michael Bridges executor and sole heir. She had details to fill in from his card in the file at the office, but the job was basically done. The last loose end tied up.

She didn't know how much of her motivation was kindness and how much cruelty, and on that question too she shut the door.

Then her appetite came back. Not emptiness and gnawing, but real appetite, she realized. She was on her way back to the freezer when the phone rang.

Probably a misdial, she told herself, since only a handful of people had the number, but she always panicked a little when it rang.

"Hello?" Cool and chilly.

"Ah, Lila, me lovely fragrant spring blossom! I've been thinkin' you might not be feedin' your pretty self well enough, and perhaps could use a decent dinner, and for all I care maybe even a flick afterward."

She giggled. "Just because I'm laughing doesn't mean I'm not highly offended. How did you get this number?"

"Same way I get the numbers of crooked politicians and Mafia bosses and reclusive celebrities. Illegal, but effective. But I wouldn't want you to be an accessory after the fact, so I'll not be tellin' ya."

"Stop that horrible fake Irish dialect."

"Ah, the County Kilkerry accent may be false, but the invitation's real. Anywhere you want—I've a two weeks' paycheck burnin' a hole in me pocket."

"You dope. In that case you can bring salad stuff and a decent wine. You just happened to catch me in one of my almost unheard-of good moods."

He whistled. "In that case open the door—I'm on me way in."

"No! Don't you dare show up in less than an hour!"

"As you say, m'dear. Any choice of wine?"

"Use your own judgment. I don't *suppose* you'll have any trouble finding the house?"

"Sweet flower, I know every antique brick and twig of ivy and wrought-iron curlicue on it. Remind me to polish that delightful lion's head door knocker for you."

"You bastard."

"Fifty-nine minutes." He hung up before she could find a last word.

Detachedly Lila watched herself start a roast, shower and shave her legs, brush her hair glossy, dress in a pretty flowered housedress she hadn't worn since before she died. She had no idea whether she was being ingenuous, satirical, gracious, sadistic, or what. She knew there was some gallows humor in it, some kind of outrageous apocalyptic showmanship, but she suspected there was more.

Michael Bridges arrived with cut flowers sticking out of a grocery bag containing half the produce department and three bottles of wine. "I didn't know exactly what you'd need, so I shotgunned it," he explained. As she led him to the kitchen he said, "If I'd known all this time you were a girl I'd have been pursuing you even more avidly."

She turned in the doorway, eyes flashing, and demanded: "What exactly was that supposed to mean?"

"It means I was too bashful to say what I really meant. Which is that I see a femininity in you I hadn't seen before, and it's very becoming and attractive."

She felt herself flushing. "Thanks, I suppose. I *was* a woman once. Now get out of my kitchen until I call you."

"Yessum, Miz Lila."

"Go. If you make me laugh, I'll send you home hungry."

They ate well and drank too much. He helped her clear up, tried to kiss her in the kitchen and was shoved away, and they took coffee and port to the living room.

When he put down his empty cup, he realized that now he had to go, or change the scenario. "There's plenty of time for a movie."

Lila shook her head. "I have to work tomorrow. I'm going to bed." Then, as if it were an afterthought, she added, "Do you want to stay or go?"

She had the satisfaction of seeing him off balance for a change. Then he recovered and said, "Given the choice, I'll stay. Must I take the couch, or have you a guest room?"

Unsmiling she said: "I'm offering you what you've been working so hard for. You've earned it. I won't wiggle my hips, but I'll spread my legs. Take it or leave it."

He looked at her for half a minute, then softly responded: "Any other woman, I'd turn her over my knee, lecture her on good manners and morals, and walk away. You ... if that's all I can have of you, I'll take it rather than nothing."

"Come to the bedroom in five minutes. You can take the cups to the kitchen while you're waiting."

He obeyed her instructions. She made many conditions, at first wouldn't let him kiss her on the mouth, and, physically, he could have found it disappointing. But once she called him "Tom," and afterward she wept on his chest and told him less than he already knew of Tom and Tibby and let him kiss the tears off her eyelids. Then sometime after the late mockingbirds had finished and before the early ones began, she woke him, shoved him abruptly away, and told him to go.

"May I dress here, or should I carry my clothes out to the street?"

"Dress in the living room. Then *go*. Be sure the door's locked behind you." He gathered up his clothes and walked around toward her side of the bed. She was afraid he would try to kiss her, but he only stood over her and said, "Good night, my sweet lilac blossom. And thank you for the gift it hurt to give." Then he was gone. She heard him fumbling in the dark as he dressed, then the click of the front door locking, then in a minute his old Toyota starting up.

The next morning she found one of his socks by the bedroom chair. She couldn't leave it there to look at and she couldn't pick it up and put it in her laundry, so she kicked it under the chair. "I'll worry about that tomorrow," she said.

Dunivan missed his regular day. He was usually in a little before lunch on Friday, and as the day went on she became more and more anxious lest he had stopped coming.

Also, thankfully, Bridges didn't show. She hoped he had given up his street-people act and she wouldn't, at least, have to fend him off at work. Though she didn't assume she was free of him.

Nor was she, even in his absence. She had to keep slamming the door, as if it were Fibber McGee's closet, on all the muck from the back of her mind that last night had stirred up: Why had she let him in her house? Why had she taken him to bed, what was she trying to prove, who was she trying to punish, what did he think of her? And why the *hell* had she spilled her guts to him? The only sane and intelligent thing she had done all evening and night was to send him away.

By quitting time she was a nervous wreck. She had a couple of scares in the traffic, ate a slice of cold roast for supper, and drank enough of the left-over port to numb her brain and remind her how little sleep she had had the night before. She was in bed with a paperback by nine. With, beside her, a ghost that might have been Tom or Michael or Fate. She realized that, unless she wanted to operate left-handed, she would have to lie where Michael had lain when it was time for her to die.

She was lying there, thumb marking her place in the paperback, wondering whether she dared add a sleeping pill to the port, when she fell asleep with the light on.

Dunivan stayed away Saturday, as did Michael, and Lila regained some equilibrium even as her anxiety increased.

When the call finally came Sunday evening, she felt a sudden flash of anger at herself for how she had been waiting for it.

"Hello." As flat as she could manage.

"Lila?" It was Michael's voice, but deferent and tentative. "Ordinarily I'd have called the lady the next day, but you seemed to need some space."

"I did and I still do. Thank you for your concern. Goodbye."

"Farewell, then." He hung up before she did, and that irritated her a little.

But later on she asked herself, "Why are you *treating* the poor bastard that way?" She knew she was leading him on, for all her showy pretense of rejection. She dimly realized she was punishing him as proxy, though she totally blocked, forgot even the train of thought leading up to it, when it came to the matter of whom he was proxy for.

One morning the next week she saw Dunivan with another phlebotomist; he had come in during her break.

Then, the week after, she gave in—because she fainted in the kitchen getting ready for work Monday—to the queasy feeling she had had, nausea and fatigue and crying spells. She put it down to stress and treated herself; she felt terminal, but she didn't want medical verification until she was ready to go.

The week after that they made her take a light schedule, and she accepted it. Then partway through the following week a thought hit her that was like a kick in the stomach.

She put off acting on the thought for a day, then the next morning she slipped into a restroom with a specimen bottle, took the kit out of her purse, and gritted her teeth.. She watched the color change, squeezed tears from under her squinted lids, and screamed in a barely audible whisper, "Goddammit, oh, goddammit, hurry up, Dunivan, hurry *up!*"

She surreptitiously went through Dunivan's old records and saw what might be a pattern of binges. Or of times in jail. His card for the period had a hiatus between the time of the accident and the trial. Her stomach knotted when she realized the significance of the missing dates, and her urge to kill renewed itself in sharp clarity.

So she could wait this one out, and she did.

He came in early the following week, looking worse than she had ever seen him. He was so jaundiced she wondered how he had ever got past the front desk.

She was minding the back desk, so she had him captive. She did the paperwork quickly, pricked his finger and flicked the droplet of blood out of the capillary tube into the little beaker of copper sulfate solution. She held her breath, prayed, used psychokinesis, and finally the dark globule sank slowly through the blue liquid. Even then, she knew it was free bilirubin in the blood and not red cell count that had sunk it.

"Just barely made it today, Mr. Dunivan. If your hemoglobin were any lower I'd have to send you away." She knew that with his patent jaundice she shouldn't have touched him—his eyeballs were yellow and his skin repulsively greenish under the fluorescent lighting—and that having gone this far she should have centrifuged the sample and suggested a referral to the clinic. "I'll take you myself. Get in the first couch over there and I'll be there in a minute."

She gathered the paperwork and fastened it to the clipboard, reached under the desk for her bag, and followed him to the couch.

She lifted his clammy hand and counted his pulse. Weak, noticeably arrhythmic, 116.

She put the manometer cuff on, pumped it up, had to listen twice before she was sure. Diastolic 98, systolic 124, less than thirty points' difference where there should be fifty.

And he stank. Not just stale booze and dirty body and sour clothes. More and worse, something metabolic.

She wrote the figures down, glanced up from the clipboard, and at the other end of the room saw Michael, very serious, slowly shaking his head. She dropped the pen, felt the blood drain from her face and would have passed out if she hadn't abruptly sat on the stool. She looked up again and he was gone. He had come and gone so quickly he might have been an hallucination.

Lila took several deep breaths and recovered enough to speak. She reached a decision, a snap decision but perhaps preordained, and spoke.

"You still don't remember me, do you, Sam Dunivan?" He looked at her in bleary confusion. "Do you remember killing my husband and daughter eight months ago?"

His yellow eyes widened round, and his face turned a duskier green.

"I was going to kill you today," she went on. "I have the weapon right here." She gestured at her purse. Paralyzed with horror, he looked as if he were trying to crawl off the couch by sliding like a slug. "But I just realized I no longer give a good goddam about you, one way or another." She reached into the purse; he sat up on the couch and cringed away from her, but it was only her wallet she brought out.

She reached into it and pulled out a ten and a five. "Your plasma's not worth buying. Your blood is falling apart, your red cells are crumbling, your liver's no good. Here's the fifteen dollars you would have got for it. You can buy booze with it and finish drinking yourself to death. Buy a cheap gun and blow out what brains you have left. Or even use it for carfare to get to the clinic or hospital."

She handed him the money, stood up and walked to the restroom. She breathed deeply, washed her face in cold water, decided she wasn't going to faint. Emotionally, she was in limbo. She knew something like cleansing tears, black despair, or hysterical laughter was ahead, but she was too drained for them now.

Lila made it through what was left of the afternoon. She left a few minutes early and got ahead of the rush, and when she got home Michael's car was there in front of the house.

"*Damn* him!" she growled. She parked in the driveway, went to the door and tried it. It was locked, but if he could get her phone number and read her mind he was certainly capable, ethically and technically, of picking a lock.

She let herself in, called him and got no answer. She went back and looked out the kitchen window and he was in the rose garden in shorts and T-shirt, pruning and weeding. She felt a sudden sense of intrusion and outrage at his presence in the garden she and Tom had put in together, whose flowers had delighted Tibby.

Angered, she unbolted the door and stalked out to where he was kneeling. "You're trespassing," she said curtly.

He smiled up at her. "Ah, and 'tis a good day to ye, acushla! . . . A shame to let a foine garden o' roses, Granada and Queen Elizabeth—I'm a Loyalist—and all, go to waste for lack o' lovin' care."

She laughed, for the first time not resenting it. Then, seriously: "This is a very private space, Michael."

"I figured it was, that's why I'm givin' it such first-rate personal attention."

"You intrusive egotistical bastard."

"Ye've been talkin' to me mither!" He flashed a wide grin, then went on more soberly: "I plan to intrude even more, for reasons I consider adequate to excuse the discourtesy."

"Just a minute. First explain your intrusion this afternoon."

He raised his eyebrows. "You mean right now?"

She shook her head impatiently. "At the office. Around three or four this afternoon."

"Not guilty, Your Honor. I was already intrudin' here. Since about half-past two—I meant to surprise you with the finished product, but it's a longer job than I figured, to do it *right*." He knit his brows. "I was thinking of you *very* seriously along about then. Frustrated, wanting to shake wrong ideas out of your head before they mess you up worse."

She didn't comment, and he went on: "Which I'm going to do now. I should have before but I was too dense and imperceptive to see it till the small hours this morning, and I've been mulling it over since."

"Do you have a permit to meddle in my personal affairs?"

"I granted myself a license to that effect." She started to protest. "Now, hush. I'm serious now, dead serious. I don't know why I was so dumb it took me weeks to see it. You've been planning to do away with Dunivan, haven't you?"

She tightened her lips and felt her face grow pale, but said nothing.

"And then yourself, that would be the only way out that you, you personally, could take." He paused for a deep breath; she wanted to speak out but couldn't. "You've been telling me that, one way or another, practically since we met."

"Michael—"

"Hush, love . . . I had to do some deep pondering on this, but I've a proposition for you. Keep your sweet little cold hands off him, and I promise you he'll die. Not that it wouldn't be a mercy, the poor miserable wretch is falling apart. Just don't ask me any questions, I won't want to tell you."

"Michael! You couldn't just coldly—"

"Couldn't I now? I've got very street-smart in a few months here. I could do it myself, with impunity, neatly and painlessly. For the price of a weekend's worth of fix, I could have it done. If you truly want him dead that badly.''

"Michael . . .''

"Don't give me a moral lecture, missy. You're ready to do it yourself, and add the sin of suicide on top of it. For me, it would be a very simple moral choice: his life and yours both, one worthless life and one good one, or his alone. No question as to what my decision would be. Just be damn sure that's what you want.''

She smiled a tight weary smile. "Are you thirsty?'' He nodded; she went in and brought back iced tea, and they sat on a wrought-iron bench overlooking the half-weeded rosebed.

"I started to kill him this afternoon. That's when I saw you—were you truly not there?''

"Cross me heart. 'Twas your conscience manifestin' itself, externalized as an hallucination o' me, the archetypal moral authority. Happens all the time.''

She giggled. "Idiot. . . . Seriously, he *is* falling apart. Advanced hepatitis at least, impending liver collapse, maybe hepatic CA. . . . Michael, can you feel pity for someone you hate, you've hated so much it's become the center of your life?''

"Compassion is for who you love. Pity is for who you don't love, nor respect. Don't let him be the center of your life any longer. He's not good enough for that exalted status.''

"He isn't. I'm suddenly, almost, *indifferent.*''

They sat there silent for a while. She discovered with mild surprise that they had been holding hands; she wasn't ready to squeeze his, but left hers in it.

Finally Lila said, surprising herself again, "I'm pregnant, Michael.''

She felt his hand tighten on hers, but he kept his voice level. "No one since me, I hope. Nobody before me, I'm sure.''

"No one but you, since Tom, till now.'' She saw him wanting to speak, but he was silent and she was glad of it. "Michael, this place is full of ghosts. Or *I'm* full of ghosts.''

"I felt 'em, this afternoon. We Irish have the second sight, you know.'' She looked at his face, and it was serious, no insouciant grin. "I think we're pretty compatible. The ghosts and me, I mean. We share a common interest.''

After a while she said, "I'm a psychological mess, still.''

"I've known that was part of the package. I see favorable changes."

She smiled up at him. A small smile, but no longer tight. "If I said, 'Hold me all night but don't do anything,' could you?"

"For now. Not forever."

"I mean for now. Day at a time, play it by ear."

"I can handle that."

It was days later before they learned that Dunivan, that same afternoon, had staggered into the side of a hurrying ready-mix concrete truck.

LIFE OR BREATH

by NELSON DeMILLE

Martin Wallace stood in a modified parade rest position and gazed out of the twenty-third floor hospital window. Across the thirty miles of flat suburban sprawl he could see the blazing skyscrapers of Manhattan.

They blinked, twinkled, and beckoned to him.

He looked at his watch. Fifteen minutes to nine. Fifteen minutes before he could leave this oppressive room and head for the lights of that enchanted island. He rocked back and forth on the balls of his feet. His reveries were broken by a sound behind him.

He turned and looked down at the form on the bed. The limp arm was tapping the night table to get his attention. He made a slightly annoyed face as their eyes met. Who else but Myra could get herself into a fix like this? But, then, he supposed that the hospital was full of bored suburban housewives who didn't know their capacity for Valium.

He stepped up to the bed. A small green plastic box sat on its stand next to the bed. A clear accordion-type plastic hose led from the box to her throat. The box made a faint, but annoying, pneumatic sound. "Myra. I have to leave, dear. Visiting hours are over. What can I bring you?" He smiled.

She looked petulant. That was her favorite expression. Petulant. In twenty years of marriage, he had labeled every one of her expressions and voice tones.

She made small grunting sounds. She wanted to speak, but nothing came out.

"You just get a good night's rest, Myra. Rest. A nice long rest." He smiled and pulled the respirator hose out of the tracheal adaptor embedded in her throat.

113

Air rushed into the adaptor and made a wheezing sound. At the same time air blew out of the disconnected hose in a continuous stream. He squeezed the open end of the hose, but it was too late. The alarm went off.

Almost immediately, a big, buxom nurse charged into the room like an enraged mother hen. "Mr. Wallace! Please. I explained to you how to disconnect that. You must squeeze the hose first, before you pull it out, so that the alarm doesn't sound."

"Sorry."

She threw him a look that medical people reserve for naughty lay people. "It's like screaming wolf. You know?"

"Sorry, nurse." He looked her full figure over. Long tresses of chestnut brown hair fell onto her shoulders and framed her pretty German-Irish face. The name tag on her breast read Maureen Hesse.

She made a huff and a puff and turned around. She called back over her shoulder as she left. "Visiting hours are almost over."

"Yes, nurse." He looked down at his wife. She had placed her hand over the gaping rubber tracheal adaptor. With the hole sealed off she was able to speak in weak, aspirating sounds. Martin Wallace preferred this to the high-pitched screech he was used to.

Myra spoke. "Don't forget my magazines." She paused as air rushed into the hole. "And get them to put a different TV in here." She wheezed. "We're paying for it." She opened her mouth and tried to gulp some air. "I want one that works. Call my mother tonight." She tried taking air in through her nose. "And talk to that doctor. I want to know *exactly* how long—"

Martin Wallace gently took his wife's hand away from the trachea adaptor. Her words faded like a slowing record. The tracheal adaptor wheezed. He began to plug the respirator hose back into her throat.

"Martin! I have more to tell you—you—" Her words were lost as the machine began pumping air back into her lungs.

"You're getting yourself excited, Myra. Now, rest. Rest. Goodnight." He walked around the bed and left the room.

At the nurses' station, he spotted Dr. Wasserman, the resident physician. He walked over to him. "Excuse me, doctor."

The young resident looked up from his charts. "Oh yes. Mr. Wallace. How is your wife doing?"

"Well, that's what I want to ask *you*, doctor."

"Of course." Dr. Wasserman put on a look of professional concern. "Well, Mr. Wallace, it could have been worse. She could have been dead."

Martin Wallace did not consider that to be worse. "What's the—how do you call it—prognosis?"

"Well, it's too early to tell, really. You see, Mr. Wallace, when you take a tranquilizer, like Valium, for instance, for extended periods of time, you begin to think you're building up a resistance to it. It seems to have no clout anymore. So instead of taking, let's say, five milligrams at a time, you take maybe twenty, as your wife did. Plus that martini—"

"Manhattan."

"Yes. Whatever. So what happened is that she had a period of anoxic cardiac arrest. In other words, her breathing and heart stopped. Maybe for as long as two minutes. This may lead to residual neurological sequelae—permanent but partial damage to the nervous system."

"Meaning?"

Dr. Wasserman stroked his chin. "It's too early to tell, really."

"Come on, doctor. What's the *worst* it can be?"

He shrugged. "She can be an invalid for the rest of her life. She may need a home respirator for a while. She may even need occasional renal dialysis. Frequent cardiac tests. There could be partial muscular paralysis. When you're dealing with the nervous system, you never know. It may take weeks to see what works and what doesn't work anymore. I mean, she was technically dead for a few minutes. How many functions come back is anybody's guess. You understand?"

"Yes." Martin Wallace glanced back toward his wife's room. He turned back toward the doctor. "How long would she live without the respirator? I mean—you know—when she wants to speak—I'm afraid to keep the hose out too long. I don't want to—"

The doctor moved his hand in a calming gesture. "That shouldn't be a concern. When she has difficulty breathing, she signals to you, doesn't she? Or she tells you."

"Yes. Yes, of course. But I was just wondering. You know. If the hose came out in her sleep, maybe."

"That's why the alarm is there, Mr. Wallace. In the event the hose comes out by accident and she can't replace it." He gave him a smile and changed his voice to a paternal scolding tone, even though he was much younger than Mr. Wallace. "You, by the way, must be more careful when you disconnect it. You can't be setting off the alarm every time. It gives the nurses a good workout, but they have enough of that anyway in the Intensive Care Unit." He smiled again. "As long as there is someone in the room or as long as the alarm system is working, there can't be any accident."

Martin Wallace smiled back, although this good news did not make him at all happy. He was asking questions with one thing in mind and the good doctor was answering him with another thing in mind. He'd have to be blunt. "Look, doctor," he smiled again, "just out of morbid curiosity—okay? How long can she live without that respirator?"

Dr. Wasserman shrugged again. "Half an hour, I guess. Probably less. Hard to say. Sometimes a patient can get the voluntary muscles to work hard enough to breathe for hours and hours. But as soon as the patient gets fatigued or sleeps, the involuntary muscles, which should normally control unconscious breathing, can't do the job. I really can't give you a definite answer. But the question is academic, anyway, isn't it? The respirator breathes for her, Mr. Wallace."

"Yes. Of course. But—" He tried to put on an abashed smile. "Just one more question. I worry about these things. I'm an accountant and I have that kind of mind. You know?" He smiled a smile that tried to bespeak professional parallelism. Neurotic complicity between great minds. "I think too much, I suppose. But I was wondering, is—is there any way the alarm system can fail? You know?"

Dr. Wasserman tapped him lightly on his shoulder. "Don't worry, Mr. Wallace. As soon as that hose comes out of the tracheal adaptor and the pumped air meets no resistance, the alarm goes off here in the nurses' station. Now, I know what you're thinking. What if Mrs. Wallace pulls it loose during the night and rolls over on it." He smiled.

That's exactly what Martin Wallace was thinking. He waited, literally breathless.

"Well, it's almost impossible to pull it loose by accident, to begin with. Secondly, she'd have to roll over on it very, very quickly. Otherwise, the alarm would go off. Then she'd have to stay in that position for some time. But you see, as soon as she had difficulty breathing, she'd move or thrash. It's a normal reaction. She's not comatose. The hose, then, would be free of her body and the alarm would sound. But anyway, in Intensive Care, we check the patients regularly. Besides, you have hired private nurses around the clock, as I understand."

Martin Wallace tried not to look glum. He nodded. Those nurses were costing him a fortune. Another one of Myra's extravagances.

But there was one last glimmer of hope. Dr. Wasserman, however, had anticipated the next question and began answering it.

"And the other thing you're wondering about is the respirator itself. Well, any malfunction in the machine also triggers an alarm. There are several alarms, actually. At least three backup alarms in that model." The doctor folded his arms and glanced at his watch. "We have a dozen spare respirators standing by. Haven't lost a patient through accident yet." He smiled reassuringly.

"Power failure?" It came out with the wrong intonation. It came out as though he were begging for one.

"I beg your pardon?"

"Power failure. Power failure. You know. Blackout."

"Oh." He laughed. "You *are* a worrier, Mr. Wallace." The doctor's smile faded and his voice became impatient. "We have auxiliary generators, of course. It's the law." He looked pointedly at his watch. "I have to make my rounds. Excuse me."

"Of course." Martin Wallace stood rooted at the nurses' station for several minutes staring straight ahead.

He walked slowly to the elevator bank. A few overstayed visitors stared wordlessly at the floor indicator. The elevator came and he stepped in. The lights blinked—22—21—20—19—

He walked out of the hospital and into the acres of parking lot. A gentle spring breeze blew the scent of newly born flowers across the dark macadam. He walked slowly through the balmy night air as though in a trance. Invalid. Partial paralysis. Home respirator. Renal dialysis.

He had come so close to losing her for good. And now this. What a monumental mess. Myra was hard enough to take when she was well—which was almost never. Twenty years of hypochondria, and never one really good fatal illness. And now this. An invalid.

He walked up to his car and got in. He lit a cigarette and looked out the side window. Three very pretty young girls walked by. They wore jeans and T-shirts. Their long hair fell over their shoulders. Their lithe bodies and lilting voices made his chest heave. He bit his lip in suppressed desire.

Myra. Painted toenails. Painted eyes. Dyed hair. Enough jewelry to drown her in the event she ever decided to jump into the swimming pool she had insisted on having built. Myra. Ridiculous fan magazines and trashy tabloids. Does Jackie O. keep a secret picture of Jack in her snuffbox? Is Robert Redford in love with Princess Grace? Who *cares*? Myra. Sitting in front of the idiot box in a crocodilian stupor. Shrieking over a game of mah-jongg, with her bitchy friends. Sitting for hours baking her skimpy brains under a hair dryer. Myra. Barren of children. Barren of a single original thought in twenty years. Myra and Poopsie. Poopsie and Myra. Of all the dogs on God's earth, he hated poodles more than any other. Myra. Professional shopper. Myra. The last novel she read was *Love Story*. The one before that was *Valley of the Dolls*. The only time she had stirred herself in years was to join a local chapter of the women's liberation movement. The Alive Doesn't Live Here Anymore Chapter. Liberation. What a laugh. Who was freer than that lazy cow? Myra. What a dud. He laughed and slumped over the steering wheel. Tears rolled down his cheeks.

Divorce. Divorce would cost him a fortune. Her death, on the other hand, would put a hundred thousand dollar life insurance policy in his pocket.

Martin Wallace pulled the rearview mirror down and looked at himself in the dim light. Not bad for thirty-nine. A few weeks at a health spa. A little suntan. New clothes. A new hairstyle. A new life.

He slumped back into the seat of his big, Myra-inspired Cadillac. He pictured the interior of a Porsche or a Jaguar.''

He looked up at the tall, bulky, illuminated hospital. Even with his medical insurance, she was costing him two hundred a day. Even flat on her back she was draining him. Her whole life was a study in conspicuous consumption. The quintessential consumer of goods and services. She even consumed more hospital goods and services than the average patient. And she never produced one single thing in her whole life. Not even the thing she was built to produce—a child. Barren. Frigid. Worthless. In his accounting firm she would be called a continuing liability. But a liability, which if liquidated, would become an asset. Liquidated.

He started the car and wheeled out of the parking lot. Within the hour he had parked his car in a midtown garage.

He began walking up Third Avenue. It was a weeknight, but the streets were alive with people on this first nice spring evening. He walked into P. J. Moriarty's. At the bar were three bachelors from his office—his subordinates of sorts.

They drank there for an hour, then took taxis to each other's favorite East Side pubs. They took taxis all over town. They walked and sang and drank.

They wound up on the West Side and had a late supper at the Act I, overlooking Times Square. Down in the street the Great White Way blazed through their alcoholic haze.

They left the restaurant. To Martin Wallace, there was pure magic in the night air and in the streets of New York as he gazed out through his clouded eyes at the lights and people swirling around him.

He separated from his friends and walked east on Central Park South and stood in front of the Plaza Hotel, overlooking the park. He finger-combed his hair and straightened his tie. Then he entered the hotel and fulfilled a longstanding recurring dream of checking in.

The marble lobby was an enchanted forest of columns and thick pile rugs. Subdued lights showed little knots of well-dressed people seated in the plush chairs and sofas. An attractive woman seemed to smile at him as the bellboy led him to the elevators.

He awoke and lay bathed in glorious late morning sunlight. He picked up the phone and ordered coffee and mixed rolls and pastry. As an afterthought—he had seen it in a movie—he ordered a pitcher of Bloody Marys.

He put his hands behind his neck and stared at the rich cream-colored ceiling. His mind wandered. On his salary, with no dependents—that is, no Myra—and with no money-sucking house in the suburbs, he reckoned that he could well afford a lifestyle like this. A nice apartment in town. A few wild nights a week like last night. An opera or a little ballet on his easy nights. A Broadway show once in a while. Sunday brunch at the Oyster Bar downstairs. Maybe he would rent a car on weekends and get out to the hinterlands once in a while. Maybe take the train from Pennsylvania Station to the Hamptons or to Belmont Racetrack. Maybe the train from Grand Central Station to the resort hotels in the Catskills or a football game at West Point. Sunday afternoon in Central Park. Saturday in Greenwich Village. A different little restaurant every night. He would have to patronize at least one bar and one restaurant enough to become one of the regulars, though, he reminded himself. He pictured scenes he had seen in movies. The possibilities for life were unlimited in this city. No house, no car, no television, no fan magazines, no Myra. He smiled.

If he had a nice windfall of, say, a hundred thousand dollars to start with, it would be even better. And all this was only a heartbeat away. Just a single heartbeat. But it kept beating, that heart. Thump.

Thump. Thump. He could hear his own heart beat heavily in his chest.

He stretched and yawned. He cleared his husky, dry throat and placed a phone call.

A woman answered. "East Park Community Hospital."

"Yes. Intensive Care Unit, please." The phone clicked.

"ICU."

"Yes. Is it still beating?"

"Sir?"

"This is Mr. Wallace. How is my darling wife, please?" He felt reckless this morning.

"Just a moment."

There was a long pause. Martin Wallace prayed.

The voice came back. "Fine, sir. Mrs. Wallace spent a comfortable night. Your private nurse is just bathing her now."

"Swell. Terrific. Thank you." He slammed the phone down and covered his face with the pillow.

There was a knock on the door.

"Come in."

The busboy entered with a rolling cart. The cart was heaped with all manner of hotel luxury. There was even a complimentary copy of *The New York Times*. Just like in the movies. But the scene paled next to the reality of the telephone call.

He signed for the breakfast and sat down heavily on the bed. He poured a Bloody Mary into a tall glass with a coating of salt on its rim. He downed it in one long gulp.

He opened the paper as he sipped his coffee and scanned it idly. The problems of the world were minuscule compared to his own, but he had developed the defensive habit of eating breakfast behind a newspaper and it was hard to break bad habits. He read, but nothing registered. His mind was elsewhere. Myra. Thump. Thump. Thump. Her heart still beat at the rate of a couple of hundred dollars a day. Thump. Thump. It had been silent for two minutes once, but thanks to the marvels of medical science, it was thumping again. Thump. Thump. Thump. It would thump for how many more years? Twenty? Forty? Sixty?

How do you divorce an invalid, even if you are willing to pay most of your salary for the rest of your life? Why not just disappear, then? That was becoming one of the most popular track sports among men these days. The hundred yard dash into obscurity. But it was a tremendous price to pay. Loss of identity. Loss of friends. Loss of professional credentials. Why should *he* disappear? Why couldn't *she* disappear? "Die! Die, damn you! Die!" The sound of his own voice scared him.

He tossed the paper on the bed. He stared at the open pages for a long second, then picked it up again. There was a lengthy article on the question of medical life-support systems. He read it intently and discovered that he was not alone in wishing that medical science would let the dying die.

He read of cases of brain dead patients kept alive for months and even years by artificial means. He read of cases similar to Myra's. Overdoses. Strokes. Partially destroyed nervous systems. Human beings snatched from the slashing scythe of the Grim Reaper, but not before suffering permanent life-wrecking infirmities. He read of the burdens of families left with slack-jawed loved ones to care for. Left with staggering medical bills rendered by smiling doctors and hospitals as the price for returning these loved ones to them as vegetables.

But what interested him more was not the horror stories of misguided humanitarianism, but rather the names of individuals and organizations who opposed these extraordinary measures taken to prolong life at any cost.

He nibbled at a big cheese Danish and a smile played across his moving lips.

He took the pass from the girl at the desk and stood in front of the elevator bank. The night was warm, but he wore a tan trenchcoat buttoned to the neck.

Swarms of visitors waited as the elevators came to collect them and carry them up into the great hospital. Martin Wallace crowded into one of the cars. He held his brown paper bag at chest level to keep it from being crushed in the press of the crowd.

In the Intensive Care Unit, he stopped at the nurses' station and exchanged a few smiling words with Miss Hesse, then walked into Myra's private room. He nodded to the attractive private nurse he was paying for. "How's she doing, Ellen?" He smiled. She, plus the other two nurses, was costing him a fortune, he reminded himself. He also reminded himself that they were not needed, but Myra had insisted.

The petite young girl smiled at him. "Fine, Mr. Wallace. Getting better every day." She rose. "I'll just leave you two alone." She smiled at both of them and left.

Myra made a weak gesture toward her throat.

Martin Wallace nodded tiredly and reached down and grabbed the hose. He pinched before he pulled and the alarm did not sound. He placed his hand over the tracheal adaptor in her throat and the wheezing stopped.

Myra sucked in a big gulp of air. "I had Ellen call you all last night."

Her voice sounded stronger today, he noticed. It had some of its old screechiness back in it. "Is that so? I must have slept through the phone. Sorry."

She looked at him with expression number three. Suspicion. "I needed my nail polish and manicure kit."

The tone was accusatory. It was supposed to provoke guilt in him, even though it was barely audible and her tonal quality was hard to control. He recognized it anyway. "Sorry."

What an incredible woman, he thought. Three days ago she was leaning heavily against death's door and today she wants her manicure kit. He stared at her for several seconds. He had an impulse to pour her bottle of skin lotion into the tracheal adaptor and watch her drown. "Sorry, Myra."

"Well, at least I see you remembered something." She pointed to the bag that he had placed on the bed. "Did you—"

He took his hand off the adaptor and air rushed in. Her words faded. "Can't have you off it too long, dear." He plugged the pinched-off hose back in with his other hand and released it. The machine changed pitch and began pumping in air. It was so easy to shut her up that it was almost comical. He could see that she was furious at being cut off. She moved her hand to the hose to pull it out, but he grabbed her wrist. "Really, Myra. That's enough talking for a while."

She tried to pull her wrist free, but he held it easily. Her other hand reached out and she pushed the nurse's call buzzer.

Martin Wallace had enough for one night. He reached inside the paper bag and took out two magazines and threw them on the night table. "I could only find two."

She looked inquisitively at the still bulging bag.

He didn't acknowledge her questioning eyes.

The private nurse, Ellen, walked in. "Yes?"

Martin Wallace smiled. "I think Mrs. Wallace wants something." He looked down at her. "I really have to go, dear. I can't stay tonight." He looked at his watch. It was only eight ten. "I'm sorry, Myra darling. I have an appointment." He looked at Ellen. "Take

care of my sweetheart, will you? I'll try to get over tomorrow afternoon. Otherwise I'll see you both tomorrow night.'' He walked to
the door. ''Goodbye.''

Ellen smiled. ''Goodbye, Mr. Wallace.''

Myra shot him look number one. Pure malice with a touch of
hatred and contempt.

He waved and went into the corridor.

At the elevator bank a chime sounded and a light lit up. He walked
over to the open car and stepped in. There were three other early-
departing visitors and one orderly. Only the lobby button was lit.
Nonchalantly, he pushed *B* for basement.

The elevator stopped in the lobby, and the doors slid open. He
moved closer to the control panel and out of sight of the guards and
reception desks. He frantically hit the *Door Close* button.

The elevator descended to the basement. The elevator doors
opened. He stepped into a long, empty corridor. Some of the kitchens
were down here, and he could smell cooking. He looked around,
then walked quickly up to a canvas laundry cart and shucked off his
trenchcoat. He threw it in the cart and buried it with dirty linen.
Under the trenchcoat he wore a white lab jacket.

Still clutching his paper bag, he paced up and down the deserted
corridors, examining doors and signs.

At the end of a long, dimly lit corridor he saw it. It was marked
Subbasement. Electrical. He opened the steel door and descended the
narrow metal staircase.

The stairwell emptied into a long, narrow corridor. He walked past
the grey painted concrete walls under the harsh glow of evenly
spaced naked bulbs that ran the length of the ceiling. He stopped at
each of several metal doors, opening each and looking inside.

Finally he came to a door whose stenciled sign was the announcement of the end of his search: *Electrics Room. Danger. High Voltage.*
He went inside and closed the door behind him.

The dimly lit room was medium-sized and crowded with the life
stuff of modern buildings. Endless tubes of wire and conduit ran
across the ceiling and tracked down the grey walls. On the far side
lay two huge diesel generators on raised platforms. Each had a
hooded exhaust over it. To the left of the generators sat a rectangular -
box labeled: *Batteries—Caution: Acid.*

It would take a barrel of dynamite to completely sabotage this
room. It would be necessary to blow up both generators, the storage
batteries, and the external city electricity source.

Every system, however, has its Achilles' heel, and he did not have to be an electrical engineer to know what the soft spot in this system was. He had to find it first, though.

He walked slowly around the room. On the rear wall were about thirty black and grey painted metal panels. Plastic label tags hung from each of them. He ran his eyes over each tag.

He smiled when he found what looked like the proper one. Mounted waist high on the wall, it was the size of a deep orange crate. It was painted a shiny, crackling black. The long switch handle on the side of the box was capable of being set in three positions: *Automatic, External,* and *Diesel.* The switch was in the *Automatic* position.

He opened the cabinet door, and it made a metallic squeak. Inside the door was a sign that said *Power Sensing and Relay Control Panel. Disconnect Diesel Junction Connector D-3 Before Servicing.* He would disconnect more than that before he was through. This was it for sure. This was the central distribution point for the sources of the hospital's power. This box decided whether or not the city's power was normal, and if not, it would then activate the diesel generators, drawing on the storage batteries, if necessary. It all came together right here in this box. The Achilles' heel. Remove the box and you removed the whole hospital's energy supply.

From his paper bag, he removed a large number ten fruit can. The top of the can was covered with aluminum foil. He removed the foil and shoved it into his pants pocket. Inside the can was packed the gunpowder from a box of fifty 12-gauge shotgun shells. It was a small charge by the standards of most bomb makers, but then he did not need much and it had the advantage of using an easily procured and nontraceable explosive.

Also inside the can was a simple wind-up alarm clock and two flashlight batteries attached to a switch. A cluster of the nitroglycerine primers from the shotgun shells was the detonator. The whole thing looked innocuous enough, especially in the foil-covered fruit can. It looked like a container that a doting husband would use to carry homemade cookies to his ailing loved one. Even one of the rare cursory inspections by the hospital guards would have aroused no suspicion.

He put his hand into the can and set the alarm for ten o'clock. He connected the wires with alligator clips. The loud ticking seemed to fill the cryptlike room. He placed the whole thing gently inside the cabinet. He wiped it carefully for prints with a handkerchief and closed the steel door. He wiped the door also. His face was covered with sweat as he turned from the wall of control panels.

He crossed the room and walked up to the door. From the paper bag he removed a piece of shirt cardboard and taped it to the door. He had wanted to letter the sign ahead of time, but it would be incriminating if by some rare happenstance a guard had wanted to look in the bag. He wrote in large block letters with a marking pen. *God Does Not Want People Kept Alive by Artificial Means. Let the Dying Die with Dignity.* (Signed) *The Committee to End Human Suffering.*

He heard voices outside the door. He stood motionless and breathless as the voices, two males, came abreast of the door. They walked by, and he could hear their footsteps retreating down the corridor. He waited.

As he waited, he looked at the sign in the dim light. He smiled. This was enough of a red herring to throw the police off for months. And if by chance they suspected a friend or relative of one of the hospital's current patients, it would make no difference. There were at least thirty people in the Intensive Care Unit whose lives depended on one machine or another. To run down the friends and relatives of each of them would take a very long time. Eventually, they might even get around to asking him to "drop by" for questioning. But so what? There would be a few hundred others, connected with the thirty or so, they would have to question also. Then there would be all the known anti-life-support-systems groups and individuals.

It disturbed him that so many others would die also, but it could not be helped, really. To play with Myra's respirator in the hospital or to see that she had an accident when she returned home was to court life imprisonment. It was no secret to their friends and relatives that he wanted her gone.

To end all the lives hanging on the machines was to scatter the suspicion far and wide. That was the beauty of the thing.

Of course there were some people who only needed the machines for a short while before they could become self-sustaining again. That was a pity. And there were even some operations scheduled at night that would never be completed. That, too, was unfortunate. But Myra had to die, and he, Martin Wallace, had to live. The footsteps and voices faded away.

Slowly he opened the door and slipped into the corridor. He went quickly to the staircase and walked up from the subbasement into the more brightly lit corridor of the basement. He threw the paper bag into a trash barrel and walked quickly over to the laundry cart near the elevators. He ripped the white coat off and threw it in the cart, then retrieved his own trenchcoat and slipped it on. He hit the elevator button and waited. He noticed that his knees were shaking as he stood staring up at the floor indicator. His head felt light and his mouth was dry, but his forehead was wet.

He could hear the elevator approach. It stopped and the doors slid open. Four visitors and an orderly stood staring at him silently. He froze. They stared.

He stepped into the car quickly and faced the control panel.

The car stopped automatically in the lobby. The doors slid open.

He turned so as not to face the guard and headed for the main doors. Every step was shaky, and he thought his knees might give out and he would topple over. He tried to swallow, but almost choked on the dryness. The doors got bigger and bigger, and soon he was pushing on one of them. Through. The foyer. More doors. Push. Outside.

He walked, almost ran, down the path to the parking lot. His hands moved in and out of his coat and pants pockets like fluttering birds. He began tearing at the pockets. Keys. Keys. There. He nearly sprinted the remaining distance to his car.

He pulled at the door handle. It would not budge. Locked. Locked. He took a deep breath and calmed himself slightly. With a hand shaking worse than he could ever have imagined, he tried to place the key in the lock. Finally, after a full minute, he got it in and twisted it.

Inside, he had difficulty finding the right key and then could not hold his hand still enough to get it in the ignition. Finally he steadied himself and put it in. He turned the key, and the engine roared to life. The sound made him jump but then soothed him. He took a long, deep breath and fumbled for a cigarette. Within forty-five minutes he would be sitting in P. J. Moriarty's with his friends.

He threw the big Cadillac into low and shot out of the parking space—directly into the path of a huge delivery van.

"Just take it easy, Mr. Wallace. You're going to be fine. Really."
He blinked his eyes. The voice was familiar. Dr. Wasserman.

The voice spoke again, but to someone else. "It was a simple whiplash. Those headrests don't always do the job. Sometimes they even cause worse injuries if they're not set properly. I suppose you had it set downward for yourself, but it was too low for him. Hit him in the back of the neck. But it's not serious."

A weak voice to his left answered. "Yes. I did most of the driving."

Myra.

Martin Wallace blinked into the overhead light. He tried to move his head but couldn't. Something was in his mouth, and he could not speak. He rolled his eyes downward as far as they would go. He could see a tube. He looked up. On the opposite wall, a television set was mounted on a high shelf. He was in Myra's room The picture was bad, and the sound was lowered so that he could not hear it. It was a commercial for Alpo. A toy poodle was being shown a can of the canine victuals by its mistress.

Another person entered the room. Martin Wallace caught a glimpse of him as he passed by. It was his family physician, Dr. Matirka. Then the face of the floor nurse, Maureen Hesse, came into view for a second, then the profile of the private nurse, Ellen.

Dr. Wasserman spoke to the others. "Whiplash. He's suffered swelling around the basal ganglia and the internal capsule above the base of the brain. Luckily, the reticular activating system was not involved. There is no loss of consciousness. He's conscious and can see and hear us. But everything from the neck down is paralyzed. He can't speak or breathe on his own. That's why I've put the intubation tube into his mouth and through the larnyx, instead of into the trachea. We've given him dexamethasone to combat the swelling. The swelling and consequent paralysis didn't begin until we got him in here, so there's almost no period of anoxia. There will be no permanent damage at all once the swelling goes down in a few days."

Dr. Wasserman leaned over him and smiled. "Blink if you understood what I said, Mr. Wallace."

Martin Wallace blinked.

"So you see, as soon as the swelling at the base of the brain goes down in a few days, your nervous system will return to normal, and we can take this respirator off. You'll leave here as good as you came in. Blink if you understand."

Martin Wallace blinked through eyes that were becoming misty. A tear rolled down his cheek.

"No need to be upset," said Dr. Matirka. He leaned over the bed. "In fact, I have more good news for you. Myra's breathing is returning to normal. She can get on fine without the respirator for extended periods. We're weaning her away from it a little at a time just to be safe, but I think she can go for at least an hour or two without it. In fact, she's off it now." He chuckled pleasantly and tapped Martin Wallace on the chest, but the paralyzed man felt nothing. Tears streamed down his face.

"Now, now," said Nurse Hesse, a little sternly, "getting upset will make it worse. You'll be fine in a few days. See, we didn't even have to make a tracheotomy opening for the respirator. When the swelling goes down, you can get up and walk out of here."

Ellen leaned over. "It could have been much worse. See, Mrs. Wallace is fine, too. You'll both be out of here in a few days."

Only the muscles above his mouth responded to his commands. His eyes blinked furiously and tears streamed down from them. His nose twitched spasmodically, and his upper lip quivered. His forehead furrowed. Even his ears wiggled just a bit.

"He does seem quite upset about something, doesn't he?" remarked Ellen.

"He'll be better when he begins to believe us," said Dr. Wasserman.

Martin Wallace fixed his blurry eyes on the television screen. The picture tube said *Ten O'Clock News*.

Myra spoke. "Turn on *Medical Center* and raise the volume for me, Ellen. I'm not interested in the news."

The lights went out.

Someone said, "Damn it."

There was a short silence.

Dr. Wasserman's voice spoke softly. "Just a second. The auxiliary generators will kick in."

Silence.

"Just a second. They'll be on in just a half second."

Martin Wallace could hear Myra's voice in the dark as he struggled to breathe.

"I'm going to miss part of the show." Petulant.

"Just a second." Dr. Wasserman's voice sounded anxious now. "They'll be on in just a half second."

But Martin Wallace knew they would not be on ever again.

DR. COFFEE AND THE OTHER TWIN

by *LAWRENCE G. BLOCHMAN*

One of the few people who could tell Fredric and Cedric Kensington apart was Rhoda Robbins, and unfortunately Rhoda was
dead. Moreover, one of the Kensington boys—they were identical
twins—was the most likely suspect of having murdered Rhoda. In
fact, one of them was seen leaving the premises shortly before Rhoda's body was found, but which twin it was the witnesses were
unable to say.

Rhoda Robbins had been the house guest of Mary Lamb, her roommate at Great Lakes University. The two girls had come down to
Northbank to spend Easter vacation on the modest ten-acre estate of
Mary's father. Rhoda had sole occupancy of the guesthouse overlooking the swimming pool (an arid leaf-blown expanse of blue tiles until
May) so she would have whatever solitude she needed to decide
which of the Kensington twins she wanted to marry. Rhoda had never
seen the twins on their home grounds, and her roommate thought she
might gain perspective by looking at them from the vantage point of
Château Lamb, dynastic seat of Northbank's banking baron.

The ninth day of Rhoda's Northbank sojourn proved to be her last.
Her demise at an hour approaching midnight caught Lieutenant of
Detectives Max Ritter standing at the refrigerator with his shirttail
hanging out, pouring himself a cold beer for a nightcap. The desk
sergeant who phoned made no apologies for disturbing Ritter's off-
duty rest; he assumed that the acting chief of the Homicide Squad
would want to make a personal appearance when the scene of the
crime, if not the victim, was important enough to make page one.

Ritter reached the Lamb guest cottage in the close wake of the
squad cars and ambulance, and in a dead heat with the first of the
technicians. Mary Lamb's hysterics had practically subsided. She had

129

stopped screaming, but she was still shaking and wasn't quite coherent.

The ambulance attendant answered Ritter's inquiring glance with a shake of his head. "No vital signs," he said. "She's not cold yet. In fact, she's hot. And she's got pinpoint pupils."

The lanky jug-eared police detective yawned as he made a preliminary survey of the corpus delicti and its surroundings. The late Rhoda Robbins sat on the floor alongside the hearth, leaning back against the bricks of the cold fireplace. The miniest of sky blue miniskirts had slipped up to reveal a frilly undergarment and a monumental run in one leg of her panty hose. Her legs were slightly parted, the unshod toes pointing to her satin slippers halfway across the room.

Ritter frowned as his gaze followed a winding trail of tarot cards scattered on the rug. Then he sniffed, and his head pivoted slowly as he tried to locate the source of the curiously appealing scent. Perched on the mantel was a red apple into which two lighted sticks of incense had been thrust, sending wisps of fragrance spiraling lazily upward.

Ritter watched the photographer recording the scene from all angles. At first glance the girl appeared to have fallen asleep. Closer inspection, however, told Ritter she was not relaxed, even in death. The muscles of her face were taut, her hands were clenched into tight fists, and her elbows made odd angles with her sides.

When the photographer had finished, the detective stooped for a closer look. He noted a tuft of blond hair clutched in the dead girl's fingers. Producing a pair of tweezers and a cellophane envelope, he worked the hairs loose, carefully placed them in the envelope, and filed it in his evidence case, which was his coat pocket.

As he straightened up, he saw Mary Lamb watching him.

"This the babe that found the body?" he asked Detective Sergeant Brody, nodding toward the girl.

Brody nodded back. "Says her name's Mary Lamb."

"Blondie, tell me what you just told the sergeant."

"Oh no! Again?"

"*And* again. And maybe still again. When did you last see this gal alive?"

"Right after dinner," said Mary Lamb. "Rhoda was seeing the Kensington twins tonight, so—"

"Both together or one after the other?"

"Separately, I suppose. I don't know in what order. Anyhow, I went to the movies with a boyfriend. We got home—oh, it must have been around eleven. I was just saying goodnight to my date on the front veranda when one of the twins came walking up the path from the guesthouse to our driveway. I shouted, 'Good night, Fredric or Cedric as the case may be,' and he waved and said 'Hi.' Then he got into his car and drove off.''

"You didn't recognize which twin?"

"No. It was dark. I can't tell them apart even in broad daylight. I don't know how Rhoda does. Did."

"What about the car?"

"They both drive red MG Midgets."

"Don't tell me they use the same license plate number!"

"Silly! I didn't notice."

"Go on."

"Well, when my date left, I saw the light still on in the guesthouse, so I called Rhoda on the interphone. We often got together here for a rap session after dates, the way we do at college. Did. Naturally I wanted to hear all the poop on what she'd decided about the twins. The phone didn't answer. I thought maybe the line was out of order or she was running a bath or something, so I skipped down the path, rang the bell, and walked in. When I saw Rhoda sitting there on the floor like this, I guess I screamed."

"Why scream? Don't you college kids always sit on the floor to protest against chairs or something? And there's no blood, no bullet hole, no sign of violence. She ain't even cold yet. Why'd you scream? How'd you know anything was wrong?"

"Well, like she looked funny. She didn't answer when I talked to her. I just knew she was dead."

"Wanta guess which twin saw her last?"

"I—I—" Mary Lamb smothered her face with her hands. When she stopped sobbing, she said, "I wouldn't dare guess. Rhoda loved them both a little. She was really having a hard time deciding, even though she said she could, you know, tell them apart."

Lieutenant Ritter pushed his warped felt hat to the back of his head and exhaled with what may have been a sound of either disapproval, exasperation, or plain weariness. He had a long night ahead of him, and interviewing people after midnight was not one of his favorite activities. Usually when confronted with an apparently insoluble enigma, Ritter consulted his personal Delphic oracle and private medical examiner, Dr. Daniel Webster Coffee. As long as the Northbank Police Department did not have a well-equipped crime laboratory and the county coroner was more proficient in ward politics than in forensic medicine, Ritter would continue to take advantage of his friend, the chief pathologist and director of laboratories at Pasteur Hospital.

After four hours of sleep, a miserable breakfast of instant coffee (which he detested), canned grapefruit juice (which he abhorred), and home-burned rye toast, Max Ritter strolled into the pathology laboratories at Pasteur.

"Hi, swami," he greeted Dr. Motilal Mookerji, the pink-turbaned Hindu resident pathologist.

"Salaam, leftenant," replied Dr. Mookerji. "More felonious huggermugger afoot this morning-time, no doubt?"

"No doubt," said the detective. He saluted the attractive dark-haired technologist who was preparing test tubes for a sedimentation test. "Hi, beautiful. Where's the wizard?"

"Dr. Coffee's in Operating Room 3," Doris Hudson replied. "We have a frozen section this morning. Come back later?"

"I'll wait." The detective sauntered into Dr. Coffee's office, made a routine tour of the walls, solemnly examining the framed diplomas and testimonials he had seen hundreds of times, then lowered his lean hams into a chair behind the pathologist's cluttered desk.

Five minutes later Dr. Coffee returned to the laboratory wearing a pale green gown and a gauze mask hanging from one ear. He handed a glass receptacle to Doris Hudson, who removed from it a snippet of tissue which she transferred to the stage of the freezing microtome. She opened a petcock, and a glacial blast shrieked from the carbon dioxide tank, burying the specimen in snow. The knife of the microtome swung repeatedly.

Doris caught the hair-thin flakes one by one on a fingertip, floated them on a salt solution briefly, then immersed them in dye. Within minutes she had them mounted like violet petals on tiny glass oblongs.

Meanwhile Dr. Coffee had dislodged Max Ritter from his chair and was seated at his microscope. When Doris handed him the slides, he slipped them under the nose of the instrument, switched on the light, and directed the beam upward. After twisting the focusing knob for a few moments he said, "Doris, go to the door of O.R. 3 and tell Dr. Green to forget about that radical resection. The tumor is benign. No doubt about it."

The pathologist then turned to Ritter. "Sorry to keep you waiting,

Max," he said, "but a young wife is going to wake up happy to learn the good news. Now, what's on your mind this morning?"

"That homicide I phoned you about last night," Ritter said. "Will you do the autopsy?"

"Dammit, Max, why doesn't the County Board finally break down and vote the money to hire a coroner's pathologist?"

"This one ain't on the cuff, doc. The coroner okayed the usual enormous pittance. Just see his name gets in the papers."

"All right then. Tell me the girl's name again."

"Rhoda Robbins. I'd swear it's homicide, but officially cause of death is unknown."

"The perpetrator is also unknown?"

"Well, yes and no."

"Max, you talk like a politician. Level with me."

"I mean he's twins. At least in my book."

"Monozygotic?"

"Translate, doc. Remember I'm just a high school dropout."

"Identical or fraternal twins?"

"Must be identical—nobody can tell 'em apart. Which brings me to the point. What can you do with hairs, doc?"

"Let's narrow your question, Max. I can tell you if the hair is animal or human. I can guess at the owner's race. I can tell roughly which part of the body it comes from, and perhaps the sex of the original owner. Will that help?"

"You can't tell which twin it comes from?"

"Identical twins? No. Practically impossible."

"But not open-and-shut impossible?"

"Oh, if certain lucky external or superimposed factors should turn up, I might hazard a guess, but testimony of that kind won't stand up in court. It never has."

Ritter fumbled in his pocket and brought forth a cellophane envelope. Dr. Coffee smiled with gratified amusement that his lectures to Max on the handling of physical evidence were beginning to bear fruit. Ritter used to store his clues in old dogeared envelopes brought up from some hidden recesses of his person.

"I'm leaving this with you anyhow," the detective said. "Do what you can."

The pathologist held the cellophane envelope up to the light and counted about a dozen pale blond hairs five or six inches long. He said, "I assume these came from the head of your most likely suspect."

"The deceased had them grabbed in her dead fingers."

Dr. Coffee opened a drawer of his desk and dropped in the evidence.

"Look, Max," he said. "I have a busy morning ahead. Another biopsy's coming up, my weekly rundown of current cases with the interns and resident is scheduled for eleven, and I still have some of Wednesday's surgicals to read. But your case fascinates me. Can we meet for lunch at Raoul's and talk about it? Say, one o'clock?"

"More wine, messieurs?" asked Raoul, the red-faced Norman proprietor of the second floor restaurant on the wrong side of the tracks. With a sweep of his napkin he brushed the flakes of French bread crust from the red-checked tablecloth, then lifted the plates that had contained a savory *civet de lapin*—rabbit stewed in red wine with onions and spices.

"Thanks, Raoul," said Dr. Coffee, "but I'll have just a demitasse dripped and some Armagnac. Okay with you, Max?"

The detective nodded. Dr. Coffee leaned back in his chair feeling quite contented, not only because he had enjoyed the *civet* (his wife refused to cook rabbit at home because it reminded her of cat) but because he was intrigued by the problem presented by the death of Rhoda Robbins. He was extremely doubtful that forensic medicine could help determine which of the Kensington twins—if either—was guilty of the crime. He wasn't even sure there was a crime and wouldn't be until after the autopsy, but he was happy to find himself involved in the age-old controversy: which was the dominant factor in the definitive formation of man's character—heredity or environment? Or as anthropologist Boaz put it, which is paramount, nature or nurture?

As Ritter had explained, Fredric and Cedric Kensington were genetically (and therefore physically) identical, but they had spent some of their formative years in surroundings that differed not only geographically but culturally. Even their emotional ambience was different for that period. If the "criminal type" theory of the early writings by the Italian criminologist Lombroso held true, the twins would be equally capable of murder. However, even Lombroso in his later years would have agreed that acquired characteristics might make Cedric more apt to kill than Fredric, or vice versa.

"You seem to be pretty sure that those hairs you gave me will turn out to belong to Fredric Kensington," Dr. Coffee said to Ritter. "Why?"

"Like I said, Fredric leaves Northbank on the midnight plane for

Toledo,'' the detective replied, ''less than an hour after the body of Rhoda Robbins turned up.''

''I hear they've got newspapers in Toledo. And if not, it's been on radio and TV all day that we're looking for him.''

Raoul set down the coffee and brandy.

''Thanks, Raoul,'' the pathologist said without looking up. ''You must have other reasons, Max, the way you talk.''

''Maybe. Of course, so far I've only talked to Cedric, but he didn't impress me as the caveman type. I know, I know, doc, you don't go along with the old Lombroso born-to-kill stuff. But these two guys don't act alike, from what people tell, even if they do look alike. They *play* at lookalikes. They love to fool people. When they first came to college, this Lamb dame tells me, one has a beard and the other just a coupla commas for a mustache. One wears Levi's and the other Brooks Brothers outfits. Now they wear the same clothes, same color shirts and ties, go to the same barber, drive the same kind of car, and try to make the same gals.''

''What do they do different then, Max?''

''Well, Fredric's more the action type. He's intercollegiate middle-weight boxing champ. He plays football. As a kid he went fishing and hunting with his old man. This Cedric is the mental type. He's editor of the college paper. He writes poetry. He collects cookbooks. He bakes popovers and French pastry. The dead babe's roommate told me the other day he once brought over a cake he baked with his own hands, for God's sake!''

''Do the twins live together?'' Dr. Coffee sipped his brandy. Ritter had already finished his at one gulp.

''Negative,'' said the detective. ''Not at college and not here. They think it's fun to turn up unexpectedly at places where people don't know which one it is. Fredric lives with his old man when he's in Northbank. Cedric has a little dough inherited from his mother, so he has his own place—an arty one room pad in an unrenewable urban ruin on the riverfront.''

During lunch Ritter had told Dr. Coffee what he had been able to learn about the Kensington twins. They had been separated for seven years before they became reunited at Great Lakes University and began working seriously at the business of being twins. When their parents' marriage broke up, Fredric and Cedric were just eleven. It had been a more or less friendly separation: George and Evelyn Kensington had come to the conclusion that each wanted something different from life.

George Kensington was a brilliant lawyer—even Evelyn had agreed—but he cared nothing about making money. He was always taking grubby little Legal Aid Society cases, or volunteering to be a friend of the court in some Civil Liberties Union defense of a poor Southern black lost in the urban jungle of the North. Evelyn on the other hand had been born to money, considered it a necessity for the enjoyment and appreciation of the finer things in life, and she intended to use her own for a creative career. She took Cedric with her when she went to live in Paris, London, and New York to compose string quartets and marry a highly successful (and wealthy) surgeon who was a patron of the arts.

Dr. Coffee reached across the table for a color photo of Rhoda Robbins that Ritter had taken from Cedric Kensington's pad. A duplicate, Ritter said, was perched on Fredric's bureau. The three-quarters' length picture portrayed a small-boned well-endowed woman in her twenties. Her smoky blue eyes were in startling contrast to her midnight-dark hair, which fell to her shoulders. Her long eyelashes appeared not to have come from a box, but the pathologist would be able to check that later. He shook his head as he handed the picture back to the detective. What a waste of youth, vitality, and sheer animal charm!

"What did Cedric the mental one have to say about her?" Dr. Coffee asked.

"He and his brother are both nuts about her," Ritter said. "So are half a dozen other big shots on the campus. Cedric said she majors in men, but she finds matrimony too restricting."

The Kensington twins, however, had given her a joint ultimatum. After all, this was their senior year. She had promised to make up her mind by the end of the Easter vacation. The twins had bought a ring jointly, leaving it at the jeweler's to be claimed by the lucky suitor. She had died, Cedric told Ritter, without announcing her decision.

Rhoda was alive, Cedric swore, when he had last seen her at about ten o'clock the previous night. He had no idea when his brother Fredric had seen her last.

"Does Cedric think Rhoda was trying to get help in making her decision by consulting those tarot cards you were telling me about?"

"Both Cedric and Mary Lamb say Rhoda was kind of a kook about this screwy mod stuff—tarot, astrology, Zen, numerology, you name it. Look, doc, I gotta get on my horse. Duty calls. Or anyhow whispers."

"Okay, Max. I'll get down to my homework later this afternoon. When I've finished, I'd like to meet Cedric Kensington at his pad. Can do?"

"Why not? Say, doc, maybe I ought to warn you. You may get Papa Kensington in your hair soon. He's been sniffing around our shop trying to pick up a scent so he can yell 'police brutality.' I told him we're not even sure Rhoda Robbins was murdered till you give the word."

When Dr. Coffee walked into his laboratory after lunch, Dr. Mookerji signaled frantically from his workbench with a large pair of shears with which he had been cutting tissue.

"World's most obstinate barrister is currently waiting inside inner sanctum," said the Hindu in a stage whisper. He handed the pathologist a calling card. "Did utmost to resist but said barrister succceded in overcoming efforts to exclude entry."

Dr. Coffee glanced at the card. "I was rather expecting him," he said. He took off his street coat, hung it up, and slipped into a white jacket before entering his office.

George Kensington rose and introduced himself. He was a tall well-built man with an unpressed tweedy air about him. His top-heavy face, broad forehead tapering to a fighting chin, was surmounted by slicked-back hair of pale gold. There was just a sprinkling of gray in his mid-cheek sideburns.

"I assume," said Dr. Coffee, "that you are the father of the Kensington twins. Are you also representing them as their attorney?"

"When or if they are charged with anything," Kensington said, advancing his lower jaw almost a full inch, "I shall certainly defend them. Meanwhile I'd simply like to assure myself that there is no skulduggery, no creation of false evidence against my boys."

"Sit down, Mr. Kensington," said Dr. Coffee, "and take the chip off your shoulder. Who told you there was skulduggery afoot?"

Kensington sat down brusquely on the edge of a chair. "I happen to know that you have some hair in your possession that you're going to try to prove came from the head of one of the Kensington twins."

"Did the police tell you that?"

"A person who saw a police detective remove some hair from the dead fingers of Rhoda Robbins informed me. The police have referred all inquiries to you. I understand you have made a postmortem examination. What did you find?"

"I won't have the gross autopsy findings until tonight. The microscopic and chemical findings—which I suspect may be extremely important in this case—may not be known for a week."

The lawyer made a gesture of impatience. "Have you considered, doctor, that Miss Robbins may have been a cardiac case?"

"I don't have to speculate. If she was a cardiac case, I will be able to say so with certainty this evening.

Kensington stood up and leaned across the desk. He shook a fore-finger at Dr. Coffee as if addressing a jury. "If you expect to intro-duce that hair as factual evidence," he said, raising his voice, "you're in for a surprise. No court in this country will let you swear that X hair came from Y's head. Your microscope can tell you no more than the ratio of the diameter of the shaft to the medulla—"

"Please, Mr. Kensington, don't start lecturing me on forensic pa-thology!" Dr. Coffee felt a flush creeping into his cheeks. Deter-mined not to lose his usual cool, he leaned back in his chair and took a deep breath. "There are other factors to be learned about hair from microscopic examination. In fact, Lieutenant Ritter is checking on some of them now."

"For instance?"

"I won't disclose any that you might manipulate, but I'll give you an example you can't use to advantage. One of your sons—Cedric, I believe—boasts he is a first-rate pastry chef. If the hairs in my possession should under the microscope show particles of flour dust clinging to them—"

"Come now, doctor, are you really going to give us the Sherlock Holmes routine?" Kensington smiled sarcastically.

Again Dr. Coffee took a deep breath. "Look, counselor," he said, "neither of your sons has been arrested or even accused. But has it ever occurred to you that one of them might really have killed Rhoda Robbins?"

Kensington's expression changed. His lips straightened into a grim line. "I might have killed her myself," he said. "She was an evil creature, a no-good rattlepate whose only aim in life was to drive men crazy."

"Not exactly a capital crime, counselor."

"She was a Jezebel, a bald-faced liar, a—"

"But both the twins wanted to marry her."

"Mad, mad. She was a complete phony, even her name. Her father has an unpronounceable foreign name. He's serving time in the state pen for embezzlement. But even if one of the twins killed her, you'll

never be able to identify him beyond a reasonable doubt. Nobody
can tell them apart.''

''Can you?''

''When they're not working at their guess-who act, yes. The years
they spent apart during their adolescence show through when they're
not play-acting.''

''Rhoda Robbins claimed she could tell them apart. Was that one
of her pathological lies?''

''Maybe not.'' Kensington was smiling to himself. ''If she went
to bed with both of them, she might know which was which. One
of the twins wasn't circumcised.''

Dr. Coffee said nothing.

''Cedric. He's the younger by fifteen minutes and his mother's
pet. She couldn't bear the idea of his being mutilated.''

Kensington got up suddenly and walked to the window. He continued talking but kept his back to Dr. Coffee as though to hide a
change of expression.

''I don't dare wonder how he would have turned out if he had
lived with her any longer,'' he said.

''How did she happen to let him go?'' the pathologist asked.

''She didn't really. She killed herself.''

''Does Lieutenant Ritter know that?''

''Nobody does.'' Kensington turned to face Dr. Coffee. His face
was expressionless. ''The death certificate, signed by her second husband, said she died of cardiac arrest, which is technically true. When
the heart stops, death ensues, even when the stoppage is caused by
some morphine derivative. You see, my wife found out that her
string quartet, which she thought had been commissioned by a music
foundation and which was roundly panned when it played, was actually subsidized by her second husband . . . Well, I must be going.''

''Just a moment, Mr. Kensington. Before you leave I'd like you
to let Miss Hudson have a few hairs for comparison. She'll try to
take them so they won't show, won't you, Doris?''

Dr. Coffee watched in silent amusement while Kensington submit-
ted reluctantly to painless minor depilation at the hands of the comely
dark-eyed technologist.

When he had gone, Dr. Coffee took Max Ritter's cellophane envelope from his drawer and summoned Doris to his office.

''Doris,'' he said, ''I want you to mount longitudinal sections of
one or two strands of this hair and the sample you just took from
our visitor. I am particularly interested in the roots and the distal

ends. Then I want you to mount cross-sections that I can examine with the micrometric eyepiece tomorrow. I expect to get some more samples for comparison tonight."

An hour later, before going down to the mortuary in the basement with Dr. Mookerji, the pathologist phoned Lieutenant Ritter.

"Max, I've had a quick look at that hair you brought me," he said, "and I think I may have a lead for you. The man whose head it came from had his hair cut recently, probably yesterday, and almost certainly within the last forty-eight hours."

"It still smells of bay rum?"

Dr. Coffee chuckled. "The tips have a sharp silhouette under the microscope. This clean line begins to change as soon as one day later."

"What about the autopsy doc?"

"I'm on my way down there now. Can you pick me up at home tonight at about eight? I promised my wife I'd come home for dinner. Seems we have a cousin in town from New York."

When Dr. Coffee and Dr. Mookerji returned to the laboratory with pertinent parts of the vital organs formerly belonging to the late Rhoda Robbins, the pathologist gave instructions to his technologist.

"Make routine sections of the usual tissue, Doris," he said, "except for the brain. You'll note that I already sectioned the brain horizontally to confirm my suspicions, but after fixation I'll want special sections from the pons and the floor of the fourth ventricle. Dr. Mookerji will show you. And make up one set with osmic acid stain just in case I've misinterpreted the gross findings."

As Lieutenant Ritter opened the door of the police car for Dr. Coffee that evening he said, "Bad news, doc. Your haircut clue is a dud. Fredric and Cedric go to the same barber—pardon me, hair stylist, Mr. Dagobert, by appointment only. They both got a haircut yesterday afternoon within half an hour of each other. Incidentally, they both have dandruff. . . . Does the postmortem show we got a murder?"

"You know I don't like to pontificate until I've seen the microscopic sections, Max," the pathologist said, "but from the gross examination I'd say we do have a homicide, even if we can't prove it's murder. From the ambulance intern's description of the immediate postmortem symptoms—the pinpoint pupils, the unusual temperature of the body—I suspected a pontine or ventricular hemorrhage—"

"Now, now, doc!" Ritter stopped for a red light.

"The microscope will show bleeding into a brain area no bigger than a peanut. I'm sure I'll find that this series of tiny hemorrhages has torn nerve fibers and destroyed nerve cells that control such vital functions as breathing and the heartbeat."

"So her skull was cracked?" The light turned green.

"No, there was no fracture. There doesn't have to be when the brain gets badly shaken up, and the girl's head was obviously banged against the bricks of the fireplace. There was a bruise at the back of her head and traces of brick dust in her hair. . . . Incidentally, what color is Mary Lamb's hair?"

"Blonde. What else?"

"You'd better get me a sample of her golden tresses, then. No word of the other twin?"

"Nope."

Ritter turned the car into the rutty road that paralleled the riverfront which, because it lay below the highwater mark whenever the spring floods engaged in their quinquennial exaggeration, had become what Ritter called "an unrenewable urban ruin." The ramshackle buildings that lined the narrow street might have been transplanted from Provincetown or Greenwich Village—rows of shoddy, self-consciously arty crafts shops, paperback bookstores full of beads, beards, bosom-length hair, fringes, and psychedelic art. Antiwar posters decorated outer walls, and antiwar protestors squatted in doorways.

Cedric Kensington's domicile was located above a gay bar and lounge with a heterogeneous if not heterosexual clientele.

When the pathologist and the detective paused on the second floor landing, the muted staccato of a typewriter in counterpoint to the strains of *The Pines of Rome* was coming through the door. Ritter knocked. The typewriter stopped, and the door opened.

Cedric Kensington was a reasonable facsimile of his father, Dr. Coffee mused—tall, well-built, with the same top-heavy triangular face and pale gold mane. He was wearing a purple dressing gown and green carpet slippers.

"Hello, lieutenant. Come in."

"This is Dr. Coffee. We're here on business. I don't have a search warrant, so you don't have to let us in. In fact, you'll have to invite us."

"You know you're both welcome," said Cedric. "I told you last night I'd do anything I could to cooperate. Please come in." Cedric threw the door open wider.

Dr. Coffee glanced around the sparsely furnished room. There were three prints on the wall, all of approximately the same period and all of the same subject—a nude bathing in a tub—by Toulouse-Lautrec, Picasso, and Charles Camoin. The typewriter was a portable on a card table, and there were two straight chairs, an easy chair, and a worn loveseat.

Cedric stopped in front of his hi-fi, the most expensive-looking piece of furniture in the room. "Shall I turn this down?" he asked Dr. Coffee. "If it bothers you—"

"Not at all," said the pathologist, "but aren't you afraid of being disowned by your generation? Respighi has been dead almost forty years."

Cedric gave a quick nervous smile. "Can't a man be under thirty and still not belong to the cult of the ugly? I admire the beautiful. That's why I loved poor Rhoda, I guess. Are you arresting me?"

"No hurry," said Ritter. "Unless you want to confess."

"Let's all sit down," Cedric said. "Confess to what? I don't even know Rhoda's dead, except from what you tell me. And why would I kill the girl I love?"

"I'm not going to quote Oscar Wilde," said Dr. Coffee. "I'm sure Lieutenant Ritter can suggest many reasons."

"For one, she turned you down," said Ritter.

"On the contrary. She agreed to marry me. She wanted to delay the announcement for a week, though, to give her a chance to let my brother Fredric down gently."

"You think Fredric found out anyhow?"

"I haven't heard from him. But it's possible, isn't it, that the Kensington twin seen leaving the premises just before the body was found last night was Fredric?"

"That's what the doc here wants to find out," said Ritter. "Are you giving us a swatch of your hair or do we have to scalp you?"

Cedric laughed. He had white, even teeth.

He seemed remarkably good-humored, Dr. Coffee mused, for a man who had just lost his fiancée, yet he was not completely at ease. His movements were jerky, his speech slow and studied, his eyelids twitchy. A high-strung lad, apparently.

"I'm going to take this hair by the roots," said Dr. Coffee jokingly. "Do you want a local anesthetic?"

"I'd rather have a general." Cedric smiled with his lips but not with his eyes. "Will you characters do me a favor? Let me make the arrangements for Rhoda's burial. No funeral, though. She didn't believe in anything, and she has no family.''

''I understand she has a father,'' said Dr. Coffee.

''Purely putative,'' said Cedric. ''She disinherited him years ago.'' He winced as he lost a strand of hair.

''Do you mind if I have a look around your quarters?'' asked Dr. Coffee as he carefully wrapped the hair in cellophane.

''Be my guest.''

The pathologist stepped into a tiny kitchenette. The gas range was spotless. The shelves were well stocked with spices. A tape recorder acted as a bookend for a dozen cookbooks. He tried a door next to a miniature sink. It was locked.

''And the bathroom, too?'' he asked.

''Sure,'' said Cedric. ''I do have indoor plumbing.''

While the police car was climbing the slope away from the river Ritter asked, ''Find anything in the medicine cabinet, doc?''

''Certainly.''

The pathologist took out a notebook, flipped it open and held it close to the dashboard lights as he read, ''Toothpaste, shaving cream, safety razor, roll-on deodorant, aspirin, baking soda, mouthwash, glycerine suppositories, Dander-oh-No scalp treatment, and two prescription items from the College Pharmacy in Academia. One was a large bottle of some oleaginous liquid, and the other was a smaller bottle which evidently contained tablets of some kind. The smaller bottle was empty. ''I'll check the prescription numbers with the pharmacy in the morning.''

''What do you do with the hair you harvested tonight?''

''I can't do a thing, Max, until you get me comparison samples from the other twin and from the Lamb girl, too. Then I'll probably send the lot over to Northbank University for analysis.''

''Can't the swami or Doris Hudson do it in your own lab?''

''We don't have the equipment needed for a job like that, Max. There's a sophisticated automated process called flame-ionization gas chromatography that can break down the components of a hair and record quantities as minute as two-tenths of one microgram. That's one ten-billionth of an ounce.''

Ritter puckered his lips in a silent whistle.

''Trouble with these ultra-sensitive instruments, Max, is that they're no better than the man who uses them. I had a professor in medical school who used to caution me when I used a microscope,

'low-power magnification, Coffee, and high-power cerebration.'
Luckily there's a team of scientists over at Northbank U. who are
up to the potential of their equipment. All the expensive and sophisticated gear they have over in the Chemistry Building wouldn't be
worth thirty cents without Dr. Mitchell, professor of molecular chemistry, and his highly capable crew.''

''You think they'll turn up something, doc?''

''I hope so. If it's at all possible, Dr. Mitchell will match the
hairs.'' Ritter changed gears as the car topped the brow of the hill
and leveled off. ''Max, do you think it's too late to call on Kensington Senior without a search warrant? I'd like to look through the
other twin's medicine chest if Papa will let us in.''

Surprisingly, Kensington Senior offered no objections, and Dr.
Coffee came away with another list. There were no prescription drugs
in Fredric Kensington's bathroom, only the standard toothpaste,
razor, shaving soap and lotion, and mouthwash.

Dr. Coffee had just gone to bed and was about to turn off the
light when the telephone rang.

''Wake you, doc?'' asked Max Ritter's voice. ''We've got news.''

''Good or bad, Max?''

''Let's say, with possibilities. You know Brody? You always say
he ain't exactly a mental giant, but he's bullheaded and he's my
champ follow-througher. Well, Brody spent the evening going
through the Lamb guesthouse again with a fine-tooth comb. This time
he found stashed away in the fingers of a glove a guy's fraternity pin
and a gold wedding ring. Inside the wedding ring there's two names,
Rhoda and Pete—''

''Great stars!'' Dr. Coffee interrupted. ''Who's Pete?''

''That's what I asked myself,'' said Ritter. ''So I called this frat
house at Great Lakes and asked for Pete. Some guy said, 'You mean
Pete Hyde?' and I said, 'Sure, is he there?' and the other guy said,
'No, he's in the infirmary. Somebody beat the hell out of him.' ''

''Max, isn't this Pete Hyde the Great Lakes football star?''

''Right. When I hung up, I got this hunch to call the police station
in Academia. It must be quite a slugger to put a six foot, two hundred
pound fullback in the hospital. The fight could have attracted attention. Follow me, doc?''

''I may be a little ahead of you, Max.''

''Right. The Academia cops have got Fredric Kensington in jail.

For assault and battery. They also charged him with second-degree arson.''

''Arson!''

''Right. I ain't sure what he burned down, but I'll get the details tomorrow. I fly at the crack of dawn. I've got to change planes at Toledo, but I'll try to get back by tomorrow night. See you, doc.''

''Happy landings, Max. Don't forget to bring me back some of Fredric's hair.''

Detective Sergeant Brody was waiting in the pathology laboratory when Dr. Coffee reached the hospital early next morning.

''Lieutenant Ritter told me to leave these with you,'' he said while the pathologist was getting into his working smock. ''He says in case you want to make with the microscope.''

Brody had followed Dr. Coffee across the laboratory and into his office. He deposited one large and one small plastic evidence case on the doctor's desk.

''Thanks, sergeant. Take a seat.'' Dr. Coffee opened the small case first. It contained a plain gold wedding band and a Greek-letter fraternity pin, lozenge-shaped and rimmed with seed pearls. ''I'll see if I can turn up something,'' he added as he opened the larger container. ''Hey, what's this?'' He riffled through a sheaf of typewritten pages.

''I dunno,'' said Brody, ''but the lieutenant said I should bring it to you after we dusted it for prints. I found it in the victim's suitcase under her panty hose and black lace nightgowns.''

Dr. Coffee gave his concentrated attention to the typescript. It was apparently a thesis by a candidate for a master's degree at Great Lakes University, someone named Christopher Blett, who was seeking higher academic honors in history, political science, or foreign affairs. It was titled ''The Influence of Gastronomy on Nineteenth Century European Diplomacy.''

The pathologist smiled to himself. It was an interesting subject, if treated in the light of Peking duck, *mao tai* and twentieth century television diplomacy, but not exactly original. Didn't everybody know how Metternich dominated the Congress of Vienna through the superlative cuisine of Austrian hostesses? Surely everyone knew that Nesselrode pudding was named for the Russian minister of foreign affairs in 1815. Everyone, perhaps, except the late Rhoda Robbins, to whom, according to the way she had been characterized, the post-Napoleonic peace of Europe might have been of minor interest.

"Who the hell is Christopher Blett?" Dr. Coffee asked Sergeant Brody.

"You've got me," Brody replied.

"Did you speak to Mary Lamb, the victim's hostess?"

"Oh, sure. She don't know. Some guy at Great Lakes U. is all she knows, she says."

"Okay, sergeant. I'll talk about it to Lieutenant Ritter when he comes back tonight."

Brody left, with an appreciative glance at the decorative legs of Doris Hudson, perched on a tall stool before her workbench as she extricated paraffin blocks from a refrigerator tray.

Dr. Coffee was skipping through the dissertation of the master's candidate who believed that the naming of delicious new dishes after the delegates to the Congress of Vienna was responsible for the maintenance of comparative peace in Europe for ninety-nine years when Dr. Mookerji waddled into his office to announce in a stage whisper, "Youngish blonde lady is awaiting without. Is requesting audience on behalf of Leftenant Ritter."

The pathologist smiled. "Show her in, doctor."

Something about Mary Lamb raised Dr. Coffee's hackles the moment she stepped across the threshold. He tried to analyze his feelings. Was it her narrow face, her thin lips, the self-consciously superior manner with which she carried her blonde head, as though to say, "Look, I may be simply dressed, but every stitch I wear proclaims money and my good taste." He told himself that he was getting needlessly emotional.

"That skinny cop told me you wanted a sample of my hair," said Mary Lamb, tossing an envelope to his desk. "I'm Mary Lamb."

"Thank you, Miss Lamb, but I'm afraid we'll have to take our own sample."

"I was hoping I could avoid being disfigured."

"Miss Hudson will treat you gently," said the pathologist. "You won't be scalped. But before you go out to be tortured, I'd like to ask a few questions. Won't you sit down?"

Mary Lamb sat gingerly on the edge of a chair; the seat might be swarming with a particularly virulent strain of staphylococcus.

"Miss Lamb, who is Christopher Blett?"

"I haven't the slightest idea. One of the cops asked the same question."

"Why would his master's thesis on Metternich's gastronomic diplomacy be found hidden under Rhoda Robbins' underwear?"

"A very good question, doctor, but I can't answer it." Mary Lamb tried to laugh; the effort turned out to be a mirthless whicker.

"When were Rhoda Robbins and Peter Hyde married?"

"Rhoda and Pete—? Don't make me laugh."

"She had a wedding ring."

"Sure, why not? It looks better when a girl goes to a motel."

"And Hyde's fraternity pin."

"Rhoda collected frat pins. Didn't mean a thing."

Dr. Coffee thought it might have meant a great deal to the Kensington twin who thought Rhoda was going to marry him. He said, "Thanks for coming by, Miss Lamb. Now let me introduce you to Doris Hudson."

When the girl had gone, Doris asked, "How do you want the hair mounted, doctor?"

"Just give me an inch or two with the tips. Probably won't show anything. She looks as if she hasn't had a haircut in months," the pathologist replied.

While Doris was preparing Mary Lamb's hair for the microscope, Dr. Coffee suddenly realized that he had not done his follow-up homework on last night's research. He picked up the phone and told the switchboard operator, "Get me the College Pharmacy in Academia."

A few moments later he said, "This is Dr. Daniel Coffee at Pasteur Hospital in Northbank. I'd like to check on the following prescriptions you people have put up." And he read the numbers. While waiting he started opening the morning's mail, throwing away half of it. "Did you say phenothiazine? . . . I see. And the other one? . . . Why the devil would he need a prescription for that? . . . I see. What percentage? . . . Thank you very much. No, he doesn't need a refill. Goodbye."

Dr. Coffee hung up. When Doris Hudson came in with the hair tips mounted on slides, he was smiling smugly to himself. "Doris," he said, "I think we have a fifty-fifty chance of solving Max Ritter's problem within the next few days."

At noon Dr. Mookerji brought the early edition of the afternoon newspapers to the laboratory. Details of Fredric Kensington's arrest in Academia were on page one.

"Academia police are holding Fredric Kensington, Great Lakes University senior, on charges of arson and assault. Kensington, a resident of Northbank, is accused of setting fire to the Shetland Print

Shop on the south side of the GLU campus, and of beating Peter Hyde into unconsciousness when he tried to interfere. Hyde is in the intensive care unit of Academia General Hospital suffering from possible concussion. An all-star fullback for the GLU Catamounts the past two seasons, he is also part owner of the Shetland Print Shop, which was totally destroyed before the fire department got the blaze under control. Kensington would give no explanation for his actions. His father, George Kensington, Northbank attorney, is flying to Academia to undertake his defense."

Dr. Coffee called George Kensington's office. His secretary reported the lawyer had left for Academia that morning.

Max Ritter arrived at Dr. Coffee's laboratory at nightfall.

"The D.A. in Academia said his arson charge takes precedence," Ritter said. "He won't release Fredric Kensington to me unless I serve him with a murder warrant. Can we charge Fredric with homicide, doc?"

"Not at this instant, Max. Maybe in a day or so. Did you bring me some of Fredric's hair?"

"Right here. No problem. He didn't object."

"You talked to him then?"

"Right." Ritter nodded. "But he didn't talk back."

"Did you ask him if Rhoda Robbins was the cause of his beating up Pete Hyde?"

"He wouldn't talk about Rhoda."

"Do the Academia police have any theory about why he burned down the Shetland Print Shop?"

"Nope."

"I have a hunch that may be worth working on later," Dr. Coffee said. "I wish you had called me from Academia before you started home."

"I shared Flight 66 with Papa Kensington coming home," the detective said.

"Did you talk to him?"

"Sure. We also shared a cab from the airfield. He tried to get bail for twin son Fredric on the arson charge, but the court said no dice as long as we've got a possible murder charge pending here."

"Well, let's get on with our hair business," Dr. Coffee said. "Dr. Mookerji, do you have those sterile test tubes ready?"

"Ready, waiting, and all neatly labeled this morning-time," the Hindu resident replied.

"Max, give the hair to Dr. Mookerji, and he'll see that it gets to Northbank University. Dr. Mitchell will be waiting at the Chemistry Building. He's been alerted."

"Let me take it over, doctor," Doris Hudson volunteered. "I pass the Chemistry Building on my way home."

Dr. Coffee had kissed his wife, shed his coat, put on his slippers, and was in the pantry surveying his bottles, trying to decide whether he should make Manhattans or martinis before dinner. He heard the phone ringing and his wife answering.

"For you," his wife announced. "It's Dr. Mookerji."

Dr. Coffee took down both the Italian and French vermouth before taking the call in the foyer. "What's up, doctor?" he asked.

"Grave contingency just now arising, doctor sàhib," came an excited voice. "Am now repairing posthaste to emergency clinic at University Hospital. Am suggesting you do likewise."

"What happened?" Dr. Coffee gripped the phone tightly.

"Doris Hudson," the resident exclaimed. "Lady was slug-mugged in occipital region."

"Is she badly hurt?"

"Unable to ascertain. Therefore am interjecting self into case personally. Have likewise advised Leftenant Ritter of situation. Goodbye."

Dr. Coffee hung up, gave his wife a brief explanation, left the Manhattan-martini question unsettled, urged his super-annuated Chevy into reluctant action, and took off for University Hospital.

He drove through the phalanx of reporters, police, and curious bystanders who had gathered outside the emergency entrance, parked in a space reserved for ambulances, and identified himself to the intern on duty. He found that Ritter and Dr. Mookerji had preceded him.

"Where's Doris?" The question was addressed to anyone listening.

Dr. Mookerji nodded his turbaned head twice to the left.

Doris Hudson was in the process of raising herself to a sitting position on a cot in the corner. When she saw the pathologist she fell back and covered her face with her hands.

"I'm just a nitwit, a numskull, and a clumsy incompetent," she moaned. "Will you ever forgive me, doctor?"

"Take it easy, Doris," Dr. Coffee said. "Are you badly hurt?"

"I'm just a little woozy. He knocked me down. I'm only groggy." She shook her head. "But he grabbed my bag."

"Were the hair specimens in it?"

"Yes."

"Any idea who it was?"

"No. He was waiting back of the shrubbery at the entrance to the Chemistry Building. He hit me from behind. I fell forward on the steps. I didn't see anything."

Dr. Mookerji, who had been making cabalistic signals with both hands from across the room, now approached the cot and whispered to Doris, "Kindly cease having regrets and guilt feelings. All is not lost." Straightening up, he confided to Dr. Coffee, "Have preserved duplicates of all suspected hairs in laboratory."

"You're a genius, doctor!" Dr. Coffee beamed. "Then we'll start over. Max will furnish us with a police escort this time."

Doris Hudson was at her workbench when Dr. Coffee reached the laboratory next morning half an hour early.

"What's the meaning of this insubordination, Doris? I distinctly told you to stay home today."

"We have a terrific backlog, doctor," Doris replied, "which is going to get bigger if I don't catch up. And besides, I don't even have a headache this morning. Do you think I'll get my handbag back?"

"I do. The mugger probably dropped it into a mailbox after he had extracted the hair specimens. The mailman will deliver it to you on payment of sufficient postage due."

"I'll be so relieved. I hate to go through the business of notifying all my credit card people. By the way, Max Ritter phoned. He wanted to come right over, but I said he couldn't before eleven. You have two biopsies this morning, you didn't finish reading yesterday's surgicals, and I'm not even going to let you look at the sections from Rhoda Robbins' brain, although they're out of formalin." Doris slid off her stool, picked up her notebook, followed Dr. Coffee into his office, and sat down beside his microscope. "Let's get to work," she said.

The pathologist spent the next three hours earning his salary from Pasteur Hospital. He was almost abreast of his workload when Max Ritter sauntered in.

"Hi, doc! Any news from the chrom—from our hair analyst?"

"I don't expect any results for at least twenty-four hours, Max.

It's a fairly complicated process even though it's automated. Did you have a stakeout on Cedric Kensington's place last night?''

"I did.'' Ritter planted one lean thigh on the corner of Dr. Coffee's desk. "Jenkins says our boy is home making onion soup when darling Doris gets conked. Got any other ideas?''

"Yes,'' said the pathologist. "You were the one who fingered our Doris last night.''

"Me?''

"Certainly. You can be sure that Fredric Kensington told his father you had taken a hair specimen, and Kensington père, either on the plane or in the taxi he managed to share with you, pooh-poohed the idea that you could prove anything in court by physical evidence about hair. Right?''

"Doc, you've got ESP.''

"What's more,'' the pathologist continued, "I'll lay you a hundred to one that you boasted of Dr. Coffee's skills in the forensic sciences, and the miracles that would be performed by Dr. Mitchell, professor by Dr. Mitchell, professor of molecular chemistry, and his automated wizardry at Northbank University.''

Ritter's prominent Adam's apple marked a difficulty in his swallowing. "Maybe I do boast a little,'' he admitted. "Do I go out and pick up Papa Kensington for mugging?''

"Wait, Max. Let's consult the victim first. Doris!'' The technician appeared in the doorway. "Do you agree to prosecute the man who slugged you last night?''

"Who was it?'' Doris asked.

"Probably a middle-aged father who thought he was protecting one of his sons from a murder charge.''

"Well, he really didn't hurt me.'' Doris was running her hands over her hips to smooth out the back of her smock. "I was scared, that's all. If I get back my bag and my credit cards and my seven dollars, I'll forget it. Should I feel sorry for him?''

"No,'' said Dr. Coffee. "Never condone violence. The man has more trouble than he deserves, but that's not the point. I think we can make a deal that will save Max time and trouble and still won't thwart the ends of justice.''

Ritter's built-in frown deepened. "I don't go for deals—unless we get the brass ring back,'' he said. "What do we win?''

"I think Kensington can tell us what we ought to know about Shetland enterprises in Academia and why Fredric Kensington wanted to burn the place down.''

"Why'n't you ask me?" Ritter inquired testily. "While in Academia yesterday I used a few unscientific old-style police methods like asking questions and taking a look-see myself at the site of arson and mayhem."

The detective described his visit to the burnt-out premises with hand gestures and head shakings. The Shetland Print Shop, he said, was not much of a shop at all—a mere hole in the wall in a two story brick building not far from the Great Lakes campus. There was no heavy equipment—in fact, no typographical gear except a light hand press, but all sorts of multicopying devices, all badly damaged. But the arsonist seemed particularly anxious to destroy the product of the copying machines. There wasn't a single unburned sheet of paper left in the place, Ritter said, "and the joint still stank of gasoline."

The Academia police, the detective continued, seem to think that the Shetland Print Shop was some sort of secret joint for commercializing on cheating in examinations.

"It can't be very secret," Dr. Coffee interrupted, "with a name like Shetland. Since yesterday I've suspected that Shetland sold not only ponies for final and mid-term examinations, but these for advanced degrees and probably term papers as well."

"What gave you that idea, doc?"

"The typescript your man Brody brought me yesterday was a dissertation by a candidate for a master's degree. Rhoda Robbins apparently had some connection with Shetland. I've been wondering if her death didn't somehow involve the Shetland operation, rather than the unrequited love of one of the Kensington twins. Max, why don't you try to find out who besides Pete Hyde owns shares in Shetland?"

"Already done, doc." Ritter produced the usual sheaf of dogeared envelopes from an inside pocket, shuffled them, and put on the reading glasses he had been wearing for the past few months. "Peter Hyde, five shares; Rhoda Robbins, five shares; Mary Lamb, forty shares."

"No shares for the Kensington twins?"

"Nope, not according to the figures the Academia cops get from the county registrar of partnerships."

"So Mary Lamb, the banker's daughter, apparently put up the capital, or most of it, to get the business started," Dr. Coffee mused. He pursed his lips and ran his long fingers through his rumpled graying hair.

"Which reminds me," said Ritter, "of what I came for in the first place. You know Brody maybe ain't a genius, but he ain't bad at plain old-fashioned unscientific detecting. He brought in all the stuff we found at the murder scene, like the red apple with the joss sticks, the tarot cards, and the gal's slippers. Well, the cards were hopeless but we found Mary Lamb's prints on the apple and the slippers."

"How did you happen to have her prints for comparison, Max?"

"Routine. We took 'em the night of the murder so we could eliminate possible unknowns. Cedric's, too. His didn't show on the apple or the slippers."

"So?"

"So I'm on my way to call on Mary Lamb. She's been lying to me. I talked to her boyfriend this morning, and he confirmed her story about saying goodnight on her front porch when one Kensington twin drove off. Only he gave me a different time. He said it happened an hour earlier than she claimed."

Dr. Coffee shook his head dubiously. "I wish you luck, Max," he said. "But don't forget she's a banker's daughter and that Papa can and undoubtedly will buy her the best lawyers on the market if you even hint that she's an accessory after the fact."

"You know lawyers don't scare me, doc."

"See you tomorrow, then. I hope we can wrap this up by that time."

The mailman arrived at the pathology laboratory in midafternoon, carrying a large official-looking manila envelope.

"Doris Hudson," he said. "There's postage due."

The technologist squealed, undeterred by the pipette she was holding in her mouth. She disencumbered herself and slid from her stool.

"My bag!" she exclaimed. "How much do I owe?"

Dr. Coffee watched the exchange of coins, the impatient ripping open of the envelope, the frowning scrutiny of the bag's contents, the smile that signaled complete restitution.

When the mailman had gone, Dr. Coffee asked, "All there?"

The smile vanished. "Except the test tubes, of course."

Dr. Coffee picked up the phone and asked the hospital operator to get him the law offices of George Kensington.

"Hello, counselor? This is Dr. Coffee. I want to thank you for returning Miss Hudson's handbag so promptly. . . . Why do you say 'nonsense?' Doris is delighted that . . . No, no, I'm sure you don't approve of such strongarm tactics, counselor. In fact, I was surprised that a crusader for the truth like you have always been—no, I'm not accusing you, but since you are the only one outside of my staff and Lieutenant Ritter who knew that it was Professor Mitchell who— yes, yes, I understand perfectly. Of course I believe you.

"Then you'll be happy to know that we had duplicates of the hair specimens and that the analysis has been proceeding splendidly. In fact, I expect to get a read-out sometime tomorrow. I suppose you'd like to be present to represent your sons. . . . Yes, of course bring Cedric. Bring the other twin, too, if you can persuade Academia authorities to release him on bond. I'll let you know when and where. By the way, counselor, when you were in Academia yesterday, I'm sure you must have looked into what financial interest the twins might have had in the combustible Shetland operation. . . . I see. No financial interest at all. Goodbye, counselor. And thanks again on behalf of Doris Hudson."

Dr. Coffee replaced the phone. When he looked up Doris and Dr. Mookerji were standing in the doorway grinning.

Ritter took Detective Sergeant Brody along when he drove out to the Lamb estate on the northern fringes of Northbank. Brody was unsurpassed in his dogged pursuit of detail.

"Thanks, but we won't come in," Ritter said as Mary Lamb opened the front door herself. "We just want you to come with us while we have another look at your guesthouse. Where's your lawyer? When I phoned, I told you to have your lawyer here."

Mary laughed. "I don't need a lawyer. Or do I really? Are you going to arrest me? For what?"

"If you've been lying to me," Ritter said, "and I think you have, I could bust you as an accessory."

"Before or after the fact?" Another laugh. "You see, I know all the words. I took a course at college last year—Law for the Citizen. Let's go, lieutenant. You can consider that I've been warned and that I know my rights."

She closed the door behind her and stepped between the two detectives. Her white pleated tennis skirt flicked saucily behind her as she swung gaily down the path, the glint of sunlight in her pale golden hair.

"I want you to go through the same routine like the night you came in and found your gal friend dead," said Ritter as the trio entered the guesthouse.

"There was no routine. I just opened the door, saw Rhoda sitting against the side of the fireplace, called to her—"

"Do it," Ritter ordered.

Mary acted out the scene with appropriate words and screams. Ritter raised his hand to interrupt her in mid-screech.

"Did you stop yelling long enough to phone for cops?" he asked. He glanced at Brody who was watching open-mouthed.

"I guess I must have. I was hysterical, but I guess I made myself understood."

"Did you go out for dramatics at college?" Ritter asked.

"Why do you ask that?"

"Because your acting is super. The performance the other night was even better. You ought to go on the stage."

"What do you mean?"

"I mean all that grief and hysterical sobbing was phony. And you didn't phone for us cossacks until you'd taken your sweet time to phony up this place but good."

Mary sat down suddenly on a couch near the hearth. Her eyes narrowed slightly as she said, "You really do think I've been lying to you, don't you?"

"So I finally get through to you," Ritter said. "Now tell me how you think Rhoda's pretty satin slippers got all the way down to the other end of the rug."

"She obviously kicked them off while she was struggling with the man who killed her," Mary said quickly.

"You say it's a man?"

"You do. You say the handful of hair she grabbed belonged to a man."

"If Rhoda kicked the slippers off, how come they land so neat, side by side? I guess you caught 'em in mid-air, because your prints were on both of 'em."

Mary's lips parted, but she said nothing.

"And on that apple, too—the only prints," the detective went on. "I guess you polished it good before you lit those joss sticks to make us believe all that jazz about Rhoda being a real genuine mystic. I bet those tarot cards were yours, too."

Mary Lamb stood up.

"Sit down, Mary's little lamb, I ain't through with you. I've got some questions about your interest in that Shetland pony business at Great Lakes U."

"I think," said Mary, "that we had better postpone this interview after all. I'd like my attorney present."

"That's your right." Ritter tried not to grin too smugly. He bowed stiffly to her. Then he nodded to Brody, who had not uttered a word. "Come on, Brody. We're about talked out. Let's go."

It was midmorning next day when Dr. Coffee telephoned Ritter at the police station.

"I've finished the microscopic protocol on the Rhoda Robbins autopsy, Max," he said.

"Is it murder?" Ritter asked.

"In my opinion, yes. Whether you and the D.A. can prove it I can't guarantee. There's no doubt the girl died from a microscopic hemorrhage in the brain. She must have grabbed the murderer's hair before he banged her head against the bricks, because she was unconscious from the moment of impact. She might have lived for a few minutes in a coma, since the ambulance attendant reported the unusually high post mortem temperature, but she was clinically dead almost instantly."

"When do you put the finger on the guilty twin, doc? Or do you?"

"Dr. Mitchell has promised me results of his chromatographic comparison by this afternoon. You want to make a Federal case of it, with television and a press gallery?"

"Don't kid me, doc. But with Papa Kensington and all his civil rights backstopping, maybe I ought to get that other twin down from Academia, even if he has to have a peace officer handcuffed to him. Whatya think, doc?"

"Suit yourself, Max. Whatever you decide, I'll be ready."

The decision was not Ritter's to make, as it turned out. It was George Kensington who took command of events and forced the delivery of the other twin to Northbank by pressuring the district attorney of Northbank County to ask for a fugitive warrant on suspicion of murder. And when Fredric Kensington was flown from Academia in handcuffs to be lodged in the county jail, his father changed hats and, as attorney for his defense, got a friendly judge to issue a writ of habeas corpus to be returned the following afternoon.

Kensington telephoned Dr. Coffee at home that night to tell him of his latest maneuver.

"I've decided to speed up the mills of God—or the wheels of justice, in case you're an atheist," the lawyer said. "I'm tired of waiting for you to spring your molecular miracles, so if you want to show off your scientific wares you'd better be in court tomorrow, doctor.''

"Thank you for warning me," said the pathologist. "If I'm called I'll be there."

The bailiff rose to his full six feet, threw out his chest, and bellowed, "All rise!"

The diminutive redheaded judge emerged from his chambers, the black robes of his dignity fluttering behind him as he mounted the steps to the bench.

The group of attorneys, principals, and witnesses rose dutifully while the bailiff's voice abated to a mumble about the superior court of such-and-such a jurisdiction being now in session and all those having business approach . . .

The audience sat down again. There was Mary Lamb surrounded by a battery of expensive attorneys, just in case her name should be mentioned in the proceedings; George Kensington sat at the attorney's table with his son Fredric still handcuffed to a peace officer. Cedric was not in the courtroom as far as Dr. Coffee could see.

An assistant district attorney was soon on his feet before the bench, objecting in a loud voice that the procedure was highly irregular inasmuch as the same counsel who had asked that the prisoner be detained on suspicion of murder was now arguing the illegality of his detention. The judge signaled with his head that George Kensington was also to approach the bench.

Dr. Coffee had come to court with Max Ritter without waiting for the promised chromatographic report from Northbank University. Ritter had insisted that the pathologist be on hand to testify in case the report was delayed. Dr. Mookerji would bring the report by hand as soon as it was ready.

The attorneys were still arguing at the bench when Dr. Mookerji appeared in the courtroom, waddled breathlessly into the witnesses area, and plumped his spheroidal form into a chair beside Dr. Coffee. He handed the pathologist a large manila envelope.

Dr. Coffee drew out several sheets of graph paper on which automated pens had drawn colored peaks and valleys, three yards of Z-folded paper strips bearing the figures and symbols of a computer printout, and the typewritten pages of Dr. Miller's interpretation of the chromatographic analysis. As the pathologist flipped through the pages the judge spoke:

"I am informed, Dr. Coffee, that you may be able to offer evidence as to whether or not the subject of this writ should be held on suspicion of murdering one Rhoda Robbins. Is that true?"

"Yes, Your Honor."

"Please take the stand."

Dr. Coffee was sworn, sat in the witness chair, and explained to the court how he had arranged to compare the hair of the suspects with the hair that Rhoda Robbins was clutching in her fingers when her body was found. He told why he had discarded several samples (they had not been recently cut) and how the hair of the two Kensington twins was finally sent to Northbank University to be compared by flame-ionization gas chromotography with the hair in the victim's fingers.

"The hair of one of the Kensington twins," said Dr. Coffee, "gave exactly the same molecular picture as the hair from the murder scene. The hair of the other twin did not."

"In what respect were they dissimilar?" the court asked.

"For one thing, there was a faint trace of sulfur which was probably produced by the phenothiazine which only one of the twins was taking as a tranquilizer and which can reach the hair. There was also a strong indication of selenium, which is the component of a scalp treatment which only one twin was using and which had obviously been absorbed by his hair."

"Are you referring to the twin now in this courtroom?"

"No, Your Honor. It is Cedric Kensington's hair that matches," said Dr. Coffee.

"Then I remand Fredric Kensington to the custody of the authorities of Academia," ruled the judge. "Where is the other twin?"

"He should be here at any minute, Your Honor," said Ritter. "I've sent for him."

It was several minutes before Detective Sergeant Jenkins entered the courtroom—alone. From the expression on his round face he might have just come from the funeral of his best friend. He handed Ritter a gray rectangular object the size of a deck of cards.

"What the hell is this?" Ritter demanded. "And where is Cedric Kensington?"

Jenkins didn't know the answer to either question. He had found the rectangular object, apparently the cartridge for a cassette tape recorder, in Cedric's pad with a note asking that it be transmitted to Lieutenant Ritter. Cedric himself had departed, Jenkins didn't know when, by devious means which Jenkins also didn't know—apparently a door leading into another apartment or the roof or some exit invisible from the street.

"Let's get on the ball and get that old dragnet going," said Ritter, outdoing himself as an unparalleled metaphor mixer, "before the scent gets cold."

The detective took off like a sprinter, the cassette cartridge clasped tightly in his hand, the assistant district attorney in hot pursuit, and Jenkins a poor third.

Dr. Coffee would have liked to join the procession, but Dr. Mookerji reminded him that they were due back at the hospital for a biopsy that afternoon. He would have to wait to learn what was on the tape.

"You are perhaps of opinion, Dr. Sahib," said the Hindu resident as they drove back to work, "that recording tape contains last will and confession of guilty twin before suiciding self in river?"

"Possibly," said the pathologist. "After all, his mother took her own life, and the boy seemed to be a sensitive character the one time I saw him. Still, he belongs to a cynical generation whose actions are not always predictable. We'll find out soon enough."

They found out that evening when Ritter brought Cedric's tape to the laboratory. It had been played earlier in the D.A.'s office for the edification of the D.A.'s and Ritter's staff. After hearing it, the detective had phoned to ask Dr. Coffee's permission to bring George Kensington along for the second playback.

The tape recorder was perched on Doris Hudson's workbench.

"I'll be long gone when you hear this, Ritter," said Cedric's voice when Ritter pushed the playback switch. "You should teach Sergeant Jenkins to examine the interior of a dwelling for alternate exits before he takes up a vigil on the exterior. I decided to split when I discovered that I was able to come and go without detection to seize Miss Hudson's handbag. No, my father didn't do it, though he did tip me off.

"Yes, I killed Rhoda Robbins, as you certainly know by now. I didn't mean to kill her. No, that's not true. For a few seconds when I attacked her I did want her dead. Temporary insanity will be my plea if you ever catch me. And it wasn't her phony promise of marriage to Fred or me that drove me mad either, although I guess for Fred her perfidy must have been pretty disillusioning, enough for him to beat up Pete Hyde. For me the trigger was the whole Shetland business—the Old Forgery, they used to call it on the campus—and the way they exploited us.

"Rhoda considered she could pay me off for writing a term paper with a few kisses and maybe a fifty dollar bonus, the way she'd seduce a professor out of his exam questions, so Shetland could sell the answers to the kids at five or ten dollars a crack. But the day I killed her I'd just found out that Shetland would sell my fifty dollar dissertations to a national syndicate for a thousand dollars or more. I guess I hated all of them—Pete Hyde the sales manager, Mary Lamb, who bankrolled the Old Forgery, and Rhoda, the talent scout—but I hated Rhoda most because I thought I was in love with her.

"Mary phoned me that you had figured out she had phonied up the scene after I left. I had nothing to do with that. That was Mary's attempt to salvage the Old Forgery before she knew Fred had set it afire.

"I make no apologies to my father or to anyone else for my contribution to throwing the educational system out of joint. I acted in complete accord with today's morality. Anything for a buck. If it pays off, it's right and good and a benefit to civilization. Honor to the corrupt if they can get away with a million. Three cheers for private enterprise. If we must die to preserve the establishment, why not murder for profit?

"Try to find me, lieutenant, on behalf of law and order. If you can get extradition papers, you may see me again. In the meantime, nuts to you. I leave Mary Lamb and Pete Hyde to your tender mercies."

Ritter shut off the recording. He turned to the father of the twins. "Kensington," he said, "your tricky little pixy of a son is going to find that the Royal Canadians are on the side of law and order, too, and they ain't all as dumb as Jenkins."

There was a long silence. George Kensington sat motionless, staring across the laboratory at an open cupboard. On the shelves were rows of glass jars containing snippets of the vital organs from previous autopsies, filed for reference. Dr. Coffee looked at him sympathetically, wondering what thoughts were going through his mind as he contemplated those pathetic reminders of mortality. Here was a man with basically kind instincts who was dedicated to humanity and to helping the underdog, yet whose reward seemed to be only disappointment and tragedy.

"Counselor," Dr. Coffee said, "your offspring seem to believe in direct action. Where did they get their violent chromosomes?"

Kensington was silent.

Ritter said, "Hey, doc, how about your theories? Who gets the decision—heredity or environment?"

"Hard to say, Max," the pathologist replied, "since Cedric's internal environment was partially dependent on a bottle of phenothiazine tablets which I found empty when we visited his pad. Perhaps if Cedric hadn't run out of tranquilizers just before he discovered that Rhoda had been playing him and his twin for a pair of suckers, our story—his story—might have taken a less tragic turn."

"Man's karma," commented Dr. Mookerji, "is depending upon deeds, not tranquilizers."

LAURA NORDER

by JOHN MORTIMER

66 L ittle Margery's going to join the battle for Laura Norder,''
Tim Oldroyd told their friends when his wife was appointed
a magistrate. Law and order was one of his favorite expressions,
something he had always "stood for," but he made it sound as
though what he was standing for was a curiously named woman,
poor old Laura who was under constant threat from delinquent youth
and the anarchist forces of the Party Opposite. When he boasted of
his wife's appointment to the minor judiciary, it was as though he
were announcing a singular and astonishing triumph of his own. As
he told her every time the subject was mentioned, which was with
embarrassing frequency, she would never have got the job if she
hadn't had the good fortune to be the wife of Tim Oldroyd, MP for
Boltingly and a parliamentary secretary at the Ministry of the Family.

Tim Oldroyd had been a pallid, shy young man until some lurking
ambition, as hidden up till then as an inherited disease, led him to
stand for the seat at Boltingly. A change came over him. He announced that he was now to be known as "Tim," in the modern
way of politicians. He became even paler and grew a paunch and a
little sandpaper mustache. His voice, always high-pitched, now
emerged as a prolonged whine of outrage. The most frequent objects
of his falsetto wrath were schoolteachers, one-parent families, unem-
ployed school leavers who went joyriding and traded soft drugs in
the town's precincts, and those who slept in wigwams or up trees in
protest at the new eight-lane super highway across Boltingly Meadows. His rage was frequently directed at his wife, and then his
squeals were weighted with sarcasm and interrupted by moments of
light laughter. "For God's sake, pay attention in court, Margerine!"
he told her. "You know how you tend to let your mind wander.

163

Don't wool-gather! The clerk's there to stop you doing anything damn silly. Just get it into your head that, in this country, people don't get stood in the dock unless they're committed something fairly outrageous. Support the police, and you won't go far wrong. Who's your chairman?''

''Dr. Arrowsmith.''

''Frank Arrowsmith's a wise old bird.'' The Oldroyds knew all the important people in Boltingly. ''Listen carefully to what Frank's got to say. Follow his instructions to the letter, and you won't go far wrong. I'm sure he won't expect you to make a contribution of any sort. Are you listening, Jerry?''

In fact his wife was staring out of the window at her garden, the lawn she mowed to a soft green velvet and the long border, set against an old brick wall, in which the flowers were all white. The garden, more than anything else in her life, was what kept her with Tim.

''Yes, I'm listening,'' she said.

''I don't suppose you've got a suitable hat?''

''I'm afraid not.''

''Pity! In the good old days, lady magistrates wore hats. Made them look imposing. That's not your line of country, is it, Margery? You couldn't look imposing, with or without a hat on you.''

From behind the coffeepot, across the polished oval table with its Laura Ashley placemats and Portmeirion breakfast china, Margery Oldroyd looked at her husband and wondered if he'd seem more imposing in a hat, a Princess Di straw perhaps, with an upturned brim and a long ribbon, or a more ornate affair with feathers and artificial roses. How would Tim look, crowned with bobbing cherries like his dreadful mother? This unexpected thought made her giggle.

''And do try not to giggle in court, Margerine.'' Her husband issued a serious warning. ''There's a breakdown of respect for all established institutions. As things are today, we really can't afford a magistrate who giggles.'' With that he left the breakfast table for the lavatory, and Bagpiper, the Scottie dog which, in the Oldroyd family, filled, inadequately, the place of a child, rose from the hearthrug and strutted off looking, in its own small way, as superior and discontented as its master.

Margery Oldroyd looked back on twenty-five years of astonishing emptiness. She and Timothy had been at Keele University together.

A quarter of a century before, at a party in the J.C.R., when Tim was a skinny student with fairish hair falling into his eyes, she had felt moved by the resolute and purposeful manner, that doomed but bravely undertaken battle against his nonexistent sense of rhythm, in which he had tried to dance alluringly to "I Can't Get No Satisfaction." She was a spritely dancer, light on her feet as plump people are, a girl with large, surprised eyes who giggled a good deal. She was attracted by something in Timothy missing in herself, and took it for an infinite ambition: she couldn't guess that it would be so quickly satisfied by becoming a parliamentary secretary and the member for Boltingly. After the J.C.R. dance she led him to her room and steered him towards the bed. When, in a remarkably short time, it was over, she smoothed back his straying lock of sandy hair and mistook his incompetence as a lover for sincerity.

Nothing, on that evening, prepared her for the stranger he was bound to become; nor for the alarming intensity with which, she found, she had grown to hate him. This hatred had been born and grew like an advanced and overactive child, even before he started calling her Margerine.

On the magistrates' training course, when they were lectured and questioned on the elements of the law and basic court procedure, Margery had found herself unexpectedly popular. She listened hard, picked up knowledge quickly, and showed no signs of giving trouble. Now her first day had come, and she was surprised at how calm she felt, far calmer than she had been at breakfast, when her hatred of Tim bubbled up from her stomach and seemed likely to choke her. Now, on the bench, she felt as though she were at a pleasant dinner party to which, she was thankful to say, her husband hadn't been invited. She sat on the chairman's left. A retired G.P., Frank Arrowsmith had the confidence of a man who, throughout his life, had found it easy to charm women. He may not have been a particularly clever doctor, but he was always a popular one. Now he sat back at ease in his high-backed, leather-seated chair, listened to tales of distress with a faint smile of amusement, and imposed fines, or brief terms of imprisonment, in the soft, reasonable voice he had used to recommend a course of antibiotics or a fat-free diet. On the other side of the chairman sat Gordon Burt, a prosperous garage owner whose skin and clothes hung loosely about his body in greyish folds, giving this squat man, Margery often thought, the appearance of a baby elephant. The first time the comparison had occurred to her she had giggled.

The new Magistrates Court in Boltingly was built of glass and concrete. Inside there was a pervasive smell of furniture polish and disinfectant, and the air conditioning hummed in a soporific fashion. During the first batch of cases, Margery's attention wandered. She thought of Tim in his office, accepting a cup of coffee from Charlotte, his inevitable researcher. Charlotte, naturally, was everything Margery wasn't, young, slender, intelligent, the possessor of a First in PPE from Lady Margaret Hall, the owner of a ''super little Lotus Elan'' which she could drive with skill at speeds Margery could never manage. A girl who, as Tim frequently told her, ''knew her opera'' as Margery never would, although whether the world of opera belonged to Charlotte and no one else, or whether the talented researcher had a private opera of her own, Margery had only once asked, to be met with a look of contempt. Charlotte, she knew perfectly well, was someone to whom Tim made love with greedy haste during lengthy lunch hours or late night sittings. She would never become Charlie, or even Lottie, although Margery had quickly been demoted to Marge or Jerry and, for some years now, to Margerine.

''If the bench pleases, may I mention the separation order made in this court?'' she heard a solicitor ask in respectful tones, as though from a long way off. Why hadn't she separated from Tim, or even divorced him? He was never tired of telling her that any hint of a broken marriage in the Ministry of the Family would severely ''embarrass the government,'' as though she cared how embarrassed the government became. When he said this, half threateningly, half in pathetic entreaty, she nursed her ever-increasing dislike in silence. Why should she separate from him and move out of the house and away from the garden she loved, to live in a rented flat in Boltingly and haggle over her maintenance, as the couple were going to haggle now in court in front of her? The story of her marriage would, she knew, have some ending, but not that one. So far as Tim Oldroyd, MP, was concerned, she thought, separation was far too good for him.

''This is the murder,'' Dr. Arrowsmith smiled and whispered, calling for attention in the way a bridge player might remind her, ''Your deal, partner.'' It was the big event in the Boltingly magistrates' day, R. *v*. Mustoe, a committal in a murder trial. Margery picked up her pencil and gave the case her full attention.

*   *   *

The man who had been led into the dock, guarded by two prison officers, looked puzzled. He wore jeans and an anorak, and he stared around the court as though he wasn't sure of its reality, or whether he was in a dream. He had brown curling hair that he wore rather long, and he had, Margery noticed, delicate hands with tapering fingers. He seemed, on the whole, to be taking little interest in the proceedings.

"Mr. Mustoe and his common-law wife Louise had been separated for some six months. She was living in a mobile home up by Boltingly Meadows, and he was sleeping, as he told the officer in charge of the case, 'rough.' Apparently he had reason to believe she had formed a relationship with a man working on the new superhighway. Er . . . um . . ." The young man from the Crown Prosecution Service shuffled his papers nervously and cleared his throat. He looked hot and uncomfortable. What's he worrying about? Margery wondered. This was only a preliminary hearing. He had nothing to do but call a few witnesses to show that there was a case sufficient to send up to the Crown Court. Mr. Mustoe's solicitor, a lined and yellowing old professional who spent every day in some local criminal court, closed his eyes, leant back, and offered no assistance.

"On the night of the twelfth of April," the prosecutor resumed uncertainly, "Mr. Mustoe was seen by several witnesses approaching the mobile home. He hammered on the door and was finally let in. Witnesses later heard sounds of quarrelling. We don't know what time Mr. Mustoe left, but in the morning Louise Rollins' partner, who had been away for several days, returned and found her dead. The cause of death—you will hear the doctor's evidence—was manual strangulation. Certain fingerprints . . ."

"Not admitted!" the old professional boomed without getting to his feet, and the young man from the Crown Prosecution Service subsided meekly.

"Yes?" Dr. Arrowsmith raised his eyebrows at the old professional, who now rose, his hands clasped together on his stomach, and boomed again, "The fingerprints are not admitted. I shall be cross-examining the officer."

"But the manual strangulation," the retired doctor probed gently. "Is that admitted?"

"Oh yes, sir. We admit manual strangulation. By *somebody*."

Gazing vaguely round the court, Mr. Mustoe, the man accused, caught Margery's eye, and for no particular reason, smiled at her.

*   *   *

"Such amateurs, these criminals! I believe they want to be caught. Why didn't that fellow Mustoe take the precaution of learning a little basic anatomy?" At half past four the committal proceedings had been adjourned until the following Monday. Mr. Mustoe was remanded in custody, and the magistrates retired to their room to enjoy their statutory tea and biscuits before dispersing. Dr. Arrowsmith stretched out his long, well-tailored legs and sipped the watery Lapsang of which he brought his own supply. "I'm not going to ruin the lining of my stomach with the prison officers' Indian you could stand a spoon up in," he always said.

"Anatomy?" Mr. Burt preferred the local brew. "How would that help him?"

"My dear Gordon, you might know all about second-hand cars, but you'd make a rotten murderer. The carotoid sinus is the place to find. Only a slight pressure needed, it wouldn't leave any bruising you'd notice, and the victim would lose consciousness and be in deep, deep trouble."

"Losing consciousness wouldn't be enough to kill anyone, though. This fellow Mustoe was out to kill her." Margery watched as the baby elephant spooned sugar into the prison officers' tea.

"Whether the victim came out alive would depend on the situation she was in. Or he. A small squeeze and they'd be helpless." The doctor had finished his chocolate biscuit and pulled out a silk handkerchief to wipe his fingers, on the backs of which Margery noticed small clusters of black hair. Hair came out from below his white, gold-linked shirt cuffs also, and encircled his wristwatch.

"Well, anyway." Mr. Burt sounded unconvinced. "Where are these carotoid whatever they are anyway?"

"Feel your neck. Gently now. Got the Adam's apple? Now on each side, little swellings . . . the carotoid sinuses."

Mr. Burt stirred his tea as Dr. Arrowsmith talked them through it, but Margery's fingers went to her neck, only a little creased by the years since she had been a student and met Tim. Now she had found the exact spot.

"I'm afraid this is rather a morbid sort of a conversation for teatime." The doctor chairman was smiling at her again. "No doubt it's a good thing for all of us that the criminal classes are so poorly educated. Now. Let's talk about something far more pleasant. How's your delightful garden, Margery? Don't I remember, when you were kind enough to have Serena and me over to dinner, your lovely white border? What was it that smelled so delicious?''

"That would have been the syringa, I think," Margery told him. "Thank you, yes. The garden's still beautiful.''

That night the Oldroyds were invited to a dinner given by the Boltingly Chamber of Commerce, a black tie affair at which Tim was to make a speech and Margery would look up at him admiringly as he painted a rosy picture of the economic situation.

Tim got home early so he would have plenty of time to change. He was greeted on the stairs by Bagpiper, who appeared embarrassingly affectionate and shot, like a bullet, at his flies. He did his best to calm the dog and then ran himself a bath.

He and Charlotte had enjoyed lunch in an Italian place in Horseferry Road and then retired to a small hotel near Victoria Station that offered reduced prices for an afternoon. Charlotte was an olive-skinned girl with thick, wiry hair, not as pretty as he would have liked her to be, and she left a musky smell on him that he was anxious to wash away. He cherished the illusion that Margery knew nothing of the way he spent his afternoons.

Tim always enjoyed his bath and avoided hotels that only offered a shower. He lay back gratefully and turned the tap on with his toe. As the warm water caressed him, the years seemed to drift away, and he was back in his student days; he sang, as he once had at a dance, "I Can't Get No Satisfaction." The noise of the taps and his singing drowned the footsteps behind him. The strong fingers that closed on his neck were like those of a lover.

Margery had been back to the house earlier. Then she waited, at the end of the garden, until she heard Tim's car. When he had gone upstairs, she stood by the back door until she heard the bath water running. He's washing off the smell of Charlotte, was what she said to herself. Then she went shopping in Waitrose, taking care to talk to as many acquaintances as possible. When she returned to the house, Bagpiper was kicking up a high-pitched yapping fuss, and water was dripping down the stairs. She turned off the tap and telephoned a Dr. Helena Quinton who had taken over the practice of Dr. Arrowsmith, now retired. Then she walked into the garden. The smell of the syringas was sweet and heavy and produced, in her, thoughts of love.

*   *   *

Margery wasn't back in court until the following Monday, for the adjourned hearing of the Mustoe committal. She parked neatly in the space marked Magistrates Only and went up to their room. Gordon Burt was always late, but Dr. Arrowsmith was there in excellent time, drinking coffee and eating a digestive biscuit; the chocolate covered ones were reserved for teatime.

"Margery, dear. I am most terribly sorry." He stood and spoke very gently, using his best bedside manner.

"Thank you. And thank you and Serena for your note."

"The funeral's tomorrow, isn't it? We'll be there, of course."

"That's kind."

"Helena Quinton said it must have been a sudden heart attack. The poor fellow was unconscious and then drowned. Of course, he'd been overworking terribly. Politics makes such terrible demands nowadays . . ."

"I blame myself."

"Why on earth?" The doctor's arm was round her shoulder. He was old, too old for work, but he had had, she knew, many mistresses and the smell of eau de cologne on his handkerchief was as strong as the smell of syringas.

"If only I hadn't gone shopping! If only I'd been there, in the house, when he came back."

"That's ridiculous."

"I felt something was wrong when I was in Waitrose. It must have been a kind of . . ."

"Telepathy?" the wise old doctor suggested.

"Yes."

"You two were very close. I know you were." There was a small silence, and he squeezed her shoulder. "We must see more of you now. We mustn't let you be lonely."

He moved away from her, it seemed reluctantly, when the pachyderm Mr. Burt arrived in a hurry. He had also written a note and spoke softly to Margery, as though they were in church together.

"The Mustoe case." Dr. Arrowsmith became businesslike now that they were all assembled. "Now, I don't know what we're going to hear today, but the evidence is already overwhelming. I suppose there's no doubt we're sending him for trial?"

"No doubt at all." Gordon Burt's mouth was half full of digestive biscuit.

"Margery?"

"Oh, Tim always said I was to pay strict attention to what you said and follow your instructions. I must do that, he told me, for the sake of law and order.''

She ran the last syllables together so they sounded like a woman's name, ''Laura Norder.'' And as she said it, she couldn't suppress a giggle.

THE PROBLEM OF THE DYING PATIENT

by EDWARD D. HOCH

"Come in and have a seat," Dr. Sam Hawthorne said, reaching for the brandy. "The story I have to tell you this time is painful for me to recollect—it almost cost me my license to practice medicine . . ."

By the summer of '35 (Dr. Sam continued), I'd started cutting back on housecalls. My office in a wing of Pilgrim Memorial Hospital was attracting more patients, and even though it was the depths of the Depression, most families in town owned a car or had access to one. Generally, it was only the very young or the very old, especially those living on the outskirts of Northmont, who still needed me to come to their homes.

One of these was old Mrs. Willis, who was in her mid-eighties and suffered from a variety of disorders. I'd been treating her mainly for a heart condition and diabetes, but now she was bedridden after breaking her hip last year. I could see her strength going with each visit I made. She'd simply lost the will to live.

Her husband had died a few years earlier, and they'd never had children. She was cared for now by a middle-aged niece and her husband to whom she'd promised the old farmhouse and its surrounding forty acres of untilled land. "It's all I've got to give them," she'd told me once after they'd moved in. "If they can put up with me, they deserve it."

I had to admit that Betty Willis, at the end of her life, was not a lovable person. She was domineering and hard to please. The niece, Freda Ann Parker, was a plain woman of forty or so who tried to take it all in stride. Her husband Nat wasn't nearly as easygoing. I'd heard him grumbling many times out of earshot of the old lady, and once he and Freda Ann had engaged in a heated argument in front of me.

About once a week I stopped by the Willis house unannounced if I had another call to make in that area. On one particular Monday morning, Freda Ann telephoned the office to make sure I'd be coming out. "She had a really bad night, doctor. I think she's dying."

"I'll be there in about an hour," I promised. I finished up with the patient I was attending and told my nurse, Mary, that I'd be driving out to the Willis place.

It was a lovely June morning, the sort of day when summer seems to stretch out endlessly. I saw some boys running along the side of the dirt road, free at last from the confines of the classroom, and remembered the summer days of my own youth. I'd grown up in the city, but the sense of freedom had to be much the same. As I topped a rise in the road, I could see the Willis farmhouse off in the distance, surrounded by a small apple orchard that was the closest to farming the Willises had gotten in recent years. It reminded me of childhood journeys to my grandfather's farm in Pennsylvania in those long-ago years before the Great War.

Nat Parker was in the orchard, inspecting the trees for possible damage from a windstorm the previous evening. He was a tired-looking man with thinning hair and a perpetual shadow of bristle around his chin. Nat seemed a good decade older than his wife, and probably was. "Did you have any damage?" I called out to him as I left my car.

"Nothing much, doc. The way it was blowing, I feared it would take half the orchard with it."

"Your wife says Betty's not good this morning."

"Well, she could be better."

I left him and went in the front door. It was always unlocked, and I knew Freda Ann would have heard my arrival. She came out of the kitchen to greet me. "I'm glad you could come," she said. "Aunt Betty's real bad, doctor."

I followed her up the creaking stairs to the second floor. Betty Willis still had the big front bedroom she'd shared with her husband for most of her lifetime. Now she lay in the ornate double bed, staring up at me as if she could see the angels coming for her.

"I'm dying," she told me.

"Nonsense." I took her pulse and listened to her heart through my stethoscope. She was certainly weak, her vital signs lower than they'd been on my last visit, but I saw no imminent danger of death.

I moved the glass of water with her dentures in it, the only thing on her night table, to make room for my bag. "You'll be fit again, Betty. All you need is some good strong medicine."

Freda Ann came into the room and stood by the door as I completed my examination. "How is she, Dr. Hawthorne?"

"Oh, I think a bit of heart stimulant should perk her up." I reached into my bag and unsnapped the compartment where I kept the digitalis. "Could you bring us a glass of water?"

She went back downstairs to the kitchen sink. The place still used an outhouse, and there was no running water on the second floor. "Do I *have* to take a pill, doctor?" old Mrs. Willis asked in a shaky voice. Swallowing was hard for her.

"Just a little digitalis, Betty. It'll get your heart pumping again." I took her temperature, though I was pretty sure she had no fever.

Freda Ann returned with the water just as I removed the thermometer. "Just about normal," I told them. "A bit low, in fact."

Betty took the pill herself and washed it down with a swallow of water. "I feel better already," she said, trying to smile.

I was just turning away from the bed when I heard her gasp. I looked back to see her lined face twisted with pain and surprise. Then her whole body sagged, and she sank back into the pillows. "Betty!" I reached for her pulse.

"What happened?" Freda Ann demanded. "What did you do to her?"

I couldn't believe she was accusing me of anything. "She's had some sort of seizure." There was no pulse, no heartbeat. I took a small mirror from my bag and held it to her nostrils. There was no clouding.

"She's dead, isn't she?"

"Yes," I told her.

"Was it that pill you gave her?"

"It couldn't have been. That was nothing but digitalis."

She stared at me with uncertain eyes. "It was so sudden. One minute she seemed fine—"

"You said yourself you thought she was dying," I replied, sounding more defensive than I'd meant to.

Freda Ann bit her lower lip, trying to decide what to do. At that moment her husband came up the stairs. "Aunt Betty's dead," she told him. "She went just like that."

He stared at the body, grim-faced. "It's for the best."

As I bent to close Betty's eyes, the unmistakable odor of bitter almonds hit my nostrils. I'd had experience with it in the past, on the night Prohibition ended back in '33. When I straightened up I said, "Something's wrong here. You'd better ring up Sheriff Lens on the phone."

Sheriff Lens had been my friend since I first arrived in Northmont to set up my practice thirteen years earlier. In many ways he was a typical country sheriff, and I'd been happy to lend a hand when he needed it. Now it seemed that I was the one who needed help.

He listened patiently to my account of Betty Willis's death and then asked, "Is there any chance you could have given her the wrong pill by mistake, doc?"

"Not a chance in the world! I don't even carry cyanide compounds in my bag."

Sheriff Lens glanced around the bedroom, seeming to take in the faded, water-stained wallpaper, the family portraits, the bit of ivy struggling to grow on the windowsill. Then his eyes fastened on the half empty glass of water on the bedside table. "Is that the water she took it with?"

I nodded. "It should be tested, though I doubt it's poisoned."

"How come?"

"No odor. I checked it right away." As I spoke, I took a small bottle from my bag—one used for urine samples—and poured the water into it. On a hunch, I also sampled the water her dentures were in.

"We'll have to do an autopsy," the sheriff said almost apologetically.

"Of course."

We went down to the sitting room where Freda Ann and Nat were waiting. "What did you find?" she asked.

"Nothing," I replied. "Is there something you think we should have found?"

Nat Parker seemed to be staring at the ceiling, perhaps studying a fluttering cobweb in one corner. Finally he said, "The old lady had a good long life. Her time was up."

His wife suddenly turned on him, close to tears. "I really believe you're glad she's gone, Nat! You couldn't stand having her in the house."

"Now, Freda—"

"It's true, you know it!"

He stood. "Maybe I should go out and check on the orchard."

Sheriff Lens cleared his throat. "We'll be taking your aunt in to Pilgrim Memorial for an autopsy, Mrs. Parker. You can go ahead and make the arrangements with the undertaker if you want to. He can probably pick her up there in the morning."

"Thank you, sheriff."

He accompanied me to my car. As I was getting in, he asked, "What do you think, doc?"

"There's a possibility one or both of them killed her," I told him, "but for the life of me I can't figure out how."

The following morning, Dr. Wolfe from the local medical society stopped by my office. Mary knew him and ushered him right in. "It's Dr. Wolfe to see you."

I laid down the medical journal I'd been reading and stood to greet him. "To what do I owe this honor, doctor?"

Martin Wolfe was a tall man in his sixties with a mane of wavy white hair. He wasn't someone you addressed by his first name unless you were his senior in years and experience. "I've come about the tragic death of Betty Willis," he said.

"I've been waiting to hear the autopsy result," I told him.

"I have it right here," he said, handing over the official form. "Death was due to a sudden paralysis of her heart, respiratory system, and brain, caused by ingestion of hydrocyanic acid. A classic case of poisoning."

"I feared as much," I said. "But I can't see how it could have happened. I never left her for an instant, The digitalis preparation I gave her came from my own bag, and the glass of water had no detectable odor."

"The water was pure," he confirmed. "It was tested. Tell me, Dr. Hawthorne, what type of digitalis preparation did you administer?"

"Digoxin. It came on the market just last year."

Wolfe pursed his lips. "I'm quite familiar with it. As you must know, it has a very narrow treatment range. The proper dose is sixty percent of a toxic dose. It was a dangerous choice of medication in someone of that age."

He was beginning to irritate me, but I tried not to show it. I said, "I might remind you, Dr. Wolfe, that Mrs. Willis died of cyanide poisoning, not an overdose of digitalis."

"A point well taken," he admitted. "But if what you say is true, I can think of only two possible explanations. Either you made a terrible mistake when you gave Mrs. Willis her medication or—"

"Or what?"

"Or you took pity on this woman and decided to put her out of her misery."

"Mercy killing."

"That's what it's called," Dr. Wolfe agreed.

"I can assure you I did neither. I was neither stupid nor criminal in my treatment of her."

"Is there a third explanation, Dr. Hawthorne?"

"I intend to find one."

"Very well." He rose to his feet, towering over the desk. "The medical society holds its regular monthly meeting one week from today. This matter is certain to be brought up. I trust you'll have an explanation by that time."

I waited until he'd left the office, unable to move from the desk in my growing fury. When Mary came in, she found me holding the two ends of a pencil I'd just broken.

"What was that all about?" she asked.

"I think you should have taken that job in Springfield," I told her. "A week from now I may not have a practice in Northmont."

"What?"

"Apparently the medical society is going to look into Betty Willis's death next week. Wolfe thinks it was either a serious mistake or a mercy killing on my part."

"That's crazy, Sam!" I was too upset to realize until later that she'd used my first name. "Is he out to get you for some reason?"

"I don't know. We've never been especially friendly, but I'm not aware of any injury I've done him."

"Could Mrs. Willis have been poisoned by her niece or her husband?"

"I don't see how." I tried to think. "It had to be them, but I can't see how they did it."

Mary went to the file drawer, removed a folder, and read through it. "The records in Mrs. Willis's folder only seem to go back a year. What about before that?"

"Before—" Suddenly I remembered. I wondered how I could have forgotten it. "Before that she was Martin Wolfe's patient."

Mary raised her eyebrows.

"I'd known her only slightly. But shortly after Freda Ann and Nat came to live there, they decided she wasn't getting the finest treatment from Dr. Wolfe. Part of the problem was that he was president of the medical society and had so many civic duties it left him with almost no time for housecalls. After she broke her hip and became bedridden, they called me, and I agreed to take her on as a patient. But there was never any hard feeling over it with Dr. Wolfe.''

''Still, it might explain his present attitude,'' she said. ''There might be a lingering guilt at having abandoned her himself.''

All that day I thought about my relationship with the dead woman and everything that had happened in the farmhouse the previous morning. I'd solved dozens of bizarre puzzles in my time, but nothing had prepared me for this simple case of a woman poisoned under my very eyes. It dogged me as I saw to my other patients and made my hospital rounds.

Betty Willis's body was laid out at the Freedkin Funeral Parlor on Main Street, right on the town square. I called there on Wednesday, the second night of the wake, and then attended the funeral on Thursday morning. There were already people muttering about keeping the body only two days instead of the traditional three, accusing the Parkers of hurrying to get her into the ground.

As I studied Freda Ann and her husband across the grave that morning while the minister intoned the traditional prayers for the dead, it was difficult for me to imagine either of them as a murderer, and I wondered why they would have felt murder was necessary. Aunt Betty was a dying woman, and her condition had been worse that very morning. There was no need for anyone to kill her unless her will contained some obscure provision with a time limit.

Thinking of that, I spotted Seth Rogers at the edge of the circle of mourners. Seth was a well-known local attorney, much liked among Northmont's older residents, and it was a good guess that he was attending the funeral because he'd acted as attorney for the deceased. When the crowd started to disperse, I caught up with him, and after a few words of formal greeting I asked him directly.

''Yes, I handled her legal matters,'' he told me. His eyes behind thick wire-rimmed glasses seemed large and fishlike. ''Not that she ever had much work for me. A little tinkering with her will from time to time, that was about all.''

''When did she tinker with it most recently?''

''Oh, it must have been a year ago—before she broke her hip. She came over to the office to sign it, I remember that.''

''And you hadn't seen her since then?''

He smiled at me. ''You cross-examine like a lawyer, Sam. As

a matter of fact, I visited her just last Friday, three days before her death.''

"Could I ask the nature of your visit? I'm not asking you to be specific, just—"

"She wanted some advice about selling off a portion of the property. But she didn't pursue it at all. I gathered it was merely a possibility for some future time.''

We'd strolled down the knoll to his car, a flashy green Cadillac Sport Phaeton with sixteen cylinders and a white convertible top. Though in many ways I preferred my own red Mercedes, I had to admit a secret fondness for this massive beauty with its five thousand dollar pricetag. "Did she seem well when you saw her?'' I asked as he got behind the wheel of the car.

"As well as she'd been lately. Well enough to be sucking on hard candy all the time I was there.''

I remembered. "It was her one weakness. She always kept a bag of it on her night table. I couldn't complain, though. She was a good patient and generally did everything I told her to.''

Seth frowned at me and leaned out the car window. "Just between us, Sam, was she murdered?''

"I wish I knew, Seth,'' I told him. "I really do.''

All that day I was aware of gazes in the street, of whispered words as my familiar car drove past the center of town. The news was getting around that my conduct in Betty Willis's final illness was under investigation—by the medical society if not by the police. Back at the office, Mary confirmed how bad things were becoming. "Three of your patents for this afternoon and tomorrow called to cancel their appointments.''

"Did they give reasons?'' I asked her.

"Well, Mrs. Mason wasn't feeling well—''

"I guess we know the real reason, don't we, Mary? The word's getting around that Betty Willis was poisoned.''

Her expression was bleak. "Everyone at the hospital knows the autopsy results, and the word was bound to spread. What are you going to do?''

"Think about it,'' I told her. "I have the advantage of knowing I'm innocent. There has to have been some other cause of death.''

She sat down opposite me. "Let's go over it step by step, Sam. Is there any possibility someone could have substituted cyanide for the digitalis pills in your bag?''

"Not a chance. You know what they look like. The manufacturer's mark is on every one. It's not something a pharmacist could duplicate in his back room. Even if one of them had been poisoned, I shook it from a nearly full bottle of a hundred. I've examined the others, and they're perfect. No one could have known who'd get the poisoned one, or when."

"How about the Parkers? Were they in the room with you and Mrs. Willis?"

"Nat didn't come upstairs until after she was dead. Freda Ann stood near the door during my examination. The only time she approached the bed was to hand me the glass of water."

"And you're certain Mrs. Willis was really dead?"

"She was really dead, Mary. There was no pulse, no breathing, no heartbeat. And she couldn't have been faking it somehow because I never left the room until Sheriff Lens arrived."

"Then it has to be the water. The glass of water. It's the only way she could have been poisoned."

"Don't you think I thought of that? First of all, when most cyanide compounds are dissolved in water, they give off a distinctive odor. Second, the half empty glass was never out of my sight after she drank from it. Third, I took a sample of the water for testing and it was perfectly all right. So was the water her teeth were in."

The next patient—one who hadn't canceled—arrived then, and our ruminating came to an end.

I slept badly that night, expecting that what had happened so far was just the prelude to a growing storm.

On Friday morning, Mary told me there'd been two more cancellations. With some free hours ahead of me, I decided to drive out to the Willis place, my first visit since Monday's tragedy. It was a fine morning, sunny and warm, and Mary was already planning a Fourth of July picnic with some of the other nurses. It would be coming up the following Thursday, two days after the medical society met. I wondered if I'd have anything to celebrate.

At the Willis farm I found Nat Parker in the pumphouse, repairing a pipe that supplied well water to the living quarters. "Good to see you, doc," he said, wiping the grease from his hands. "Thanks for coming to the funeral yesterday."

"It was the least I could do. How's Freda Ann holding up?"

"Oh, it's a bit hard on her, but I think we both know it was for the best. The old lady wasn't doing nobody any good wasting away up there in that bed. Whatever you done, I thank you for it.''

"Whatever I—? Look here, Nat, I didn't do a thing to hasten her end. I certainly didn't poison her, if that's what you're getting at!''

"No, no, of course not. I just meant whatever sort of accident happened. We take no stock in this talk that's goin' around town. You were a good doctor to her. She always spoke highly of you. She told us once you done more for her than old Doc Wolfe ever did.''

"Did he ever come around to see her after I took her on as a patient?''

"Heck, no. At least I never seen him out here.''

I went up to the house and found Freda Ann washing out some things in the kitchen. "There's lots to be done,'' she said, brushing the dark hair back from her forehead. "I've been cleaning out her bedroom and closets, washing the curtains and bedding.''

"Has Sheriff Lens been out to see you?''

"He came by again last evening, full of questions. He still thinks my aunt was poisoned.''

"She was, Freda Ann. There's no doubt about it.''

"I don't know how it could have happened with you sittin' there right by her bed!''

"I'm sure that's what the sheriff is trying to determine. Tell me something. Was it just you who took care of your aunt, or did your husband sometimes tend to her needs, too?''

"Are you kidding? Nat stayed as far away from her as he could. He wanted to put her in an old folks' home, but I figured she was leaving the place to us in return for taking care of her and we had to do something to earn it.''

"Have you spoken to the attorney since her death?''

"Mr. Rogers? Yes, he telephoned to arrange a meeting in his office. Nat and I are going in on Monday morning.''

"Any problems?''

"No, I just have to sign some papers. The property come to me, along with a small bank account and some stock she owned.''

"I wonder if I could see her bedroom again. I'm just trying to get clear in my own mind what happened.''

"Certainly.'' She led the way upstairs to the second floor. "I want you to know that Nat and I both think this business of the medical society holding a hearing next week is ridiculous. We have every confidence in you.''

"I appreciate that.''

I stood for a moment in the doorway, studying the bare bed and the scant furnishings. Without curtains, the morning sun streamed in the window, bathing everything in a golden glow. I sat on the same cane-backed chair I'd sat in the previous Monday, thinking about all that had happened since then. "Was Seth Rogers here last week?" I asked Freda Ann.

She nodded. "On Friday. He stayed about a half hour."

"Were you in the room while they talked?"

"Heavens, no. She always kept her legal and financial affairs strictly to herself."

I walked to the window and looked out, shielding my eyes from the sun. I could see Nat out in the yard, carrying his tools from the pumphouse. Then I turned and looked at the bare bedside table. "Was she buried with her teeth in?"

"Of course." Freda Ann looked at me strangely. "What an odd question to ask."

The weekend dragged on. I had two patients Saturday morning, and when I'd seen them both I stayed in the office going over Betty Willis's records. Mary poked her head in once and asked if I'd be attending the Fourth of July picnic. "We've got about twenty people so far," she told me.

"I don't know, Mary. Right now I don't think my heart would be in it."

She understood. "I'll ask you again later," she said.

The next time the office door opened it was Sheriff Lens. "I was hopin' I'd find you here, doc."

"What's up, sheriff?"

He came in and sat down. "I'm still workin' on the Willis case. Folks want some action, but I don't know what to do. Should I arrest the niece, Mrs. Parker?"

"Your only alternative is to arrest me, sheriff."

"Don't talk foolish, doc!"

"Martin Wolfe doesn't think it's so foolish."

"Don't worry about him. He's just a lot of talk."

"If the medical society believes him, they could take away my practice."

"They don't think you murdered her, doc. They just think you might have made a mistake of some kind."

"For a doctor, it's pretty much the same thing. If I made a mistake, I murdered her."

Sheriff Lens took out a package of chewing tobacco and opened it as he spoke. "I been thinking about it and comin' up with all these crazy theories—the sort you'd think of."

"For instance?"

"Well, maybe Mrs. Parker or her husband poisoned the old lady's false teeth."

I had to smile at that one. But would the truth, if I ever discovered it, be any less bizarre? "Cyanide kills instantly, sheriff—within seconds. She didn't have her teeth in her mouth all the time I was there. And if she'd been poisoned before I arrived, she'd have been dead already."

"What went into her mouth while you were there?"

"The digitalis pill and a little water." I remembered something else. "And my thermometer. I took her temperature."

"Could someone have gotten to it and poisoned it?"

"Not a chance. I don't even carry it in my bag. It's right here in a little case inside my coat, with my pen and pencil."

"Well—"

"Believe me, sheriff, I've been all over the possibilities already. Betty Willis couldn't have been poisoned, but she was."

"What are you going to do, doc?" Sheriff Lens asked.

"I'll attend the hearing on Tuesday, of course. I'll abide by their verdict."

"If they say you can't practice here—"

"There are other places besides Northmont." I managed a weak grin. "Maybe I'll become a veterinarian. They might let me treat animals."

"Doc!"

"Go on, sheriff. I'm only kidding."

"I have to appear at the hearing on Tuesday. I been tryin' to trace any local purchases of cyanide compounds, but that's tough to do. A lot of photographic chemicals, like reducing or toning agents, have cyanide bases. People have little darkrooms at home for developing pictures, and they go out and buy the stuff over the counter."

"They can even buy the stuff if they *don't* have darkrooms," I pointed out. "And the cyanide can be easily extracted."

He still looked unhappy. "What should I tell them on Tuesday, doc?"

"The truth," I reassured him. "It's the only thing you can do."

Only one of my patients showed up on Monday, and I noticed people had stopped whispering when they saw me in the street. They didn't need to anymore—everyone knew I was a suspect in Mrs. Willis's death.

"I'm going with you," Mary announced Tuesday morning as I prepared to leave for the hearing.

"Nonsense—someone has to take care of the office."

Her clear blue eyes sparkled. "I've already arranged for one of the girls to answer the phone. I'm going along, Sam."

At that moment I had too much on my mind to argue with her. I merely shook my head in resignation and started for the door. She followed along and slid into the seat of the Mercedes next to me.

The hearing was scheduled for ten thirty, and we were there early. The medical society served a three-county area, renting office space in the new Northmont Bank Building. A conference room had been set aside for the hearing, and when I entered I saw that Dr. Wolfe and two other physicians I barely knew were already seated at the end of a long table.

Wolfe gave me a half friendly smile. "Take a seat anywhere, Dr. Hawthorne. I believe you know Dr. Black and Dr. Tobias. They're representing the other counties in our group."

We shook hands all around, and I introduced Mary. "This is my nurse, Miss Best."

Wolfe cleared his throat. "A pleasure to see you again, Miss Best, but this isn't a public hearing. I'll have to ask you to wait outside."

Mary retreated with some reluctance, and I faced the three of them alone. "What questions do you gentlemen have?" I asked.

"This is an informal hearing, not a trial," Wolfe told me. "First off, let me say we've all admired your dedication and high visibility in Northmont during the years you've been practicing here, doctor. I'm certain no one believes for a moment that any deliberate act was involved in the poisoning of Mrs. Willis. We simply want to determine if her death was the result of some preventable error on the part of yourself or someone else."

"There was no error," I insisted. "I gave her digitalis, the drug I intended to give her. The autopsy found it in her stomach."

"We plan to call two others to speak to the circumstances of this tragedy—Freda Ann Parker and Sheriff Lens. Do you have any objection?"

"None whatever," I said.

We listened to Freda Ann tell her story, about phoning my office when her aunt's condition seemed so bad, about my arrival, and about fetching the glass of water for me. They asked very few questions. Then it was my turn. While Freda Ann took a seat against the wall, I told them what I knew of Betty Willis's condition on Monday morning a week ago, of my decision to treat her with digitalis, and of her sudden seizure and death.

"You knew immediately that she'd been poisoned?" Dr. Wolfe asked.

"Yes. The odor of bitter almonds was unmistakable. I witnessed a similar poisoning a few years ago."

"And you told Mrs. Parker to telephone Sheriff Lens?"

"That's correct."

Wolfe held a whispered conversation with the other two doctors, and they decided to call the sheriff in for his story. He entered the room with seeming reluctance, glancing at me as he took his place at the table. His questioning was brief as he told of receiving the call and arriving at the house to find me still waiting in the bedroom with the dead woman.

When he'd finished, Dr. Wolfe said, "That'll be all for the moment, sheriff. Dr. Hawthorne, could we review the evidence with you?"

"Certainly."

Sheriff Lens took a seat against the wall near Freda Ann Parker as Wolfe turned to me with another attempt at a smile. "Let me quickly review the facts of the case, Dr. Hawthorne. Please correct me if I'm wrong. When you arrived at the house, you found Mrs. Willis confined to bed as she had been for the past year. Your diagnosis was that she needed a heart stimulant but otherwise was in no danger of death. You were alone with the patient during the examination, except that Mrs. Parker came to stand in the doorway. She brought a glass of water to wash down the pill you prescribed, and almost immediately Betty Willis expired, with an odor of bitter almonds pointing to the presence of a cyanide compound. Sheriff Lens was summoned, and you remained with the body until his arrival. The unfinished glass of water was never out of your sight, and when it was later tested, it was found to be free of any poison. Is that a fair summary of the events?"

"It is," I conceded.

The other doctors consulted again, then Wolfe said, "I think we have all the facts. There will be a ten minute recess."

The three men remained at the table while the rest of us filed out. Mary was waiting in the hall. "What happened?"

"They're considering the verdict," I told her.

"What do you think?"

I patted her arm. "It doesn't look too good."

Sheriff Lens joined us, nervously unfolding his package of chewing tobacco. "I don't see how they can do anything to you, doc. They got no evidence. All they're saying is that they don't know how she died, so you musta been responsible."

I was annoyed at everyone just then, even the sheriff. "Where did you pick up this habit of chewing tobacco all of a sudden?"

He put it away, looking chagrined. "Well, Sam, I was just tryin' to relax."

Dr. Wolfe appeared at the door to motion me inside. The others remained in the hallway.

When I was seated at the table, he began to speak. "Dr. Hawthorne, as I stated at the beginning, this is not a trial but an inquiry. Nevertheless, we have found sufficient circumstantial evidence that the death of Betty Willis could only have been caused by the mistaken administration of—"

Chewing tobacco.

I was remembering Sheriff Lens and his chewing tobacco. It was like chewing tobacco, in a way. The flavor mattered more than anything else.

"Excuse me for interrupting, Dr. Wolfe," I said, "but I've just thought of something."

"Unless it has a bearing on Mrs. Willis's death—"

"It does."

"Proceed, then."

I leaned forward on the desk. "Betty Willis had one small vice. She always kept a bag of hard candy next to her bed. It was there as recently as the Friday before her death, when her lawyer, Seth Rogers, paid a visit, but it wasn't there on Monday when I went to see her. Only a glass of water with her false teeth was on the bedside table."

"If her teeth were out, she couldn't have eaten anything anyway," Wolfe pointed out.

"She could have had a piece of hard candy. She could simply have sucked on it and let it dissolve in her mouth. And that's how she was poisoned. The cyanide was injected into the center of the hard candy. It was dissolving into her mouth all the time I examined her without my knowing it. When it dissolved enough to release the cyanide, she died."

"Do you have any proof of this theory?"

"The absence of the traditional bag of hard candy is proof enough for me. Freda Ann Parker *had* to remove it after Mrs. Willis took a piece of it because she'd probably poisoned it and couldn't risk my examining it."

"Why Freda Ann and not her husband?"

"She's the one who tended to Betty. She would have offered the candy, and only she could have removed the bag. Nat was rarely in the room, and his presence would have been suspicious. And it was Freda Ann who phoned and urged me to come out because the woman was dying. She wanted Betty to die in my presence, to re-move any blame from herself. She didn't realize the odor of the poison would be immediately obvious to me."

"Why would she do such a thing if Mrs. Willis was dying anyway?"

"That's just the point—she wasn't dying. Her condition had been fairly stable, and Seth Rogers found her as well as usual on Friday. His visit, on a minor matter, is what triggered the fatal events. Freda Ann must have feared her aunt was about to change her will. She knew it hadn't been done yet because there were no witnesses to sign any document, but she decided to tell me that Betty Willis was dying, and then make the lie come true. Maybe Betty asked the lawyer out there to frighten her deliberately, never knowing it would lead to her murder."

Dr. Wolfe looked perplexed. "How will we ever prove this?"

"I suggest we begin by calling Sheriff Lens in to our meeting," I said. "It was him and his chewing tobacco that made me remember Betty Willis and her hard candy."

"The rest of it was easier than I could have hoped for," Dr. Sam Hawthorne concluded. "Freda Ann had given her husband the bag of hard candy to burn with the rubbish, but he was suspicious and held it out. He turned it over to Sheriff Lens, and we found poison in four other pieces. Freda Ann received a long prison term—I don't recollect what ever happened to Nat.

"The good folks of Northmont more than made up to me for their suspicions during that terrible week. I went to Mary Best's picnic on the Fourth of July, and it was a happy day without the hint of a crime. In fact, it wasn't until late that summer—but, no—I have to save something for next time."

POOR DUMB MOUTHS

by BILL CRENSHAW

"I tell you that which you yourselves do know,
Show you sweet Caesar's wounds, poor, poor dumb mouths.
And bid them speak for me."

Julius Caesar, *III.ii*

"Same deal, Adam. Five bucks an hour, ten hours tops. Anything over ten's a freebie." McMorton thumbed the folder with a thumb unnaturally soft and pink, a thumb streaked from pinching the moist end of his unnaturally brown and foul cigar.

Adameus Clay took the folder from him delicately and with some disgust, though it didn't show on his face. Disgust rarely showed on his face. He almost always appeared to be smiling, even in his sleep. It was a physiological quirk that he had often regretted, though he had to admit that in the long run it had probably done him more good than harm. But the run had been long indeed, and just when the end was in sight, five years until early retirement, along came the twins and . . .

"Adam. You hearin' me?"

"Of course, Marvyn."

"Well, don't space out on me, hear? I mean, brother-in-law or no brother-in-law, you space out, you're through. Jiminy. Like I was saying, this one shouldn't be more than a four hour job. An hour with the beneficiary, an hour on the reports, an hour writing it all up. I'm giving you an extra hour for fumbles." McMorton leaned far back in his swivel chair, which Clay thought a dangerous thing to do, given all that bulk, and somehow grinned around the cigar clamped between yellow-tinted teeth. Clay knew what was coming because the same thing came at this time every time. "But this one's

189

so easy," said McMorton, "that even a Ph.D. could do it." Then
he laughed, the one sound that by itself could twist Clay's face into
a reasonable facsimile of disgust. "Well, good to see ya and all,
Adam, but I'm a busy man, busy man. I don't get paid to sit on my
duff like you high foreheads do."

Clay bit back a torrent of abuse, thinking particularly of Kent's
torrent against the wormy Oswald in Act II of *King Lear*. To all
appearances, however, he was still smiling vaguely. He forced his
next words out with difficulty. "Uh, Marvyn, I need more money?"
Somehow it came out as a question.

"Yeah, so do I. Five bucks. Period."

"You pay other claims investigators more."

"*Other* claims investigators? You an investigator? Look, Adam,
old bean, old chap, I'm doing you a favor, right? Gift horse, right? I
mean, I'm going out on a limb here. Ever hear of nepa, of nepa . . ."

"Nepotism." Clay shuddered at the implications of the words and
closed his eyes against the sight of the primary implication and its
fat cigar.

"Right. I could lose my job."

Clay could see that McMorton was about to laugh again, so he
stood up quickly. "Well, thank you anyway, Marvyn. My best to
Ruth. I'd better be . . ."

But it was too late, and it was beyond laughter and into guffawing.
"Of course, if you find fraud here"—McMorton broke up completely
for some long seconds—"fraud here, Acme Home and Casualty will
pay you fifteen percent of a hundred and eighty G's. That's . . .
that's . . ."

"Twenty-seven thousand dollars," murmured Clay wistfully.

"Yeah." Guffaw turned into bellow. "Fat chance."

Which was the term Adameus Clay used to refer to his brother-
in-law from that moment on.

Clay felt guilty all the way to the hospital.

He should be grateful, he knew, and he felt guilty that he wasn't
more grateful, but it was hard to be grateful to Fat Chance. He had
even calmly and rationally drawn up a list of all the reasons that he
should be grateful—his brother-in-law was providing extra money,
was letting him work at a job for which he had no training, had not
let age stand in the way. But for every reason to be grateful, there
was an equally compelling reason to punch Fat Chance's potato

nose—you call that money, no one needs training for this, age deserves some respect.

"Oh, well," he sighed as he eased into the parking lot, "make virtue of necessity."

But it was hard to make virtue of this. He hated what he was about to do. After carefully wiping all traces of Fat Chance's smeared thumbprints off the folder with a handkerchief that he promptly threw away, Clay had scanned the summary report for main points. Auto accident six weeks ago at dusk. Bridge abutment. One dead, Susan Cannon, good but not bestselling writer of inspirational novels. One survivor, husband and beneficiary, Henderson Cannon. Multiple injuries—broken bones, dislocations, contusions, lacerations, punctures. A man severely injured and not yet out of the hospital, a man undoubtedly still grieving, a man to whom a hundred and eighty thousand dollars probably meant nothing at this point in his life. And here I am, he thought, about to go through the pointless and cruel exercise of quizzing him about the accident just so the proper forms can be filled out in double triplicate. Clay had trouble just talking to strangers, but this kind of invasion . . .

He realized that he was still sitting in the car, engine running, trying to avoid the inevitable. For thirty seconds more he considered the possibility of driving back to Fat Chance's office and tossing the file on his desk in a gesture of righteous contempt. Then he heard what he feared was a new rattling cough from the engine and immediately cut off the ignition. "Necessity is indeed the mother," he sighed as he got out and locked up carefully, checking the doors twice. The maroon hood of his 1948 Studebaker shone with rich depths. He had owned the car for thirty-five years, had spent embarrassing sums maintaining and restoring her, had named her Brunhilde. He needed money, but even to think of selling her now . . . he wiped at an invisible spot on the paint with a new handkerchief, then headed for St. Ebenezer's visitors' entrance, pausing once behind his car to make sure he had lined it up precisely between the lines of the parking space.

He finally found Room 5501. "East Wing," the orderly had said with a faint smirk. West Wing it was, last room in West Wing. Clay had walked the entire lengths of the two fifth floor corridors to find that out, and now he was sweating slightly and unpleasantly. He pulled down his coat, straightened his tie, took a deep breath, and knocked softly.

No answer, but the sounds of the television filtered through the door. He knocked again and pushed the door open just enough to put his head into the room. Cannon was sitting up in his bed, still bandaged in places, sections of the *Wall Street Journal* spread around him. He was giggling at the television. On the screen the coyote was riding a rocket into a wall of red sandstone while the roadrunner beep-beeped across the desert highway. Another giggle.

Clay cleared his throat. "Mr. Cannon?" He said it twice more before Cannon heard and turned to him, apparently embarrassed and angry as he killed the sound of the television with his remote control.

"Why don't you try knocking?" he growled.

"I did. I'm sorry." Clay gave himself a mental kick in the pants for the apology. It was like saying "Thank you, officer," to the policeman who wrote you a ticket. He had done that once, too. "I'm sorry to disturb you, that is," he added, trying to make some sense out of it. "I'm Adameus Clay, a claims representative from . . ."

Cannon giggled again. "What kind of name is Adameus?"

Clay shrugged and spread his hands as if in apology, looking for all the world as if he were smiling. "You may call me Adam."

"Claims rep, huh? Well, where the hell have you been? I knew the lawyer threat would work. You guys are trying to stiff me."

"No, Mr. Cannon, let me assure you that we are not. And please accept my apologies for the delay." Now I'm apologizing for Fat Chance, he thought. This just isn't worth it. "May I sit down?"

"Yes, you may sit down, Pops, but not in here. You go sit in accounts receivable and straighten up this bill."

Clay was frozen with his hand on the chair he had been pulling out, his unsmile transfixed as if nailed to his face. "I'm not sure I follow you, Mr. Cannon."

Cannon sank back onto his mountain of pillows. "Another nerd. You'd better follow me. I didn't pay outrageous premiums just to have you dance away when I have an accident. I know my rights, Pops. When I buy health insurance, I expect it to pay off when I need it."

"Mr. Cannon, I'm here about life insurance, not health. Your late wife's policy, sir. My condolences." Clay congratulated himself for maintaining his composure.

Cannon looked blank for a moment. You're not from Mountain Valley Mutual?"

"No, sir. I'm from Acme."

"Oh. *Oh.* Well, why didn't you say so, Pops? Those guys at

Mountain Valley haven't paid one penny on my bill here, and it's a bill, let me tell you."

Clay was suddenly in a hurry just to get it done and get out. "I hate to intrude on your hour of grief, Mr. Cannon, but I'm afraid I have a few questions to ask you."

"You insurance people are all alike, you know? Here I'm thinking that you might be ready to hand over the check, in person even, but no, you snivel in here with phony condolences and more questions. Is it about the accident?"

Clay still stood by the chair. "Yes, I'm afraid so."

"Forget it, Pops. Get out. I don't want to see that little balding head poke around my door again unless it's preceded by a hand with a check in it. I've been over that accident a dozen times. You've got reports, the police have reports, Mountain Valley has reports, all God's children got reports, and they've all got the same bottom line. I want my money or I really will sue."

Clay didn't care if he did sue. He might enjoy seeing Fat Chance suffer a bit. But he did care about his hair, or what was left of his hair, especially with the twins. When they were twelve, he would be seventy, and he wanted at least to *look* young for them, but his hair had perversely begun thinning faster this year. So when Cannon made a reference to his little balding head, Clay looked almost angry, which meant he was furious. "There are some details, Mr. Cannon, that we need to check out." It was the only thing he could think of to sweep to his revenge.

"That's it, Pops. You're sued. You and Everest and everybody. Take your four eyes and get out of here."

"See you in court, Cannon," Clay said before stalking from the room. He'd heard it in a movie once. It sounded good now. But in the elevator it sounded not so good, and he did pour out Kent's torrent of abuse, but he aimed it at himself, muttering in spite of the quizzical faces behind him. So much for extra money, he thought. Well, at least when Fat Chance fires me, I can tell him off. So there is a good side to every situation.

But when he found that someone's bumper had taken a two inch wide strip of paint off the driver's door before putting a double-fist sized dent in Brunhilde's front fender, he was convinced that the only side this situation had was an underside.

When the call came from Fat Chance two days later, it wasn't at all what Clay was expecting. Fat Chance wanted to know where the report was. No, Cannon hadn't called him, why should he? Well, being sorry wasn't good enough. The report was on his desk by Friday or Adam could pick up pocket change someplace else.

Clay was unaccountably pleased. He had expected to be fired and was in part looking forward to it, but now he found himself eager for the second chance. And secretly he was glad for the excuse to put aside his writing, which he could scarcely admit he was doing, even to himself. He thought his short fiction was good; publishers didn't. So now he was trying to write a hot pink romantic novel under a pseudonym, but he found the obligatory sex scenes embarrassing or amusing, and what he wrote, as he himself recognized the morning after, had all the seductiveness of a commencement address. To electrify the scenes, he was researching heaving bosoms, firm backsides, and the allure of the water- or sweat-drenched body on television commercials, and as long as he wrote exactly what he saw, the passages did seem to have some juice, but any embellishment on his part was viciously satirical. The need for money drove him on, but his pseudonym was Maress Beard, an anagram of "embarassed." The novel's title was *Love Me Now, My Love*. Any excuse to put it aside was welcomed. Even Fat Chance.

So Clay for the first time approached his assignment with some eagerness. He wanted the paperwork done double quick now, and he would put in for three and a half hours even though the work would cost him six easy, just to stay on Fat Chance's good side. He'd had *sort* of an interview with Cannon; he had accident reports, insurance applications, even the newspaper account of the accident, so he could fill out most of the forms and fudge what he didn't know. He told himself that this was all a formality anyway. Acme would pay off, but only by the numbers.

Clay dropped the manuscript of *Love Me Now, My Love* into the bottom drawer and spread Acme's paperwork across his desk. He'd have to start all over, read thoroughly this time. He began with the ambulance report and was struck again by the conglomeration of Cannon's injuries, wincing at each cold detail. The emergency room write-up was even worse. He put both reports aside. He'd get to them later.

He picked up Acme's own information, beginning with the application for Mrs. Cannon's insurance. It was dull reading, mostly statistical, the have-you-ever-had, is-there-a-history-of variety, but he read line by line, detail by detail, unable to break his scholarly approach to serious reading even for this. When he finished, he found himself chewing on two of the details—the policy was six months old; there were no other life policies on Mrs. Cannon with other companies.

Mountain? he thought, staring off blankly. Mountain? Something about Cannon and a mountain? Mountain Valley, of course, but there was something else. As he thought of Cannon, he found himself running his fingers through his thinning hair and he was suddenly angry. "Everest," he said aloud. Didn't Cannon say something about Everest? And wasn't that an insurance company? Life insurance or health?

He found Everest Insurance ("The Pinnacle of Protection") in the Yellow Pages. Even if Cannon had lied on his insurance application to Acme about not having other life policies, would that give Acme grounds to negate the policy? And if it did, did Cannon deserve that kind of treatment from him? "Vengeance is petty, Adameus," he said as he finished dialing, but he didn't hang up.

He didn't get far, either. He could almost see the sneer on the secretary's face when she said, "We don't just give out information on clients to any Joe who calls, y'know, bub." She hung up before she heard his apology. Then he was angry again. Rudeness made him angry. There were no decent standards left. What had happened to courtesy, to respect? He called back. The same secretary answered.

"Hello," said Clay, lowering his voice and rounding his vowels, "I'd like to speak to someone about taking out a group health insurance policy. I run a small business, fourteen employees, and we're interested in . . ."

"I'm sorry, sir," she answered in a voice distinctly more polite now, "but we don't carry health. Now if your company needs life or fire or casualty . . ."

No, he told her, and thank you. She told him to have a nice day.

So, he thought. No health. Acme's file showed the health policy at Mountain Valley, the company Cannon had mentioned. Maybe he meant a man named Everest. He called Mountain Valley and asked to speak to Mr. Everest. No one by that name. Just to be sure, he called Acme and Everest, asked both the same question, got the same answer. So perhaps Cannon *had* meant Everest Insurance, and perhaps he *did* have a life policy on his wife there. And maybe with other companies, too. For a moment Clay entertained the thought of murder, a diabolical plot to get rich from his wife's apparently accidental death. He imagined calling every insurance company in the area and finding that Cannon had a huge policy on his wife at each one. "Pops" brings murderer to justice. More important, Adameus

Clay makes better than a year's salary in a week. Invest ten thousand dollars each for the twins now and they'd be able to go to college even if he were . . .

"Cut it out, Adameus," he muttered. "Five dollars an hour and you're being Walter Mitty here." But he went back to the police report anyway.

It was gruesome. The car had hit the bridge abutment almost head on, impact on the passenger side. The car was virtually sheared in half. Woman apparently dead on impact, thrown through the windshield into the concrete pillar. Male driver wearing seat belt, multiple injuries. There were no skid marks. Investigating officer says mechanism of accident consistent with driver falling asleep at the wheel and drifting straight into abutment. Theory backed up later by victim interview: Victim claims to remember driving, then to remember waking up in hospital. Feels he fell asleep at the wheel.

There was more, but Clay wanted the reports he had seen earlier, the ambulance and emergency room reports with their lists of injuries. He found them. For the woman, no life support given at the scene. Man had to be extricated from the car with heavy tools and "jaws," whatever they were. The injuries were listed more specifically on the emergency room report, and Adam had to reach back into his own college physiology class to remember what all the words meant—open fracture of the left clavicle, fracture of the right olecranon process, anterior dislocation of right shoulder, fracture of ribs eight through ten left side, lacerated liver and spleen, ruptured bladder, crushed metacarpals on right hand, broken nose, laceration of scalp, face, and neck, crushed right ankle. Clay shuddered and fought nausea, almost feeling the pain in each part of his own body as he read the report. He rubbed his elbow fitfully.

No, he thought, there's no murder here. Death was riding too close for murder.

He finished filling out the report as quickly as he could.

The next day, before his first class, he took the report to Acme. He found himself badly shaken by the descriptions of the accident and injuries. He'd had nightmares all night, filled with screaming brakes, splintering glass, twisting metal, bodies flying to pieces, blood. It took him fifteen minutes more than usual to get to Acme, certain that every other driver was out to get him.

He gave the ungrateful Fat Chance his work, took his seventeen dollars and fifty cents without grace, got back into Brunhilde, and crept to the university, parking at the far side of the lot. He usually ate lunch at home, but today he would have chanced the Ptomaine Tower, as the students called the dining hall, rather than drive again. But the twins needed food, too, so he reluctantly climbed back into Brunhilde, stood his briefcase in the passenger seat, buckled in, and took his chances in the streets. At the Winn Dixie he parked as far away from the other cars as he could, and even though he spent his seventeen fifty and then some, he had only one bag to show for it, full of junior meats and strained prunes and the like, and the bag was heavy, so he was tired and irritated and sweating by the time he balanced it in front of his briefcase and strapped himself in again.

Driving was worse than ever. He felt absolutely paranoid until he finally saw his house two blocks away, and he was just feeling safe when some idiot in a jeep with a bumper made out of steel pipe jerked away from the curb and stalled out right in front of him. By all the laws of physics, he knew he couldn't stop in time, but his reactions were fast and instinctive—he slammed on the brakes, cut the wheel to the left, flung his right arm to the grocery bag, and hit the jeep.

He realized that someone was asking him if he were okay. He looked around. The jeep was mashed into his front end, steam hissed from his radiator, jars of baby food were on the dash, the floor, in his lap, strained prunes and tapioca pudding oozing into the carpet. He shook his head. His head hurt. "People in the jeep okay?" he asked.

"We're fine," said the teenager with the unbuttoned shirt at his window. "Are you okay?"

Pain shot through his right shoulder and elbow and lodged in his hand. He looked down at his hand and realized that something might be broken. Slowly he turned to face the anxious boy. "Eureka," he said, his eyes watering with pain even as he smiled.

They gave him something for the pain after they took X-rays and punched, kneaded, prodded, and probed. He was glad that Ginger was in the emergency room with him, even more glad that she had ridden with him in the ambulance. He had been near hysteria, not from the pain or fear, but from the absurdity of it all—two blocks from home, his house in sight, his precious car bleeding water and anti-freeze and spouting steam, and him immobilized by the idiots from the jeep. He wanted to get home, to see the twins, to tell Ginger he was all right. He heard his own voice babbling, saw his left hand pointing to his house. "No sir, you stay right there, we've called an ambulance, don't move, you might hurt yourself, stay put, sir." A girl was crying somewhere. His frustration was blinding. Finally he made someone understand and someone ran to his house and got his wife. Only then had the sense of helplessness faded.

Now here in the hospital lobby it was back again, only slightly dulled by the painkiller. He held the phone away from his ear to protect his eardrum from Fat Chance's howling. "You're a real pip, Adam, you know that?" The voice carried far in the room. Heads turned. "I know you're serious because you don't have a sense of humor. And if you're serious, you're nuts. Now why don't you go home, go to bed, and . . ."

"Marvyn, have you still got the report?"

"It's right here on my desk. I'm not touching it until Monday morning. I've got a big meeting now, Adam old chap, so I'm going to hang . . ."

"Just look at the injuries, okay? Just open the file and look. Don't they strike you as odd? Marvyn? Are you there, Marvyn?"

"You're off your doodle, Adam. You're bonkers. Goodbye."

Hearing the dial tone was something of a relief.

"He didn't believe you," said Ginger. It was not a question.

Adam didn't really respond to her remark until they were in the cab, and even then he talked as much to keep his mind off the fact that he was on the streets again as to discuss the problem.

"Well," he said. "Well."

"Well?" said Ginger, teasing.

"Well, he's probably right, Ginger. He deals with this sort of thing daily. I don't know anything about it. Imagine my reaction if he was to tell me I had mistranslated a section of *Beowulf*."

"Were."

"What?"

"You said 'if he was,' Adam. You don't make that kind of mistake unless you're upset. Try to relax."

He lapsed into a long silence. Defeat settled like dust on his shoulders. He'd smashed his car. He'd hurt himself and frightened his wife. He'd missed his afternoon classes. He was underpaid, he hadn't saved, he couldn't sell his writing. He was too old to drive, to teach, to think. There wasn't enough money, wasn't enough time, wasn't enough anything. And he'd made a fool of himself in front of Fat Chance—of all people.

"And I use the word loosely," he mumbled.

"What?" said Ginger.

"What?" answered Adam, looking up suddenly as if he'd been caught sleeping in class.

"What did you say, Adam?"

"Damn," he said, surprising even himself. "Driver, take us to 2607 Craig Road, please."

Dark eyes squinted in the rearview mirror. "That okay by you, lady?"

"Yes," said Ginger, and they sat in silence until the cab came to a halt.

"Wait," Clay ordered as he got out of the cab. The driver shrugged and lit a bent cigarette.

Just act as if you know what you're doing, Clay thought as he lengthened his step into what he hoped was a purposeful stride toward Fat Chance's office.

"Marvyn still in, Miss Andress?" he asked almost casually as he passed the desk and reached for the office door.

Miss Andress half rose as if to stop him. "No, Mr. Clay. He's gone for the day."

"Fine," he said as he opened the door. "He said he'd leave a folder on his desk," and with that he was in the office. It wasn't a lie exactly, he told himself, any more than Marvyn's meeting. But at the sight of the desk he felt his confidence drain again. It was chaos, paper piled everywhere. Not a square centimeter of desk top was visible. He walked around the desk and stood at Fat Chance's chair, his eyes dancing furiously for the report. The secretary appeared in the doorway.

"Ah, Miss Andress. Now I understand why my brother-in-law requires such a competent secretary." He waved his left hand vaguely, looking helpless. "If you'd be so kind . . ."

Miss Andress allowed a smile to twitch at her lips. "Exactly what do you need, Mr. Clay?"

"The Cannon file, please."

She plucked it from the mess with a dextrous flick of a magician's wrist.

"You amaze me, Miss Andress. Marvyn would be lost without you, I'm sure."

Another twitch encouraged him.

"Indeed," he continued, "I dare say that he is often lost despite you?" He made it lilt like a question, this time intentionally, and received a genuine smile in return.

"I'll pretend I didn't hear that, Mr. Clay."

"I'll pretend I didn't say it, Miss Andress."

They allowed themselves a small laugh as they left the office.

"I hope you don't have much you need to do, Mr. Clay. Those reports can be so tedious."

"Not much, Miss Andress." Just the name of the ambulance attendant, he thought. "Good day."

He was beaming as he got back into the cab. "Home, James," he announced.

The driver jerked his thumb at his I.D. "That's Jimbo, Mac."

"Adam," said Ginger as she reached for his hand, "are you all right?"

"All right?" He kissed her cheek. "I was terrific."

It didn't take long for Adam to feel his confidence drain yet once more. The ambulance that had picked up the Cannons was based in DeWitt, in the next county, a rural county with miles of narrow country roads twisting away from the interstate. Too far for a cab. That meant hiring a sitter. It also meant riding in Ginger's '72 Volkswagen Beetle on those roads where traffic came at you just inches away, and the Bug lacked for Adam the comforting dead weight armor of excess steel. He spent a restless night and decided finally to go, shame winning over fear, because Hogan Lewis, the EMT he had reached, had changed his plans in order to meet with Adam the next morning, and Adam was too embarrassed to call back and cancel.

He survived the drive by concentrating on what he was after and on trying to discover exactly how he had gotten himself into this situation. Why was it so important to pursue this? Cannon's insult? Fat Chance's laughter? This is idiocy, he thought. He had no experience in these matters. Surely he could accept Fat Chance's opinion as valid. Good Lord, he thought suddenly. Is it that I'm seeking Marvyn's approval? The idea horrified him.

"Do you like your brother?" he asked, then realized how strange it must sound since he had said nothing at all for the last fifteen minutes.

Ginger kept her eyes on the road. "Really beautiful country, don't you think?"

"Which one of you is the changeling?"

She smiled and patted his knee.

What he wanted, he finally decided, was a second opinion. He wanted to understand the mechanism of injury.

"Oh, yes, I remember that accident well," said Lewis over a second cup of coffee at his kitchen table. "We're a volunteer service in this county, Mr. Clay. Not enough action around here to support a paid service. We don't see as much as the city units do, thank God. That accident was one of the worst. I remember it too well."

"Did anything . . . do you think . . ." Adam broke off and stared at his coffee, glancing first to Ginger at his right before looking back at Lewis. "I don't know quite what to ask, Mr. Lewis. I've read the reports and the injuries strike me as unusual. But I'm not an expert in these matters."

"Neither am I. Yeah, lots of injuries, bad ones. But it was a bad wreck. You can't believe what the car looked like."

Adam swallowed and found it hard to swallow. "I'm sorry," he said. "This must be unpleasant for you."

"It is," said Lewis. "Not real good for you, either, from the way you look."

Adam felt that Lewis was waiting for something from him, but had no idea what it was. "I imagine these ambulance calls can be very trying."

Lewis shifted back in his chair. "Can be."

I'm losing him, thought Adam. What am I doing wrong? "Lots of blood sometimes?" He could think of nothing else to say, but that sounded terrible even as he said it.

"Sometimes," said Lewis.

Ginger's hand brushed Lewis's arm with the lightest of touches. "Mr. Lewis, I guess we should have made it clear that whatever suspicions we have are directed at the occupants of the car only." She met Lewis's eyes for a half second before adding, "Could I have some more coffee, please?" and she reached for the pot.

Lewis leaned forward, put his elbows on the table, and stared into Adam's eyes. "Not that time," he said. "Not *enough* blood that time."

"What do you mean?"

"Mr. Clay, you've got to picture what things are like. It's just getting dark. Winter then, remember. I'm sitting down right here, halfway through my supper, when the call comes in. We get out there, it's really dark, but there's headlights and floodlights, the cops' blue lights flashing, our red and whites flashing, big clouds of exhaust fumes, and there's what might have been a car and what might have been people. Noise, dark, cold, adrenalin, death, okay? The woman was dead, anybody could see that right off. The ER doctor wouldn't even let us unload her. We took her right to the morgue. You can't get all of that out of you right away. Something bothered me later that didn't bother me then. There wasn't enough blood at the scene. There was blood around her, on her, but not enough." He paused a second. "To tell you the truth, Mr. Clay, I think she died some time before she went through the windshield."

Clay let his breath out slowly and loudly. "Thank you, Mr. Lewis. I thought that something was wrong here. It is quite a relief to hear you say that."

"No more than it is to me."

"Could I ask you about the husband? He . . ."

"Banged up really bad."

"Anything unusual about the injuries? I have a list here." He passed the emergency room report to Lewis.

Lewis read for a few moments in silence. "Thought that was right," he said softly.

"What, Mr. Lewis?" asked Clay.

"Oh, I see where the broken ribs got the liver. That's what I thought in the field, but no way to tell for sure out there."

"Can you describe the mechanism of injury for the ones on that list? For the liver and ribs?"

"I can try. The guy was wearing his seat belt and shoulder harness way too loose. He'd smack into them hard. The harness could have gotten the ribs, or he might have had the belts so loose that he got a little of the steering wheel. Belt that loose could help that bladder rupture, too, especially if it's full. Broken left clavicle and, uh, yeah, these deep abdominal contusions—same thing, seat belt too high, shoulder harness too loose."

"Pardon me for saying this, but I thought you said you weren't an expert in these matters."

"A lot of this is textbook answers, Mr. Clay. And I saw that wreck. I *saw* it, understand?"

Adam nodded.

"Let's see," Lewis continued. "Crushed ankle probably from the car just buckling back on his foot. The passenger side was displaced almost six inches back. Lacerations from flying glass. Broken nose? Could be steering wheel, could be missile of some sort. Broken hand, same thing. Fracture of the olecranon process? Now that's harder. That's this bone here, sticks out behind your elbow, part of the joint. Usually takes a direct blow or some strong leverage to break it. Something loose in the back seat, on the ledge, maybe, smacked it from behind. Dislocated shoulder, maybe whatever got his elbow. Maybe just impact. It was a hell of an impact.''

"Have you ever connected the husband with your belief that Mrs. Cannon was dead before impact?''

Lewis looked uncomfortable. "Got to, don't you? But I don't see how.''

"Have you ever fallen asleep at the wheel, Mr. Lewis?''

"Sorta nodded off once or twice. Hitting the shoulder woke me up.''

"Where were your hands when you woke up?''

Lewis sat straighter, closed his eyes, and raised his hands. "On the steering wheel still,'' he said.

"So were mine, when it's happened to me. If Cannon went to sleep at the wheel, then I think that's where his hands would be, too. But that makes those injuries difficult to explain.''

"Maybe he woke up.''

"If I had been he and had waked up, I would have hit my brakes. There were no skid marks. I would have swerved. He didn't. Now, Mr. Lewis, would you find all of this easier to explain if Mr. Cannon had hit that bridge on purpose? And would you find broken metacarpals, dislocated shoulder, and fracture of the olecranon process easier to explain if Mr. Cannon had been using his right arm and hand to prop up the body of his dead wife so that she would in fact go through the windshield and hit that abutment, thereby duplicating the expected mechanism of injury and mangling her beyond . . .''

"Of course,'' whispered Lewis, sinking back into his chair as if suddenly tired. "That's why his belts were so loose—so he could reach over. Her body smashed his arm into the dash on its way out. Why didn't I see it before?''

"I didn't see it, either,'' said Clay, raising his bandaged right hand, "until it happened to me.'' He winced at the pain in his shoulder and elbow and quickly added, grinning ruefully at Ginger, "With a bag of groceries, that is.''

"You're nuts, you know that? Fruit-cake. Bananas.''

Fat Chance paused long enough to remove the bitten-off butt of his cigar from his tongue. Clay took advantage while he could.

"Let me lay it out for you, Marv." He'd heard that the night before on a *Dragnet* rerun. He found he was watching more cop shows. "It seems to me that you can't lose here. You forward my report to your boss. One of three things happens. One—he follows up and I'm right and we prove it. You get part of the credit for saving the company big bucks. Maybe a promotion. Two—he follows up but we can't get enough evidence to prove the theory. You're still due for congratulations for hiring good people and for making the company sharper on elaborate fraud cases. Three—I am, as you say, a dessert plate. You blame me and can me and never have to see me again except at family reunions. At best you're a hero. At worst I'm your goat."

Fat Chance stared at Clay while absently picking bits of tobacco from his tongue. "You're right," he said finally. "Nuts, understand, but right."

"Let me talk to him."

"No way. I'll send the report up."

"If I'm wrong, he'll have me to chew out in person. He won't have to chew you to get me."

Fat chance hit his intercom. "Shirley, see if Mr. Carroll can see Mr. Clay. Tell him it's about possible fraud. Buzz me when you know."

"That's Dr. Clay," said Clay with a genuine smile, "but we'll keep that a family secret, eh, Marv?"

Clay deposited twenty thousand of his bonus in trust funds for the twins. He spent something over three thousand dollars of the rest on a very friendly word processing system to help him write his torrid romance. He gave the rest to Ginger, insisting that she spend it on something frivolous. She had the dents and holes taken out of Brunhilde, had her repainted and polished, and parked her shining in the driveway as a surprise. The rest she invested.

Everybody was happy. Everest was happy, and paid him a thousand dollars, which was nice of them, if cheap. Mountain Valley Mutual offered Clay a job, which flattered and amused him, and which he politely declined. Even Fat Chance was happy. After Acme, Everest, and Mountain Valley Mutual had convinced Mrs. Cannon's parents that an exhumation would be wise, and after an autopsy found that the heart had been skewered clean through by a thin, round, sharp object, like an ice pick, and after Cannon had pled guilty to reduced charges, Fat Chance even threw his arm around

Clay and said to his boss, "Yes-sir, Mr. Carroll, real proud of this brother-in-law of mine. Threw him this case special. Knew if something smelled, he'd find it." And Clay had stood there, apparently smiling.

So everybody was happy, but Clay had been happiest longest of all. Almost from the first moment that he had edged into Mr. Carroll's chrome and glass office to make his pitch for fraud, he had known things were going to work out.

"How do you do?" he had said. "My name is Adameus Clay."

"Adameus?" puffed Carroll. "Don't you mean Amadeus?"

Clay shrugged apologetically. "My mother meant Amadeus."

"Did she, by thunder?" Carroll boomed. "Well, my name is A. Belk Carroll. *My* mother, bless her soul, named me for her favorite department store and her favorite brand-name patent medicine. Can you guess what the 'A' stands for?"

Clay looked down at the letterhead on the report he was holding. "Acme?" he ventured.

"I've never forgiven her for that," Carroll said, "until now. Sit down, Adameus. I think we're going to like each other."

And they did.

THE RESIDENT PATIENT

by ARTHUR CONAN DOYLE

In glancing over the somewhat incoherent series of Memoirs with which I have endeavoured to illustrate a few of the mental peculiarities of my friend Mr. Sherlock Holmes, I have been struck by the difficulty which I have experienced in picking out examples which shall in every way answer my purpose. For in those cases in which Holmes has performed some tour de force of analytical reasoning, and has demonstrated the value of his peculiar methods of investigation, the facts themselves have often been so slight or so commonplace that I could not feel justified in laying them before the public. On the other hand, it has frequently happened that he has been concerned in some research where the facts have been of the most remarkable and dramatic character, but where the share which he has himself taken in determining their causes has been less pronounced than I, as his biographer, could wish. The small matter which I have chronicled under the heading of "A Study in Scarlet," and that other later one connected with the loss of the *Gloria Scott,* may serve as examples of this Scylla and Charybdis which are forever threatening the historian. It may be that in the business of which I am now about to write the part which my friend played is not sufficiently accentuated; and yet the whole train of circumstances is so remarkable that I cannot bring myself to omit it entirely from this series.

It had been a close, rainy day in October. Our blinds were half drawn, and Holmes lay curled upon the sofa, reading and rereading a letter which he had received by the morning post. For myself, my term of service in India had trained me to stand heat better than cold, and a thermometer of ninety was no hardship. But the paper was uninteresting. Parliament had risen. Everybody was out of town, and I yearned for the glades of the New Forest or the shingle of

Southsea. A depleted bank account had caused me to postpone my holiday, and as to my companion, neither the country nor the sea presented the slightest attraction to him. He loved to lie in the very center of five millions of people, with his filaments stretching out and running through them, responsive to every little rumour or suspicion of unsolved crime. Appreciation of nature found no place among his many gifts, and his only change was when he turned his mind from the evildoer of the town to track down his brother of the country.

Finding that Holmes was too absorbed for conversation, I had tossed aside the barren paper and, leaning back in my chair, I fell into a brown study. Suddenly my companion's voice broke in upon my thoughts.

"You are right, Watson," said he. "It does seem a very preposterous way of settling a dispute."

"Most preposterous!" I exclaimed, and then, suddenly realizing how he had echoed the inmost thought of my soul, I sat up in my chair and stared at him in blank amazement.

"What is this, Holmes?" I cried. "This is beyond anything which I could have imagined."

He laughed heartily at my perplexity.

"You remember," said he, "that some little time ago, when I read you the passage in one of Poe's sketches, in which a close reasoner follows the unspoken thoughts of his companion, you were inclined to treat the matter as a mere tour de force of the author. On my remarking that I was constantly in the habit of doing the same thing you expressed incredulity."

"Oh, no!"

"Perhaps not with your tongue, my dear Watson, but certainly with your eyebrows. So when I saw you throw down your paper and enter upon a train of thought, I was very happy to have the opportunity of reading it off, and eventually of breaking into it, as a proof that I had been in rapport with you."

But I was still far from satisfied. "In the example which you read to me," said I, "the reasoner drew his conclusions from the actions of the man whom he observed. If I remember right, he stumbled over a heap of stones, looked up at the stars, and so on. But I have been seated quietly in my chair, and what clues can I have given you?"

"You do yourself an injustice. The features are given to man as the means by which he shall express his emotions, and yours are faithful servants.''

''Do you mean to say that you read my train of thoughts from my features?''

''Your features, and especially your eyes. Perhaps you cannot yourself recall how your reverie commenced?''

''No, I cannot.''

''Then I will tell you. After throwing down your paper, which was the action which drew my attention to you, you sat for half a minute with a vacant expression. Then your eyes fixed themselves upon your newly framed picture of General Gordon, and I saw by the alteration in your face that a train of thought had been started. But it did not lead very far. Your eyes turned across to the unframed portrait of Henry Ward Beecher, which stands upon the top of your books. You then glanced up at the wall, and of course your meaning was obvious. You were thinking that if the portrait were framed it would just cover that bare space and correspond with Gordon's picture over there.''

''You have followed me wonderfully!'' I exclaimed.

''So far I could hardly have gone astray. But now your thoughts went back to Beecher, and you looked hard across as if you were studying the character in his features. Then your eyes ceased to pucker, but you continued to look across, and your face was thoughtful. You were recalling the incidents of Beecher's career. I was well aware that you could not do this without thinking of the mission which he understood on behalf of the North at the time of the Civil War, for I remember you expressing your passionate indignation at the way in which he was received by the more turbulent of our people. You felt so strongly about it that I knew you could not think of Beecher without thinking of that also. When a moment later I saw your eyes wander away from the picture, I suspected that your mind had now turned to the Civil War, and when I observed that your lips set, your eyes sparkled, and your hands clenched, I was positive that you were indeed thinking of the gallantry which was shown by both sides in that desperate struggle. But then, again, your face grew sadder; you shook your head. You were dwelling upon the sadness and horror and useless waste of life. Your hand stole towards your own old wound, and a smile quivered on your lips, which showed me that the ridiculous side of this method of settling international questions forced itself upon your mind. At this point I agreed with you that it was preposterous, and was glad to find that all my deductions had been correct.''

"Absolutely!" said I. "And now that you have explained it, I confess that I am as amazed as before."

"It was very superficial, my dear Watson, I assure you. I should not have intruded it upon your attention had you not shown some incredulity the other day. But the evening has brought a breeze with it. What do you say to a ramble through London?"

I was weary of our little sitting room and gladly acquiesced. For three hours we strolled about together, watching the ever-changing kaleidoscope of life as it ebbs and flows through Fleet Street and the Strand. His characteristic talk, with its keen observance of detail and subtle power of inference, held me amused and enthralled. It was ten o'clock before we reached Baker Street again. A brougham was waiting at our door.

"Hum! A doctor's—general practitioner, I perceive," said Holmes. "Not been long in practice, but has a good deal to do. Come to consult us, I fancy! Lucky we came back!"

I was sufficiently conversant with Holmes's methods to be able to follow his reasoning, and to see that the nature and state of the various medical instruments in the wicker basket which hung in the lamp-light inside the brougham had given him the data for his swift deduction. The light in our window above showed that this late visit was indeed intended for us. With some curiosity as to what could have sent a brother medico to us at such an hour, I followed Holmes into our sanctum.

A pale, taper-faced man with sandy whiskers rose up from a chair by the fire as we entered. His age may not have been more than three or four and thirty, but his haggard expression and unhealthy hue told of a life which had sapped his strength and robbed him of his youth. His manner was nervous and shy, like that of a sensitive gentleman, and the thin white hand which he laid on the mantelpiece as he rose was that of an artist rather than of a surgeon. His dress was quiet and sombre—a black frock-coat, dark trousers, and a touch of colour about his necktie.

"Good evening, doctor," said Holmes cheerily. "I am glad to see that you have only been waiting a very few minutes."

"You spoke to my coachman, then?"

"No, it was the candle on the side-table that told me. Pray resume your seat and let me know how I can serve you."

"My name is Dr. Percy Trevelyan," said our visitor, "and I live at 403 Brook Street."

"Are you not the author of a monograph upon obscure nervous lesions?" I asked.

His pale cheeks flushed with pleasure at hearing that his work was known to me.

"I so seldom hear of the work that I thought it was quite dead," said he. "My publishers gave me a most discouraging account of its sale. You are yourself, I presume, a medical man?"

"A retired army surgeon."

"My own hobby has always been nervous disease. I should wish to make it an absolute specialty, but of course a man must take what he can get at first. This, however, is beside the question, Mr. Sherlock Holmes, and I quite appreciate how valuable your time is. The fact is that a very singular train of events has occurred recently at my house in Brook Street, and tonight they came to such a head that I felt it was quite impossible for me to wait another hour before asking for your advice and assistance."

Sherlock Holmes sat down and lit his pipe. "You are very welcome to both," said he. "Pray let me have a detailed account of what the circumstances are which have disturbed you."

"One or two of them are so trivial," said Dr. Trevelyan, "that really I am almost ashamed to mention them. But the matter is so inexplicable, and the recent turn which it has taken is so elaborate, that I shall lay it all before you, and you shall judge what is essential and what is not.

"I am compelled, to begin with, to say something of my own college career. I am a London University man, you know, and I am sure that you will not think that I am unduly singing my own praises if I say that my student career was considered by my professors to be a very promising one. After I had graduated I continued to devote myself to research, occupying a minor position in King's College Hospital, and I was fortunate enough to excite considerable interest by my research into the pathology of catalepsy, and finally to win the Bruce Pinkerton prize and medal by the monograph on nervous lesions to which your friend has just alluded. I should not go too far if I were to say that there was a general impression at that time that a distinguished career lay before me.

"But the one great stumbling block lay in my want of capital. As you will readily understand, a specialist who aims high is compelled to start in one of a dozen streets in the Cavendish Square quarter, all of which entail enormous rents and furnishing expenses. Besides this preliminary outlay, he must be prepared to keep himself for some years, and to hire a presentable carriage and horse. To do this was quite beyond my power, and I could only hope that by economy I might in ten years' time save enough to enable me to put up my plate. Suddenly, however, an unexpected incident opened up quite a new prospect to me.

"This was a visit from a gentleman of the name of Blessington, who was a complete stranger to me. He came up into my room one morning, and plunged into business in an instant.

" 'You are the same Percy Trevelyan who has had so distinguished a career and won a great prize lately?' said he.

"I bowed.

" 'Answer me frankly,' he continued, 'for you will find it to your interest to do so. You have all the cleverness which makes a success- ful man. Have you the tact?'

"I could not help smiling at the abruptness of the question.

" 'I trust that I have my share,' I said.

" 'Any bad habits? Not drawn towards drink, eh?'

" 'Really, sir!' I cried.

" 'Quite right! That's all right! But I was bound to ask. With all these qualities, why are you not in practice?'

"I shrugged my shoulders.

" 'Come, come!' said he in his bustling way. 'It's the old story. More in your brains than in your pocket, eh? What would you say if I were to start you in Brook Street?'

"I stared at him in astonishment.

" 'Oh, it's for my sake, not for yours,' he cried. 'I'll be perfectly frank with you, and if it suits you, it will suit me very well. I have a few thousands to invest, d'ye see, and I think I'll sink them in you.'

" 'But why?' I gasped.

" 'Well, it's just like any other speculation, and safer than most.'

" 'What am I to do, then?'

" 'I'll tell you. I'll take the house, furnish it, pay the maids, and run the whole place. All you have to do is just to wear out your chair in the consulting room. I'll let you have pocket money and everything. Then you hand over to me three quarters of what you earn, and you keep the other quarter for yourself.'

"This was the strange proposal, Mr. Holmes, with which the man Blessington approached me. I won't weary you with the account of how we bargained and negotiated. It ended in my moving into the house next Lady Day, and starting in practice on very much the same conditions as he had suggested. He came himself to live with me in the character of a resident patient. His heart was weak, it appears, and he needed constant medical supervision. He turned the two best rooms of the first floor into a sitting room and bedroom for himself. He was a man of singular habits, shunning company and very seldom going out. His life was irregular, but in one respect he was regularity itself. Every evening, at the same hour, he walked into the consulting room, examined the books, put down five and three-pence for every guinea that I had earned, and carried the rest off to the strongbox in his own room.

"I may say with confidence that he never had occasion to regret his speculation. From the first it was a success. A few good cases and the reputation which I had in the hospital brought me rapidly to the front, and during the last few years I have made him a rich man.

"So much, Mr. Holmes, for my past history and my relations with Mr. Blessington. It only remains for me to tell you what has occurred to bring me here tonight.

"Some weeks ago Mr. Blessington came down to me in, as it seemed to me, a state of considerable agitation. He spoke of some burglary which, he said, had been committed in the West End, and he appeared, I remember, to be quite unnecessarily excited about it, declaring that a day should not pass before we should add stronger bolts to our windows and doors. For a week he continued to be in a peculiar state of restlessness, peering continually out of the windows, and ceasing to take the short walk which had usually been the prelude to his dinner. From his manner it struck me that he was in mortal dread of something or somebody, but when I questioned him upon the point he became so offensive that I was compelled to drop the subject. Gradually, as time passed, his fears appeared to die away, and he renewed his former habits, when a fresh event reduced him to the pitiable state of prostration in which he now lies.

"What happened was this. Two days ago I received the letter which I now read to you. Neither address nor date is attached to it.

'A Russian nobleman who is now resident in England [it runs] would be glad to avail himself of the professional assistance of Dr. Percy Trevelyan. He has been for some years a victim to cataleptic attacks, on which, as is well known, Dr. Trevelyan is an authority. He proposes to call at about a quarter past six tomorrow evening, if Dr. Trevelyan will make it convenient to be at home.'

"This letter interested me deeply, because the chief difficulty in the study of catalepsy is the rareness of the disease. You may believe, then, that I was in my consulting room when, at the appointed hour, the page showed in the patient.

"He was an elderly man, thin, demure, and commonplace—by no means the conception one forms of a Russian nobleman. I was much more struck by the appearance of his companion. This was a tall young man, surprisingly handsome, with a dark, fierce face, and the limbs and chest of a Hercules. He had his hand under the other's arm as they entered, and helped him to a chair with a tenderness which one would hardly have expected from his appearance.

" 'You will excuse my coming in, doctor,' said he to me, speaking English with a slight lisp. 'This is my father, and his health is a matter of the most overwhelming importance to me.'

"I was touched by this filial anxiety. 'You would, perhaps, care to remain during the consultation?' said I.

" 'Not for the world,' he cried with a gesture of horror. 'It is more painful to me than I can express. If I were to see my father in one of these dreadful seizures, I am convinced that I should never survive it. My own nervous system is an exceptionally sensitive one. With your permission, I will remain in the waiting room while you go into my father's case.'

"To this, of course, I assented, and the young man withdrew. The patient and I then plunged into a discussion of his case, of which I took exhaustive notes. He was not remarkable for intelligence, and his answers were frequently obscure, which I attributed to his limited acquaintance with our language. Suddenly, however, as I sat writing, he ceased to give any answer at all to my inquires, and on my turning towards him I was shocked to see that he was sitting bolt upright in his chair, staring at me with a perfectly blank and rigid face. He was again in the grip of his mysterious malady.

"My first feeling, as I have just said, was one of pity and horror. My second, I fear, was rather one of professional satisfaction. I made notes of my patient's pulse and temperature, tested the rigidity of his muscles, and examined his reflexes. There was nothing markedly abnormal in any of these conditions, which harmonized with my former experiences. I had obtained good results in such cases by the inhalation of nitrite of amyl, and the present seemed an admirable opportunity of testing its virtues. The bottle was downstairs in my laboratory, so leaving my patient seated in his chair, I ran down to get it. There was some little delay in finding it—five minutes, let us say—and then I returned. Imagine my amazement to find the room empty and the patient gone.

"Of course, my first act was to run into the waiting room. The son had gone also. The hall door had been closed, but not shut. My page who admits patients is a new boy and by no means quick. He waits downstairs and runs up to show patients out when I ring the consulting room bell. He had heard nothing, and the affair remained a complete mystery. Mr. Blessington came in from his walk shortly afterwards, but I did not say anything to him upon the subject, for, to tell the truth, I have got in the way of late of holding as little communication with him as possible.

"Well, I never thought that I should see anything more of the Russian and his son, so you can imagine my amazement when, at the very same hour this evening, they both came marching into my consulting room, just as they had done before.

" 'I feel that I owe you a great many apologies for my abrupt departure yesterday, doctor,' said my patient.

" 'I confess that I was very much surprised at it,' said I.

" 'Well, the fact is,' he remarked, 'that when I recover from these attacks my mind is always very clouded as to all that has gone before. I woke up in a strange room, as it seemed to me, and made my way out into the street in a sort of dazed way when you were absent.'

" 'And I,' said the son, 'seeing my father pass the door of the waiting room, naturally thought that the consultation had come to an end. It was not until we had reached home that I began to realize the true state of affairs.'

" 'Well,' said I, laughing, 'there is no harm done except that you puzzled me terribly; so if you, sir, would kindly step into the waiting room I shall be happy to continue our consultation which was brought to so abrupt an ending.'

"For half an hour or so I discussed the old gentleman's symptoms with him, and then, having prescribed for him, I saw him go off upon the arm of his son.

"I have told you that Mr. Blessington generally chose this hour of the day for his exercise. He came in shortly afterwards and passed upstairs. An instant later I heard him running down, and he burst into my consulting room like a man who is mad with panic.

" 'Who has been in my room?' he cried.

" 'No one,' said I.

" 'It's a lie!' he yelled. 'Come up and look!'

"I passed over the grossness of his language, as he seemed half out of his mind with fear. When I went upstairs with him he pointed to several footprints upon the light carpet.

" 'Do you mean to say those are mine?' he cried.

"They were certainly very much larger than any which he could have made, and were evidently quite fresh. It rained hard this afternoon, as you know, and my patients were the only people who called. It must have been the case, then, that the man in the waiting room had, for some unknown reason, while I was busy with the other, ascended to the room of my resident patient. Nothing had been touched or taken, but there were the footprints to prove that the intrusion was an undoubted fact.

"Mr. Blessington seemed more excited over the matter than I should have thought possible, though of course it was enough to disturb anybody's peace of mind. He actually sat crying in an armchair, and I could hardly get him to speak coherently. It was his suggestion that I should come round to you, and of course I at once saw the propriety of it, for certainly the incident is a very singular one, though he appears to completely overrate its importance. If you would only come back with me in my brougham, you would at least be able to soothe him, though I can hardly hope that you will be able to explain this remarkable occurrence."

Sherlock Holmes had listened to this long narrative with an intentness which showed me that his interest was keenly aroused. His face was as impassive as ever, but his lids had drooped more heavily over his eyes, and his smoke had curled up more thickly from his pipe to emphasize each curious episode in the doctor's tale. As our visitor concluded, Holmes sprang up without a word, handed me my hat, picked his own from the table, and followed Dr. Trevelyan to the door. Within a quarter of an hour we had been dropped at the door of the physician's residence in Brook Street, one of those sombre, flat-faced houses which one associates with a West End practice. A small page admitted us, and we began at once to ascend the broad, well-carpeted stair.

But a singular interruption brought us to a standstill. The light at the top was suddenly whisked out, and from the darkness came a reedy, quavering voice.

"I have a pistol," it cried. "I give you my word that I'll fire if you come any nearer."

"This really grows outrageous, Mr. Blessington," cried Dr. Trevelyan.

"Oh, then it is you, doctor," said the voice with a great heave of relief. "But those other gentlemen, are they what they pretend to be?"

We were conscious of a long scrutiny out of the darkness.

"Yes, yes, it's all right," said the voice at last. "You can come up, and I am sorry if my precautions have annoyed you."

He relit the stair gas as he spoke, and we saw before us a singular-looking man, whose appearance, as well as his voice, testified to his jangled nerves. He was very fat, but had apparently at some time been much fatter, so that the skin hung about his face in loose pouches, like the cheeks of a bloodhound. He was of a sickly colour, and his thin, sandy hair seemed to bristle up with the intensity of his emotion. In his hand he held a pistol, but he thrust it into his pocket as we advanced.

"Good evening, Mr. Holmes," said he. "I am sure I am very much obliged to you for coming round. No one ever needed your advice more than I do. I suppose that Dr. Trevelyan has told you of this most unwarrantable intrusion into my rooms."

"Quite so," said Holmes. "Who are these two men, Mr. Blessington, and why do they wish to molest you?"

"Well, well," said the resident patient in a nervous fashion, "of course it is hard to say that. You can hardly expect me to answer that, Mr. Holmes."

"Do you mean that you don't know?"

"Come in here, if you please. Just have the kindness to step in here."

He led the way into his bedroom, which was large and comfortably furnished.

"You see that," said he, pointing to a big black box at the end of his bed. "I have never been a very rich man, Mr. Holmes—never made but one investment in my life, as Dr. Trevelyan would tell you. But I don't believe in bankers. I would never trust a banker, Mr. Holmes. Between ourselves, what little I have is in that box, so you can understand what it means to me when unknown people force themselves into my rooms."

Holmes looked at Blessington in his questioning way and shook his head.

"I cannot possibly advise you if you try to deceive me." said he.

"But I have told you everything."

Holmes turned on his heel with a gesture of disgust. "Goodnight, Dr. Trevelyan," said he.

"And no advice for me?" cried Blessington in a breaking voice.

"My advice to you, sir, is to speak the truth."

A minute later we were in the street and walking for home. We had crossed Oxford Street and were halfway down Harley Street before I could get a word from my companion.

"Sorry to bring you out on such a fool's errand, Watson," he said at last. "It is an interesting case, too, at the bottom of it."

"I can make little of it," I confessed.

"Well, it is quite evident that there are two men—more, perhaps, but at least two—who are determined for some reason to get at this fellow Blessington. I have no doubt in my mind that both on the first and on the second occasion that young man penetrated to Blessington's room, while his confederate, by an ingenious device, kept the doctor from interfering."

"And the catalepsy?"

"A fraudulent imitation, Watson, though I should hardly dare to hint as much to our specialist. It is a very easy complaint to imitate. I have done it myself."

"And then?"

"By the purest chance Blessington was out on each occasion. Their reason for choosing so unusual an hour for a consultation was obviously to insure that there should be no other patient in the waiting room. It just happened, however, that this hour coincided with Blessington's constitutional, which seems to show that they were not very well acquainted with his daily routine. Of course, if they had been merely after plunder they would at least have made some attempt to search for it. Besides, I can read in a man's eye when it is his own skin that he is frightened for. It is inconceivable that this fellow could have made two such vindictive enemies as these appear to be without knowing of it. I hold it, therefore, to be certain that he does know who these men are, and that for reasons of his own he suppresses it. It is just possible that tomorrow may find him in a more communicative mood."

"Is there not one alternative," I suggested, "grotesquely improbable, no doubt, but still just conceivable? Might the whole story of the cataleptic Russian and his son be a concoction of Dr. Trevelyan's, who has, for his own purposes, been in Blessington's rooms?"

I saw in the gas-light that Holmes wore an amused smile at this brilliant departure of mine.

"My dear fellow," said he, "it was one of the first solutions which occurred to me, but I was soon able to corroborate the doctor's tale. This young man has left prints upon the stair carpet which made it quite superfluous for me to ask to see those which he had made in the room. When I tell you that his shoes were square-toed instead of being pointed like Blessington's, and were quite an inch and a third longer than the doctor's, you will acknowledge that there can be no doubt as to his individuality. But we may sleep on it now, for I shall be surprised if we do not hear something further from Brook Street in the morning.''

Sherlock Holmes's prophecy was soon fulfilled, and in a dramatic fashion. At half past seven next morning, in the first dim glimmer of daylight, I found him standing by my bedside in his dressing gown.

"There's a brougham waiting for us, Watson," said he.

"What's the matter, then?"

"The Brook Street business."

"Any fresh news?"

"Tragic, but ambiguous," said he, pulling up the blind. "Look at this—a sheet from a notebook, with 'For God's sake come at once. P. T.,' Scrawled upon it in pencil. Our friend, the doctor, was hard put to it when he wrote this. Come along, my dear fellow, for it's an urgent call."

In a quarter of an hour or so we were back at the physician's house. He came running out to meet us with a face of horror.

"Oh, such a business!" he cried with his hands to his temples.

"What then?"

"Blessington has committed suicide!"

Holmes whistled.

"Yes, he hanged himself during the night."

We had entered, and the doctor had preceded us into what was evidently his waiting room.

"I really hardly know what I am doing," he cried. "The police are already upstairs. It has shaken me most dreadfully."

"When did you find it out?"

"He has a cup of tea taken in to him early every morning. When the maid entered, about seven, there the unfortunate fellow was, hanging in the middle of the room. He had tied his cord to the hook on which the heavy lamp used to hang, and he had jumped off from the top of the very box that he showed us yesterday."

Holmes stood for a moment in deep thought.

"With your permission," said he at last, "I should like to go upstairs and look into the matter."

We both ascended, followed by the doctor.

It was a dreadful sight which met us as we entered the bedroom door. I have spoken of the impression of flabbiness which this man Blessington conveyed. As he dangled from the hook it was exaggerated and intensified until he was scarce human in his appearance. The neck was drawn out like a plucked chicken's, making the rest of him seem the more obese and unnatural by the contrast. He was clad only in his long nightdress, and his swollen ankles and ungainly feet protruded starkly from beneath it. Beside him stood a smart-looking police-inspector, who was taking notes in a pocketbook.

"Ah, Mr. Holmes," said he heartily as my friend entered, "I am delighted to see you."

"Good morning, Lanner," answered Holmes; "you won't think me an intruder, I am sure. Have you heard of the events which led up to this affair?"

"Yes, I heard something of them."

"Have you formed any opinion?"

"As far as I can see, the man has been driven out of his senses by fright. The bed has been well slept in, you see. There's his impression, deep enough. It's about five in the morning, you know, that suicides are most common. That would be about his time for hanging himself. It seems to have been a very deliberate affair."

"I should say that he has been dead about three hours, judging by the rigidity of the muscles," said I.

"Noticed anything peculiar about the room?" asked Holmes.

"Found a screwdriver and some screws on the wash-hand stand. Seems to have smoked heavily during the night, too. Here are four cigar ends that I picked out of the fireplace."

"Hum!" said Holmes, "have you got his cigar holder?"

"No, I have seen none."

"His cigar case, then?"

"Yes, it was in his coat pocket."

Holmes opened it and smelled the single cigar which it contained.

"Oh, this is a Havana, and these others are cigars of the peculiar sort which are imported by the Dutch from their East Indian colonies. They are usually wrapped in straw, you know, and are thinner for their length than any other brand." He picked up the four ends and examined them with his pocket lens.

"Two of these have been smoked from a holder and two without," said he. "Two have been cut by a not very sharp knife, and two have had the ends bitten off by a set of excellent teeth. This is no suicide, Mr. Lanner. It is a very deeply planned and cold-blooded murder.''

''Impossible!'' cried the inspector.

''And why?''

''Why should anyone murder a man in so clumsy a fashion as by hanging him?''

''That is what we have to find out.''

''How could they get in?''

''Through the front door.''

''It was barred in the morning.''

''Then it was barred after them.''

''How do you know?''

''I saw their traces. Excuse me a moment, and I may be able to give you some further information about it.''

He went over to the door, and turning the lock he examined it in his methodical way. Then he took out the key, which was on the inside, and inspected that also. The bed, the carpet, the chairs, the mantelpiece, the dead body, and the rope were each in turn examined, until at last he professed himself satisfied, and with my aid and that of the inspector cut down the wretched object and laid it reverently under a sheet.

''How about this rope?'' he asked.

''It is cut off this,'' said Dr. Trevelyan, drawing a large coil from under the bed. ''He was morbidly nervous of fire, and always kept this beside him, so that he might escape by the window in case the stairs were burning.''

''That must have saved them trouble,'' said Holmes thoughtfully. ''Yes, the actual facts are very plain, and I shall be surprised if by the afternoon I cannot give you the reasons for them as well. I will take this photograph of Blessington, which I see upon the mantelpiece, as it may help me in my inquiries.''

''But you have told us nothing!'' cried the doctor.

''Oh, there can be no doubt as to the sequence of events,'' said Holmes. ''There were three of them in it: the young man, the old man, and a third, to whose identity I have no clue. The first two, I need hardly remark, are the same who masqueraded as the Russian count and his son, so we can give a very full description of them. They were admitted by a confederate inside the house. If I might offer you a word of advice, inspector, it would be to arrest the page, who, as I understand, has only recently come into your service, doctor.''

"The young imp cannot be found," said Dr. Trevelyan; "the maid and the cook have just been searching for him."

Holmes shrugged his shoulders.

"He has played a not unimportant part in this drama," said he. "The three men having ascended the stairs, which they did on tiptoe, the elder man first, the younger man second, and the unknown man in the rear—"

"My dear Holmes!" I ejaculated.

"Oh, there could be no question as to the superimposing of the footmarks. I had the advantage of learning which was which last night. They ascended, then, to Mr. Blessington's room, the door of which they found to be locked. With the help of a wire, however, they forced round the key. Even without the lens you will perceive, by the scratches on this ward, where the pressure was applied.

"On entering the room their first proceeding must have been to gag Mr. Blessington. He may have been asleep, or he may have been so paralyzed with terror as to have been unable to cry out. These walls are thick, and it is conceivable that his shriek, if he had time to utter one, was unheard.

"Having secured him, it is evident to me that a consultation of some sort was held. Probably it was something in the nature of a judicial proceeding. It must have lasted for some time, for it was then that these cigars were smoked. The older man sat in that wicker chair; it was he who used the cigar holder. The younger man sat over yonder; he knocked his ash off against the chest of drawers. The third fellow paced up and down. Blessington, I think, sat upright in the bed, but of that I cannot be absolutely certain.

"Well, it ended by their taking Blessington and hanging him. The matter was so prearranged that it is my belief that they brought with them some sort of block or pulley which might serve as a gallows. That screwdriver and those screws were, as I conceive, for fixing it up. Seeing the hook however, they naturally saved themselves the trouble. Having finished their work they made off, and the door was barred behind them by their confederate."

We had all listened with the deepest interest to this sketch of the night's doings, which Holmes had deduced from signs so subtle and minute that, even when he had pointed them out to us, we could scarcely follow him in his reasonings. The inspector hurried away on the instant to make inquiries about the page, while Holmes and I returned to Baker Street for breakfast.

"I'll be back by three," said he when we had finished our meal.

"Both the inspector and the doctor will meet me here at that hour, and I hope by that time to have cleared up any little obscurity which the case may still present."

Our visitors arrived at the appointed time, but it was a quarter to four before my friend put in an appearance. From his expression as he entered, however, I could see that all had gone well with him.

"Any news, inspector?"

"We have got the boy, sir."

"Excellent, and I have got the men."

"You have got them!" we cried, all three.

"Well, at least I have got their identity. This so-called Blessington is, as I expected, well known at headquarters, and so are his assailants. Their names are Biddle, Hayward, and Moffat."

"The Worthingdon bank gang," cried the inspector.

"Precisely," said Holmes.

"Then Blessington must have been Sutton."

"Exactly," said Holmes.

"Why, that makes it as clear as crystal," said the inspector.

But Trevelyan and I looked at each other in bewilderment.

"You must surely remember the great Worthingdon bank business," said Holmes. "Five men were in it—these four and a fifth called Cartwright. Tobin, the caretaker, was murdered, and the thieves got away with seven thousand pounds. This was in 1875. They were all five arrested, but the evidence against them was by no means conclusive. This Blessington or Sutton, who was the worst of the gang, turned informer. On his evidence Cartwright was hanged and the other three got fifteen years apiece. When they got out the other day, which was some years before their full term, they set themselves, as you perceive, to hunt down the traitor and to avenge the death of their comrade upon him. Twice they tried to get at him and failed; a third time, you see, it came off. Is there anything further which I can explain, Dr. Trevelyan?"

"I think you have made it all remarkably clear," said the doctor. "No doubt the day on which he was so perturbed was the day when he had seen of their release in the newspapers."

"Quite so. His talk about a burglary was the merest blind."

"But why could he not tell you this?"

"Well, my dear sir, knowing the vindictive character of his old associates, he was trying to hide his own identity from everybody as long as he could. His secret was a shameful one, and he could not bring himself to divulge it. However, wretch as he was, he was still living under the shield of British law, and I have no doubt, inspector, that you will see that, though that shield may fail to guard, the sword of justice is still there to avenge.''

Such were the singular circumstances in connection with the Resident Patient and the Brook Street Doctor. From that night nothing has been seen of the three murderers by the police, and it is surmised at Scotland Yard that they were among the passengers of the ill-fated steamer *Norah Creina,* which was lost some years ago with all hands upon the Portuguese coast, some leagues to the north of Oporto. The proceedings against the page broke down for want of evidence, and the Brook Street Mystery, as it was called, has never until now been fully dealt with in any public print.

AUNT RUTABAGA

by ARTHUR PORGES

Even if his Aunt Melba had been bright, warm, witty, charming, and beautiful, Mark Hamilton Whipple would still have sacrificed her for his own benefit without a qualm. That she was, in fact, air-headed, selfish, cold, and so plain that as one detractor—she had many behind her back where the money wasn't obtrusive—said, she looked as if she'd fallen out of the Ugly Tree and hit every damned branch on the way down, was not a factor in his decision to insure his own financial security.

He was himself, and he knew it, no Errol Flynn for looks, although he never said so aloud, and as cold as a frozen snake. No, what made his operation Counter Aunt a vital necessity, and soon, was her blasted lifestyle. She drank heavily, everything from cheap beer to Jack Daniel's and French champagne; smoked several packs of cigarettes daily; and ate enough junk food, full of saturated fat and chemicals barely known to science, to give indigestion to a dozen burly truckers. At age fifty-two, she already had severe emphysema and a congestive heart for which she took, when she remembered, not always the case, a variety of medications. She was often in and out of the hospital, and Mark was sure she would die there sooner rather than later, probably in a matter of months. Her death in itself did not concern him; there was no love lost between them; but while she was alive he got a hundred thousand dollars annually from her late husband's considerable estate. On her death that income ceased, and all the money went to various charities, there being no other heirs.

In short, it was up to him to keep her alive, yet there was no chance she'd reform and become a nonsmoking, ever-sober vegetarian. That hundred thousand was absolutely essential to his survival

225

as a happy, untroubled, relaxed playboy, the only role he was fit for, having no marketable skills and no work experience whatever, since his late uncle Alexander P. Whipple had reluctantly, aware of the boy's numerous deficiencies, put him on the Gravy Train for the life of Melba.

There was only one solution, far from perfect, much of a gamble, and not easy to implement, but at worst at least equal to his present situation, and at best, one that would guarantee his income for years to come.

He began by investigating her insurance policy and was reassured on that score. The shrewd A. P. Whipple had bought a really ironclad document, one that would pay for any amount of hospitalization for any length of time, for any ailment or ailments, for all doctor's bills, for everything down to the last five dollar tissue and seven fifty aspirin tablet.

Mark had visited his aunt several times in the hospital, not out of compassion it should be emphasized. Rather, as a born opportunist and exploiter, he always tried to stay in her good graces in case something happened to his annuity and he had to call on her for help, unlikely as such assistance might be what with her greed and selfishness.

But a useful bonus from such visits was his familiarity with hospital routine, now so vital to his plan. While Melba and he had engaged in a small talk, her suspicious gaze often on his bland face, Mark, with his basically good mind and powers of observation, noted and retained many details about patient care, from the respirator that attached to Melba's nose and mouth and was in turn connected to a mysterious electronic cabinet that beeped a warning and alerted the nurses if anything went wrong, to the timing of pulse and temperature readings. For example, when Melba dug messily into the box of chocolates he'd brought, she loosened the mask unintentionally so that the monitor went into a loud trill of alarm and a nurse hurried in to check. At the time he was merely amused, if wryly, but now the information was critical to his success.

The plan was basically simple in concept: Aunt Melba must be made into a vegetable, kept alive by machines for—how long? Well, Mark had read about such patients lasting for years, with nobody allowed to disconnect them legally as long as the closest relatives objected. And as her only close relation, he would evince great horror at the idea of cutting off the life-support equipment. The insurance company would hate him, but there would be nothing they could do, thanks to the airtight policy A. P. Whipple had paid so much for in 1980 dollars. Come to think of it, Mark reflected, maybe he could sound them out, very obliquely, about paying him, say, a hundred and fifty thousand a year for life if he gave permission—why settle for his present income if he could do better? But that would keep. For now, it was the operative details that mattered.

The brute-force obvious idea would be to pull the mask from her face for six to eight minutes, by which time the brain would die, so to speak, for lack of oxygen. But that option had an obvious, fatal flaw: the box would beep, a nurse come running, and the airflow be restarted in moments. Besides, she'd cry out, fight him, make a fuss; no good; impracticable. There was a better way he'd found out about. If one could inject a hefty dose of some potassium compound into the blood, the heart would stop almost instantly, like a switched-off light bulb. No need to puncture her, which wouldn't be possible surreptitiously anyhow; just inject some potassium chloride, easily obtainable either as a salt substitute or a health supplement, into the IV bag hanging by Melba's bed. He could do it quickly, casually, with his back to her, blocking any view of the act. Then, the moment her heart stopped and she fell back against the pillow, he'd snatch the mask—this was his lovely solution; he was proud of such ingenuity—and breathe into it himself, so aborting the warning system. He needed only six to eight minutes, and would watch through the door's glass panel for any unwelcome visitors. At worst, if anybody did come in, he could immediately restore the mask and let the beeping start. The nurses would charge in and restart Melba's heart—if they could. If not, and she died, he'd lose his gamble, but nothing could be proved against him. Even if there was an autopsy and the potassium contamination was found in the IV bag, it would be thought some error in the preparation of the solution. On the other hand, if his aunt survived he could try again later.

Actually, it went without a hitch. Within seconds of his injecting the solution, his aunt gasped, her eyes rolled up and went glassy-blank, and she fell back. He grabbed the mask, put it on, and took several deep breaths. There was no alarm, and since nobody approached the room, he was able to allow almost nine minutes, more than enough for irreversible brain death. His Aunt Melba, the feisty, unloveable woman so fat in her tacky yellow robe, was now the Giant Rutabaga, the vegetable that insured his income. Nobody seemed suspicious; rather they shared his obvious grief over so unfortunate a development. He even managed a bit of moisture in his eyes.

When after five months there were no glitches, no nasty conse-
quences, Mark began to relax, feeling himself home free and quite
pleased with the world he had so neatly manipulated.

He did get a brief scare when some eager beaver of a doctor
wanted to try some kind of new medication, an injection, that showed
some promise in bringing flat electro-encephalographs back to life,
reviving dead brains, as the researcher put it.

Although taken by surprise, Mark was quick to protect himself.
With a great show of pious anger, he refused the offer, objecting
that Melba was no guinea pig for dangerous experiments. "For all I
know," he fumed to the doctor, "your crazy stuff could kill my dear
aunt. No way, doctor; I'll never allow it." It could have been hairy:
what if she actually woke up? To be sure, she'd probably had no
idea what he'd done to her, and the IV bag was long gone, but he'd
be back at Square One, with her drinking, smoking, over-eating, and
again likely to die soon.

Safe for now, he was still uneasy, so he sounded out the insurance
company as he'd thought of earlier. They were intrigued but didn't
bite. Rather than pay him a hundred and fifty thousand dollars a year
for life, which might be fifty or more years in his case, they preferred
to gamble that Melba would die naturally or somehow be disconnected from the life-support machinery.

Three events, not obviously related, but perhaps part of the complex tapestry woven by the Three Fates, Clotho, Lachesis, and
Atropos, changed everything.

First, Mike Hallinan, the agent from the senior Whipple's insurer,
Moran, Adler and Musgrave, came by one evening to offer Mark a
company annuity of fifty thousand a year for ten years if he'd give
permission to unplug his Aunt Melba. Mark was tempted, but not
much. There was every indication from hospital personnel he'd
sought out and carefully cultivated with free drinks that the patient
was physically stable and might well hang on indefinitely, and a
hundred thousand a year was indubitably better than fifty. No question about that, so the risk was worth it. As it turned out, that was
a bad decision.

The second event, much more public, involved the work of a sharp
investigative reporter who, having got wind of the Melba Whipple
case, carefully researched it, learning that by keeping her alive, although citing compassion and unwillingness to "lose" his beloved
aunt, her nephew, an idler, a womanizer, and a quintessential ne'er-
do-well, gained a fat income by most standards and might enjoy it

for years. The report in the local paper was headlined CONCERN OR GREED?, and few readers had any doubt about the answer.

And finally, the third and definitive event: after a loud and bitter quarrel about the morality of maintaining the hapless Melba in a coma with his current girlfriend, a six foot tall, titian-haired showgirl, Mark brutally cast her off for his latest bedmate, a petite brunette. He had been far too cautious to tell the redhead about the syringe of potassium chloride, but she had suspicions about just how Melba ended up a vegetable.

The very next day a tall, flame-haired, beautiful virago screaming, "I'll fix that parasite SOB!" charged into Melba's room brandishing a tire iron, wreaking havoc on all the life-support equipment, battering the delicate complex into rubbish. It took several husky guards to restrain her, and by then Melba's heart had stopped for good.

The tragicomic end of L'Affaire Whipple, as one observer called it, came just a few months later, when Mark, broke, despondent, and more than a bit tipsy from cheap red wine, stumbled into the path of a fast-moving minivan. It flung him forward and up in a classic parabola that would have intrigued a physicist. He just missed, unfortunately for him, a relatively soft lawn, to land instead in a rock garden belonging to a small, pricy restaurant, which—another irony in a case full of them—was featuring Pêche Melba.

When the paramedics came, some eighteen minutes later, they were able to stabilize his fibrillating heart, but at the hospital Mark's brain gave a dead flat reading on the screen. It stayed that way for three days, after which the state, finding no heirs and concerned about mounting costs at a tax-supported facility, had him disconnected.

And so, wielding her golden shears, the cold, classic serenity of her lovely face undisturbed, Atropos deftly cut Mark's thread.

ONE DEADLY SIN

by ANTHONY MARSH

D r. Sam Pitman was fat (rotund was the expression he preferred) and congenial. He had to be, so he said, since as pathologist at the Bishops Community Hospital his traffic was much more with the dead than with the living, and being rotund and congenial was his only defense against falling into a morbid frame of mind. Not that he was incapable of unpleasant emotions; his secretary, Miss Plumbley, had the faculty of arousing in him the deepest anger. As he passed through the outer office of the pathology department that morning, she was seated at her desk nonchalantly filing her already over-manicured fingernails.

Stifling his feelings, Sam bade her a curt good morning, then passed through to his own office. This was a large room where he kept his files, textbooks, and high-powered microscope. It was a center point of the department; the wall facing his desk consisted in its upper part of a thick glass panel through which he could overlook the laboratory. Here the technicians, men and women, mostly young, sat at the long workbenches or walked busily up and down the aisles attending to their duties. They all wore the same knee-length white coats, which gave the place a sort of science fiction aspect. The thick glass of the panel filtered out most of the sound, so that, staring through it, he had the impression of watching a silent movie.

He sat at his desk in quiet frustration for several minutes. He had wanted to fire Miss Plumbley long ago, much to the amazement of some of his colleagues, but the power that maintained Miss Plumbley on her unwelcome pedestal was the gay, debonair Bob Marlowe, president of the medical staff. No staff employee could be hired or fired without the consent of the medical executive committee, and if the president said no, the executive committee said no; that is the way things were done at the Bishops Community Hospital, particularly while the president was Bob Marlowe.

To work, Sam Pitman told himself and, purely out of habit, opened the door at the far side of his office which connected it with the brightly lighted autopsy room. He stared for about three seconds, then withdrew hastily and stormed back to the outer office resolutely.

"Miss Plumbley!" His voice boomed with anger, but she looked across at him calmly, almost impertinently.

"Yes, doctor?"

"Why didn't you inform me there was a body in there for post-mortem examination?"

"But there isn't, doctor."

"Don't tell me there isn't. I say there is. It's your job to notify me of these things. I'd have come in a little earlier if I'd known. The relatives or the funeral directors may be waiting for the body."

"But there isn't a body," she said, fiercely.

He gripped her arm. "Come on, I'll show you."

Miss Plumbley drew back. Although for the past ten months she had worked little more than twenty feet from the autopsy room, she had never actually been in there. She turned pale and pulled her arm free. "Okay. I'll take your word for it."

"Then where are the papers? Where is the relative's consent? Where is the chart? How am I supposed to know what I'm looking for? What have you done with the clinical record?"

She dropped the nail file into the open top drawer and began rummaging through the papers on her desk. There were not many on it, and it rapidly became obvious that she had no information at all about this particular corpse.

Dr. Pitman stamped out angrily and returned to the autopsy room. The body was laid out on the special white-tiled table and covered with a white sheet that drooped halfway to the floor.

Dr. Pitman pulled away the top of the sheet and stepped back, horrified; he was staring into the familiar features, still debonair though not so gay in death, of Bob Marlowe. He threw the sheet over the face again and strode back to Miss Plumbley's office. Trembling, he leaned against the door jamb.

"Do you know whose body that is?"

She was finally showing some signs of concern. "No, doctor."

"It's Dr. Marlowe!"

Her deep blue eyes opened wide, and her pouting lips fell apart. "Dr. Robert Marlowe?"

"Yes, Robert Marlowe, the president of the medical staff. My God, I saw him only last night; he presided at the monthly staff meeting. He must have been admitted during the night and died. Surely you've got some record, Miss Plumbley."

She began to leaf rather stupidly once again through the sparse papers on her desk.

He exploded, "For heaven's sake, stop dawdling. You're the most incompetent person I've ever met." He strode out into the corridor and to the opposite side of the hospital where the admissions office was located.

An alert, middle-aged woman in an immaculate nurse's uniform looked up at him. "Good morning, Dr. Pitman. My, what's the matter? You don't look well."

"I'm all right, Mrs. Rogers." He sat down heavily in the chair opposite her. "When was Dr. Marlowe admitted? Who's his doctor?"

"Dr. Marlowe?"

"Yes, he was admitted as a patient here. Which ward did he go to?"

"It must have been before I came on. Let me look at the book." She ran an efficient finger down the huge ledger in front of her. "No, I can't see his name here. When would he have been admitted?"

"It must have been after eleven o'clock last night; that's when the staff meeting ended; I saw him there as I was going out."

She ran her finger down the list again. "There were only four admissions during the night, one obstetrical, one child with appendicitis, one woman of sixty-nine with a stroke, and a man from a street accident."

"Who was the man?"

"His name is Donald Griffith. He's twenty-four."

"Nobody else?"

"No. There must be a mistake somewhere."

"There's no mistake, Mrs. Rogers. Dr. Marlowe's body is lying in my autopsy room right now."

Her jaw dropped. "Dr. Robert Marlowe?"

"Yes, the staff president. If *you* don't have a record of it, maybe he was brought in dead and taken straight to the autopsy room, though it ought to be a coroner's case."

She was looking very distressed. "They're supposed to notify this office anyway so that we can keep our census in order. Gracious me, what could have happened? Poor Dr. Marlowe. Perhaps they know about it in emergency. Let's go and check.''

He followed her to the emergency department. The front desk was empty, and she sat down to study the record book, a ledger similar to her own. The young nurse in charge came out. "Did you have any D.O.A.'s during the night?" Mrs. Rogers asked her.

The girl shook her head. "No, there's nothing in the book."

"I can't see it, either," said Mrs. Rogers.

Dr. Pitman was growing frantic. "Did anybody at all die during the night? Any one of the patients?"

They both shook their heads.

He pinched his thick cheek. "I must be seeing things. Would you mind coming back and looking at the body with me, Mrs. Rogers?"

"Of course, doctor." She fell into step beside him.

Miss Plumbley was standing nervously at the door of her office as though ready to flee the ghost of the departed staff president. Mrs. Rogers gave her a nod, but Dr. Pitman walked by without seeming to notice her. They passed through his office where a few curious eyes glanced at them through the glass panel. He went ahead of her into the autopsy room, stretched out his arm, hesitated for a brief moment, then drew back the white sheet. Mrs. Rogers gasped.

"My goodness, it is Dr. Marlowe. How did he get here?"

"That's exactly what I've been trying to find out ever since I arrived in the hospital this morning."

"But it's impossible, doctor."

He dropped the sheet back into place. "We can't both be crazy, Mrs. Rogers."

She stepped backward haltingly. He followed her out of the room and closed the door. They sat down on either side of his desk, saying nothing for several seconds. There were more eyes looking at them through the glass.

"What are you going to do?" she asked.

He tightened his lips. "I don't know. This situation is entirely without precedent."

"Perhaps you could discuss it with Dr. Rochester. I know he's in the house; he passed by my office a minute or two before you came along."

"Yes, I suppose he would be the best man. He's vice-president of the staff." He picked up the phone and dialed the switchboard. "Would you page Dr. Vaughan Rochester for me?"

Dr. Rochester's name came over the loudspeakers, and a few moments later he had answered his page.

"This is Sam Pitman," said the pathologist. "Could you come right over to my office; something very serious has happened."

"I'll be there immediately," Dr. Rochester answered.

There was a short delay, then he came in, a big man, over six feet tall, and broad-shouldered, with square features and close-cropped gray hair. He had been quite an athlete in his day and still looked very husky. He moved with the athlete's smooth precision, but there was a deep, fixed intensity in his gaze.

"What's going on, Sam? Why did you send for me?"

Dr. Pitman was tired of reciting his piece. "Come with me," he said briefly.

He hastened into the autopsy room, Dr. Rochester walking sedately behind him. Without ceremony he uncovered the face of the dead doctor.

"Bob Marlowe," said Dr. Rochester in a matter-of-fact tone.

"My God, is that all you can find to say?"

" 'Thou shalt not take the name of the Lord thy God in vain, for the Lord will not hold . . .' "

"Look, Vaughan, this is no time for a prayer meeting. What are we going to do? We have no idea how he got here."

Mrs. Rogers, who had followed them as far as the door, was pointing to a chair in the far corner. "What's that over there?"

Sam Pitman went across to the chair. Arranged on the seat was a set of clothes, neatly folded, the shoes on top. He touched them gingerly. "They're Bob's clothes. That's the light gray suit he was wearing last night, and I'd recognize those Italian woven shoes anywhere."

Dr. Rochester had followed him and was leaning over his shoulder. "Yes, they're Bob's clothes, no question about it."

Dr. Pitman stared at his colleague's immobile features incredulously. "What do you suggest we do?"

"Do? You're the pathologist here. The man's in your department, all ready for you. Get on with your examination and find out what he died of."

"But I don't have any records. I don't even have a consent for an autopsy."

"Then get one. Call up Mrs. Marlowe. I'm sure she'll be quite willing. Now, if you'll excuse me, I have some patients waiting for me upstairs." He walked out as though this were a morning like any other morning.

Dr. Pitman almost staggered back to his office and collapsed into his chair. The nurse seated herself opposite him. "Mrs. Rogers," he said, "tell me quite frankly, what is your impression of Dr. Rochester? You've known him longer than I have. Would you say that he is quite normal?"

She stared thoughtfully across the room for several seconds, then said, "He's a very good doctor, Dr. Pitman, very dedicated. Of course, we know he's a very religious man, and that makes him a bit different from the rest of the people around here."

"Heaven knows I'm no atheist myself, Mrs. Rogers, but this isn't religion; the man's positively weird. I call him in and show him the body of the president of the medical staff. We both saw him alive last night and apparently in good health. He suddenly appears on my postmortem table without any explanation, and all Dr. Rochester can say is examine the body and find out what he died of. If this is religion, he must be in some strange state of ecstasy."

"I agree with you it's all very irregular," she said. "Would you like me to call Mrs. Marlowe, or will you do it?"

He wiped his forehead with the back of his hand. "No, you call her, Mrs. Rogers. I'm going to talk to the police."

"I'll speak to her from my office, poor woman," she said, and left.

He went out and called to Miss Plumbley, who was still stationed at the outer door. "Would you get back to your desk and call the police for me. That's at least something you can do."

Inspector Richard McCallister came over with remarkable speed. As he told Dr. Pitman, when a reputable pathologist claims that he has a dead body that he can't explain, a good policeman doesn't waste time asking questions; he comes, but fast. The inspector was a lean man whose features reflected a fleeting smile every time he spoke. The voice that emanated from his thin lips was surprisingly strong.

Sam Pitman felt reassured for the first time that morning; he wished he had called the police earlier instead of consulting with that visionary way-out colleague of his. Relaxed now, he gave a steady, systematic account of everything that had happened that morning, including the unaccountable reaction of the staff vice-president, Dr. Vaughan Rochester.

Inspector McCallister smiled when he heard the name. "Yes, I know Dr. Rochester well. We belong to the same church. I would say that he is a little more devout that I am; in fact, he's one of the deacons. He has an obsession about the Seven Deadly Sins. Whenever he gets to read the lesson, which is quite often, he recites them at both ends. Any member of our church could give you the list in his sleep: Pride, Covetousness, Lust, Anger, Gluttony and . . .''

Dr. Pitman interrupted him, playfully running a hand over his own prominent corporation. "Gluttony, that's me, and I only eat enough to keep a bird alive, but when I tell Vaughan that, he looks sour and says I must be referring to a three hundred pound ostrich."

"Then there's Envy and finally Sloth."

The pathologist grinned, pointing to the outer office. "There sits Sloth out there, but she's coming to her reward, now that Bob Marlowe has gone."

"What sort of man was Dr. Marlowe?"

"I didn't have too much to do with him outside the official business of the hospital. He wasn't my type, rather shallow, a social climber; had a reputation as a ladies' man. Still, it was a good year under his presidency; he was in especially good form last night. Boy, it's going to be rough next year under Vaughan Rochester. What am I saying, next year? Next year's here. With Bob Marlowe gone like this, Vaughan Rochester is already president. From now on there are going to be no more medical or social gatherings, just prayer meetings."

"I'd like to see the body if I may."

Dr. Pitman's features became set again as he led the way through the connecting door. The inspector walked slowly around the cheerless autopsy room, looked over the clothes on the chair without touching them, then came back to the table. He peeled the sheet off completely, taking care not to disturb anything beneath, and stared down at the corpse, examining it from all angles.

"Has anybody touched anything here?"

"Not since I arrived."

"That's good. I can't see any signs of violence, at least not on the front of the body, can you, doctor?"

"No."

Inspector McCallister replaced the sheet and pointed to a door about six feet from the foot of the table. "Where does that lead?"

"To a raised ramp on the parking lot. The bodies are taken out that way after we have finished with them and loaded into a hearse or ambulance. They are brought in here from the wards on a trolley through there.'' He pointed to a third door on the adjacent wall.

"So that if Dr. Marlowe's body did not come into this room by the orthodox route, it could have been brought in directly from the outside?''

"Yes.''

"And there are not too many people around at night. It could have been brought in unnoticed that way.'' The inspector opened the door and walked out onto the short ramp. He tried the handle on the outside; it did not turn. "I see you need a key to unlock it from out here. Do you have one, doctor?'' McCallister asked.

"Yes.''

"Who else?''

"The janitorial staff has one. There's one at the switchboard.'' A startled look appeared on Dr. Pitman's face. "Bob Marlowe had one himself. The staff president always has a set of master keys. He could have let himself in and . . . Oh, no, that's ridiculous.''

"There's one thing that is not ridiculous,'' said the inspector. "If Dr. Marlowe had been murdered, whoever had the body would also have the keys, and would naturally assume that they belonged to his home or his office.''

The phone rang in Dr. Pitman's office; he went in to answer it, then said, "Mrs. Marlowe has arrived, inspector. We have a special room for interviewing relatives. Would you like to see her in there?''

"Say that I'll be over in a minute. Now, doctor, we both agree that there is something radically wrong here, and I'm going to make a full, formal investigation. That means that nothing must be touched until my men have been over here, taken photographs, checked for fingerprints, and so on. I'll have to regard this room as the *locus delicti* and start here. Please see that nobody is allowed to come in till my men have arrived. May I use your telephone?''

"Take my chair,'' said the pathologist. "Dial 9 if you want outside.''

After Inspector McCallister had phoned through his instructions he said, "I'll see Mrs. Marlowe now. Perhaps your secretary will show me where to find her. I'd like you to stay here and keep guard over the autopsy room. My men should be here in a few minutes.''

Miss Plumbley seemed glad of any excuse to put as much distance as possible between herself and the pathology department. She chatted amiably to the inspector all the way to the visitors' room, and it took all his firmness to persuade her to accept her dismissal and to understand that he wanted to go in alone.

Lucille Marlowe rose from the sofa as he came in. Mrs. Rogers, who had been keeping her company, excused herself and left. Mrs. Marlowe was a trim woman in her middle forties, of medium height and tastefully dressed, not beautiful but of pleasant overall appearance. Her expression was serious, but there were no signs of tears, shock, or deep sorrow.

"I'm Inspector McCallister," he said.

She held out her hand. "How do you do, inspector." Her voice was remarkably firm; he wondered for a moment if she knew what had actually happened.

"Did you have a chance to talk with Mrs. Rogers?" he asked.

"Yes, she's a very kind person."

"She told you about your husband?"

"About his body's being found here, yes."

"Doesn't this come as a surprise to you?"

"Naturally." Her voice was still devoid of emotion.

McCallister's wonder increased. "You appreciate that nobody knows how your husband's body got here. There is a possibility of foul play. That's why the police . . . Why I have been called in."

"I gathered that was the reason."

"You seem to be taking all this with remarkable calm, Mrs. Marlowe."

"I'm not the screaming, hysterical type."

"Were you expecting anything to happen to your husband?"

"No."

"When the body was first discovered in the morgue, Dr. Pitman naturally assumed that he had been taken ill in the night and been brought into the hospital as a patient. Do you know if he was ill?"

"He appeared quite well when I saw him last."

"When was that?"

"After dinner last night, about seven thirty. He left for the staff meeting at the hospital."

"So he never came home after the meeting?"

"No."

"Weren't you worried?"

"I assumed that he had been caught up with some medical emergency and he had to stay with it."

"Did he often have emergencies like that?"

"No."

"Wouldn't he have called home or sent a message to say that he had been held up, just to let you know that he was safe?"

"He might have."

"But he didn't, and you made no effort to find out what had happened to him. You might, for example, have called the hospital."

She stood in front of him, rigid and a little paler, biting her lips.

He continued very softly. "You'll pardon me for being frank, Mrs. Marlowe, but I find your attitude a little strange. I have to ask you, would you say that your relations with your husband were satisfactory?"

"They could have been better."

"I see. You weren't in the process of divorce?"

"We hadn't come to that."

"The situation wasn't hopeless then?"

She shrugged. "I don't know, inspector. I would have found out in time."

"Are you interested in learning the cause of your husband's death?"

"Of course I would like to know."

"The suggestion has been made that since your husband's body is here, Dr. Pitman be permitted to perform the postmortem examination. If you are willing to consent to this, I am prepared to authorize it."

"I have met Dr. Pitman once or twice socially, and I hear he's a good pathologist. I'm willing to let him do it."

"I'll pass that on." He held out his hand. "Do you have transportation home?"

"I have my car outside."

"I'll get in touch with you as soon as I have some concrete information."

He left the room hurriedly with the sensation of having just emerged from an icebox. When he got back to the pathology department his men were already at work. Most of the photographs had already been taken, and one man was delicately dropping the dead man's clothes, garment by garment, into individual cellophane bags. The fingerprint men were busily dusting the tiles on the autopsy table and searching diligently for likely prints. The presence of the investigating team had produced a minor frenzy in the laboratory. Every few seconds one of the technicians would gravitate surreptitiously to the glass partition and peer through the open door of the autopsy room trying to glean details of what was going on.

The inspector sat down with Dr. Pitman until his men should finish.

"Well," asked the pathologist, "what did Lucille Marlowe have to say?"

"She was no more helpful than anyone else so far, but she did give her consent for you to perform the autopsy."

"Why me? Surely you didn't take that part seriously."

"Why not? What better place? The body's all laid out for you, ready."

"But . . ."

"Oh, I'm sorry, doctor, perhaps I was a bit hasty. You're not squeamish, I hope."

"No, it's not that. I've done postmortems before on people I've known. Once the soul has left the body, so to speak, it's all the same to me."

"Then what's holding you back?"

"Well, this is a little unorthodox, isn't it? I mean this sort of case usually goes to the coroner's pathologist."

"Firstly, let me say, doctor, that I haven't got where I am today by consistently following orthodox methods. Secondly, aren't you taking it for granted that this man has been the victim of foul play? Look, the body is undisturbed in your morgue; you're an experienced pathologist; go ahead; take the bull by the horns."

For a moment there was an expression of doubt on Dr. Pitman's face, then his customary broad grin came back, forming deep creases on his cheeks. "Put that way, inspector, it's a challenge I can't refuse. However, there is one thing. Supposing I don't find any obvious cause of death, like a knife wound in the back—if you'll pardon the expression—the problem of poison or some other subtle cause arises. My laboratory is only set up for routine medical pathology; I don't have the facilities for complete forensic analysis."

"Let me have specimens of the organs, and my chemists will be only too happy to oblige you."

"Right, then it's a deal." The pathologist stretched out a hand across the desk, but before Inspector McCallister could grasp it, the commanding sound of shattered glass reached them even through the thickness of the window. Dr. Pitman straightened. "What now?"

McCallister turned quickly to see one of the women technicians lying prone on the floor, the fragments of a chemical flask strewn around her. For a second Dr. Pitman was at his side, then he made a dash for the outer office and ran into the laboratory. The inspector followed close behind him.

By the time they reached the scene, the young woman was staggering to her feet, being assisted by two of her fellow technicians. Bits of glass were falling from her clothing, tinkling on the floor. One of them must have cut her chin, from which blood was oozing.

"What happened?" asked Dr. Pitman.

"She fainted," said one of the young men. "I saw her go pale, then whoops, down she went, flask and all. I was standing on the other side of the bench; otherwise I would have tried to catch her."

"Did you hurt yourself, Pat?" Dr. Pitman brushed the blood from her chin with his forefinger. "Hm, only a surface wound."

Still dazed, Pat shook her head. "No I'm all right."

She was a striking looking girl, with dark hair and eyes that stood out vividly against the temporary pallor of her skin. Inspector McCallister noted how well the white technician's coat hung on her slender figure.

Dr. Pitman was feeling her pulse. "It's a bit rapid," he said. "I think you ought to go down to emergency and let the man in charge check you over. Why don't you fellows help her down there?"

The color was coming back to her cheeks now, giving them a radiant glow. The wound on her chin began to bleed more briskly and a dark red drop fell onto her white lapel, but she seemed unaware of it, for she shook her head again. "No, really, I'll be all right."

The doctor took her gently by the shoulders and started her off toward the door. She continued on her way, supported by a colleague on either side. He watched them go.

Dr. Pitman muttered all the way back to his office, then stood behind his desk frowning.

"What's bothering you, doctor?"

"I don't know. The whole family seems to be acting strangely today."

"What family?"

"That was Patricia Newark; she's Dr. Rochester's niece. You might ask me how an old sourpuss like that could have such a beautiful niece. I don't know the answer to that one, but they're acting strangely. I wonder what came over her."

Inspector McCallister offered no comment. The last of his men were leaving the autopsy room. He looked at his watch. "I have to get back to my other work. It looks as if the coast is clear for you to begin now. Good luck, doctor. Give me a call if you find anything interesting.''

"Yes," said the pathologist absently. He pulled off his coat and hung a rubber apron over his paunch.

As the inspector left he saw that Miss Plumbley's office was deserted. Perhaps she was out on her coffee break. It did occur to him that she might have left for good, she had looked so scared each time he had seen her out there.

As he got into his car he had a glimpse of Dr. Rochester just driving off in his big black sedan. He nearly caught up with him along the street but was parted from him by a traffic light. The signal turned green, and a couple of blocks farther down he saw the black sedan parked outside Mary Anne's Cleaning Establishment. The well-built doctor was crossing the sidewalk, holding up a dark blue suit on a hanger. Inspector McCallister drove on.

He was glued to his desk for the next two hours, then a preliminary report came to him from his laboratory. He studied it thoughtfully for several minutes, reading it and rereading it, then picked up the phone. "Is Jarvis there?" He waited for Jarvis to come to the phone. "Go over to Mary Anne's Cleaning Establishment on Park Street immediately, and pick up a dark blue suit left there by a Dr. Vaughan Rochester this morning. Hurry; I hope they haven't got to work on it yet."

His secretary came in. "It's getting late, inspector. Would you like a lunch tray sent up?"

"No thanks, Molly, I'm going over to the Bishops Community Hospital. I'll pick up something in the cafeteria there." He ran down to his car.

When McCallister walked into the autopsy room, Sam Pitman was just completing his examination. He pointed to a row of wide-necked bottles all neatly labeled. "There are the specimens all ready to go. Will you have one of your men pick them up, or shall I have them sent?"

"I'll get someone to pick them up. I gather that you haven't found any obvious cause of death."

The pathologist pursed his lips. "Well, yes and no."

"Could you be a little more explicit, doctor? What's the yes, for example?"

"Well, Dr. Marlowe seems to have had a coronary attack."

"Surely he either did or did not."

"Unfortunately, it's not as simple as all that."

"Tell me, what did you find?"

"He had a fresh blood clot in the left coronary artery of his heart."

"What would cause that?"

"Coronary artery disease; hardening and narrowing of the vessels."

"Did he have that?"

"Oh yes, and the heart was enlarged. He must have had a raised blood pressure for some time."

"Wasn't he being treated for this?'

"Not as far as I know."

"Wouldn't that be rather unusual for a doctor?"

"On the contrary, doctors are among the worst offenders in this respect. Bob Marlowe may even have been trying to treat himself. We make all sorts of jokes about this kind of thing, you know; a doctor who treats himself has a fool for a patient and a bigger fool for a doctor, and so on, but we all do it. Come to think of it, I haven't had a physical myself for years."

"Hm, let's come back to Dr. Marlowe. You say his coronary arteries were diseased and he had a fresh blood clot in one of them, but you're still not sure this is what killed him. I don't want to appear naive, but I fail to see your problem."

"It's the strange circumstances of the whole case, inspector. You see, if Dr. Marlowe had died as a patient in this hospital, or even if he had suddenly dropped dead in the street and been brought in here, and if I had found what I found just now, I wouldn't be looking any further for the cause of death. But things being what they are, my index of suspicion is raised very high."

Inspector McCallister smiled. "Why don't you leave the suspecting to me, doctor? I understand that this is what is known as coronary thrombosis. Are you trying to tell me that Dr. Marlowe could have survived this, or are you suggesting that it could have been brought about by some human agency?"

"He could certainly have survived. A large number of people do."

"Then why do people die at all from coronary thrombosis?"

"In this sort of case, it's from what we call ventricular fibrillation. To put it simply, in certain cases, the ventricles of the heart suddenly go into spasm and stop pumping. That's the end, of course."

"Why does it occur in some cases of coronary thrombosis and not in others?"

"Nobody knows really, some sensitivity of the heart muscle, some temporary inhibition. For example, this may occur while the patient is under medical care, say in the hospital. If you have the proper apparatus ready and use it within about five minutes, you can sometimes start the heart up again, and the patient will recover.''

"Very interesting, but you're not sure if that's what happened here, this fibrillation?''

"There's no way of telling. Frankly, I don't know what to think. I just can't believe that Bob Marlowe had a heart attack last night, let himself into this room, took off all his clothes, folded them up neatly and laid them on that chair, climbed up onto the slab, draped himself with the sheet, then went into fibrillation and died. Do you believe that?''

The inspector's smile took on an impish quality. "If it helps with your hypothesis, you might be interested to know that Dr. Marlowe's car was found in the hospital parking lot.''

"I don't have a hypothesis.'' The pathologist ran his finger along the row of labeled bottles. "I want your lab to do every conceivable test on these organs. If they come up with nothing, I'll have to accept the coronary thrombosis as the cause of death. After that, we can start working on a hypothesis, at least, you can.''

"Fair enough. By the way, how's that beautiful technician of yours, Miss Newark?''

"Oh, she'll be all right. It was just a fainting spell and a little cut on the chin. Something must be upsetting her; I don't know what it is. Still, we sent her home for the rest of the day.''

"I'm glad it was nothing serious. I'll send someone over for those jars.'' The inspector went out.

Before going to the cafeteria he stopped in at the personnel office. A bright, chirrupy young woman looked up at him. "Can I help you, sir?''

"I had a message to deliver to Miss Newark, Patricia Newark. They tell me she had to leave early. Would you be kind enough to give me her address?''

"One moment, sir.'' The girl opened a metal filing cabinet beside her desk, riffled through it, then scribbled the address on a piece of paper; it was in an apartment house a few blocks away from the hospital.

He thanked her and continued on to the cafeteria where he joined a couple of his patrol officers. They had just brought in some victims of a street accident and were passing the time over a cup of coffee while they awaited the doctor's report.

Inspector McCallister was through in about fifteen minutes; then he drove down to the apartment house. Miss Newark looked startled when she opened the door to him. Her beautiful features were drawn, and there were unmistakable signs of weeping. She wore a small patch on her chin.

"Do you remember me?" he asked. "I was with Dr. Pitman this morning when you passed out in the laboratory."

"You're from the police."

"Yes. May I come in?"

She stepped back to let him pass, closing the door behind him. He was standing in a fair sized living room furnished in a rather stark style which scarcely appealed to him, but he tried to be complimentary. "It's delightfully simple and modern in here." He looked down. "And I must say I admire your carpet."

She forced a smile. "That's the most luxurious thing I have in here. I like to lie on it when the chairs get too hard."

"May I offer you a cigarette?"

"No, I don't smoke, but you may if you want to."

He lit one for himself. "May I sit down?"

"Please, do."

He took one of the high-backed armchairs while she poised herself uncomfortably on the edge of an ordinary chair.

"How long have you worked at the Bishops Community Hospital, Miss Newark?"

"About two years now."

"You like it there?"

"I love it."

"You enjoy being a lab technician?"

"It's very exciting work."

There was an uneasy look on her face, and every word she uttered was guarded. He stared at her for a moment, then seemed to fall into deep thought, drawing hard on his cigarette. He pulled it slowly from his mouth and let his hand fall on the arm of the chair. A roll of ash dropped onto the carpet, and he suddenly came to life. "Oh, pardon me, I've soiled your beautiful carpet."

"It doesn't matter," she said flatly. "It's not the first time it's had ash spilled on it. I'll clean it later."

"I won't hear of it." He snatched some tissues from his pocket, dropped to his knees, and began brushing vigorously at the ash, sweeping it into one of the tissues.

She held out her hand. "Thank you very much. I'll put it in the garbage."

"Please don't bother." He thrust the tissues back into his pocket and pulled an ashtray toward him. "I'll take care to use this next time. Now, you're probably wondering why I came here."

"I assumed it wasn't a purely social visit."

"Of course not. It's about this unfortunate affair of Dr. Marlowe."

"Why do you come to me?"

"I was hoping you might have some information you could give me which would throw some light on the mystery."

"Why me?"

"The thought occurred to me when you passed out this morning when all that commotion was going on over the body."

"That had nothing to do with it."

"Nothing at all?"

"Well, I suppose I was upset. After all, we all knew Dr. Marlowe very well, him being staff president, too. But I have my own personal problems."

"You wouldn't want to tell me about them?"

She shook her head, staring at him sullenly. He stood up. "You're sure there's no information you can give me about Dr. Marlowe?"

"No." Her lips fastened together.

"I'm disappointed."

She let him out without a goodbye. He drove back to the station.

The report which he particularly wanted did not reach his desk until the middle of the next morning; his men had carefully double-checked everything. After he had read it he asked his secretary to call Dr. Rochester.

"What is it?" asked the stern voice.

"I'd like to come over and talk to you, doctor."

"About this business of Robert Marlowe?"

"That's right."

"I've got a very busy schedule today. How much time do you want?"

"Fifteen to twenty minutes should do it."

"Let me look at my appointment book." There was a pause. "You'll have to wait till two thirty this afternoon."

"I'll be there," McCallister stated.

Dr. Rochester saw him at precisely two thirty. "What did you want to tell me, inspector?"

"I'd like to start off with a question. What was the particular sin that Dr. Marlowe committed?"

"I'm quite sure you didn't come here to discuss theological matters."

"It may well turn out to be a theological problem, doctor. Would I be correct in saying that the sin in question would be Lust?"

"What are you talking about?"

"I interviewed Mrs. Lucille Marlowe at the hospital yesterday, and I was greatly impressed by two things; first, her remarkable composure for a woman who has suddenly become a widow, and second, I discovered that her husband had never returned home after the staff meeting the previous night and that she had done nothing to ascertain his whereabouts. She was not aware that anything had happened to him till Mrs. Rogers called her from the hospital. When I questioned her about her lack of curiosity, she gave me the rather unconvincing explanation that she assumed that her husband had been detained by some medical emergency. If such a thing had happened to you, doctor, wouldn't you have notified your wife so that she wouldn't be unduly alarmed?"

"I probably would."

"Of course you would. No, the fact of the matter is that Mrs. Marlowe was used to her husband's staying away all night, but not for professional reasons. He was, as Dr. Pitman put it, a bit of a ladies' man."

"I regret to say that this is quite true. My late colleague was an exceeding immoral person. But why do you come to me with all this stuff?"

"Because, unfortunately, Dr. Rochester, it concerns you personally. One of the ladies in question was your niece, Miss Patricia Newark. In fact, after that staff meeting, instead of going home, Dr. Marlowe went straight to Miss Newark's apartment."

Dr. Rochester's deep-set eyes fixed themselves on the inspector menacingly. "You are making a very serious allegation, you know. I trust you are in a position to prove it."

The smile that flickered over McCallister's face only served to intensify his expression. "Let's stop playing, Dr. Rochester. Allow me to reconstruct for you what actually happened. While he was at Miss Newark's apartment, Dr. Marlowe had the misfortune—her misfortune—to suffer a fatal heart attack. Your niece very wisely called you and asked for your help. You went over, removed the body, transported it in Dr. Marlowe's own car to the hospital morgue, stripped it, folded the clothes, and then left the corpse ready for your colleague, Dr. Pitman."

"You really believe this fantastic story, inspector?"

"It's a strange thing that lying is not included among the deadly sins, doctor, but I'm sure you don't enjoy it, nevertheless. To save you further embarrassment, let me tell you that I have incontrovertible evidence for every statement I have made. The first pointer came when my men examined the dead man's suit. It was of a light gray color, rather gay, the sort of color Dr. Marlowe might have been expected to wear. Careful examination of the front of the suit showed the presence of some dark blue fibers from the suit of another man who, for example, might have thrown the body over his shoulder to carry it out. I happened to remember that I had seen you taking a dark blue suit into the cleaners that morning, and I took the liberty of requisitioning your suit from them for examination. The fibers matched unmistakably; there were also some gray fibers on the right shoulder of your suit."

"I see," growled Dr. Rochester, "and where does my niece come into all your ingenious sleuthing?"

"On both suits there were some other fibers, short, broken pieces of nylon of different colors; my experts told me those must have come from a certain type of carpet. They were most profuse on the back of the gray suit, where the corpse had presumably lain, and on the knees of the blue suit. I assume that you had knelt down beside the body, perhaps to attempt resuscitation, or maybe merely to enable you to pick it up; I can only guess there, of course. We found some similar fibers in Dr. Marlowe's car, which you left in the parking lot.

"Yesterday afternoon I paid a brief visit to Miss Newark in her apartment and was able to obtain a sample of fibers from her carpet. Once again, they matched unmistakably. Need I say more?"

The broad shoulders sagged for the first time. "It's my punishment for the sin of Pride. I told myself I was doing it to protect my niece's reputation, but it was my own reputation I was thinking of as a professional man, vice-president of the medical staff, a deacon of the church; I couldn't tolerate a scandal in the family."

"I know exactly what happened, and I can understand your motives in removing the body," said the the inspector, "but tell me, what possessed you to put on this bizarre production, carrying the corpse over to the hospital and laying it out on the autopsy table? Why didn't you drive the car down the street and leave the body behind the wheel? It would have been found, taken over to the city morgue, an autopsy would have been performed, and everybody would have assumed that the heart attack had occurred where he was found. No one would ever have connected it with your niece."

The doctor nodded grimly. "That's what I intended to do originally, but when I got the body out to the car I realized what a serious mistake I was making. Doing it that way I was conniving with my niece, even condoning her misconduct. I didn't want her to get that impression. I think that we are too permissive today with our young people and their loose-living morality. I wanted her to be punished, so I took the body over to the hospital, laid it out in the autopsy room, and did my best to get the postmortem performed right there. I knew that she would have to come to work that morning within a few feet of her lover's body. I hoped that would teach her a lesson she'd never forget."

"I'm sure she will never forget it," the inspector said, with feeling.

The usual hard look had gone out of Dr. Rochester's eyes. "I know you've come to arrest me. Can I ask you a small favor? Could you wait until this evening when I've seen all my patients? They all have appointments, and they are expecting me to attend to them. I'm sure you know I won't run away."

"You misunderstand me. I have no intention of arresting you."

The hard look returned. "Look, inspector, because we both belong to the same church, I expect no special privileges or favors. You have your duty to perform as a police officer."

McCallister regarded him solemnly. "It's not a question of special privileges, doctor. It's just that I'd be hard put to it to find a charge against you. You found the body of a man who had died of natural causes and transported it to the autopsy room of the hospital. That happens many times every day in slightly less dramatic circumstances. Oh, I suppose I could pull something out of the book, but it would have to be something highly technical and rare, hardly sufficient to warrant the scandal that would envelop you, your niece, poor Mrs. Marlowe, the hospital, everybody. No, I told you when I came in that it might turn out to be a purely theological matter. If you will permit me to quote from the book of Romans, 'Vengeance is mine; I will repay, sayeth the Lord.'

"I propose to leave you in His hands." Inspector McCallister rose. "I'll see that your suit is returned to you, Dr. Rochester, duly cleansed."

ANOMALIES OF THE HEART

by ASHLEY CURTIS

Maple looked at Basram. He looked at his bare black feet, his scrawny legs, his western shorts. Basram's eyes looked dirty, but at least they didn't have flies crawling around them, like most babies' eyes around here did. He reckoned that Basram was about eleven years old, though it was very difficult to tell, and Basram himself said fourteen.

Every day, Basram led Maple around the outskirts of the village, over the hard, packed dust, around the great juniper trees, past the emaciated herds of cattle and the flocks of goats tended by children, over the dry wadis where the men dug deep for water for their animals. And always Basram carried in his right hand a long, thin, rectangular box hammered together from the remnants of boards he had probably found around the hospital. The handle of what must once have been a suitcase was screwed into one side of the box, and it was this that Basram held in his right hand. It was his weapon. Not the box, but what was in the box.

No one was going to mess with Basram. It was his own idea. He needed it because his father was not Lambanu. He would never be a warrior like most of the young men around here, and he had only a mother to look after him. He went to the Mission school, and carried a snake perpetually at his side.

Basram had another box as well. It was much shorter and somewhat fatter, just big enough to hold a rat. When it was time for the snake to eat, Basram hooked the two boxes together and lifted up a sliding door between them. Except for these rare variations in its life, the snake lay stretched out inside Basram's box, carried about as if it were a collapsible fishing rod.

Maple went to the hospital every day, and always saw the same

251

thing. He walked down the main street, the only street of Tingu, raising dust at every step. On his left and right, on the porches of the one room boxes that were their homes, their restaurants, their grocery stores, the women sat, lethargic, with small piles of tomatoes or garlic or onions at their feet. Though they were happy to sell to you, they made no effort to attract your attention, had no sales pitch, and seemed indifferent to whom you bought from. It had given Maple an uncomfortable feeling on the first day, and he had had Basram do his shopping every since.

At the bottom end of the town he reached the gates of the Mission Hospital where a crowd of people, potential visitors, stood about but were not let in. He sometimes turned around and looked back up the street at the village. There was not much to see. Even the little houses were mostly hidden by the dusty bushes that grew along the road. A few hundred yards up the gentle slope the road simply stopped, and somewhat higher, though in the same line, a vague, white building with a gabled roof (the only one in Tingu) brought the village definitively to an end. This was the police station, Basram had said. But Maple had yet to see a police officer, or any movement at all around the house.

The gatekeeper, a wizened old man with a stick, let Maple into the hospital grounds without questions—in deference to his whiteness, he supposed. Once inside, things looked different. There were flow-erbeds, there was water and the sound of a generator pumping elec-tricity. Maple always had an eerie feeling at this point, just inside the gate. He supposed it was what they called déjà vu: he had the sudden, shocking sense that he had lived through exactly the same moment before. It was not just because he had come through the hospital gate at approximately the same time, with approximately the same attitude, the day before and the day before that; it was not just a similarity but rather an exact repetition that he felt. He tried to shrug it off, for he could not find its cause and he did not think that he believed in such things anyway.

The hospital itself was on his left, a U-shaped structure, also one story but made of plastered-over cinder blocks, cleanly painted, fresh. Immaculate nurses walked about, many of them white, in pale gray habits with a crucifix about the neck. They smiled at him as he walked by.

Sometimes he did not go directly to Schmidt-Grohe's room. Some-times he walked softly through the gardens to the back of the com-pound from where, over a small, inviting metal gate, he could look into the doctor's quarters. He saw a flagstone terrace with flowers everywhere, and odd bits of sculpture peeking out from various corners and niches. When he came at lunchtime he smelled garlic broiling in olive oil, roasting meat, the pale, damp smell of boiling pasta. He had several times considered asking if there were not an extra room back here, but he had never got up the courage. Nothing had been offered him, and he did not want to presume. Only, when he entered the courtyard of Mama Haja's in the evening (and he no longer did so without Basram at his side), and felt his stomach sink, and scorpions, snakes, and giant cockroaches scuttled across his mind, he was often on the verge of running back to the hospital, jumping that gate, and demanding that he be given a bed, clean, with real sheets, a shower, the security of sealed walls and window screens. But he did not; he walked on, Basram by his side, unlocked the padlock that held closed the plywood door, pushed it open, and stepped back, as if to let whatever creature might meanwhile have entered his abode slip out without resistance or cause for fright. Then Basram, understanding, would go in and shine the flashlight in the corners and shake out the sheets. And Maple would say thank you to the boy and bring out the matches and the gas cooker, the tank of water, the bread, the oily cheese, tomatoes, garlic—sometimes a zucchini, if one had been featured in the little piles before the women's feet (and if there was a zucchini in the pile before one woman's feet, there was, uncannily, a zucchini in every single pile). And Basram would start to cook their dinner while Maple lay down gingerly on the bed, tucked the mosquito netting in all around him, and sweated, staring at the ceiling, telling himself to rest.

Every day he would walk through the flower gardens of the hospital, sometimes pausing at the doctor's gate (while, at other times, he did not have the heart), but inevitably making his way through the open wards to Schmidt-Grohe's room, and there he would see always the same thing.

The first time he had made this trip was engraved clearly in Maple's memory. He remembered reaching the hospital gate, knocking on the glass to gain the attention of the gatekeeper.

"Do you speak English?"

The man had stared at him, a big smile on his face, the whiff of liquor on his breath, his left hand holding a small stick with a big knob at its end.

"Schmidt-Grohe?" Maple had tried.

Maple had turned to look into the courtyard. He saw a boy jump up from a green bench by the fence (it had been a long time since Maple had seen such a bench, like a bench in an American park) and run across the yard to one of the grated windows. The boy's small hand rapped on the glass, his arm poking through the bars. Maple saw mothers suckling babies on other benches, old men sitting with crutches at their sides, and then, to his delight, a white nurse walking briskly down a path. He gestured to the gatekeeper, who remained smiling, and then he hurried towards this woman. She had a wrinkled, kindly face, spoke broken English with a thick Italian accent, and told him where Schmidt-Grohe could be found.

Maple thanked her. He followed her instructions, turning left at the end of the building. He saw the second wing of the hospital extending in front of him but turned left again through the open entryway and found himself in the interior courtyard. A lawn, scantily green, occupied the space in front of the main building and between the two wings, the center of the U; at the far end of the lawn a heavily vined fence put an end to the hospital grounds. Inside, roofed concrete walkways lined both the main building and the wings, and every few yards a door opened into one of the rooms. On these walkways young children played, or sat, or screamed, or lay asleep; dark black children, naked except for the shockingly clean white of a massive set of bandages on one part of their bodies: an entire leg or, more often, a whole side of the head was wrapped in plaster or white gauze. Others, without bandages, were simply misshapen—an arm so scrawny that it might belong to an insect, or a great protrusion sticking out from the forehead, so that the child looked like a creature from another planet.

Maple followed the walkway to the third door on the left. It was open, as the nurse had promised. He stepped gently inside.

The room was mostly bare. Straight ahead he saw the large window, one of its big panes open and its blind pulled most of the way down. The sharp shadows of the outside grating sent black parallel lines all the way down the blind. Beneath the window was a ratty gray and white flecked sofa on which sat Schmidt-Grohe's traveling bag and, next to it, open but face down, a black paperback book. The doctor, dressed in a white uniform, stood at the wall to Maple's right, noting something down on a clipboard, while a large bed with bars on its sides like a baby's crib stood heavily against the left-hand wall. In this bed, contorted into an unnatural but monumental position like a piece of antique sculpture representing the agonies of some great hero, of Prometheus or Hercules, Maple's friend lay motionless—though "lay" is not the word for such a twisted position, and one would better say humped or torqued or mangled. His legs were under a white sheet, curled up as they might be by a man lying on his side, but his torso then twisted in the opposite direction, his back rose up into the air, and his head, buried in the pillows, faced the wrong way; as if it hadn't learned of the position of his legs. Maple was reminded for an instant of some great sea creature surfacing and twisting in the air before submerging again into the deep water, but this thought did not stay for long, for his attention was consumed by the great red, irregular circle that took up most of Schmidt-Grohe's back. It was a red he had never seen before— impossible to guess the texture from the color, whether a liquid scab was building on the poor man's skin or whether the skin itself was gone and one was looking at the meat that hides inside a man like sirloin in a cow. Maple could not look at it for long, for a mutinous feeling was rising up through his intestines. He turned to face the doctor.

"How is he?" Maple asked.

The doctor looked at him a moment with his ambiguous eyes. His thin white hair was combed straight back, his face and hands were tan, his eyes rich but troubling, and he exuded both a strength and an evasion. Maple remembered their first meeting—it had been just the day before—himself sitting at the Safari Lodge, a tropical fruit cocktail on the table in front of him, waiting for Schmidt-Grohe to return from making inquiries. They had been looking for a driver to take them around the park because the van that they had hired in Nairobi wouldn't start. It had been lucky, Schmidt-Grohe kept repeating, that they'd even made it to the park. It would have been no picnic to be broken down at night in the semi-arid land that stretched for hundreds of miles on either side of the miserable dirt road from Isiolo. It was after all lion country, buffalo and leopard country— not to mention the snakes and insects that gave Maple the particular creeps. But they had made it to the lodge, and the next morning the van had just refused to start; the driver had called Nairobi; they could have a replacement only on the following day; and so Schmidt-Grohe was "inquiring," as he put it, to see about a vehicle for the day. He had returned with this Dr. Agnelli, who spoke English very well, who regularly came on his day off to the Lambanu Park, and who would gladly take a couple of visitors around. He would show them, too, places where he knew the animals would be—unlike the drivers from Nairobi, who had no idea.

Then it had all happened so fast. They had stopped the van— "Lions around here, I'm so sure of it!"—and Schmidt-Grohe, the damned fool, had got out with his fancy camera, the doctor screaming, "No!"; then Schmidt-Grohe's piercing scream, the sickening sound of his body slamming against the body of the van; the doctor jumping over the seats to the back door, opening it, pulling in the body, while Maple, petrified, stared at the red juice that poured through the back of the ripped safari shirt and waited for the lion to jump in the van and finish them all off. Then the doctor, frantic, "Start the car, goddammit, back to the lodge," and Maple, in spite of himself, sliding over to the driver's seat, somehow getting the van started and in gear, and tearing over the hot grasses back to the dirt road, following the river up towards the lodge; the lodge finally looming into sight, and Maple himself finally opening his mouth to say, "We're almost there."

"Goddammit, no!" the doctor yelled above the noises of the jolting van. "They can't do anything for him at the lodge. We go direct to Tingu hospital. Out of the park, keep going, straight out of the park, don't stop there at the gate, just go!"

And Maple, as in one of his dreams where he is the only one who can save somebody's life, and, acting mechanically but with great bravery, does so, pushed the gas pedal down even harder, tasting a fear, an excitement, a brush with reality that he had never known before, and ran right through the exit gates while the black men in green suits emerged, shouting, from their little huts—but they were soon well in the distance. "Left on the main street," the doctor shouted, and on reaching the pitted, dusty, stone-ridden disaster of a road, the doctor asked him for a little box kept in the glove compartment and as an aside muttered, "Go left, go left," while in the background, though he could not see him, Maple heard the lingering moans of his traveling companion.

Maple had driven, hard and awkwardly, left down this road on which, the day before, they had come from the right, from Isiolo and comparative civilization. He did not know where he was going, observed only that the landscape became drier, rougher, wilder, that one no longer saw even the roadside settlements or stray mud huts that they had seen on the way from Isiolo to the park. Schmidt-Grohe moaned in the back of the van, but there was an absolute limit to the speed at which one could drive along this stretch of road that might yesterday have been bombed, so many were the craters and the washouts that wracked the suspension of the van. It took well over an hour and a half, he later reckoned, before they reached the first fork and the doctor instructed him to take the right; and three minutes later they were at the bottom of the little village he now knew, and he was backing up to the gate of the Mission Hospital.

A great commotion had arisen in the crowd that was perpetually waiting at the gate. Maple stayed in his seat until Schmidt-Grohe, on a stretcher carried by two men, disappeared into the compound with the doctor at his side. He had wanted to get out of the van, but this crowd of black people was not inviting him to mingle. Most wore dingy western clothes and broken shoes, but some—young men, tall, lean, and powerful—were got up in some tribal fashion. Their beautifully madeup faces were accentuated by a chain of golden metal that ran from ear to ear along their perfectly smooth, black cheeks, drawing a strong, fascinating line through the depression between lip and chin. They held long spears at their sides with a short sword in a sheath about the waist, tucked into the short red cloth that was their only covering. He later learned they were the warriors of the Lambanu—something Basram would never be.

He had waited in the driver's seat, fretting, hot, while people from the crowd outside came up to the windows of the van, saying things to him in a language whose sounds he did not even begin to recognize. Finally, after what seemed like hours, a black nurse in the same gray habit he would later see on the Italian sisters made her way starkly through the crowd. She stood at the window by the driver's seat and stared at Maple for a moment.

"Your friend hurt bad," she stammered at him. "He be here long time. He maybe die."

Then, peremptorily, "Get out."

Maple had not been expecting such an order. He did not like it. Nevertheless, he opened the door and stepped out of the van.

"Place to stay," the woman curtly said. She looked about her. "Boy!" she called imperiously, pointing at a shabby looking creature sitting against the fence with a strange, long wooden box at his side. "Boy!"

And Basram, for a price of several shillings (and this was to become a refrain with him: "Mister, you have a shilling for your boy? One shilling, mister, shilling, please?"), had taken him to Mama Haja's, where he was able, for what was undoubtedly an outrageous price, to rent a "house." He had not forgotten to grab his bag from the back of the van, and he thanked Schmidt-Grohe's paranoia, which never for a moment let a single one of his possessions out of sight, for the fact that he had anything with him at all. As he picked it up, he saw what the people from the crowd had been staring at in the back of the van. A white towel still hung from the back seat, and Maple, who had always been told that blood turned dark brown, even blackish, once exposed for long enough to the air, was shocked at the still bright red color of the liquid on this towel, and reflected that his friend must have bled copiously right up to the very end of the drive.

The doctor hung the clipboard back up on the wall. He stared at Maple for a moment before answering.

"I have to change his dressing now. It is a terrible wound."

The doctor paused and let his eyes travel about the room.

"You are probably wondering why I brought him here, why we did not go to Isiolo, which we would have reached more quickly and where the road is not so bad."

He stopped and bit his lip, and in this pose looked both humble and extremely powerful. Maple blinked his eyes with an exaggerated force.

"It is because," he said, taking up his own question, "the hospital in Isiolo is not like this hospital. The doctors are not competent. The administration is messy. We would have had to wait, even in the emergency room, longer than it took us to get here. You don't understand how this can be, perhaps, for you come from America. But I tell you it is so.

"You have seen the children, playing out there on the pavement? They are my children. They are children who have walked through fires, who have played too near a river full of crocodiles, who have been partly eaten by a wild dog in the night. They come here, and I put them back together as best I can. I have been here thirty years, you know. I have experiences with fixing people after they have played with animals.

"I would do better if I had better equipment," he went on. "Not with these, the animal cases, but the others. There are among the children here, you see, many anomalies of the heart. It is essential ... but that's not the point."

He let out a sigh and then continued, looking down at the ground.

"I am afraid, though, that it would not have made any difference for your friend." He gestured over at the bed. "It is severe. He will not live. Save for a miracle, he will not live."

Maple had drifted over to the sofa, where he now sat down. He felt an undeniable relief at the doctor's words. He glanced down at the book beside him: *Mord in Mesopotamien.* He looked down at his feet. "I have to explain," he said. "This man is not really my friend. I hardly know him. We met only two days ago and decided to go on safari together, but only to save money. I really don't know him at all."

The doctor said nothing. He glanced over at the bed and the motionless, twisted creature on it.

"There's really no reason for me to stay here, I suppose," Maple ventured.

The doctor moved over to the bed. He readjusted something that Maple could not see.

"It would be good," the doctor said slowly, "if you would stay until . . . until he seems to be improving, or, more likely, until he has really died."

The doctor turned away from the bed now and focused his full attention on Maple. His voice modulated softly as he spoke.

"I say this out of humanitarian grounds. Your friend is probably going to die—in a strange country, of strange wounds. He has a family—I do not know what—but he must have a family, a mother or a sister or a child. I have seen enough to know that such a case is very difficult for them. Everything is so uncertain. They are informed by their embassy; there is a document from the Interior Ministry; there is perhaps a letter signed by myself. But they know nothing—who I am, what kind of government reigns here. It is too strange. They suspect foul play, or they suspect that he is really still alive, a hostage of some tribe or of a terrorist or brainwashed by the Hare Krishnas—it is all so vague. Perhaps one of them comes down here, visits the ambassador, rents a vehicle and comes to Tingu to see me. I tell them what I know—and still it is too vague, too strange, too foreign. They don't know who I am—the town of Tingu horrifies them with its primitive, slow life—they leave less certain even than when they arrived."

Maple was still staring at his feet. He knew how this would end, and knew, too, that he would acquiesce, and not out of strength but out of weakness, out of an inability to say no to a more authoritative man.

"But if a person, a western person—" the doctor's voice shifted strangely, becoming vaguely aggressive "—having nothing to do with this country, with black people, poverty, a person whose motives they can understand, someone who goes on holiday for a safari—" a bit of sarcasm, almost of anger, became more and more clear in the doctor's voice, while his eyes seemed to grow duller, to lose their power, to withdraw "—if they can meet someone like this," he said sharply, "someone who knows what happened, someone who shares, to some extent, their horror of this strange, foreign world, shares their life of comforts, running water, flushing toilets, antiseptic, central heating—" The doctor paused at this bitter crescendo, which almost frightened Maple. Then he changed, all of a sudden, back to his earlier, gentle, kindly mode. His face relaxed, his eyes sparkled again, and his voice became peaceful, knowledgeable, understanding: "If they only meet you, and you can tell them what you saw, and how it happened—then they have a clean death on their hands. They mourn, they grieve, and they forget. They can perform the rites of grief correctly—and then they can move on. Do you see what I mean?"

Maple nodded reluctantly. A practical thought had just struck him for the first time. How did one get out of Tingu? He had not yet seen a bus—he doubted that there was a bus. Certainly no taxi. He was not sure that he wanted to try to hitch a ride with one of the two or three vehicles that entered and left the town each day. And then, as though he had read his thoughts, the doctor went on:

"Of course, I cannot compel you to stay against your will." And he addressed an ironic smile to Maple that disturbed him with its strange look of complicity, as though the two of them were in on something Maple did not quite understand. "Nevertheless, I must tell you that it is sometimes easier to come to Tingu than to leave. There is a bus that leaves every third day—you will see it tomorrow on the street if it has not broken down somewhere. But it is so packed always that it is difficult to get on, particularly for a white man. Besides, it is not safe, riding on such an overloaded bus, and there are many accidents. Sometimes a truck comes, making a delivery, and if you pay them money you can get a ride back out—but this is chancy and, besides, illegal, and they are often caught at the roadblock just outside of Isiolo.

"The easiest way out, of course, is with the hospital van. But I can't simply offer you a ride, for it is constantly in use—it is our ambulance, our supply truck, our portable pharmacy. But Gerard is making a supply trip to Nairobi in about a week, and he could easily take you along. And by then we should know about your friend."

Maple thought of the cockroach, if it had really been a cockroach, if something of that size could be a cockroach at all, that he had surprised with the flashlight in the middle of the night when he had wanted to go out to the latrine. He had not gone; he had waited until the morning, wrapped up tight in the mosquito netting, his bladder almost bursting, wide awake. He grimaced but nodded his head.

"Yes, I understand," he said.

"It is very kind of you," the doctor replied.

One morning, for a few extra shillings, Basram led Maple along a largely overgrown path into the hills outside the village. It followed a dry streambed out of which, from time to time, emerged a buried metal pipe. They left the village much farther behind than they had on any of the previous days. Maple learned that this pipeline had been a Peace Corps project seen through by a volunteer named Peter, who had lived for two years in the little cubicle in which he himself had spent the past four nights. Before this project, there had been no source of water in the village, and the people had had to seek it at the bottom of the deep holes that they dug in the dry wadis. Maple could hardly imagine living in such conditions; he didn't see how he could have survived without the pump in the middle of the village from which drinkable water was so easily obtained. He felt a pride in the work of the Peace Corps, and when they reached their destination, the "dam" that Peter had built sent a rush of warm feeling up his spine which spread out, tickling his scalp. He almost started to feel tears in his eyes as he looked at the humble engineering project, and in the same glance caught the unselfconscious, angelic face of Basram, gazing into the water where tiny tadpoles swam. It was simply a concrete wall, no more than four feet tall and seven wide, and the amount of water it dammed up was no more than might fit into a very large bathtub; yet it was enough to provide for all of Tingu.

He felt more optimistic when they reached the village after this excursion. He was almost certain that Schmidt-Grohe would be dead soon, and had the feeling that Gerard's trip was only being held up by this event. He also felt more confident himself somehow, and though he could not place exactly why, it had perhaps something to do with the discovery that this Peter had lived in his own room for two years, with the fact that it had been a white man who had laid these pipes that gave him water, with the fact that, on the walk today, his usual fears had been distant. Perhaps he was just getting used to it, this life. Or perhaps he was so desperate that he did not notice enough anymore.

This last thought grabbed him as they entered the courtyard of Mama Haja's. Was it, perhaps, not that he was braver or more confident but only tired and getting foolhardy? The thought upset him. The picture that he was expecting to see again this afternoon, of Schmidt-Grohe contorted on that metal, railed-in bed, a bed that almost resembled a medieval instrument of torture, depressed him more, and he became less sure that Schmidt-Grohe would ever die. He tried to shake these thoughts and go back to the ones that had sustained him on the walk back through the land of reddish dirt with its occasional tall trees, with the beautiful, indolent picture of the herds of particolored goats and the young, perfectly black children watching over them from the shade of trees, holding long, smoothly whittled sticks in their small hands.

"Where is Peter now?" he asked. "Do you know?"

Basram looked at him uncomprehendingly.

"Peter, from the Peace Corps. Where did he go when he left Tingu?"

"I don't know," Basram finally answered. "Mister wants cheese?"

"Yes, cheese. With tomatoes, Basram. You don't know where Peter went? To America?"

Basram did not reply. They ate hard, dry tomatoes and oily, mealy cheese in silence. Maple had again the feeling, suddenly, that this would be the day, that he would enter the hospital room and the bed would be empty, the bag gone from the sofa—or perhaps another man would lie, bandaged after his own fashion, in the bed—and this would be his ticket to go home.

"Heaven," Basram finally said, out of the blue.

"What?"

"Peter went to heaven," Basram said. "Mister wants tea?"

The glimmerings of confidence that Maple had felt that morning were thoroughly gone by the time he approached the hospital gate in the afternoon. Something seemed awry. He had got out of Basram that Peter had died just before he was to leave the town, but Basram hadn't wanted to talk about it anymore. He felt a new uneasiness, occasioned not only by this news about the man he was coming to see as his precedessor but also, as he approached the gate, because of the strange feeling of déjà vu that he received without fail whenever he entered the grounds of the hospital. It was more than a feeling of repetition—he had utterly convinced himself of this—of performing the same actions day after day, of seeing the same thing once he reached Schmidt-Grohe's room; something more specific, more eerie always struck him, and always just as he entered the hospital grounds—and he felt that it was something he could localize if he only concentrated hard enough. He passed the gatekeeper and smelt the sticky scent of alcohol—some terrible liqueur, cherry or peach or something of the sort—and wondered if it was not this unique, ugly smell that triggered it—and then, as he slipped through the gate, he saw something that knocked the wind out of his gut. The same women, or women like them, were sitting on the benches nursing babies; and men with crutches hobbled about in brief circles before sitting down again; and a small boy got up and ran across the yard, knocking through the metal grating on the glass of a big windowpane. Maple felt suddenly sick, nauseated; he stumbled over to an empty bench. He tried to collect himself. The same boy, running over to the same window. He stared down at his feet and felt the sweat breaking out on his neck. He breathed in deeply. The outlines of his shoes were fuzzy against the ground.

He knew he had to look up at the hospital building, knew he had to place which window the boy had run up to and knocked on. He knew also which window it was bound to be. He looked up quickly, just long enough to see that he was right.

He looked down again at the ground, to calm his stomach. A few paltry blades of grass poked through the dust between his shoes. He felt a tingling on the balls of his feet, as he often did when he looked down from a tall building.

But how? What could they be doing in the room, to get it ready for his visits, whenever the little boy tapped on the glass? He stared down at his shoes but only saw the boy.

Then the body echoed in his sight. It had been too unnaturally twisted, and each time too much the same. He should have known something was wrong—known, also, from the strange way the doctor sometimes spoke. And it became clear to him, suddenly, that Schmidt-Grohe was dead; had been dead, probably, for days—perhaps, even, he had been dead upon arriving at the hospital. His wish of the last several days had just come true—but now he did not want it anymore. Why were they concealing it from him? He did not even know how they had kept it from him—was that Schmidt-Grohe's corpse there on the bed? If so, why didn't it stink by now? Or was it the body of another man, contorted, the face hidden, so that he would not notice it? Had he ever noticed that it breathed?

He sat bolt upright, staring at the window. The boy had left it and gone back to sitting near a flowerbed. Should he confront the boy? It was a stupid idea: he couldn't speak his language, and he would only give himself away. And this brought home to him that he should not do anything to show he had found out; he would have to make his visit, ask his usual questions, and go home. But what could possibly be going on? Why did they—who? The doctor? Was it Peter in that bed? This thought, which seized him suddenly, gave him the worst fright of all though it didn't make a bit of sense. He brushed it away. Why would the doctor want to keep him here? And he remembered then the first words the doctor had addressed to him. They had been an excuse. "You're probably wondering," he had said, "why we didn't drive to the hospital in Isiolo." Maple had not been wondering this at all. But clearly it was on the doctor's mind. Could it not be that, with Schmidt-Grohe already dead, it had become clear to the doctor that he had made the wrong choice in bringing him to Tingu? And was the doctor afraid of this getting out, and his being disbarred, or whatever happened to doctors when they had made severe mistakes? It was a slender thread. And Maple remembered then the rest of the conversation during that first visit, and how the doctor had been so anxious that he not leave Tingu, and had perhaps greatly exaggerated the difficulties of leaving, in order to keep him there. But why? What could the doctor want to do with him? And Maple turned his face away from the window and looked back over towards the gate, for there could only be one answer to that question.

He knew that he should, but he simply could not go into the room right now. It was too much for him; he would give himself away. It was not unbelievable that he might come into the hospital grounds without visiting: he had often, after all, walked around a long time before going to Schmidt-Grohe's room, and he might not have the stomach for it now. He stood up and glanced back at the doctor's quarters resting in their quiet, western peace, and was glad that he had never had the courage to inquire about a room.

Maple strode out the gate and up the street of Tingu, trying to think. But his senses were so assailed by unwanted noises, by the shrill screech of a bird coming at irregular intervals, the chirping of some kind of cricket, by the heat that beat down on him and the sweat it unloosed on his forehead, by the pounding of his heart, which seemed to have taken up a new position right between his ears—not to mention the regular approach of boys, boys of Basram's age and younger, with their soft refrain of "Shilling, mister? Shilling for a boy?" He saw at the end of the street in front of him the mysterious building, half hidden in vegetation, that was the police headquarters, and his instincts quickly told him it would be exactly the wrong place to go. He reached the square where Peter's pipeline delivered water to a standing section of pipe. The people grasped a lever, plunged it down, and out came the cool, clear stream. There was a crowd around the tap. Maple sat down on a stump in the shade of a tall tree, out of sight of almost everyone.

He sat for a long time on the little stump. When he finally got up, he made his way into the pale blue building Basram had once disappeared into when Maple had asked him for a beer.

Night fell. Basram cooked a stew over the stove at dusk, and they shared the meal silently. When it was thoroughly dark, Maple sent Basram into the hut to get him his dark sweater and told him that he would be going for a walk.

"Mister, you want Basram should come? A shilling?" the boy asked.

"It's okay, Basram. I'll be fine.

"And Basram," he said on a whim, "you don't have to wait for me tonight. Go see your mother. Sleep at home tonight, I'll be okay. Here, take these shillings to her." He handed Basram several bills and watched his eyes open enormously wide. "These are for your mother, not for you. I have more for you, later. Take these to your mother, okay?"

Basram took them, nodding, dumbstruck, and was gone.

There was no one on the street. Occasionally he saw, from the tiny, thin windows at the very tops of the little boxlike houses, the faint glow of yellowish light from a kerosene lantern or a candle and heard loud chatter coming from inside. As he neared the hospital, the hum of the generator became louder until it even overcame the sharp sound of the crickets rubbing their legs together in the tall grasses all around. Soon a rectangle of brighter yellow light came into view, and as Maple got nearer to the gate, he made out the dark shape of the gatekeeper behind his window, elbows on the table, his chin resting on his hands. Maple approached the window, but the man did not see him. He was asleep.

Maple tapped lightly on the glass. The man's head jerked back, and he had to adjust his eyes for a minute before he could see who was there. He broke into a smile, and though his teeth were yellow, and even partly black, they stood out sharply against the darkness of his skin. He smiled and nodded at Maple, but then shook his finger at him as a means of saying no. He twisted his wrist, and pointed at the watch he wore. The watch, Maple noticed, said four o'clock, and the second hand was not moving, but the message was still clear.

Maple reached into his pocket and pulled out a little pink glass bottle. He held it up to the window so the man could see. They had had only one kind of liqueur at the little store, a sickly smelling mango flavored liquid, and Maple had been sure he recognized it from the gatekeeper's breath.

The man's smile, if possible, grew even bigger. But still he did not move to open the gate. He slowly shook his head, and once again held up his broken watch against the windowpane.

Maple reached again into his pocket. He took out a twenty shilling note, and held it up next to the bottle. The man's eyes widened; he put his finger to his lips, edged out of his booth, and quietly released the latch of the gate. Maple slipped through and handed him the money and the bottle. The man smiled, nodded his head, and bowed his emaciated body. Then he returned to his little cell.

There was only one room lit up on this side of the hospital. It was one of the windows at the far end, and Maple knew that it was Schmidt-Grohe's. He crept up to it from the side and leaned his back against the wall right next to it.

He was astonished, as he stood still and collected himself, to hear breathing, loud, as though it were almost in his ear. It was a slightly asthmatic breathing, interrupted often by the beginning of a cough, or by the loud sniffling of a congested nose. He saw that the window-pane right next to him was open. He moved his head back slowly until he could look in sideways and saw something so unexpected that for a moment he was not sure if he had screamed.

Schmidt-Grohe sat on the sofa, his head right next to, almost lean-ing up against, the bottom of the open pane. Maple was so close to him that he could see the individual hairs on his head, wetly combed across his scalp, and even the flecks of dandruff dispersed randomly about it. Schmidt-Grohe was entirely alive—in fact, entirely healthy—just as he had been a week before when Maple had first met him in Nairobi. Maple exhaled carefully. It was so inconceivable, so ludicrous—so beyond his grasp—that he hardly even felt that he existed anymore. Logic was by the boards. He made no judgment, only stood and listened to Schmidt-Grohe's wheezing breath. Then, slowly, he began to inch his head towards the window, with a mind to looking directly into the rest of the room. He placed his face right on the wall, and slid it slowly, excruciatingly slowly, evenly, towards the window's edge—and then suddenly he froze. He heard a voice.

"Like Jesus Christ!" the voice said, and though it was the doctor's voice, it was so different from the way he had ever heard the doctor speak that he was not quite sure.

"Like Jesus Christ!" the doctor exploded, ranting, almost shouting. "Like Jesus Christ our Savior, who died so we should live, and in whom truth and glory . . ." He deflated. He ran out of steam, and his mad voice became quite normal once again, frighteningly normal, almost casual, as he rounded off his theme: "He will die so that the children live. Herr Schmidt will have his tropical island, and Dr. Agnelli will have his echocardiogram. Echocardiogram," he repeated, as if in a trance. "Echocardiogram in Tingu. Yes."

Schmidt-Grohe's head jerked forward. He muttered a series of guttural German words that must have been indecent. Then he said in English, almost whining, groveling, "I can't do it. I will not do it."

"You don't have to do anything," the doctor spit at him.

"I won't let *you* do it either, dammit," Schmidt-Grohe replied, with more force in his voice. "I come to this stinking country, live like a damned savage, grovel around in cheap hotels until I find the correct idiot—but this is for a witness, dammit! *Augenzeuge!* Not a . . . not a . . ."

"Victim," said the doctor calmly. "You are right. But now things have changed. And why have they changed?" And the doctor left his calm behind as if it were a little parcel that one might forget beside one on a bench, and suddenly was yelling once again, in a voice that twisted on itself with hate: "Because the white man is the king! Because even the black man acts that way! And when a white man dies, a rich, spoiled, pampered idiot who drinks his cocktails at the lodge and drives around in cars to take his idiotic photographs of animals and says he goes on a 'safari'—they need to see the body of this idiot. But when a black man dies, a warrior, a man who lives on God's good earth like God made him to live—in thirty years, thirty years, they have never asked to see the body of this man. Even here, even here.

"I am sorry," he said. "It is my mistake. I should have foreseen it, even here. But it is *my* mistake, and *I* will put an end to it.

"I will have the machine," he stated, with the deep, active accent of finality. "I will have this machine. You can have your island or not—I will have this machine. My children—my children will have this machine."

Maple leaned his back against the wall and stared across the yard. Beyond the square of light cast through the window everything was dark. He faintly made out darker blacks against the lighter blacks, bushes, flowerbeds, the benches, the sharp horizon of the fence—and above it all the perfectly clear sky, full of stars he had never seen in the Northern Hemisphere, stars shining, also, with an intensity that he had never known. He exhaled softly and was surprised at the calm and swiftness with which he took in and evaluated what was happening. It was some kind of insurance scam, he thought, the old story of pretend you're dead and have your wife collect, and he was to have been the witness to the death—only something had gone wrong. Somebody—probably the mythical police—needed to see the body, and so now Maple was to take on a new role.

Dr. Agnelli, it was clear, had gone crazy. Maple's uneasiness with him had not been simply paranoia. He had cracked under his thirty years of dealing with almost unmentionable suffering, and, perhaps in no small part, from dealing with it from the comfort of his quarters, his statuary, his pasta and his olive oil. And Maple could even see some of the logic to the cracking: after the last few days with Basram, watching the children with their goats, watching the lithe strides of the warriors, the golden chains against their deep black chins, the redness of the earth, the bareness of it all, Maple felt, too, that if he had to choose now between saving Basram's life or saving that of one of the young boys who rode their racing bicycles around his neighborhood at home, something would drive him to save Basram first. He exhaled gently. He was getting much too philosophical. He would have to leave, and quickly. He would have to make a plan. He regretted sending Basram off tonight.

The doctor's voice, once again gentle, kindly, reached out to him again.

"It has already happened once," he said.

"What?" Schmidt-Grohe was subdued, resentful, but his fight was gone.

"There was a white man living in the house where Maple is sleeping now. He did a lot of good work for the town. He was a good man." The doctor paused. "And then he wanted to go away. He was going to go to acting school, to become an actor." He spoke with a sadness, with resignation. "I tried to convince him to stay. And he did think about it. But in the end he decided to become an actor. He dreamed of living in New York."

It seemed as if the doctor were reaching deep into his memory for something hard to say. He was silent for a long time.

"And then, the night before he was to leave, a snake slipped in through the window of his little house—the same house Maple is in now. And the next morning he was dead."

Schmidt-Grohe did not say anything.

"I'll get a boy," the doctor said. "Wait for a minute, and I'll get a boy."

The door opened and the doctor's footsteps started up and then faded away again. Maple dared to move his face into the light. He saw Schmidt-Grohe sitting motionless on the couch. The paperback book lay on the floor in front of him. Maple heard, and then saw, the doctor return. The doctor stood by the door anxiously.

"A boy is coming," he said. "I have sent."

Schmidt-Grohe did not reply.

A minute later Basram came into the room.

Basram did not leave by the front gate. He jumped over the little fence that cordoned off the doctor's quarters and then made his way through a hole in the wall that surrounded the compound. Maple did not have time to think. Everything was turned so upside down that he barely even felt betrayed. He only knew that he wanted to go after Basram, that he needed to keep him in his sight.

He followed at a distance, over the gate and through the wall. He knew where Basram would be going. Keeping to the bushes on the right, he followed as Basram skirted the fences and small hedges that bordered the little back yards of the houses that abutted the main street. Halfway up the town, Basram turned into a path that led through undergrowth and over a tiny, dried-up stream. Maple did not follow. He would be able to see enough from where he was.

Basram soon came to a wall. He clambered up its loose stones, and now stood right next to the back of the blue cubicle in which first Peter and then Maple had spent their countless sleepless nights.

Maple watched, spellbound, as Basram steadied himself, holding the corrugated metal roof of the house in his left hand. A little window no more than a few inches high with bars across it cut into the wall just underneath the roof. Basram worked delicately, carefully. He leaned the front end of his funny box on the sill of the window, then lined it up with one of the square holes in the grating. He stepped back, holding the other end of the box in his right hand. He looked about him for a moment and then, once again intent on the mission before him, fiddled with his fingers on the front of the box and finally lifted his left hand away, holding the little square of wood that was the sliding door. He stood back, holding the box at its far end with both hands, peering forward uncertainly from time to time to monitor the progress of the snake.

There was for Maple, whose normal ideas and fears had been on hold ever since he had seen Schmidt-Grohe's resurrection on the couch, something heartrendingly beautiful about what he was watching, about where he stood as he watched Basram's silhouette move in the faint light of the stars. Behind him breathed the semi-arid land, the red dirt stretching away forever with its brown, waving grasses and the astounding, sudden greens of its big trees; it was laden with its vastness, with the humility of the mud huts that the humans built and called their homes, with the grandeur of the cats and buffalo who ruled this wasteland in the night. Above him the sky hung down its unknown constellations and the Milky Way shone so brightly that it seemed a ribbon and not just a cloud, vaster than he had ever seen it, mirroring the vastness of the land beneath. In front of him, as in a pantomime, he saw the play of his own death enacted for him, blackness on blackness under the black sky, and he reflected that few people could boast of having watched, as untouched spectators, their own murder being carried out. For that was what was happening: Basram was pulling the trigger, administering the poison, turning on the switch of the electric chair. Basram was killing him, and he was watching it, the only spectator, standing in the middle of an amphitheater without bounds.

Maple began to walk away. Then a sudden rush of anger overwhelmed him. His face grew hot, he felt the muscles in his arms tense up. Tears—which seemed to be pushing upward the entire length of his body, streaming cumulatively to his head from all his arteries and veins, rushing up out of his heart—put an unbearable pressure on his eyes, a pressure that did not let up even when it all poured out upon his face, flooding his skin with liquid heat. He was going to have to go back to the boy, grab him by the neck, smack him, kick him, rub his face down in the dirt and show him how a person acted to another person, show him, prove to him that friendship had a meaning, that there was such a thing as human feeling . . .

His eyes cleared, and his mind. Basram would be finished soon. Maple walked away, and quickly. He had no more choice.

He followed the road out of Tingu, and at the fork he took the left. It could not be more than fifty miles. He tried not to think about the length.

The animals were out at night, he knew. Once he made it through the night, he would probably be okay. The animals detected fear. He walked straight down the center of the road. He tried to avoid kicking stones.

The night was silent. He heard nothing rushing through the undergrowth. He heard no roars. He did not hear the scream of death. He felt the animals about him, animals on every side, but he did not hear a sound. His sneakers scuffed along the road. The road was empty. He walked straight ahead. The stars were changing in the sky.

He walked in a trance, straight through the night. Time had stopped moving. There was only the regular, light, easy scuffing of his sneakers on the road. There was not even any breeze. There were only his steps, strong, confident, and muscular. He was going away.

The stars changed, finally, so much that they all disappeared. There was a freshness and almost a moisture to the early dawn. Maple felt hopeful. The greatest danger is over now, he told himself. Though his belly hurt with emptiness and his knees and hips were aching terribly, he knew somehow that he would make it through the day.

He walked on through the daytime, jumping out of the way and hiding in the bushes when he heard a vehicle. The vehicle passed, and he emerged to walk again. His tongue was stuck, not just to the roof of his mouth but everywhere, to all the skin inside his cheeks. He forced himself to swallow, and seemed to squeeze down little balls of cotton cased in sticky mucus. He did not feel his legs moving but only felt a burning pain located vaguely down below his hips. It was not more than fifty miles. He was sure it was not more than fifty miles. He had driven it himself. He had driven, yes, he, he had driven, driven Schmidt-Grohe, driven the doctor, he had driven them to Tingu. He had heard the moans. He had seen the blood. He had turned the key. . . . He tried to concentrate on his steps, the one and then the other, and then the next, down the center of the road. He could not keep them, now, for more than three in a row. He could not count to more than three.

He stopped being there. He was not there anymore. He would wake up, suddenly—his head would jerk against his chest and he would see his feet, stepping, first the one, then the other, then the next—and then he would not be there anymore, and he only knew that he had not been there when his head jerked down again against his chest, and he saw his feet, and was surprised; and because he was surprised he knew that he had not been watching his feet, that he had not been there, because he was surprised to see his steps. And then he looked at his steps curiously, looked down at his shoes, looked at the texture of the laces—and the texture of the laces rubbed against his eyes, and the cold, shiny eyelets, the round metal dough-nuts, like machines; the canvas with its crisscross pattern, and the crisscross became magnified, and he saw the huge crisscrossing of the threads, and the sharp diamonds on the rubber, the little diamonds patterning the rubber at his toe, and the thin stripes of blue, and the places where the blue had been scuffed off: and suddenly it was a shoe again, taking a step, on the red dirt, against the stones, one step, another step. And then he was surprised, and saw his foot taking a step, and then another step, against the road, against the stones . . .

It was a white man, actually, who found him, a white man driving a white van. The van was almost new, and so the white man drove it carefully and concentrated hard upon the road ahead. At first he thought it was a large stone, and then a dead animal, some kind of antelope, and it was only after he was very near that he saw it was a human being, and a white one at that. Killed by Shiftas, the man thought, or by an animal—but what the hell was he doing here, in the middle of the road? At least thirty miles from the game park, which was the only thing of interest for a white man in these parts. And then, when he bent down, he saw that Maple was not dead. He was breathing faintly, and his pulse was very slow, but he was certainly alive.

The man stood by Maple's side for a moment. He reached up with his right hand and scratched the back of his ear. He did not know if he should get involved. He would be in for a lot of paperwork and wasted time if this man were to die in the back of his van. On the other hand, the man had no obvious wounds on him and might just be exhausted or stricken by the heat. In that case he could possibly get a reward for having saved his life. He looked like an American, and that probably meant money. And after all, it was not far to Tingu Hospital, where he was going anyway—he had business to arrange with the doctor there. He was to get the doctor an echocardiogram, and he thought that he could do it for a very reasonable price.

He decided to risk it after all. He swung the van around and, after opening the big back door, grabbed Maple underneath the shoulders and managed to pull him in. He closed the back door, slipped into the driver's seat, and told himself (and it was not the first time, either, that he had told himself this very thing) that although his business was not always clean, he had a conscience of a sort and did good in his own peculiar way.

LIFE AFTER LIFE

by *LAWRENCE BLOCK*

When the bullets struck, my first thought was that someone had raced up behind me to give me an abrupt shove. An instant later I registered the sound of the gunshots, and then there was fire in my side, burning pain, and the impact had lifted me off my feet and sent me sprawling at the edge of the lawn in front of my house.

I noticed the smell of the grass. Fresh, cut the night before, and with the dew still on it.

I can recall fragments of the ambulance ride as if it took place in some dim dream. I worried at the impropriety of running the sirens so early in the morning. They'd wake half the town.

Another time, I heard one of the white-coated attendants say something about a red blanket, and I recalled the blanket that lay on my bed when I was a boy almost forty years ago. It was plaid, mostly red with some green in it. Was that what they were talking about?

These bits of awareness came one after another, like fast cuts in a film, with no sensation of time passing between them.

I was in a hospital room—the operating room, I suppose. I was spread out on a long white table while a masked and green-gowned doctor probed a wound in the left side of my chest. I must have been under anesthetic—there was a mask on my face with a tube connected to it—and I believe my eyes were closed. Nevertheless, I was aware of what was happening, and I could see.

There was a sensation I was able to identify as pain, although it didn't actually hurt me. Then I felt as though my side were a bottle and a cork was being drawn from it. It popped free. The doctor held up a misshapen bullet for examination. I watched it fall in slow motion from his forceps, landing with a plinking sound in an aluminum pan.

"The other's too close to the heart," I heard him say. "I can't get a grip on it. I don't dare touch it, the way it's positioned. It'll kill him if it moves."

Same place, an indefinite period of time later. A nurse saying, "Oh God, he's going," and then all of them talking at once.

Then I was out of my body.

It just happened, just like that. One moment I was in my dying body on the table and a moment later I was floating somewhere beneath the ceiling. I could look down and see myself on the table and the doctors and nurses standing around me.

I'm dead, I thought.

I was very busy trying to decide how I felt about it. It didn't hurt. I had always thought it would hurt, that it would be awful, but it wasn't so terrible.

But it was odd seeing my body lying there. I thought, you were a good body. I'm all right, I don't need you, but you were a good body.

Then I was gone from the room. There was a rush of light that became brighter and brighter, and I was sucked through a long tunnel at a furious speed. Then I was in a world of light and in the presence of a Being of light.

This is hard to explain.

I couldn't tell if the Being was a man or a woman. It could have been both, or maybe it changed back and forth—I don't know. It was dressed all in white, and it emanated a light that surrounded it.

And in the distance I saw my father and my mother and my grandparents—people who had gone before me—and they were holding out their hands to me, and beaming at me with faces radiant with light and love.

I was drawn to the Being, which held out its arm and said, "Behold your life!"

And I looked, and I could see my entire life. I don't know how to describe what I saw. It was as if my whole life had happened at once and someone had taken a photograph of it. I could see in it everything that I remembered in my life and everything I had forgotten, and it was all happening at once and I was seeing it happen. I would see something bad that I'd done and think, I'm sorry about that, then I would see something good and be glad about it.

At the end I woke and had breakfast and left the house to walk to work and a car passed by and a gun came out the window. There were two shots and I fell and the ambulance came and all the rest of it.

And I thought, who killed me?

The Being said, "You must find out the answer."

I thought, I don't care, it doesn't matter.

He said, "You must go back and find out the answer."

I thought, no, I don't want to go back.

All of the brilliant light began to fade. I reached out toward it because I didn't want to go back, I didn't want to be alive again. But it continued to fade.

Then I was back in my body.

"We almost lost you," the nurse said. Her smile was professional, but the light in her eyes showed she meant it. "Your heart actually stopped on the operating table. You really had us scared there."

"I'm sorry," I said.

She thought that was funny. "The doctor was only able to remove one of the two bullets that hit you, so you've still got one in your chest. He sewed you up and put a drain in the wound, but obviously you won't be able to walk around like that. In fact, it's important for you to lie absolutely still or the bullet might shift in position. It's right alongside your heart."

It might shift even if I don't move, I thought. But she knew better than to tell me that.

"In four or five days we'll have you scheduled for another operation," she went on. "By then the bullet may move of its own accord to a more accessible position. If not, there are techniques that can be employed." She told me some of the extraordinary things surgeons could do. I didn't pay attention.

After she left the room, I rolled back and forth on the bed, shifting my body as jerkily as I could. But the bullet did not change position in my chest.

I stayed in the hospital that night. No one came to see me during visiting hours, and I thought that was strange. I asked the nurse and was told I was in intensive care and couldn't have visitors.

I lost control of myself. I shouted that she was crazy. How could I learn who did it if I couldn't see anyone?

"The police will see you as soon as it's allowed," she said. She was terribly earnest. "Believe me," she said, "it's for your own protection. They want to ask you a million questions, naturally, but it would be bad for your health to let you get all excited.''

Silly bitch, I thought. And almost put the thought into words. Then I remembered the picture of my life, and the pleasant and unpleasant things I had done and how they had looked in the picture.

I smiled. "I'm sorry I lost control," I said. "But if they didn't want me to get excited they shouldn't have give me such a beautiful nurse."

I didn't sleep. It didn't seem to be necessary. I lay in bed wondering who had killed me.

My wife? We'd married young, then grown apart. Of course, *she* hadn't shot at me because she'd been in bed asleep when I left the house that morning. But she might have a lover. Or she could have hired someone to pull the trigger for her.

My partner? Monty and I had turned a handful of borrowed capital into a million-dollar business, but I was better than Monty at holding on to money. He spent it, gambled it away, paid it out in divorce settlements. Profits were off lately. Had he been helping himself to funds and cooking the books? And did he then decide to cover his thefts the easy way?

My girl? Peg had a decent apartment, a closet full of clothes. Not a bad deal. But for a while I'd let her think I'd divorce Julia when the kids were grown, and now she and I both knew better. She'd seemed to adjust to the situation, but had the resentment festered inside her?

My children? The thought was painful. Mark had gone to work for me after college. The arrangement didn't last long. He'd been too headstrong, and I'd been unwilling to give him the responsibility he wanted. Now he was talking about going into business for himself. But he lacked the capital.

If I died, he'd have all he needed.

Debbie was married, and expecting a child. First she'd lived with another young man, one of whom I hadn't approved, and then she'd married Scott, who was hardworking and earnest and ambitious. Was the marriage bad for her, and did she blame me for costing her the other boy? Or did Scott's ambition prompt him to make Debbie an heiress?

Who else? Why?

Some days ago I'd cut off a motorist at a traffic circle. I remembered the sound of his horn, his face in my rearview mirror, red, ferocious. Had he copied down my license plate, determined my address, lain in ambush to gun me down?

It made no sense. But it didn't make sense for anyone to kill me. Julia? Monty? Peg? Mark? Debbie? Scott? A stranger?

I lay there wondering but didn't truly care. Someone had killed me, and I was supposed to be dead. But I was not permitted to be dead until I knew the answer to the question.

Maybe the police would find it for me.

They didn't.

I saw two policemen the following day. I was still in intensive care, still denied visitors, but an exception was made for the police. They were very courteous and spoke in hushed voices. They had no leads in their investigation and just wanted to know if I could suggest a single possible suspect.

I told them I couldn't.

My nurse turned white as paper.

"You're not supposed to be out of bed! You're not even supposed to move! What do you think you're doing?"

I was up and dressed. There was no pain. As an experiment, I'd been palming the pain pills they issued me every four hours, hiding them in the bedclothes instead of swallowing them. As I'd anticipated, I didn't feel any pain.

The area of the wound was numb, as though that part of me had been excised altogether. I could feel the slug that was still in me and could tell it remained in position. It didn't hurt me, however.

She went on jabbering away at me. I remembered the picture of my life and avoided giving her a sharp answer.

"I'm going home," I said.

"Don't talk nonsense."

"You have no authority over me," I told her. "I'm legally entitled to take responsibility for my own life."

"For your own death, you mean."

"If it comes to that. You can't hold me here against my will. You can't operate on me without my consent."

"If you don't have that operation, you'll die."

"Everyone dies."

"I don't understand," she said, and her eyes were filled with sorrow. My heart went out to her.

"Don't worry about me," I said gently. "I know what I'm doing."

* * *

"They wouldn't let me see you," Julia was saying. "And now you're home."

"It was a fast recovery."

"Shouldn't you be in bed?"

"The exercise is supposed to be good for me," I said. I looked at her, and for a moment I saw her as she'd appeared in parts of the picture of my life—as a bride, as a young mother.

"You know, you're a beautiful woman," I said.

She colored.

"I suppose we got married too young," I said. "We each had a lot of growing to do. And the business took too much of my time over the years. I'm afraid I haven't been a very good husband."

"You weren't so bad."

"I'm glad we got married," I said. "And I'm glad we stayed together. And that you were here for me to come home to."

She started to cry. I held her until she stopped. Then, her face to my chest, she said, "At the hospital, waiting, I realized for the first time what it would mean for me to lose you. I thought we'd stopped loving each other a long time ago. I know you've had other women. For that matter, I've had lovers. I don't know if you knew that."

"It's not important."

"No," she said, "it's not. I'm glad we got married, darling. And I'm glad you're going to be all right."

Monty said, "You had everybody worried there, kid. But what do you think you're doing down here? You're supposed to be home in bed."

"I'm supposed to get exercise. Besides, if I don't come down here how do I know you won't steal the firm into bankruptcy?"

My tone was light, but he flushed deeply. "You just hit a nerve," he said.

"What's the matter?"

"When they were busy cutting the bullet out of you, all I could think was you'd die thinking I was a thief."

"I don't know what you're talking about."

He lowered his eyes. "I was borrowing partnership funds," he said. "I was in a bind because of my own stupidity and I didn't want to admit it to you, so I dipped into the till. It was a temporary thing, a case of the shorts. I got everything straightened out before that clown took a shot at you. Do they know who it was yet?"

"Not yet."

"The night before you were shot, I stayed late and covered things. I wasn't going to say anything, and then I wondered if you'd been suspicious, and I decided I'd tell you about it first thing in the morning. Then it looked as though I wasn't going to get the chance. You didn't suspect anything?"

"I thought our cash position was light. But after all these years I certainly wasn't afraid of you stealing from me."

"All these years," he echoed, and I was seeing the picture of my life again. All the work Monty and I had put in side by side—the laughs we'd shared, the bad times we'd survived.

We looked at each other, and a great deal of feeling passed between us. Then he drew a breath and clapped me on the shoulder. "Well, that's enough about old times," he said gruffly. "Somebody's got to do a little work around here."

"I'm glad you're here," Peg said. "I couldn't even go to the hospital. All I could do was call every hour and ask anonymously for a report on your condition. Critical condition, that's what they said. Over and over."

"It must have been rough."

"It did something to me and for me," she said. "It made me realize that I've cheated myself out of a life. And I was the one who did it. You didn't do it to me."

"I told you I'd leave Julia."

"Oh, that was just a game we both played. I never really expected you to leave her. No, it's been my fault. I settled into a nice secure life. But when you were on the critical list, I decided my life was on the critical list, too, and that it was time I took some responsibility for it."

"Meaning?"

"Meaning it's good you came over tonight and not this afternoon, because you wouldn't have found me at home. I've got a job. It's not much, but it's enough to pay the rent. I've decided it's time I started paying my own rent. In the fall I'll start night classes at the university."

"I see."

"You're not angry?"

"Angry? I'm happy for you."

"I don't regret what we've been to each other. I was a lost little girl with a screwed-up life, and you made me feel loved and cared for. But I'm a big girl now. I'll still see you, if you want to see me, but from here on in I pay my own way.''

"No more checks?''

"No more checks. I mean it.''

I remembered some of our times together, seeing them as I had seen them in the picture of my life. I went and took her in my arms.

Later, while Julia slept, I lay awake in the darkness. I thought, this is crazy. I'm no detective. I'm a businessman. I died and You won't let me stay dead. Why can't I be dead?

I got out of bed, went downstairs, and laid out the cards for a game of solitaire. I toasted a slice of bread and made myself a cup of tea.

I won the game of solitaire. It was a hard variety, one I could normally win only once in fifty or a hundred times.

I thought, it's not Julia, it's not Monty, it's not Peg. All of them have love for me.

I felt good about that.

But who killed me? Who was left on my list?

I didn't feel good about that.

I was finishing my breakfast the following morning when Mark rang the bell. Julia went to the door and let him in. He came into the kitchen and got himself a cup of coffee from the pot on the stove.

"I was at the hospital,'' he said. "Night and day, but they wouldn't let any of us see you.''

"Your mother told me.''

"Then I had to leave town the day before yesterday, and I just got back this morning. I had to meet with some men.'' A smile flickered on his face. He looked just like his mother when he smiled.

"I've got the financing,'' he said. "I'm in business.''

"That's wonderful.''

"I know you wanted me to follow in your footsteps, Dad. But I couldn't be happy having my future handed to me that way. I wanted to make it on my own.''

"You're my son. I was the same myself.''

"When I asked you for a loan—''

"I've been thinking about that,'' I said, remembering the scene as I'd witnessed it in the picture of my life. "I resented your independence, and I envied your youth. I was wrong to turn you down.''

"You were right to turn me down.'' That smile again, just like his mother. "I wanted to make it on my own, and then I turned around and asked you for help. I'm just glad you knew better than to give me what I was weak enough to ask for. I realized that almost immediately, but I was too proud to say anything. And then some madman shot you and—well, I'm glad everything turned out all right, Dad."

"Yes," I said. "So am I."

Not Mark, then.

Not Debbie either. I always knew that, and knew it with utter certainty when she cried out, "Oh, Daddy!" and rushed to me and threw herself into my arms. "I'm so glad!" she kept saying. "I was so worried."

"Calm down," I told her. "I don't want my grandchild born with a nervous condition."

"Don't worry about your grandchild. Your grandchild's going to be just fine."

"And how about my daughter?"

"Your daughter's fine. Do you want to know something? I've really learned a lot these past few days."

"So have I."

"How close I am to you, for one thing. Waiting at the hospital, there was a time when I thought, God, he's gone. I just had this feeling. And then I shook my head and said, no, it was nonsense, you were all right. And you know what they told us afterward? Your heart stopped during the operation, and it must have happened right when I got that feeling."

When I looked at my son, I saw his mother's smile. When I looked at Debbie, I saw myself.

"And another thing I learned was how much people need each other. People were so good to us! So many people called and asked about you. Even Philip called, can you imagine? He just wanted to let me know that I should call on him if there was anything he could do."

"What could Philip possibly do?"

"I have no idea. It was funny hearing from him, though. I hadn't heard his voice since we were together. But it was nice of him to call, wasn't it?"

I nodded. "It must have made you wonder what might have been."

"What it made me wonder was how I ever thought he and I were meant for each other. Scott was with me every minute, except when he went down to give blood for you—"

"He gave blood for me?"

"Didn't Mother tell you? You and Scott are the same blood type. Maybe that's why I fell in love with him."

"Not a bad reason."

"He was with me all the time, and by the time you were out of danger, I began to realize how close we'd grown, how much I loved him. And then when I heard Philip's voice I thought what kid stuff that relationship of ours had been. I know you never approved."

"It wasn't my business to approve or disapprove."

"Maybe not. But I know you approve of Scott, and that's important to me."

I went home.

I thought, what do You want from me? It's not my son-in-law. You don't try to kill a man and then donate blood for a transfusion. Nobody would do a thing like that.

The person I cut off at the traffic circle? But that was insane. How would I know him? I wouldn't know where to start looking for him.

Some other enemy? But I had no enemies.

Julia said, "The doctor called again. He doesn't see how you could check yourself out of the hospital. He wants to schedule you for surgery."

"Not yet," I told her. "Not until I'm ready."

"When will you be ready?"

"When I feel right about it," I told her.

She called him back and relayed the message. "He's very nice," she reported. "He says any delay is hazardous, so you should let him schedule the surgery as soon as you possibly can."

I was glad he was a caring man, and that she liked him. He might be a comfort to her later when she needed someone to lean on.

Something clicked.

I called Debbie.

"Just the one telephone call," she said, puzzled. "He said he knew you never liked him but he always respected you and he knew what an influence you were in my life. And that I should call on him if I needed someone to turn to. It was kind of him, that's what

I told myself at the time, but there was something creepy about the conversation.''

What had she told him?

"That it was nice to hear from him, and that, you know, my husband and I would be fine. Sort of stressing that I was married but in a nice way. Why?''

The police were very dubious. It was ancient history, they said. The boy had lived with my daughter a while ago, parted amicably, never made any trouble. Had he ever threatened me? Had we ever fought?

"He's the one," I said. "Watch him," I told them. "Keep an eye on him.''

So they assigned men to watch Philip, and on the fourth day the surveillance paid off. They caught him tucking a bomb beneath the hood of a car. The car belonged to my son-in-law, Scott.

"He thought you were standing between them. When she said she was happily married, he shifted his sights to the husband.''

There had always been something about Philip that I hadn't liked. Something creepy, as Debbie put it. Perhaps he'll get treatment now. In any event, he'll be unable to harm anyone.

Is that why I was permitted to return? So that I could prevent Philip from harming Scott? Perhaps. But the conversations with Julia, Monty, Peg, Mark, and Debbie, those were fringe benefits.

Or perhaps it was the other way around.

They've prepared me for surgery. And I've prepared myself. I'm ready now.